The Persian Asteroid

The Persian Asteroid

Hyrum W. Hawks

Sparkling Draconic Unicorn Publishing

To my wife, whose encouragement is my earthly anchor to optimism.
To my children, who laugh at my dumb jokes, mostly.
To Seth, my friend and business partner who keeps me on track.
To Brad, who encouraged me to the end.
To the Iranian people-Women, Life, Freedom.

Day 0

Casey Scarlett stood in front of a seething, restless mob, his sense of danger spiking as he stepped up to face his fate. He scanned the crowd, seeing his men held captive among them. He prepared his only weapon... And clicked on the presentation, making it full screen.

Casey chuckled to himself at this thought as he gave his presentation to the 'mob' of engineers at the conference. A mob of NASA, ESA, and JAXA scientists and engineers, as well as their counterparts in private industry from around the world. They were a seething, restless mob. His was the last presentation before the afternoon coffee break, and if they were like him, they were sleepy and a bit hungry.

"In conclusion, our patent pending technology will enable the use of orbital space debris as the fuel for outbound asteroid retrieval missions and use an asteroid to provide the fuel to bring the captured asteroids home."

Polite applause sounded in the classroom. The university hosted this space resources conference every year and attendance was excellent, but these were mostly the same people he'd been harassing about his team's inventions for years. In fact, Casey had given this same speech four times in the last two months. Maybe repetition would beat into their heads what a revolutionary approach this was. Maybe they had all fallen asleep during his presentation. Either way, he had gone well over his time again, so they told people to ask him questions during the break. Casey immediately began second guessing how he'd said everything, especially the conclusions. Did he emphasize the right parts of the technology for this audience? Did he put too much emphasis on the business case? Did his jokes land, or was he trying too hard?

As he headed from the podium out among the flimsy desks, the smell of decades of college students mixed with coffee and cheap pastries gave him nostalgia for his time in college. The smell was identical to the fragrance of engineers and scientists confined to a classroom for three straight days. *Does the classroom receive the smell from the occupants, or the occupants from the classroom?*

He'd met his two best friends in college in a freshman English class. All three were engineers and gravitated towards each other with an instant sense of camaraderie. Perhaps it was an aura that engineers had to set them apart? Perhaps it was their shared annoyance at having to take English at all? Most likely, it was the fact they were all wearing shirts with math equations on them to the first day of school. Impossible to know. Those friends had since become his business partners. Glancing towards his seat, he saw both of them give him nods of approval, easing his worry and causing him to smile. Manuel, gentle soul that he was, would have encouraged him even if he'd bombed. Blake would have harassed him without mercy if he'd bombed, meaning he'd done a good job. Both were visionaries, and their combined skill sets were formidable.

Blake Landry was a hulking man risen from backwoods Alabama who had become a mining guru and economics genius but had started life as a mechanic. He stood out in the mining industry, not just for his height, but for his race. There were not a lot of black men in mining, though that number was growing because of him. Manuel Navarro was of average height and had been born an astrodynamicist and rocket engineer, though he didn't know it until he got a scholarship to come to the U.S. from Spain. ESA was furious that NASA had stolen him. Manuel always did complex math during all presentations that did not discuss higher level math. He was tan and handsome but did not care, blissfully unaware of his tendency to turn heads, even in his early forties. Casey was from a mining town in Montana and was pale even by mining industry standards, and not nearly as handsome as either of his partners. He was reasonably tall and fairly strong, but Blake still dwarfed him. Casey was also the spokesman and systems engineer, coming up with the most insane ideas and connecting the pieces together. And they were all just about broke.

Casey glanced at the door, the smell of the pastries calling to him, his heart longing to go to the snack table in the foyer. He told himself that his active mind needed fuel, though his gut said he still had a bit of a mass and energy imbalance to rectify. But there were people to talk to, relationships to develop, and funding to secure. For several minutes, he fielded compliments from a variety of old acquaintances on the presentation, some of which he assumed were sincere. They would ask for details on some part of the concept and then query when a prototype would be ready. The same stock answers were comfortable fallbacks. Those details are proprietary for now while we work out the technology. We're waiting on commitment from investors or for small business grants.

The space industry had huge money for anything related to satellites and for the companies that had tech that were part of 'strategic plans' that year. But asteroids were not in the hot seat. Moon bases as a preparation for Martian settlement were the big game in town.

Which was why Casey found himself arguing with a fiery NASA engineer, Dr. Devon, only a few minutes into the break.

"Look Casey, we all know that asteroids are fascinating. I want to mine them, too! But we can't split our focus. The moon is where we've sunk the last decade of effort, both NASA and the private sector. If we start funding asteroid retrieval missions, we'll never meet our moon mission objectives. I don't think anyone will fund this in the next two decades. I know I won't recommend it to anyone."

Casey fumed. This was the same nonsense she had spouted for so long that other people were believing it, drying up his team's already fading funding streams. The smug look on her face as she minimized his dreams drove him crazy.

"I appreciate your concern, Stacy, but our team demonstrated that a small player in the game could afford this. A small country, like South Korea or New Zealand, or even a large business, could easily fund us and start a regular delivery of 10-meter diameter asteroids into a safe orbit around Earth for mining and processing and start building space stations within 10 years! We only need to build and flight test. We completed the engineering. We did that on our own dime. With a launch cost down below two thousand dollars per kilogram to low-Earth orbit, our first phase system can launch for as little as half a million and our second for only two million more! The economics are clear. The moon and Mars are not nearly as good an investment. They're good, but not thousand-fold returns on investments in just a decade level good."

As the flow of the conversation waned, a younger man in an immaculate suit and wearing an elaborate kufiyah stepped up and raised a hand, then stepped back, blushing. Casey turned his body to face him, taking a closer look. Late twenties, early thirties. Handsome. And timid. Casey gave him a smile.

"Dr. Devon," the man said with a slight stammer, "I am sorry to interrupt, but may I steal Mr. Scarlett for a question on his technology?"

Casey excused himself from Dr. Devon and followed the man to the back of the room. Manuel continued the argument in his absence by bringing up orbital dynamics equations while Blake would break in and translate into English for those who were not so well versed in elliptical mathematics.

"Mr. Scarlett, it is an honor to meet you." The man spoke with a refined British accent, with only a trace of something else. He was tan with a well-kept beard and features that reminded Casey of his time in the Middle and Near East. "I am Hamid Yazdani, head of the investing arm of Fitch and Port Financial, based in the City of London. What you said resonated with me on many levels. My company is in the business of making grandiose dreams come true. Our senior partner read a book that inspired him to invest in space. He wants to make his mark as the funding source of an audacious space venture. If what you are saying about your technology is true, then I intend to finance your company in its entirety."

The room's lights flashed, indicating the break was about to end. Hamid sighed. "Never enough time at these events. Can I take you and any of your team here out to dinner this evening? We can discuss next steps."

Casey tried to speak, but the only result was a choking sound as his eyes bugged out a bit. He turned and coughed to give himself a chance to let his brain process this news and then school his face. Turning back, he said, "That would be delightful," with only a slight squeak to his voice.

Hamid smiled. "Wonderful, I will see you at Abejas at 7 pm?"

"Yes, that would be lovely."

"Then I will go make the arrangements." With that, Hamid turned and left the conference hall.

Casey waited until he was gone, then pumped both fists in front of himself, eliciting a few amused looks from people in the back. He turned and saw his partners staring at him, waved them to follow, and bolted into the foyer without checking to see if they were coming. He did not see Hamid, so he paced, hands shaking. Seeing the break table, he walked to it and grabbed a plate, skipped the fruits, and filled his plate with cheese and crackers.

"Well, Manuel," a resonant voice drawled, "we know what it means when he breaks his diet. He has either really good news or really bad news."

Casey, insides writhing with the equivalent of a couple of alley cats brawling, roughly set his plate down. Little squares of cheese tumbled to the table, and he gave Blake a withering stare. Blake and Manuel both laughed, making Casey smile broadly.

"I don't know why I am still on this stupid diet. It's all Manuel's fault." Casey slapped his slightly protruding gut.

"You blame me, your savior?!" Manuel placed a hand on his heart and took a melodramatic step back. "Two years ago, you were as fat as Blake and now you are... well, less fat. If you continue, you will be as handsome as one of those annoying Chris's from the movies. Never as handsome as me, tragically."

"But while you two are miserable," Blake picked up Casey's plate and popped a cracker with a hunk of cheese on it into his mouth, "I'll be happy."

Casey knew this could go on until the sun swallowed them up, so he reined in his desire to continue aboard the runaway train of dumb jokes and got to the point.

"I think it is good news. Well, maybe. That guy in the kufiyah ... Oh, blast, I already forgot his name!" He slapped himself on the forehead. "Hamid. Don't remember his last name. Anyway, he represents some London finance company that wants to 'make its mark on the space industry,' and he was so impressed by our presentation that he wants to meet us for dinner tonight to discuss financing us!" Casey felt himself choking up.

Blake smiled and smirked while popping more cheese and crackers into his mouth. "You're both such babies. I haven't cried in my entire life."

Manuel crossed himself piously as he openly wept, even as he smiled, which made Casey tear up.

"Stop that, Manuel. You know I'm a sympathy crier."

"Blake, you're a liar." Manuel punched him on the shoulder. "I saw you cry last time we watched Apollo 13!"

Casey smiled with gratitude. Nothing like these two to give him a boost. He dove right back into the fray.

"Manuel, not only does he cry at Apollo 13, but I make him cry when I won't stop calling 'ore' 'dirt.' He gets so mad."

Blake opened his mouth to protest the horrors of abusing geologic terminology for the thousandth time, but Manuel stopped him by throwing another cheese cube in, making Blake glare with a smirk.

Manuel got them on track this time.

"So, Hamid, you say? Out of London? We should do some homework on this guy before dinner."

Casey sagged and started pacing again.

"Well, it would have helped if he'd given me a card, but I have, as usual, forgotten to listen when people tell me things. You'd think after decades of practice I'd have it down! I'm glad I remember the restaurant. Abejas, here in Golden. I say we ditch the rest of the session and prep for this meeting."

"Good, the meeting is boring." Manuel smiled with his usual relief at avoiding crowds. "No one is talking about astrodynamics! Just going on and on about the probe crawling into that lava tube on the moon next month. So dull. Anyway, I need a new notepad. I filled mine up doing derivations. I took a new geometry that I found in a journal based on polyhedra in five dimensions and phase shifted it. I hypothesize the extra dimension after the four of normal spacetime is an expansion dimension. Then I made some simplifying assumptions and got Einstein's Lorentz transformation to fall out!"

"I don't know what that means, but it sounds important." Casey slapped Manuel on the shoulder. "We can stop and get you a new notebook on the way."

###

Casey paced back and forth across his musty, threadbare motel room, using all three paces between walls, as he spoke to his wife, Esin, on the phone.

"And so, we are meeting Hamid at a restaurant in 20 minutes!"

"That's amazing! You think this is the one?"

"I do. This will be how we get funded and get this mission to finally happen! This time next year, we could have our first phase in orbit collecting space debris!"

"And then we can replace the fridge?"

"Esin, my love, if this goes through, we can finally redo the entire kitchen."

"Casey, you know I don't need that. I spent the first decades of my life in a village where electricity was a rumor, not a reality. I make do. It would be nice for us to have a fridge that doesn't need one of us to rebuild it every three months..."

Casey hung his head, lost in a moment of sadness. She had lived on little the first 15 years of her life, then she lived on even less in a refugee camp. For the first years with him, he'd given her the American dream, though on a farm with a proper fence, not the illogically useless white picket variety. Then she convinced him to pursue his true dream of shifting to being an outer space engineer. They'd tightened their belts, made do, and did without. Then tightened the belts more. But success was always one more grant or conference away, and it was only Esin's part-time job as a handywoman and the farm that Blake and Manuel's wives, Jane and Rosa ran that kept all three of their families afloat.

"You haven't needed a lot of things this last several years. You and the kids have had to put up with a lot to let me pursue this dream of mine. But you won't want for money from tomorrow on. I better go soon or the adrenaline of talking to you will run out halfway through this dinner."

"If you wouldn't pace while you talked, you wouldn't be so hyped up!"

"But imagine how fat I'd be if I stopped pacing. My thirties killed my metabolism."

"You were a scrawny thing when I met you," she teased, her voice still causing a flutter in him after all these years.

"Hold on, I know English isn't your first language, so I'll correct you. I was svelte. Or skinny, at most. Not scrawny. That word implies a gangly youth with minimal muscle mass."

"Excuse me, Mr. Professorman. But don't you worry. You were an adorable, scrawny young man."

Casey sat and sighed. "I knew I loved you about 30 minutes after I met you. It was when I asked you for a crescent wrench, and you handed me a pipe wrench."

The smile in her voice was so strong that Casey could see it in his mind's eye. "Which was most definitely what you would have asked for if you had not been so googly eyed over me. Good thing I was paying attention to learn how to do the job."

He put on a dramatic, tragic voice and flung himself onto his squeaky mattress, probably from the Nixon administration. "Yes, and you loved it so much that now you do all the household maintenance, to my eternal shame as an engineer! I have to lie to the engineers at the office or they'd revoke my license! To let a non-engineer do maintenance in your own home! The tragedy!"

"It's your own fault. I wouldn't have known how fun it was if you hadn't taught me on our first date."

"Hardly a date when it involves repairing a well in a refugee camp. But that's besides the point."

"Casey, my bluebird, you must focus and go. Remember, I'm proud of you. Remember that when the anxiety tries to take you. Remember, when the depression lies to you and says you are not worthy, you are a hero to me and your children. And remember. I love you."

He smiled, his heart happy as she repeated the mantra to keep the pain in his heart at bay; keeping the emptiness and panic at bay.

He replied, "I love you, my hummingbird, and I believe you more every day."

Casey, Blake, and Manuel entered the Mexican restaurant at precisely 6 pm, the smell of the kitchen making Casey ravenous. Happily, they found Hamid already there and so were soon several bowls deep in tortilla chips and salsa. Business cards exchanged, they all knew Hamid's full name and business, though it was too late to do any research without appearing rude.

Blake kicked the conversation off with his usual directness.

"So, you want to fund us, eh? When we're done with this project, there are more in the pipeline."

"Blake," Casey admonished, "let the man enjoy some chips before you ask him to get out the checkbook. Besides, you know that people with full stomachs are more likely to spend money on crazy ventures than people who are grumpy and ill fed."

"Quite true." Hamid smiled and picked up his menu. "Now, I've never had Mexican food, but Dr. Devon recommended it, and I took a chance on it."

Casey hesitated with a chip partway to his mouth. "How do you know Dr. Devon?"

Casey felt a tension build, his lips compressing and his eyes narrowing. He glanced at his partners, who also looked displeased.

Hamid apparently read their expressions correctly. "Oh, yes. Well, I only know her from a conversation we had yesterday over the break table. I was commenting on the lack of interesting flavors, and she recommended this place. I suppose you aren't big fans of hers?"

Blake scowled, but Manuel spoke first. "She is our bête noire, you might say. She has prevented us from getting critical funding on our project several times."

"Well, consider her your unexpected heroine." Hamid chuckled. "Your responses to her provocations piqued my interest." He pointed at his menu. "Now, what is a chimichanga?"

They enjoyed a discussion of the intricacies of Mexican cuisine and intrigued Hamid with the idea of each of the dishes. In the end, they ordered a variety and shared so they could all try some of everything.

Blake, more verbose when full and now stocked for the famine of waiting for their entrees with plenty of chips and salsa, began his own line of questioning. "So, Hamid, how do you like it in London? Is the lack of spice killing you?"

Casey fought not to wince. He realized this would be their last chance for funding before they had to give up and go back to consulting. He prayed Blake wouldn't overwhelm Hamid with his humor.

Hamid gave his tiny, polite smile. "Growing up in London with English parents, I did not partake of many spices. It was in my teen years that I discovered ethnic restaurants. I have never looked back, though I never tried Mexican."

"He who controls the spice, eh?" Blake asked with a grin. "While your friends experimented with drugs, you experimented with seasonings?"

Hamid's mouth twitched into a slight smile. "You could say that, yes. So, where are you all from?"

Casey explained and then asked, "You were born and raised in London?"

"Originally, I am from Afghanistan," Hamid explained, "but moved to London as a refugee when I was about eight. I was adopted."

"Blake and I spent a lot of time in Afghanistan," Casey said with a smile. "My wife was a refugee. I learned Persian there, and from her." Casey turned to Manuel. "The Arabic pronunciation of Persian is Farsi. Arabic doesn't have a 'P' sound." He turned back to Hamid. "Anyway, I pick up the local languages when working overseas. Blake and I automated mines and oil wells in Turkey, Saudi Arabia, and Afghanistan, and I always love to practice with native speakers."

Hamid raised both eyebrows. "You have the advantage of me and will know Afghanistan better than I do. You met your wife in America?"

Casey leaned back in his chair and smiled, gazing into the distance without seeing the restaurant at all. "No, she was still in a refugee camp, and Blake and I were spending our off time fixing a well for the camp. She had been in the camp a few years, and I was able to pull some strings to get her to Montana. Blake and I obtained some leverage on some important people, if you know what I mean. She went to the university in my hometown and about a year later, she became my wife."

Hamid's eyes widened. "That is an amazing story. She was a very lucky woman to escape from those camps."

"And he'll tell it any chance he gets," Blake said with a chuckle. He leaned towards Hamid and spoke in hushed tones. "Casey's a hopeless romantic. You'll never meet a man more devoted to his wife, or more annoying about it."

Casey punched Blake on the shoulder, grinning.

Hamid glanced between them. He took another chip and dipped it before speaking.

"But you said you were there with Blake. How did you and Blake each shift from mining and oil and gas to outer space?"

"The Martian," Casey and Blake said simultaneously.

Manuel piped in, "They mean the book. The movie was alright, but not nearly as good as the book. But I also helped. I was smart and went into aerospace from the start. I like applied math, so astrodynamics and rocketry. When they read the Martian, they called me, and we started our own company. They said, 'Manuel, you are way cooler than Matt Damon and we want to be like you.' We've all been pursuing it ever since. They are yet to be anywhere as cool as Matt Damon, let alone me."

"It helps that Manuel had all the contacts," Blake said, "and we both worked in mining, so our experience made for an easy transition into outer space mining."

"That is the perfect segue," Hamid said, pushing the chips away with wide eyes as the meal came.

Casey knew that feeling. He probably ruined his appetite on chips and salsa before the meal came 90% of the time.

"Please, explain to me the orbital system you have designed," Hamid asked.

Manuel dived right in, ignoring his meal being set down and speaking in complete obliviousness as everyone else started to eat. Hamid got far more than he likely expected from that little question. Casey watched with shaking hands as Hamid's interest turned to slight confusion. He and Blake looked towards each other, and Blake's normally unflappably calm face showed signs of a war with his internal nervousness. Casey would have intervened, but he knew Manuel was about to give the coup de gras that he always ended with. Besides, it was a chance to take a few more bites and settle his stomach before he had to talk again.

"And so, the orbital intercept is possible with our thrusters with minimal fuel because the specific impulse is extremely high while still maintaining a reasonable thrust!" Manuel, who could have spoken on orbital mechanics for several hours, saw the look of confusion on Hamid's face and tried, "Well, extremely high is relative to other ion engines. It's an incremental improvement. It's not as high as a theoretical fusion engine or something, but that would require solving the magnetic field containment problem." Manuel's eyes refocused, and he glanced at Hamid's face, apparently seeing the confusion lingering, so he turned a pleading look to Casey. Manuel was making progress reading facial cues.

Casey fought down panic and leapt into the fray, rescuing Manuel from his own intelligence. "What Manuel means is that our thrusters are both efficient and high thrust. When combined with our asteroid capture and mining systems, we can bring an asteroid in with better fuel consumption and faster orbital periods than any proposed system before."

"Could you do it in a year?" Hamid asked.

"With the right funding, sure," Casey assured him, picking up and putting down his fish taco. "Phase 1 launch could definitely be accomplished within a year. It will require a large team and a concerted effort. Phase 2 follows the timeline I showed no matter what, as astrodynamics is a cruel mistress."

Hamid rubbed his chin, looking at them with what Casey hoped was respect. Hamid took another bite of the enchilada, which was clearly his favorite, while the three of them all gave each other nervous smiles. He studied their charts on Casey's laptop while he chewed.

Hamid set down his fork and knife, wiped his lips carefully, then gave his tiny smile and said, "Your data looks thorough and complete. Your technology appears well considered. I have had background checks done on all of you, of course. You are all family men, with more children than average. I also have children." Hamid paused, eyes wandering for a moment. Then he turned his attention back to them. "You have no vices?"

"If you mean, do we drink or the like, then no." Casey felt himself relax a bit. If this was where the conversation was going, perhaps they were doing well. "We all agreed when we were friends in college that alcohol and drugs were illogical and detrimental."

"We have not agreed, however, on whether food is a vice," Blake drawled. "And we all do have one significant, very controversial vice."

Casey and Manuel looked at Blake with concern, always aware that Blake's impulsivity could be unpredictable.

Blake smiled with a lopsided grin and a twinkle in his eyes. "We all waste a lot of money on Legos."

Blake... Casey thought. *Oh, please, please Hamid, don't think us too weird.*

Hamid, who had been rather reserved in his emotional tells, broke into a smile at this. "I have the same vice, my friends! I have every single space set, including one from 1964. It is decided. I will invest in your company. You will come with me to London to finalize the deal, of course. I have a private jet at the Denver Airport. It has plenty of room for all of us. I hope you have your passports?"

"Yes, we always travel with our passports, but you haven't finished your due diligence," Casey protested. "You were gracious enough to sign our non-disclosure agreement, but this seems so fast!"

Hamid waved a hand dismissively. "I understand your concerns, but I have been looking for the right opportunity in space for months. You are the one. Let me assuage your concerns. Please give me your banking information. I will wire $50,000 to each of your accounts as a gesture of good faith, and to provide for your families while we are working through contract negotiations. Whenever lawyers get involved, things take too long, and I wouldn't want them to suffer needlessly. I am sure this has been a very expensive endeavor. It is time you begin to recoup your investment."

"Could we have a moment to discuss it between us?" Casey stammered.

Hamid nodded and arose, carefully setting his napkin on his seat.

"I will visit the restroom and give you a few minutes to discuss my offer. Keep in mind, the money is no strings attached. If we cannot come to an agreement, you will keep the money. That is how serious I am about this."

He walked away from their table, leaving three very stunned men behind.

"Did he say what I think he said?" Manuel asked.

Blake snorted. "If you think he offered us a cool fifty grand each to go to London, plus he wants to fund us, then yeah."

"That's a lot of earnest money..." Casey said with caution. "This seems a bit too good to be true. Is he trying to rob us?"

"Two questions," Blake said. "One, do any of us have more than a grand in our bank account? And two, do we have a choice not to take this offer?"

"Not if we want to see this project happen," Manuel noted. "You heard Dr. Devon, that heartless spoilsport. If the money clears our bank accounts, we go."

"Blake, is this Abu Dhabi crazy or Turkmenistan crazy?" Casey asked, picking up a tortilla chip and putting it back in the bowl.

"I don't see how anything could ever top Turkmenistan," Blake muttered. "I still have nightmares about that bus ride. It's more like Lagos crazy, minus the bakery you set on fire."

"I did not set it on fire. I only knocked over the candle."

"Which set it on fire."

Manuel held up both hands and they stopped to look quizzically at him.

"You two are insane, but the real question is, do we do it?"

Casey smiled, his eyes misting over with relief. *My wife will get that new kitchen.*

Blake and Casey both nodded agreement as Hamid approached their table, sliding into his seat with a soft smile on his face.

"Have you decided?"

Casey, Manuel, and Blake all looked at each other, smiling. Casey broke the silence.

"Can we call you Haj Hamid?"

"I suppose that would be alright." Hamid smiled.

"Alright, let's do it! We'll need to stop at our hotel and get our bags."

Twelve hours later, their pilot came on the intercom and announced, "We are now on final descent into London. I apologize. We are arriving in the rain so you can't see the sights. Please fasten your seatbelts."

Casey smiled as Blake stirred but did not wake. Blake lay in his luxurious seat in a partial fetal position, his CPAP mask lending him the air of a man in a hospital. A very nice hospital. The poor man was truly too tall and broad for any normally designed human seat, even the seats on a luxury corporate jet. Casey and Manuel had slept a bit but had been up for hours, too excited to take advantage of the luxury accommodations. The flight attendant had pampered them, and the meals had been gourmet.

"Mr. Blake," the flight attendant said, coming to stand over the slumbering giant. "Mr. Blake? It is time to put your seat up." She patted him on the shoulder, her face paled, and she turned to Casey. "Mr. Casey, sir, is Mr. Blake dead?"

"No need to trouble yourself." Casey winked, quite used to Blake's sleep patterns. "If he isn't up by the time we are landing, I'll wake him up in a violent manner that leaves no evidence."

Blake snorted, startling the flight attendant. She gave up, sighed dramatically, and went to get ready for landing.

Someday I'll take my wife in first class, Casey thought. *We'll go to the Maldives. Or somewhere truly exotic, like Arkansas.*

Laughing at his own joke, he restored his attention to Manuel, who had been conjugating verbs in Spanish for him. This was not the most effective way to teach or learn Spanish, but Casey got a bit out of it, and it made Manuel feel appreciated. Manuel had not slowed at the announcement, but finished conjugating 'defenestrar,' which Casey had asked him to do on a whim.

"We're almost there?" Manuel asked.

"El orangután defe… wait… defenestraba el bocadillo de jamón," Casey grinned and replied, "And I feel like I've run a marathon. Even reclined, sleeping on a plane is exhausting. But thank you for the Spanish. I will never speak as many languages as you, but I'll add Spanish to the list soon."

Hamid walked in as Manuel smiled and said, "Then I can teach you Portuguese, Italian, French, German, Dutch…"

Hamid laughed and bowed his head in respect. "That would be an impressive feat."

Casey nodded, though he had no intention of learning those. Spanish was important in the U.S., of course, but he only had so much time each day and only so many years left. Why learn languages his partner already spoke when he could learn ones that would be useful in business?

"We'll never speak as many as Blake." Casey raised his voice louder. "Of course, he only speaks four dozen languages because all he knows in any of them are swear words. He calls it a hobby."

Blake made a grunting sound, but otherwise didn't acknowledge the jibe.

"Very uncouth," Manuel said with a frown. "He gets the conjugations wrong half the time."

Hamid spread his hands and smiled softly. "We had a delay, but will land in a few more minutes." The smile faded as he turned to their sleeping giant. "Blake." He stood closer and said, "Blake! We need you to sit up for the landing."

Blake made no sound, though his machine pulsed air in and out.

"I got this." Casey stood and walked to the galley, where he grabbed a giant bottle of water. He returned to Blake's side and shook it. "Sit up or I pour this on your head."

Blake swore, then sat up, his grumbling echoing in his mask. Manuel cheerily greeted him. Blake ripped off his mask and replied with one of his favorite vulgarities in Icelandic. Casey had never bothered to translate, but Blake said it involved a goat. Why did so many swear words involve goats?

Casey smiled, then winked at Hamid. "Blake, you're positively a delight when you first wake up. But don't worry. You'll get your coffee soon enough. Maybe we can get you some good Turkish coffee from Cafe Nazar in Lampton. If they're open."

Blake, continuing to swear under his breath, situated himself.

"I will never understand why they don't make seats big enough for a normal sized person," Blake muttered.

"Because even if you lost every ounce of fat and muscle on your body," Casey replied, "you'd be a foot taller and a foot wider than 99% of the population."

"Bah," was all Blake had to say in response.

Had Blake ever gone running with Casey and Manuel, maybe he would have fit in a seat better. However, he stated it was 'torture' and was 'covered under a secret portion of the Geneva convention.' To be honest, Casey hated running, but did it for Manuel's sake. And because his doctor said it would help with his anxiety and depression. He wasn't sure if this was true. Either the exercise or the medicine kept his mental health stable, and he wouldn't risk giving up either. Not when he'd been so close to giving up not long before switching to working on outer space projects.

"I will go prepare for landing." Hamid left with a bow.

Manuel had pulled out his notebook and now spoke excitedly.

"So, I derived the equations needed to describe the fields, but I don't think it will work."

Casey blinked, not having any context to understand what Manuel was talking about. Mind racing, he guessed. "Are you talking about that thing you were talking about at Abejas?"

"Yes," Manuel said, face confused at Casey's ignorance.

Casey smiled. This was part of being friends with Manuel. He would pick up conversations they had finished days, weeks, or even years earlier and continue them as if they had been in the middle of them.

"So, why won't it work?" Casey asked, knowing he would not understand much. He knew all the words but did not know they went together that way.

"Magnetic fields cannot be used to effectively make artificial fusion occur. Not at any reasonable scale in an energetically positive way. That's why there are stars."

Casey nodded sagely, putting his thinking expression on. The one that others assumed meant he understood and was formulating a response. It meant, 'What in the world is he talking about and how do I respond coherently?'

He went for a question in response, which was always safe with Manuel. "What other fields could you use? There are magnetic fields, electric fields... Umm... Other fields..."

"That's not a distinction that matters. Electromagnetic fields are basically the same thing, mathematically."

Casey reached deep into his 'Useless Trivia from High School Physics' file and said, "What about gravity? Isn't it a field?"

Manuel sat back, cocked his head, and sat staring at him without blinking. Casey began his usual game and counted up from zero, reaching 57 before Manuel blinked several times, grabbed his notebook, and began scribbling furiously.

Casey smiled and let him work.

A quarter hour later, they bumped and bounced to a fairly dignified, safe landing. *No motion sickness. Nice plane.* As they taxied, he pulled out his phone and checked for service. They'd had intermittent internet over land and none at sea. Now they were at civilization again, he hoped to send his wife a message.

She'd preempted him. He chuckled as his phone blew up with incoming messages. Clearing all, he dove straight to their chat, containing over 18 years of messages. This was the home to their triumphs, tragedies, and mundane requests to pick up milk at the store. It was one of his most precious sources of comfort on trips, because there, synced to the cloud for safety, he could read a strange view of the story of their life.

He quickly caught up, enjoying every scraped knee for his young children and the crushes and drama of his teenage children. Part of him mourned he couldn't be there to be a full part of their lives, but he was there in part by his wife reaching out to tell him. Though he didn't mind that he wasn't there to help choose their new kitchen. She informed him she would finish by the time he got back if she could help it.

We just landed, he wrote. *It's very dark here.*

It's always fun when you are overseas to think of you on the other side of a giant ball, she replied.

I haven't been to London in years. I hope I can bring you here soon. Are you going to do the whole kitchen yourself or hire help for once?

I will do every last bit of it myself. I've had this planned for two years.

Hamid walked out of the cockpit.

"I never told you, but I am an amateur pilot, both fixed wing and rotor. I take every opportunity to practice that I can and was our pilot for most of the flight."

"Excellent flying, Haj Hamid." Hamid impressed Casey. Most scientists did not have time for hobbies.

"I did not want to scare you, but I was piloting on that landing," Hamid said with a shy smile.

"Well, we're not dead, so good job," Blake grunted.

Casey rolled his eyes. "What my barbarian of a friend means is, 'I'm still half asleep so I can't form a polite sentence, but you did an excellent job.'"

Blake grunted again. "Yeah, that."

Hamid seemed nervous, but continued to speak. "There was one time I was flying a helicopter into Derby when a freak storm slammed into us. It was me and my wife and I was so scared. But my wife is a dear thing and sung to me, calming my nerves. I landed without difficulty."

As the engine spun down and the flight crew opened the door, Hamid stared at the ground, wrung his hands, and shifted from foot to foot. "My friends, I have to apologize to you. I have not been entirely honest with you. You are all far too trusting. Of course, seeing fifty thousand dollars in your bank accounts would be very convincing. And fear not, your families are provided for. I am not a monster. But..." Here he paused.

Two large men in military uniforms came on board the plane. Casey quickly typed on his phone before Hamid walked among Casey and his team and took their cell phones. Tears welled in Hamid's eyes.

"My real name is Hamid Jabiri, of the Iranian Space Agency. These men are joining us for the last leg of our flight. We are refueling here in Morocco and will fly directly to Iran." Hamid paused and appeared to collect himself and his voice became wooden, like a bad recital. "Your mission is the same. We are going to build your spaceship, we are going to capture asteroids, and we will return them to near-Earth orbit. But Iran will be the nation to lead this. We will stake our claim to space decisively and bring peace to our homeland."

It was worse than Casey could have dreamed. Iran, enemy of freedom, oppressor of women, and all-around despotic nation. Casey fought the panic welling in his heart, threatening to swamp his senses.

Hamid walked away but paused and turned to face them. "I truly am sorry for the deception. You are all wonderful men. This would be easier if you were all knaves, like the Ayatollah says all Westerners are. But you are not, so I apologize, deeply."

With a bow, Hamid turned around and walked into the cockpit. The two soldiers sat down in the front of the cabin, swiveling their chairs to face the three devastated men, handguns on their laps. Casey knew his face was ashen. He looked to his friends. Manuel looked more confused than fearful, which made sense. Manuel had never joined Blake and him in danger. Blake's face was nothing but grim lines. With his complexion, he could never be called 'pale,' but Casey knew him. That look meant he was ready to break something. If he hadn't already attacked, there was no chance of escape. Yet. Casey fought to breathe.

The flight attendant came up to Casey and spoke with jarring cheerfulness. "Breakfast is being loaded onto the plane. Can I get you some coffee or tea while we refuel?"

Esin sat plastered in sheetrock dust among the debris of a kitchen remodel she had begun almost the moment the money cleared the bank and stared at her phone in confusion. Casey's last message read, "Well, I'm not surprised sos." He had never typed 'sos' to her before. Even if he did, he'd have typed it with proper spelling and punctuation. Not lowercase. She texted back, asking him what he meant, but he had stopped typing. Then his avatar showed him go offline.

She waited for a full minute, unsure of what to do. She had learned what SOS meant when she arrived in the U.S. nearly two decades earlier as a young adult refugee. Afghanistan had been a hard life and there was no sending SOS to anyone. She'd fought her own battles and left her enemies buried in the sand.

Until Casey came into her life, the first man besides her father to treat her with genuine respect and dignity. For over 18 years, he had been a companion and partner to her. He'd had many times when he asked her for help in emergencies. Never once had he sent her a literal SOS.

When no further messages came, she pulled out Casey's personal laptop and signed in, her hands shaking. Thank goodness she had finally memorized his latest ridiculously long password. She pulled up his phone locator, and it searched for his phone.

Last known location: Rabat, Morocco, 2 minutes ago.

Her eyes widened and she froze with mouth agape. Every few minutes, she refreshed the location.

3 minutes ago.

No flight to London would fly to Morocco first.

4 minutes ago.

He texted me that he had landed in London. He thought he was in London.

7 minutes ago.

He sent an SOS. No. No, it can't be.

10 minutes ago.

Closing the laptop, she rose and paced the room. She began to mutter to herself, waving her hands as she negotiated with herself. Finally, she sank to the ground, beat her fists on the pile of downed sheet rock next to her, and sobbed.

Silence reigned on the flight until after they'd taken off.

Alright Casey, pull yourself together. Sure, we've been kidnapped by a psychotic government run by extremists and murderers. Sure, your best friends are in the same boat and your families are going to be left father- less. Sure, they expect you to build a space mission that is first of its kind in a year. But really, how is that different from some of the more bizarre situations you've been in?

Casey realized he had not been breathing in far too long.

Manuel broke into his escalating thoughts and asked, "You speak the language, right Casey?"

Casey replied mechanically, "I learned it partly in Afghanistan, at an iron mine in Bamyan province, and mostly from my wife. But Iran and Afghanistan have different accents. Kind of like British versus American English, but a little more severe. I should be able to understand it and be understood. Mostly."

"Alright, we need you to do your thing, Casey." Manuel pointed to Casey's notebook. "You need to list our resources. Start with lan- guages."

Casey knew what Manuel was doing. Casey had taught Manuel this exact trick. Get Casey talking about things that were not panic inducing and use it to ease into the panic.

"Besides Persian, I learned Turkish while automating a mineral processing plant at a gold mine in the Munzur Mountains along the Euphrates River. And a few other jobs. I learned Arabic mostly while in Saudi Arabia at the Ras Tanura refinery doing some seismic work. Blake was with me for all the jobs. Saw each other more than our wives."

"Don't remind me." Blake shuddered.

Casey felt his heart grow a tiny bit lighter, so he punched Blake, picked up his notebook, and continued. "I did the systems engineering;

Blake did the mining engineering and geology. That was when you were working for NASA."

"Write it down," Manuel said.

Casey picked up his notebook and wrote, 'Resources, Languages: Persian, Turkish, Arabic (Casey).'

The flight attendant handed out hot towels to each of them. Manuel refused and continued his questioning.

"I never asked. How did you learn the languages and Blake didn't?"

Casey felt the panic rise and fall and rise. He fought it the one way he knew. *Laugh. Don't let them win.* "Because he's a lazy shlub."

Blake chimed in with mock indignation. "No, because I had better things to do than study languages."

"Like getting the high score in Angry Birds?" Casey quipped

Blake leaned back, allowing the diligent and clueless flight attendant to place the next meal. "Exactly. Those birds weren't going to avenge themselves. And I was also getting the lay of the land and keeping you out of trouble. You had the field training of a civilian."

"Yes, you were in the Army before college, sabemos, sabemos," Manuel interjected. "So, soldier, give us a... what is it called?"

Casey frowned, the situation feeling real and the beginnings of panic rising in his chest. "Situational report."

Blake also frowned, but his priorities were elsewhere. He spoke to the flight attendant.

"Could I have another roll? Actually, give me the rest of your rolls. Basically, any bread on this plane."

When the flight attendant left, clearly confused, he turned back to them and spoke without his usual humor.

"Sitrep. We screwed up and got ourselves kidnapped by a ruthless but decaying dictatorship. They're taking us to Iran, a regime controlled by the ayatollahs with a weakening iron fist. They enforce Sharia law with rigor and don't tolerate dissent, though most of the people are in rebellion against their leaders with protests and violence escalating. The government is especially vicious toward certain minorities, religious and ethnic. Assuming the people around us speak English, we will have to watch what we say carefully, as they have a lot of spies among the populace. Technically, there isn't supposed to be any interconnection between the U.S. and Iran. The State Department has a blanket 'Do Not Travel' statement for Americans going to Iran, though you can get a visa from Iran of late. I'm surprised they didn't try to hire us."

"Tea, coffee, wine?" The flight attendant handed Blake a sizable bag of rolls.

"Manuel is former NASA," Casey explained, stealing an extra roll for himself from the bag. "No way the State Department would let us go to Iran. Missile tech is something they hold tight."

Blake slowly chewed on a roll, which he had buttered liberally. He swallowed, tapped his chin, and continued. "Either way, someone in their government wants to do this outside of normal channels and probably to save face internationally. Kidnapping from American soil could cause a huge incident. If word of our presence there leaks, the U.S. will demand our release. Iran will try to spin it that we went willingly. The money in our bank accounts will probably get traced to the Iranians, so they'll cite that as evidence that we came without duress. However, if I know Casey, he blabbed every bit of the details of the deal to his wife, who will tell the police everything when we come up missing and the investigation will show we never landed in England. But this is going to be a very hush-hush operation for as long as they can get away with it."

Casey processed the information, replying, "I hope we're in the west, near Turkey. I have friends..."

Blake shook his head, giving a warning glare as the flight attendant walked by, taking coffee to their babysitters. "Assume anything we say is being monitored from now on. We need to speak as obtusely as possible."

"So, I can speak normally?" Manuel asked.

Blake and Casey stared at Manuel incredulously, but Manuel couldn't maintain the straight face, so he winked at them, bringing all three to soft laughter.

Casey sat back and relaxed his vice grip on the armrests. Feeling some of the panic he had been feeling ebb.

"I guess we finally got the funding, even if Dr. Jerk Face said we wouldn't," Manuel said. "Congrats, team."

The three of them exchanged looks and then they laughed until they cried.

Casey finally reined in his hysterical laughter, took a deep breath, and spoke.

"Well, this is a horrendous situation, but I can't think of two goofballs I'd rather be with. We may be doomed, but at least we'll die building a spaceship with a wisecrack on our lips."

###

Hamid sat in the cockpit. The dull roar of the wind and the engines comforted him with memories of his years in the Imperial Iranian Air Force. The words from the cabin brought the opposite emotion. The men were more solemn than they had been, but somehow, they were cracking jokes! They were laughing!

His thoughts were a jumble. This was his first overseas operation, and he'd accomplished his mission objectives without a misstep. He had kidnapped a team of engineers to build a spacecraft that would bring glory to his homeland, or more likely, to General Telebi. Why did it make his heart hurt? These were infidels who defied the will of Allah, living a life of decadence and sin. Except they weren't, and he never had believed that every American could be so bad. These men had families, spoke with admiration of their wives, loved their children, and worked hard. Nothing like the government preached them to be. More like what the protesters said. He shuddered, thoughts of his family reminding him of what was at stake.

Laughing voices came through his headset. Manuel was speaking.

"So, what's the food like? Do you think they'll be smart enough to feed us well? Because if I am starved and tortured, they'll get lousy results. My wife told me that I am a figurative bear when hungry."

"You are not a literal bear," Blake said. "I've had some amazing Iranian cuisine in my day. Trust me, the food will be delicious. Hey, I thought of a movie. You guys ever seen Bridge Over the River Kwai?"

"Yeah, great movie," Casey said. "Worth another watch when we get home."

"I have not seen it," Manuel replied with obvious curiosity. "What is it about?"

Hamid ignored their currently meaningless conversation and shifted in his seat to get more comfortable. He had to have his report prepared for his superiors by the time he landed. He had to justify himself on every step he had taken. It irked him, as he was a scientist and was trying to explain details of extreme technical intricacy to a group of ignorant generals and politicians who didn't know the difference between Neptune and Pluto. Sighing, he typed.

Having asteroid-derived space stations in orbit will not only provide the prestige of being a spacefaring nation, but will also provide an additional source of income as we rent berths to other nations. We will even have the opportunity to charge exorbitant fees to the Great Satan, the United States, as they will have no one else to turn to without being left behind in the new space race completely.

Casey's voice broke into his thoughts. "I believe we'll get out of this somehow, gentlemen. God has never forsaken us. Yes, we were kidnapped by a government that not only tortures and kills its enemies, but sometimes its own friends. So, yes, it's possible we may die. But I don't think we will. I have a feeling that if we are true to our convictions, we will make it home to our children."

"I may not believe in your religion," Blake drawled, "but your instincts have never led us wrong. Except in that sales call in Sudan."

"You would bring up the rental car," Casey replied with a laugh. "But did I not convince that nice man to tow it back to town with his camel? And did we not get a great meal out of it?"

There was a pause and Blake spoke. "Manuel, your face... What's wrong?"

"Why did you eat the camel?"

Hamid struggled to tune out the laughter and his troubled thoughts turned to the pictures of the men's children they had shown him. They were so proud, with children as old as twenty. He was still a young father. His oldest was not quite 6 years old. What would his children think if they knew that he'd stolen three fathers from their children? He steeled himself to write the next section. He may have flown jets, but he was a scientist first. As a scientist, he abhorred the violence his superiors craved. But it was this or they would hurt his family. He'd also have no job without this project. This was his only shot at leaving the poverty of his youth behind. He felt nauseous.

Further, the ability to control asteroids first means the ability to drop asteroids from space onto enemies of the Islamic Republic. This power will only last until the enemy gains the same power, at which point they will be able to stop our attempts, and we theirs. Time is of the essence, or this upper hand will be lost.

Casey's voice, barely loud enough for him to hear over the noise of the plane, cut through him like fire. "Dear God, we pray this day for Hamid and our captors that you will soften their hearts, and they will see fit to give us our freedom. If not, bless us to know what to do to return home to our families. And bless Blake to stop sniggering during my prayers..."

Hamid remembered his former science teacher who had spoken out against inhumane treatment of political dissidents. The Revolutionary Guard had dragged Hamid and his professor's students to come and watch as they stoned the teacher and his entire family to death. Hamid shuddered and tried to ignore the prayer and type again, the remembered screams of the children making each meaningless platitude he wrote a torture.

Esin walked into Google headquarters ready to cause a stink, which would have been very noticeable, as the place smelled... Like there was no smell at all. *Why is there no smell?*

Surprisingly, they were very accommodating, especially when she showed them her husband's power of attorney. He had made a permanent one fifteen years earlier when he traveled overseas so much. She had full rights to act in Casey's name. Considering how useless the Google online help system was, the in-person people were very helpful.

After legal had cleared it, the specialist led her back to his glass-walled office. "Of course, I'd be glad to help you find your husband. What a strange set of circumstances. You're sure he didn't just try to disappear?"

"Yes, it is against his nature. His last known location was Morocco," Esin began.

"But his phone was shut off at that point?"

"Yes, but it was an android. You guys can track it further, can't you?"

"Afraid not. Not without the phone power being on. Tracking powered down phones is only for silly sci-fi movies."

The office was bizarre, with high-chairs, a desk to match, and bean bags around the floor and one on a low table. He gestured her to the last bean bag, where she sagged into the squishiness under the weight of the bad news. How else could they find him?

Then she sat up, eyes alight with the spark of an idea. "We can't track his phone but... Can we track his path in another way? Can you analyze Google searches that are abnormal by location?"

He leaned forward, chin in his hands, elbows on the desk, feet dangling like a child in the large chair. "Yes, we analyze searches like that regularly. What did you have in mind?"

She felt the first glimmer of genuine hope she'd had in days and spoke quickly. "Please, look for searches starting 4 or 5 days ago and up to today where they went from very few or no searches for 'asteroid mining' and then spike to many searches."

The specialist's eyes betrayed surprise, and he sat up, typing and clicking like he was trying out for a movie role as a hacker. Except he did so for far longer than a movie hacker could have gotten away with.

"Well, this is quite a distinct result. In the U.S., it appears there was a spike in Colorado, though it tapered off quickly."

"No, that's where things started. What about internationally?"

"There are several IP addresses in Iran that went from no searches for those terms to an extremely high number of searches, some ongoing. Tehran, specifically their government offices, had an increase. However, an IP address in Urmia had the most dramatic spike."

Esin stood, smiling for the first time in a week. "That's it! They took him there." The pieces all fell together in her mind. She realized someone in Iran had kidnapped her husband to build them his asteroid mining probe. This was no investment firm. It was the Revolutionary Guard!

The specialist's eyes were the size of saucers. "It's like an adventure movie. Kidnapped by the Iranians!"

"But this is real life." Esin put her hands on his desk. "And my husband is a real-life hero, not an action movie hero."

The specialist sighed. "I wish I could offer you more help."

"You may be able to." Esin leaned close to him and whispered. "Can you use any backdoor or underhanded means to get me some names? Can we narrow it down to some specific people?"

"Well... I'm not supposed to but..." The man fidgeted, looking from his computer to the ceiling, then to her, where she sat with face drawn and forlorn. "Well, this is only between us, as this is a special case. Let me see."

He typed for a few minutes, which was not nearly as exciting as movies made hackers out to be. His face also made some strange contortions, which she focused on to prevent excessive fidgeting. He finally smiled.

"Bingo. This guy does not use his VPN correctly and does everything logged into his personal account from government offices. Sloppy. Firouz Telebi. General."

###

Casey stood and stared without flinching as the menacing bear growled and threatened him and his men. The rage in the bear's eyes was nothing to the courage in his heart, but even a mighty hunter would balk at infuriating a dangerous beast like this.

General Telebi stood close enough for Casey to smell the alcohol on his breath. Odd that Telebi could get away with it while he would put others to death for doing the same. The privileges of power, Casey supposed. Why anyone would let a dangerous beast like this have alcohol… They stood in Telebi's opulent office; guards having brought them down to explain to the general why they were not making some kind of Herculean progress on the rocket system. The room was full of an odd collection of beautiful art, shelves of liquors, and some downright hideous trinkets probably bought from flea markets. Telebi was a stocky man, bordering on obese, of middling height, with a once handsome face hidden by a graying beard. And he was angry, poking Casey's chest with a swollen finger for emphasis.

Given, he was probably always angry. Telebi spoke with a mix of cold anger and occasional hot outbursts, saying something about ingratitude and incompetence. Casey put on his best poker face. Unless depression and anxiety overwhelmed him, Casey could school his face to say anything. Right now, it said nothing. Telebi continued to stare at him in rage as Hamid translated.

"The general insists you explain again why you cannot do everything you need to do in the space he provided for you and with the resources on your laptops in the 3 months he desires. I apologize, he is unaware of engineering realities. I am theoretically in charge of the entire project, but he appreciates being informed. Intermittently.”

Telebi stormed away to pace behind his desk while Casey thought, *Well, he sure did tone that translation down. He left the entire bit about goats and orifices out.*

Casey breathed in to speak, the smell of alcohol and mildew reminding him of the time he went to a frat party in college. There were some bears at that party, too. This bear would have to back down in the face of reality or the prize would be unreachable. “Haj Hamid, we will do the work you assign, as we are captives with no choice, but we can’t very well function in a vacuum. We cannot design a mission without full access to all schematics for the rockets you have, the hardware you expect us to interface with, and the control systems you intend us to communicate with. Further, a single barracks room without a desk is hardly sufficient for what you asked us to build. Plus, we must have access to at least some amount of the internet to find references, besides the obvious need for occasional entertainment to allow our minds to relax so we can do our jobs. I do not desire to incur the general’s wrath, but our laptops are insufficient to design an entire mission, let alone one that is, in final scope, akin to the Apollo missions. We can do Phase 1, since you have told us you already have several rockets built and available. With a large team. But we can do nothing in three months. This first mission, if the rocket is truly ready, we could finish in three years.” Casey screamed inside. He could not be away from his family for three years with no contact. He thought a moment more, then added, “And, Mr. Jabiri, I beg you. I need my medications to be successful in any measure. I know they are only for anxiety and depression, but those are real medical concerns.”

Hamid raised an eyebrow at that, face awash with terror. He relayed the message to the general, who listened with growing anger. The general replied in a near scream, throwing pencils and pens at Hamid. Hamid spoke with passion and terror but deference while the general stormed around the office. Hamid let the words and objects bounce off of him without reaction. Casey caught 80% of what Hamid said and about 20% of what Telebi replied, meaning he was thoroughly lost. Hamid was most definitely not telling Telebi everything.

Casey glanced over at Manuel and Blake. Manuel was humming to himself quietly, probably brainstorming orbital paths they might use. Blake saw Casey's look and rolled his eyes at the general, then he scooted close to Casey, drawing Manuel over, too.

"Okay, I doubt General Teletubby bugged his own office, so let's talk. First, Apollo? This isn't 1/100th of that."

"Hyperbole to get more resources and slack. And nice nickname choice."

Blake dusted some fake dust off his lapel and smirked. "Yes, thank you. When someone tees up a shot like that, you have to take it."

"A sports metaphor? You haven't watched sports since... ever."

"I'd totally have gone pro if I hadn't blown out my knee."

Manuel's eyes widened. "You played sports? Was it football?"

"Croquet. Now shut up. I have friends that stayed in the Army, and they feed me non-classified chatter. Probably some classified, too, but I'll never tell. Anyway, we're at the Urmia Research Center, and it is bad news. Weird stuff happens here. Space mission development must be a recent addition. But I'd wager my first born that it's locked down harder than a teenager when you try to take their phone."

A pencil bounced off Hamid's head and flew among the three of them.

"That metaphor made no sense," Casey replied. "But from what I can understand of this oaf's rantings, Teletubby is a bloodthirsty nut job, but may be the 'quick to anger, quick to calm' type. I think we have a chance for sympathy with Hamid, but not this guy. Hamid is definitely pandering to him, but he has a boundary that he's sticking to. He insists that the general treat us well."

Another pencil bounced off Hamid's nose. The general had impressive accuracy.

"We need to figure out how to get privacy for a longer talk," Blake whispered. "Try to figure out how they're bugging us."

Telebi spun and marched to stare out his window as Hamid turned back to them, his face compressed and red, his fists clenched. "General Telebi still will not allow me to provide you with the medications, as he insists this will 'toughen you up.' However, he has *graciously* agreed to provide you with larger facilities and supervised access to our schematics and the internet. I will provide you with my best technician, name of Sarosh. He's young but is by far the best English speaker and is exceptionally clever. He'll be running things someday and will get things setup for you. Oh, and he is my brother."

Hamid took a breath. "I will continue negotiations at a later time, when he calms down. Telebi says that absolutely, without fail, you must finish in a year. I do apologize for the general. He says that if you do not finish in time, he will kill you and send men to kill your families." Hamid hung his head. "And mine." He lifted his head, facing them with an intense, pleading look on his face. "Please don't judge my people based on him."

Casey put on a fake smile and glanced at the floor littered with pencils, pens, and knick-knacks. "Of course not, Haj Hamid. But that is at least some good news. Let's leave the general to his murderous musings and get to work."

Esin,

I believe someday I will make it home and so I will fill this notebook with letters you will not see until I escape. I will hide it where I hide all the mementos I love to look at and fill it with the things of my heart. And my liver. Maybe my spleen. Whatever organs feel like sharing.

We are walking a razor's edge. This does not feel like real life. This feels like one of those stories I love to read. But those aren't supposed to happen to real people. Not to me. A wicked government has taken us captive. They charged us to bring asteroids back 'for the glory of Iran.' That I will not do. But I feel I must make them believe I will. And I must carry much of this burden myself, as Manuel is incapable of lying and Blake doesn't have a filter. I will be spokesman, as I have always been.

They're keeping us in an old barracks. The walls are bare, so we'll fill them. The room echoes with the drip of a leaky faucet in the bathroom. We'll fix the faucet and play forest sounds from our laptops. The air is stale and damp. We'll figure that one out. Maybe we'll pretend we're in Florida. Not much we can do with 90% humidity! But for every problem, I'll think of a solution. Because that's what you would do. I tease you about your overwhelming optimism, but I think I will miss that attitude in short order. So, since you aren't here to be my hummingbird of optimism, I will have to croak out my best rendition of your tune. Hope I don't shatter any glass...

I had a decent amount of my medicine with me, but the general won't allow me to get more. He says it's an indulgence. I am tapering down to make it last a bit less than two months. Hopefully, I'm not hit too hard by withdrawals. I'm also doubling my exercise regimen. But I'm scared. I know the adrenaline of crisis will last a time, but once this becomes routine, I'll be on my own. But I believe in Jesus' grace, and I will endure despite all. I will return to you.

Love ever,

Casey

Casey hid his notebook and went to the shower, the dim lighting and the creeping mold on the walls adding to his sense of foreboding and imminent overwhelm. He knew he'd be showering after exercising in the morning, but sleep was elusive, and he had no mindless videos to lull him to somnolence. The shower was the next best thing.

The water hit him, and he backed out, turning the heat down even more. Casey always hated the moment the water hit his body, but especially hot water. He turned it to lukewarm and stood, letting the water cascade over him. He mindlessly rotated on occasion, keeping his skin from getting cold.

His mind raced as he played scenarios in his head. During shower time, he would tell entire stories in his head as he stood there. If depression took him, he'd sit and tell sad stories. Today's stories were alternate versions of this week.

'Hello, Mr. Scarlett. I'm Hamid Jabiri. I want to fund your asteroid ventures.'

'Mr. Jabiri, I'm pleased to meet you. Here is my card.'

'And here is mine. Can we do dinner tonight?'

'But of course.'

His mind shifted back to his team.

'Blake, you've got friends in strange places. Do a background check on this guy, please.'

'You bet… So, the financial institution is valid, but my contact took it a step deeper. It's a front for an Iranian firm.'

He mumbled, "No, no, no, they wouldn't have been so sloppy."

'You bet… So, the financial institution is valid, but this Hamid is new there. Started a few weeks ago. We should be cautious. Not sure he has the time there to be offering funding.'

Stop it, he shouted to himself. *You did what you did. Made-up scenarios and self-recrimination will not get you out of this. Stop it.*

Casey continued to circle. As quickly as he told himself to stop, he continued in a new story.

Manuel flipped the switch, triggering the bomb. The back wall of the barracks blew out, exposing the grass of the compound's field.

'Go, go, go,' Blake shouted, and they ran through the rubble strewn field towards the far wall. No one could see them because they'd killed the power to the building.

As they reached the compound's main gate, they saw a jeep with two men in it, looking confused. Blake grabbed one and Casey the other, and they knocked them out and then climbed in the jeep, Manuel in the back. Racing towards the wall, they burst through the chain-link fence and drove away.

Racing behind them, a pair of motorcycles were fast approaching. Manuel, rummaging in the back, pulled out a machine gun and quickly mowed the two cyclists down. Racing along, they crossed the distance to approach the Turkish border.

Abandoning their jeep, they crawled across the border, under razor wire, until they emerged on the Turkish side. Casey called out to the Turks in their own language, where they received them with much rejoicing.

"That wasn't very realistic," he mumbled. "Manuel has never even fired a gun."

He began another version. Then another. Eventually he tired and headed to bed, feeling further from a solution than he had when he started.

###

"And so, I need to go to Turkey to meet with a general about how to get my husband back."

Esin's sister-in-law, Sue, stared at her from across her kitchen table like she'd grown a second head. And maybe a third. "Esin, I've known you since my insane big brother showed up with you at our house and asked our parents to give you a place to stay." She reached for her hand and placed it on Esin's. "And I am so grateful for that day. You've been my dear friend and sister ever since. So, I say this with all my love." She took a deep breath and continued. "Have you lost your ever-loving mind!?"

Esin smiled wanly, glancing down at her cup, the smell of the herbal tea battling with her anxiety. "My heart is troubled, Sue. I feel I must go and see this out. Casey is going to need me before the end. He risked his life rescuing me. I must risk mine for him."

Sue stood and started pacing across the floor that, until recently, had been linoleum and was now bare wood.

"If it were only you and him, I'd call that super romantic and give you a hug and send you on your way. But with him gone, all your children have left is you! If you go to Turkey, what are you going to do? Perhaps you can get them to send special forces in to rescue him, but why would you have to go?"

"It has to be me. I don't know why, but it does." Esin glanced at Sue with her face scrunched in sorrow. "Sue, please, this is already hard enough. I need your understanding and support. I have the strongest feeling that I have to go and that I will spend months there. Perhaps longer. I need your help. I need mom and dad's help."

"Esin..." Sue's eyes swam with tears. "How can you ask me to send you into danger? To risk leaving your children orphans. We don't even know if Casey is alive."

Esin stood and spoke quietly but with a piercing vehemence, "He is alive. I tracked him to Iran. He's there. General Nacar has been monitoring things. He's alive."

Sue shook her head. "Why aren't we getting the police involved? The FBI? The CIA?"

"Sue, the Iranians transferred each of them fifty thousand dollars! You know how the government will react. This has to be us. Jane and Rosa are running interference on the business front. I need you and our parents to keep the children out of trouble. They are Casey's children, you know. They get some wild notions. Remember how Matthew built a crossbow for launching cantaloupes last summer?"

Sue sat down, eyes welling with tears even as she laughed. "Maybe I'm too scared. Maybe it's because my intuition isn't attuned to your life." Her shoulders slumped. "Alright, I'll be here for the children. I'll help you. But I do not know what I'll do if one of them builds something insane."

Esin came around the table and sat down next to Sue.

"I'll warn them to only build things that are partly insane."

The two of them laughed, cried, and then laughed until it was time to act.

Casey stared at Blake's workbench. Chaos reigned, as usual. There were gadgets and gizmos aplenty, though there were no singing teenage mermaids, and what they'd make of this mess was anyone's guess. In true Blake fashion, he'd covered almost every square inch in something, including photographs of his family in frames he'd welded from scrap metal while their handler Sarosh looked on in befuddlement. But at the center, there was a fancy-looking drone. "Blake, what in the world are you working on?" He sniffed the air. "Were you soldering?"

"Shh, it's a surprise for you both."

Manuel lifted his head up with wide eyes, though he didn't look nearly as stressed as Casey felt. Still doing applied math, Manuel had probably forgotten where they were.

"Well, that's not unbearably cryptic." Casey rolled his eyes. "Anyway, when do Manuel and I get our picture frames? We want to mope over our families, too."

"As soon as they get me more gases for the dumb welder." Blake rolled his eyes. "Now, I'll show you the surprise in a minute. Now be quiet. I want to focus."

They went back to work, and after a few more rounds of annoyed curses, Blake flipped a switch on the device. That resulted in some happy curses. They stared at him as he fiddled a bit more, then yelled across the bay. "Sarosh, could you do me a huge favor and go grab us some parts?"

Their minder and internet lackey, Sarosh, looked up from his computer with a haggard expression. Casey guessed he was about twenty. Clever and cautious, he had orders to read every word of any website they wanted him to search before he gave them the saved html file or pdf for their use. They didn't need much, but his English was not nearly up to reading technical journals, like Casey's Persian wasn't up to reading much of anything. Sarosh was behind by about 200 requests and was so stressed he had even stopped talking to them to improve his English. Now he read and occasionally wept when they added more requests to the list.

"What parts, Mr. Blake?"

"I sent an order request to the electronics shop," Blake said with careful enunciation, though his accent made that less helpful than it should have been. "I need to test your electronics to verify they can handle the loads we'll need. You look like you need a break, anyway."

Sarosh closed his laptop. "Yes, Mr. Blake. I could use a break."

"Take your time." Blake winked at Sarosh. "In fact, I doubt we'd notice if it took you an hour to get back."

Sarosh appeared confused, then the implications crept over his face. "Yes, it may take me an hour to get back. Very busy down there." With a brightness to his step that they hadn't seen in days, Sarosh headed right out the door.

Casey cocked his head and raised an eyebrow, to which Blake laughed.

"Merry early Christmas. With Sarosh out of the way for a bit, we're free to talk."

"You sneaky man," Manuel said with a laugh. "You learned how to redirect personnel for personal benefit in the Army, too?"

Blake winked. "That's classified."

Manuel frowned. "Then what is that you were making?"

"Micro-drone. I had the plans on my computer, and they had the parts." He flicked another switch, and a tiny buzzing device took off and flew straight up, then straight back down.

"Anyway, that was to clear my mind, though we can probably use it for equipment inspection if they ask why I made it. But with Sarosh gone, we can talk freely."

He cleared his throat, then struck a pose in his seat like he was doing a poetry reading. "I will begin by insulting General Teletubby. He is a lecherous beast of a man. I can't repeat half of what they say about him in the lunchroom, mostly because they only say half of it in English."

Manuel frowned. "What if they are monitoring us over snooping devices?"

Casey shook his head, a smile spreading on his face. "Sarosh is their monitoring device. If they had listening devices in the lab, Sarosh would never have said what he just said to us out loud. Plus, they gave us these labs last minute. I bet they didn't have time to prepare a listening system. Or the budget. This isn't some movie where they have time to plant devices and then the staff to monitor them. The regime is in shambles from the protests, strikes, and international sanctions. Hamid is always complaining about not having enough personnel as it is!"

"Actually, we should first talk about Sarosh." Blake spoke with a level of seriousness Casey hadn't seen since the police in Namibia held them for a few hours. No sense of humor, those guys. "We need him out of here if we're going to get anything done or speak freely at all. How do we do it? We can't have him reporting to his big brother."

They sat pondering for a moment, then Manuel shrugged. "We requisition him some noise canceling headphones. He loves to listen to loud music on that ancient iPod of his, but he seems to have only one working earbud."

Casey laughed out loud. "You devious man, that's great! Blake, quick, add to the requisition to the electronics shop that we need noise canceling headphones. I've seen some people wearing them among the general's idiot staff. We can give them to Sarosh as a gift of appreciation for his hard work."

Blake was already typing, "Justification... Testing the audio output of the asteroid grabbing mechanism and interference with acoustic devices."

Manuel narrowed his eyes at him, "But that doesn't make any sense and isn't true."

"We're lying to them," Casey explained.

Manuel's eyes lit up. "Oh, right. We have to lie to them. They're the bad guys."

"They are definitely the bad guys," Blake replied. "At least, some of them. We have to figure out how to get away. I've been coming up dry on ideas on how to get out of this base. It's locked down something serious. It's odd. We appear to have near unlimited leash to run on, but the moment we go towards the outer doors, we're stopped by a half-dozen men."

Casey jumped in. "Agreed on the escape, but unless someone has ideas, let's first talk about the mission. The two go hand in hand. I've done a broad analysis of the documents they gave us."

"You skimmed them," Blake translated.

Casey continued, putting on his best stern face. "A broad, high-level executive analysis. We may have what we actually need to do this in a year, with some shortcuts. There are some key things they're holding out on us regarding the rockets, but we can get everything ready while we ferret that out."

Blake pulled out his notebook and Manuel poised himself at his computer. *This is what we do*, Casey thought to himself, feeling panic shouting at him to give up and mope.

"Manuel, now we have the rocket specs, do an analysis of what payloads we can take to what orbits. My guess is LEO is our limit, even with a very light payload. Analyze the potential for staging. Odds are, one stage isn't enough for our system, so we'll likely have to do two. In short, be creative."

Manuel smiled, having typed everything Casey said, and then asked, "How creative? Can I try alternate rocket engines? I have some breakthroughs for using a spinning, oscillating EM field to produce null spacetime, and I think it could lead to a fusion containment system which would allow for fusion-based rocket engines."

Casey raised an eyebrow. "Umm... That would be nice, but let's stick to the rockets they have for the asteroid mission. You can pursue that other thing in your spare time."

Manuel grinned more broadly, then got right to work. Casey knew Manuel knew what to do better than Casey, but hearing it gave Manuel a sense of drive he never had from solo work.

Casey turned to Blake. "Fortunately, you finished, more or less, until we learn from Manuel what we actually have to work with. Our designs are complete, our equipment lists are ready for parts ordering. So, I need you to pretend you're a mechanical engineer and start figuring out how we're going to attach our payload to these Iranian buckets and modify our designs accordingly. Work the Iranian engineers ragged collecting information for you and doing all those mechanical analyses our contractors are always going on about."

Blake jotted his notes down. "And of course, we sabotage the mission at the end. Alright, on to the escape. Any ideas?"

Manuel looked up from his computer and spoke. "Break out and flee to the nearest border?"

"If we can get out, that's fine," Casey said. "I think the nearest border is Turkey, but it'll be tough. Couple days of walking while patrols look for us unless we get a vehicle. Then we have to get across the border without getting shot. I have only been shot at crossing one border and it is-"

"Two," Blake interrupted. "You always forget Tijuana in college."

"But I got shot at *in* Tijuana, not at the border."

Blake ignored this obviously convincing argument and stated, "I don't think you two have the tactical training to do a daring escape, even if Casey and I have been in a few scrapes in the past. I know I'm not in the physical shape. If we escape, we need inside help."

Casey pondered on this. "Hamid or Sarosh. Or both. They are brothers."

"I could build us a rocket on the roof, and we could escape that way," Manuel said.

Casey laughed. "If you can figure that one out, more power to you."

Manuel nodded. "I will. Well, we should write down ideas and talk about them as we distract Sarosh." He then got back to work.

Blake nodded and also got back to work. Casey sat and stared at his computer, then leaned back and stared at the ceiling. With assignments made, he felt hollow inside. He had so much to do, but it hurt to face the emptiness. Anxiety wasn't always the sharp pain of panic. Sometimes it was the silent agony of the vacuum.

Blake stopped typing and looked at him. "Manuel, he has that look. Casey, you okay?"

"Fine."

"Liar. You're the one that taught me that 'fine' means nothing. Panic or hollow? Hollow, right? That's your hollow look."

"Look, I know the two of you are hurting just as much as me, so I'm not going to burden you-"

"Casey, we miss our families, sure, and we hate being in captivity. But you're the one with a medical problem. My PTSD doesn't hardly act up anymore, and mostly around fireworks. So, sure, it hurts, but I can deal with it."

"And I don't miss anyone when I'm working," Manuel added. "I forget that I even exist when I'm working. I don't think I feel time like you two. Do I miss my family? Yeah. But I cope by working all the time."

Casey breathed in deeply. "Right. Right. No, I'm not fine. Hollow."

"What would your counselor say?" Blake asked, a sly grin on his face.

Casey sighed and considered the question. "She'd ask if I might be overthinking. She'd ask me if I was taking too much on myself. Then when I told her I had to take on everything on my plate or people would die, she'd ask if I was taking too many expectations on with what I had to take on. Am I expecting perfection when all I should expect is effort?"

Blake made a face like he was trying to be Zen, though it appeared more like he was constipated, making Casey smile despite the pain. "I'm your counselor and just asked you those questions. Now answer them."

Casey leaned back, taking the question seriously, even if Blake was a clown. "I am expecting perfection because my life is on the line. And not just my life, but the lives of my friends. And the future prosperity of our wives and children."

"Can you do anything about this right now?" Blake cocked his head and raised a single eyebrow while steepling his fingers.

"Yes, Doctor Freud, I can do the engineering they are asking of me. I can figure out a way to escape. I can figure out how to stop them from doing terrible things."

"Are you doing all you can?"

"Yes, but I worry that I'm still not doing enough."

Blake paused and frowned. "Okay, I don't know the answer to that one, since I'm feeling the same."

"Not me," Manuel said. "Should I feel that?"

"No, you're doing great Manuel." Casey frowned, stood, and began pacing. "My counselor would say, 'Of course you aren't doing enough. No human ever does. Why should you be special?'"

They all pondered on that for a minute, nodding and thinking together. For once, none of them could think of anything funny to say. Then Casey picked up the remote for Blake's drone and started flying it around the room.

"Manuel, Blake... As Blake mentioned, do we all concur we can't actually succeed at this? It would be the death of many, giving access to asteroids to the ayatollahs."

Staring at the drone, Manuel nodded. Blake grunted in the affirmative.

"Then we can't just succeed at the engineering task to stay alive. We have to sabotage it in a way that they can't tell it was us. And escape in the process."

The drone clattered to the ground. Blake stood and took a turn.

"Agreed," Blake added. "Now if we could Iron Man it out of this, we'd be set. But as none of us want to be the guy left in the cave to die, and none of us wants a redemption arc to suffer through... Well, we'll have to figure out how to get all three of us out of here. I like the idea of making other people die for us instead."

"What about Iron Man 2?" Casey asked, eyes alight with mischief.

"That is the most ridiculous excuse for an engineering sequence I have ever seen!" Blake raged. "He just happens to have the parts in his house to build a miniature particle accelerator? And he can do it in what, an afternoon? I mean, the supercomputer calculations alone would take days, even if we assume Jarvis is some kind of AI. And then jack hammering through that floor by itself would leave him worn out and probably crippled, unless he was secretly a daily jackhammer user."

Manuel spoke loudly but with his usual casual calm. "Oh, I also have something to talk about. I stole Sarosh's server login info. Sadly, not his laptop login, but it's a start."

The drone bounced off the ceiling, then tumbled towards Blake, who caught it.

"Nice," Blake said with a huge smile. "Lax password security for the win."

"Yes," Manuel continued, "while it isn't quite as good as access to the internet or anything, it means we have full access to their engineering and research. I've been dumping files onto my jump drive. They didn't search us thoroughly. I could have had a weapon! But as we suspected, I've found this center is also bad news. They're researching nuclear and biological weapons. So... Can we make a computer virus and wipe out their research?"

Blake steered the drone expertly around the room, doing loops around pipes and light fixtures. "None of us are that type of hacker, nor are we living in a cheesy 80s movie." He then used the drone to buzz Manuel's head, which Manuel ignored.

"Even if we had a virus," Casey explained, "there are probably hard copies and isolated servers in this building or in Tehran."

Manuel dropped his head. "Okay, so what do we do?"

Casey leaned forward, tapping his chin, and staring down at the floor, panic welling in his heart, his breathing becoming more rapid. How could he bear this up?

Blake landed the drone neatly on his desk, then tapped Casey's desk, making Casey look up.

"Casey, you're trying to take the entire load on yourself again, aren't you? We talked about this ten seconds ago."

"Yeah, yeah, but now it's the panic. But how can you tell so easily?"

"Your wife warned me of your tells years ago. Besides, I've known you over 20 years. You've got to let us share the load. We know you're the spokesman, but you have to let us share the rest."

Manuel nodded his concurrence. "I trust Blake on this, since for all I can tell from your face, you're breathing."

Casey laughed and sat up straight. He fought his breathing under control, following his therapist's advice and going to his happy place. Maybe a decade of therapy was worth it. After a time, he stood up and took the drone controller from Blake and lifted it in the air. "Alright, what do we do?"

"We wanted funding to do the research, right?" Manuel asked with a sly grin. "Well, we do it. We do it well. But what we give them, we make sure it'll never work, but they'll never know it."

Blake frowned. "Even doing the job wrong could take months. And they're going to expect us to build hardware."

Casey spoke with a smile as the drone circled his head like a buzzy halo. "We said earlier that we need to turn Hamid or Sarosh to our side. That's too small. We need to turn the entire research center staff to our side. We've all seen the news. Discontent is deep in this country. They hate the Revolutionary Guard. I think I know how to exploit it."

Blake snorted. "What? Kidnap them and hold their families hostage?"

Casey grinned. "No, something far more devious. We make them love us so much they turn to our side."

Blake and Manuel stared incredulously at him with identical expressions of confusion. Casey simply smiled and hummed along to the buzzing drone.

###

Casey watched as Sarosh walked back into the construction lab looking much more relaxed. They all called out a friendly greeting. It was a large lab and they all had their own desks, so the greetings came from many directions. Sarosh smiled with delight at the attention and delivered the packages to Blake, who thanked him loudly and got right to work opening them up.

Sarosh sat at his desk and his face wilted, the work clearly daunting him. He put his one earbud in, sighed, and opened the laptop.

They all watched as the buzzing sound caught Sarosh's attention. He glanced around, but with only one ear open, he apparently couldn't identify it. He took out the earbud and triangulated the sound better. Casey nearly laughed as Sarosh's eyes widened as he caught sight of the drone carrying a pair of headphones as it settled down to rest on his desk.

"Now disconnect the drone," Blake called. "I'm giving you the head-phones, not the drone."

Sarosh released the drone and held the headphones up. "Why did you deliver the headphones to me?"

"They're a present. You've done such hard work. We're trying to make your load lighter."

Sarosh held them in awe, the fresh plastic shining in the florescent lights of the lab. Casey would have to convince them to shift to LEDs. As *Joe Versus the Volcano* taught, fluorescent lights sucked your soul. Maybe he could convince Sarosh to have a movie night.

Then Sarosh sniffled. He stood, turned to Blake, and bowed, thanking him for the headset. Blake marched over and stood him up.

"None of that now. You don't bow. We're your friends, so we take care of you." He gave him a shoulder hug and then turned to face Sarosh's laptop.

Casey fought to not laugh at the giant next to the weeping young man.

"Now see, here is the real problem." Blake put on his best fatherly voice. "Your assignment. What can we do? We need these documents. I need to know the tensile strength of austenitic steel or other gobbledy-gook. So, how are you going to get it to me without reading reams of useless stuff?"

The question caught Sarosh's attention. He sniffed, then stood up straighter. "We give you only what you need."

Blake nodded. "Yes, that is a first step. But how do you know what I need? I need 3 pieces of data in a file. What are those? I don't know until I ask for the document. What's most logical?"

"Give you all the files and you can sort through what you need and what you don't."

"Yes. That's the solution."

"But they said I am to read everything you want in case they contain hidden messages."

"Hidden messages? In data tables for stainless steel? In manufacturer's websites who don't know we're here?"

"That is true. Very illogical."

"Sarosh, your job is to keep *us* from putting messages out *there*. What would we even do with a message if we got one?"

Blake waited as Sarosh processed this. Then Sarosh stood as tall and happy as he ever had.

"Mr. Blake, you will be as a father to me, for you have saved me from the insanity of days and days of meaningless work of no value. I will provide you with what you ask, and you can interpret what you need. And I will have time to do my actual job!"

Casey gave them a thumbs up and Sarosh sat down to play with his new headphones, then knock out all of their requests.

"You were mentioning you like cooking," Blake said, winking at Casey. "I'll introduce you to some cooking channels to watch in your spare time."

###

"Yes, General Telebi, they are making substantial progress." Hamid trembled as he stood in Telebi's office. The man's very presence made him so nervous. "I review their designs every evening and make sure they are doing their job."

"How often do you beat them? Describe it to me." Telebi sat smoking a cigar behind his desk, a glass of dark liquid in a tumbler in his hand.

If Hamid weren't so nervous, he'd have laughed at the general. His entire appearance was that of a villain from an old movie in an evil lair.

"Sir? Describe it to you?" Hamid tried to school his face, but he feared his shock was apparent.

"Yes. I am a civilized man." He puffed on his cigar, his fat cheeks moving in and out like a bizarre fish. "I do not participate in violence. I let others do it for me. But I do enjoy watching. But for now, describe it to me."

Hamid's mind raced. He felt an immense amount of disgust at this realization. The general wanted him to beat the Americans and then report on it. *The Americans. What would they do? What would Casey do?*

Lie.

"I do not want them to know that the beatings are coming, so I have only done so three times, sir. I do not want them to be unable to do their work, so I beat them on their calves. I use..." *What would you use to beat someone? This is not part of a normal person's life!* In desperation, he spoke two words in English. "Riding crop." *Where did that come from? I've never even ridden a horse!*

"What the devil is... whatever you just said?"

Hamid pulled out his phone and did a search, showing the general the offending article. The general literally giggled with delight.

"That looks hideously painful. I must get one! Tell my secretary to buy me one. You can go. Good work. Keep it up. I expect great punishments from you, yet!"

Hamid walked out of the office in a daze, telling the glassy eyed secretary of the general's latest bizarre obsession.

I'm going to have to search for torture methods. How will I explain this to my wife? His eyes widened in horror. *I'm going to have to explain this to the Americans!*

Casey,

I know you're probably not getting your emails, but in case you can read them and not reply, I want to make sure you have word from me regularly.

I tracked down where you are. You'd be proud of me. But I haven't told anyone in the U.S. because I have a distinct feeling that if I do, things will not go well for any of us.

I went through everyone in your contacts list. One of the Turks, General Nacar, was most solicitous. He said you had done him a great favor and he would not rest until he had found you. I will make sure that he has no rest.

The children are well, if very concerned. They love you very much and are confused, of course, why you aren't there. I can't tell all of them the details, but Matt figured things out. You would be proud of him. He turned 16 two weeks after you disappeared and has concluded he has to be the man of the house until you return. He helps to still the little ones during scripture study and prayer, has taken over your chores, and has begun to do car maintenance, relying on internet video tutorials to learn. He intends to start his own business doing car maintenance to help pay the bills. I told him we have savings, and that school comes first, but he just laughed and said that he finishes school while at school, and that Uncle Blake always tells him he better learn a trade to pay for college. He is so much like you, it hurts.

I ever pray for you. With all my love,

Esin

###

Esin,

Good news. On the friendship front, Blake has totally won over our assistant, Sarosh. I think he's supposed to be our minder, but Blake was kind to him twice, and now Sarosh is as devoted as a whipped puppy feeling a gentle hand.

You would be proud of me. I've never been great at making friends before, but I am making progress with Hamid. Besides my two partners, I don't think I have had a real friend last long enough to get to know them. But Hamid is a scientist and we're slowly working our way into his trust. I think he liked us from the beginning. I think he feels guilt for kidnapping us. So, we are making it a point to be as friendly and inclusive of him as we can, despite him being our captor. We realized right away that the real enemy is Teletubby. That man is awful. He ordered Hamid to beat us regularly! Hamid lied to him that he was beating us. So, we have to pretend he beats us regularly, in case Teletubby asks us about it. What a joke!

Anyway, we had some other progress this week. Manuel has the Iranian rockets figured out in his orbital models. It's a matter of minutes and he can change parameters. He keeps telling us about some new rocket design he's working on using fusion, though he won't tell us the details as he doesn't know if he can make it work. I'm encouraging him, but my understanding is... limited. His drawings are a bunch of discs in strange patterns. Looks like something out of scifi.

Blake is snarkily getting our hardware designs integrated into their rocket couplings. It's a real joke. Manuel says the rockets appear to be very similar to some Apollo era designs. Very archaic but functional. Makes you wonder where they learned rocketry!

Speaking of jokes, my medication situation is hilarious, but only if you like dark comedies. Despite tapering, I'm having withdrawals and a return of my bad anxiety and depression. The withdrawals aren't too bad, but the panic attacks and hollowness are there. I wish you could reply to these letters. This is crisis mode, so I anticipate I'll be good for a few months. I know you're praying for me, as I can feel it. I'm praying for you and the kids.

###

Hamid pored over the Americans' work every night after they had gone to bed. They insisted on getting 8 hours of sleep and plenty of breaks, rightly pointing out that their work was mental, and that poor sleep or overwork would produce terrible results. Considering that he was supposed to be torturing them, they were sleeping soundly while he was the one being tortured. Hamid could not sleep. His life was on the line with this project, and he could not find the peace that those three seemed to have about the whole situation.

When he asked them how they could smile and laugh when they were hostages, Manuel had been spokesman. "If you think about it, we are in a very humorous situation. It's almost like we are in one of those silly movies that Hollywood makes. We are behind enemy lines, with crazy captors like General Teletubby who want us tortured, and not a one of us is a superhero or billionaire ready to save the day. It is comedic!"

He still couldn't believe they called General Telebi 'Teletubby.' If he found out... But Hamid would protect them... Somehow. And yet... What made them so resilient?

He also had concerns about these designs. He could look at their filed patents and know that they were designing a system that should work, but no one had tested it in space. They had talked a big talk, but as he reviewed their presentations, he realized they had clearly laid out a multi-phase process, and he had deceived himself in his enthusiasm and ignorance. The design was not flight ready, like he had assumed. It was all flight test ready, meaning they were ready for ground tests and then to go up on a rocket for proof. They couldn't send this to an asteroid this year. Their first phase design was to send a small device to capture a first piece of orbital debris and use it to fly around and capture many pieces of debris, proving they could fly and capture an asteroid. Then they would build the full-scale mission in phase two and send it after an asteroid using the debris the first phase had collected as fuel for the second phase.

Hamid stood and marched out of his office and headed to the American suites, as his personnel were calling them. Far from a suite, it was more of a repurposed barrack. He marched past their snoozing guard, in the door, and flipped the light on.

Not a single one of them stirred, but the room took his breath away. He hadn't been in here since the first day, and the state of the room amazed him. An enormous American flag draped along one wall. Pictures of their families and images from Hubble and JWST covered the rest of the wall. And it was all made on printer paper. This explained why they'd run through two sets of color cartridges in the last two weeks. Did the guards never come in here at all?

"Gentlemen, I am sorry to wake you, but I insist on asking you a question."

Casey and Manuel stirred, while Blake didn't even flinch. Casey sat up and raised an eyebrow at Hamid. "Sobh bekheir, Haj Hamid. How can I help you?"

"Why does Blake not wake up?"

Casey glanced at Blake with a smirk. "Blake has trained himself to sleep through anything, perhaps as a psychological 'middle finger' to his time in the Army where sleep was so often interrupted. It would take physical force to wake him, and he would become violent in the struggle. So, unless you have a mining, mechanical, or geology question, I recommend we let sleeping giants lie."

Hamid looked to Casey and then to Manuel, who were both smiling at this last quip. They truly seemed unconcerned with their captivity. They had to be concerned. Didn't they? Were they just amazing actors?

He settled himself onto one of their chairs and leaned forward, forearms on his knees. "I have studied your designs and plans and do not see how we can have a mission to an asteroid this year."

Casey sat up straighter, his brow wrinkling with confusion. "We never told you the mission could return an asteroid to Earth in a year. If you recall from my presentation, we anticipated it would take 10 years to start making money, meaning to asteroid return. Our design is one for a patient investor. The first asteroid capture will occur after about a 3-year series of slow, high efficiency orbital maneuvers. We will then take 7-years to return to Earth orbit by further slow, high efficiency maneuvers. We did tell- you we could have our first phase underway in a year, which we can. That's what we have been designing for the last month. A first phase that can interface with your rockets. Your largest rocket can just reach orbit, if we make a few tweaks, and then we can put our first phase probe into service, capturing space debris and collecting it to a single location. In another year, we can have the larger probe built and launch it to intercept the first probe, steal all of its orbital debris, and then use it as the fuel to go to the asteroid. The second phase uses the results of the first phase."

"You see," Blake said groggily, eyes still closed but CPAP mask pulled away from his face, "space is really big, and things take a long time. And if you let Manuel explain astrodynamics to you, you'll begin to understand time dilation." He seemed to wait for Hamid to laugh. With no laugh, Blake opened his eyes and saw that Hamid had begun to shake. "Because of boredom..." Blake said lamely, then wisely gave up on the joke, putting his mask back on.

Telebi would never accept a multi-year ramp up followed by a 10-year mission. He wanted prestige now! Telebi was a military man, not a scientist or engineer, and he gave Hamid great leeway in the how, but not in the what. Hamid's mind reached about in desperation.

"What would it take to get an asteroid and return it in a year?"

Manuel whistled softly and Blake, who had closed his eyes again, chuckled and spoke. "A rocket bigger than the Burj Khalifa..."

Hamid turned to Manuel, who nodded slowly, eyes glazing over as he began mumbling, "Unless you could contain the reaction with spacetime nullification and use that to accelerate the particles..."

Hamid ignored Manuel's incomprehensible ramblings and slumped back in the chair, eyes unfocused, shooting past panic and straight to frozen dread. General Telebi had ordered the last person to seriously disappoint him flogged.

Casey spoke quietly, "Hamid, I'm sorry. I thought you knew. We showed you everything in our presentation at the restaurant. We were completely honest with you, even if we are very optimistic. Now, we could lie to you now and say we are on track to do everything, but we won't."

"Cannibalization," Blake muttered, then rolled over, facing away from them.

Manuel shot from leaning on his elbows, eyes glassy in his own world, to sitting up stock straight in a moment, mouth making a silent 'O.' Casey frowned for a moment, then his eyes brightened, and he smiled deviously.

Hamid looked from man to man, confused at their obvious understanding of that one word. "What does that mean? I mean, I know the word, but not in a space context."

Casey stood and paced, speaking with a professorial tone. "We have assumed all along that our probes would be ride shares. Very few payloads go to orbit on a dedicated rocket. That's like having your own car. It's convenient, but it's very expensive. We assumed we would go up like most of the other satellites. On the equivalent of a crowded bus. Every seat taken with a satellite, and we get one seat. Then it would eject us and we'd have to scavenge orbital debris to produce the thrust we need to get to intercept."

Hamid nodded. "Yes, standard satellite protocols."

Casey grinned. "But you intend to launch us on our own dedicated rocket, which we plan on being two stages. We can use the upper stage of your rocket as the fuel we need to go to the asteroid. We will literally cut apart the entire upper stage, bit by bit, and feed that to our probe. The probe will melt, ionize, and spit the results out the back end as propellant. That cuts a whole year off of our process, as we don't have to scavenge the fuel we'll need for the mission. We can shift to focus on the asteroid probe, which is already fully designed."

Blake rolled over; eyes wide open. He swore, ripped his mask off fully, and shouted, "I'll have to spec out another robot to handle climbing around an upper stage! I hate teleoperations with time lag! That means using a poorly developed AI package."

"Hah! It was your idea!" Casey threw a sock at Blake. "And anyway, the robots you designed can handle collecting a large pile of debris. What makes this different?"

Blake closed his eyes and frowned. "Distance and load balancing. Plus, AI machine learning is still slow and problematic. It finds cancer when looking for donuts. Bah. You wouldn't understand."

Hamid's eyes had widened with excitement, but then his mind returned to the real bad news. "I may be in charge of all science and engineering for this project, but my superiors expect results far sooner than the 10 years it will take to go to and retrieve the asteroid. They expect results in a year."

Casey stood and walked to Hamid, placing a hand on his shoulder. "Then you spin the story. You tell them that while the asteroid portion of the mission will take 10 years, we can launch the first phase mission to act as a hugely prestigious short-term asset."

Blake rolled back over and muttered, "Garbage collector."

"What do you mean, garbage collector?" Hamid hated confusion, and this conversation was one thing after another.

Manuel spoke so fast Hamid struggled to follow him. "Orbit around earth is overflowing with space junk. Debris that is flying around in orbits we aren't sure of due to the perturbatory effects of the Earth, moon, sun-gravitational interaction. In fact, even Jupiter's gravity has minor perturbatory effects..." Casey made a slight sound with his tongue and Manuel paused, glanced at Casey, smiled, and continued. "Ah, but I am going into the weeds. In short, one of the side benefits of our first phase probe is that it collects that space junk for use as fuel!"

Hamid felt intrigued but unconvinced. "But what prestige is there in being a garbage collector? Telebi may be more figurehead than day to day leader now, but he is still the ultimate authority. He dines with the Ayatollah at least yearly!"

Casey sat and turned to him. "Because you can charge other nations for cleaning up their junk, and because you will be able to hold it over the heads of the U.S., China, Russia, and the EU, that they were not responsible enough to clean up after themselves and so Iran had to do it for them. Heh, none of the big 4 have done much past token work on debris mitigation."

"Because politicians always punt problems down the road." Blake pulled his blanket over his head. "Now, can we go back to bed?"

Hamid glanced at Manuel, who was nodding vigorously. They both appeared to ignore Blake, so Hamid did so as well.

Casey walked over and sat next to him. "Don't worry, we're here to help!"

Hamid shook where he stood, sweating the upcoming presentation. He had spent the last few days closeted with the team, asking them question after question to put in his presentation to the general and his senior staff. Casey had answered most of the questions, though he occasionally asked one of the others for some obscure detail that he did not know.

Arriving 15 minutes early, he carefully set up his presentation so it would be ready the moment the general arrived. He then arranged the seats with the irrational precision the general's staff insisted. Coffee and snacks were ready and waiting on the table for the general's whim.

As usual, he could hear them coming for several minutes before their arrival. Besides the incessant shouting, you could tell the general was coming by the shouting and cursing of the general and the nearly palpable smell of subservience of his minions. With a rush of noise, they came barreling into the room and spread out to their seats immediately. Hamid stood, ready to begin as soon as the general turned to look at him.

"General Telebi and esteemed staff. Thank you for your kindness in overseeing this project. I am ready to give you a full update on the status, as detailed in my report."

"Yes, yes. Get on with it," Telebi said, taking a sip of the flask he kept on his belt. He held it towards Hamid, shaking it invitingly.

"Thank you, but it is forbidden." Hamid had become adept at turning down the general's daily attempts to get him to drink. Hamid took a deep breath and drove into his fears. "To the mission progress. The mission design is complete and if you turn to page 1, you can see the time frame detailed in my report. We are in week 3 now. They anticipate a preliminary design review in three and a half weeks, with equipment ordering commencing immediately upon approval of the design. Their preliminary equipment list shows that a significant amount of the custom work is already available for welding and fabrication in house, and I have already ordered a few long lead items, as we discussed."

One of the staff, Colonel Kazmi, a lanky man who rumor said had been born without a sense of humor, interrupted, making Hamid's stomach drop. "Custom work? Long lead items? What do you mean? Can't we just buy all the parts?"

"Colonel, the probes have to have frames built that have never been built before." Hamid relaxed a bit as he spoke of engineering issues. Real issues. "These are first time builds. And some of the items needed are only made overseas and we have to order them. As some of them are EU and American built, we have to smuggle them out through holding companies."

The colonel persisted. "This will get expensive. Are you-"

Telebi shouted, "Shut up, Kazmi." He then bounced a pencil off the colonel's head.

Hamid continued, amused by someone as deserving as Kazmi receiving the abuse, but hands still shaking at the reminder of Telebi's temper. "Construction will commence in several stages. We will build the body of the probe by week 12. The equipment will arrive between weeks 12, for the bulk of items, to week 24, for the longest lead items. We have planned launch for week 52. This allows for an assembly schedule of 24 weeks. Flight qualification tests will begin upon completion of construction in week 36 and should take about 6 weeks. Re-work of any subsystems that fail in flight qualification should take another 8 weeks. This is an extraordinarily compressed time frame. They know of only one other system that has gone from technology readiness of 4 to 9 in a comparable time, and it still took 18 months."

Kazmi interrupted again. "If we worked these Americans harder, perhaps we could get this down to 6 months? I understand you allow them a full 10 hours for personal time and sleep!"

The general slashed a hand at Kazmi again. He'd already thrown his pencil. "You idiot, these aren't disposable day laborers! These are geniuses that need sleep, so their brains work. They need exercise, good food, and only strategic beatings for morale. That's why you're all forbidden from going into the research wings. Bumbling fools, you'd ruin their genius."

Hamid felt the only moment of appreciation for the general in his life. The man didn't understand compassion or kindness, but when Hamid had shown him literature (provided by Manuel via Sarosh) proving that sleep deprivation, poor diet, and no exercise reduced mental productivity, the general's selfishness bowed to expediency. Hamid noted to himself with amusement that Casey would have added that Teletubby had ignored the literature on torture, despite it all. He fought back a smile and continued.

"We will then mount the assembly on the rocket and go through pre-launch checks, which will consume the rest of our scheduled time. We have begun constructing the launch facility, with diggings underway now."

"What do you mean by diggings?" Kazmi asked.

"He means they are digging holes, you moron," Telebi shouted, taking another hit from his flask.

"But why do we need holes?" Kazmi asked, proving once again why nepotism was so effective at producing astonishing results.

"Colonel Kazmi," Hamid explained, "have you seen how tall a rocket is?"

"Well, yes," Kazmi said. "But they did not have holes."

"Actually, sir, they had massive holes."

"But there were no holes!"

"They filled them with cement, Colonel Kazmi."

"But then they wouldn't be holes anymore!" the colonel shouted.

"No, you're right," Hamid said, exasperated. "But we have to have holes now to make sure we don't have holes then."

"So, why dig them in the first place if we are going to fill them up again?"

Hamid stood, mind reeling. If he didn't know better, he would have assumed Kazmi was having a laugh at his expense. But Kazmi had never had a laugh in his life.

"There is one hole you are forgetting about, sir," Hamid said.

"Which hole is that?"

The one in your head, Hamid thought. Instead, he replied diplomatically.

"The tunnels for the hot gases from the rocket to escape from underneath the launch pad."

"Why didn't you say that in the first place instead of spouting nonsense about digging holes and filling them up?"

"I do apologize, sir. It won't happen again. May I continue?"

"Yes, but no more talk of digging unnecessary holes." Kazmi then leaned back, victorious.

"This is an extremely aggressive schedule, requiring the use of thousands of technicians and tens of thousands of contractors. Casey has made a master schedule, which I summarize in the report, that controls all tasks of everyone in the project. Happily, he had already made one for this project before we acquired his services and only had to modify it for our rockets."

"This is boring," General Telebi interjected. "I have you to take care of these details. Even the idiots here can read schedules to me." Telebi stared daggers at Kazmi, who sat fuming but silent under this verbal abuse.

Telebi continued. "I want you to tell me the details the reports can't hold. How are the Americans? Are they sufficiently in awe of our facility and cowed to do our bidding? Do the staff quake as they see the abuse you heap upon them? Do they fear me as they should? They must know that if they fail, they will most assuredly die. Hah, I will probably never let them go, anyway. Now, no details. That's for the two of us. Some of these idiots," he glared at Kazmi, "get squeamish."

Hamid never considered telling the truth. You couldn't tell Telebi that the Americans were quickly becoming the most popular people in the facility, friends with the cleaning ladies, maintenance techs, engineers, and staff. Especially Manuel, who would go out of his way to talk to anyone he passed and was learning Azerbaijani, the local dialect, in his spare time. That would not make General Telebi a happy man.

He led by fear, his senior staff a band of lackeys and bootlickers of the most egregious variety. Happily, the lackeys had hardly ever come to the research sectors, and none of them ever will now with the general forbidding them. The only other people that had the misfortune of the general's ill treatment were the senior scientists and engineers from each department.

"Yes sir, they are most assuredly in awe of our facility and are eager to do your will. I can assure you; they fear you exactly as much as you deserve."

The general laughed. "Excellent. Now, Kazmi, get me that bowl of fruit. There better be plums. Hamid, tell me about the rocket again. I'm so happy that we got those designs from NASA. Made our work so easy."

Kazmi reached a hand towards the fruit bowl and the general slapped it, then grabbed a peach and tossed it to Hamid.

###

Blake had baked three very large sheet cakes and hung a sign up in the breakroom that read, "Teletubby Appreciation Day!" Casey smiled as he helped to hand out slices of cake to dozens of staff, making sure the cleaning ladies and maintenance techs got their slice, too. When asked what the sign said, Casey would say it was in honor of their boss. Those that spoke English squinted at the sign, some doing quick internet searches. Before the day was over, everyone outside the general and his staff knew what that sign said. No one dared tell, though, as they feared the general would demand why they hadn't torn the sign down immediately.

Casey saw Hamid walking down the hall past the cafeteria, returning from his update meeting with the man of the hour, shoulders slumped and eyes downcast. He called out, "Hamid!"

Hamid stopped, then peered through the open double doors into the cafeteria.

"Has the general's riding crop come in!?" Blake handed out another slice of cake.

Hamid lifted his eyes to the ceiling. Casey wondered if he was praying for patience or asking for rocks to fall on him to hide him. Or Blake.

Casey ignored the provocation and shouted into the hall. "Blake was feeling munificent and wanted to share his culinary skills with our guests. I convinced him to use a recipe instead, so he baked sheet cake, an American tradition. Please, come have a slice."

"Yes, I'm so munifi-something that it oozes out of my pores." He waved a slice towards the door.

Hamid sighed so dramatically they could see it from 20 feet away and headed towards the break room. As he saw the sign, his eyes grew wide, and he spoke with a mix of awe and fear in his voice.

"You called him that for everyone to see?! He could kill you. He threatens to kill me nearly every time I see him, and I have never even crossed him!"

Casey tapped his temple and wiggled his eyebrows. "We can read the building, Mr. Jabiri. There is no back and forth between the staff and the common man. Word is that most of the staff have participated in the recent protests. No one likes our liquor-addled friend. They fear him. Besides, all the non-scientists are ethnic Azerbaijanis. They have no love for the guard. Now, here's your cake. Enjoy yourself. I assume things went smoothly."

Hamid took the cake, then held it in his hands while he unloaded. "Telebi used to be a great man. Never a good man, but a great man. He rose through the ranks of the military on skill, not nepotism. But he reached the limit of his competence and exceeded it in his present position. He is military overseer of all research projects. But he cares nothing for any of the details! He didn't even care about the schedule. I could have lied. He does not care what a near impossible task he's given us. He only wanted to know you feared him. Then he spent 45 minutes asking me about the rocket and then rambling about nonsense. He talked about plums and his walnut orchard for half of it, then complained about some other general for the rest." Hamid glanced up at the sign. "I told him you feared him exactly as much as he deserved."

Blake began laughing at this so hard he had to sit down, his weight sagging the flimsy cafeteria chair while Casey joined him with a merry chuckle. Manuel, who had been teaching some Spanish to one of the engineers who spoke English in exchange for Azerbaijani lessons, came over and asked in on the joke. When Hamid told him, Manuel gave them his assessment with an air of finality.

"He deserves to be feared like a rabid dog who needs to be put down."

"You know they sometimes monitor what is being said," Hamid remonstrated.

Blake, wiping his eyes, asked, "Who? Who monitors it? I've talked with the IT staff. There is no real monitoring."

"How do you speak to the IT staff?" Hamid was clearly confused.

"I make Casey translate. And back to my point, the general's staff speaks pitiful English. They couldn't understand us if they even tried. I met the guy who oversees monitoring us. He's over there, eating a piece of my cake. Great guy. Speaks English about as well as I speak Spanish."

"You speak Spanish?"

"Enough to curse someone out, order food, and tick people off."

Hamid paled. "I thought..."

Blake laughed. "Hamid, I have a problem with speaking before I think. I thought I had to be careful of what we said. But if someone is monitoring us, they've let me say a lot of stuff without getting in trouble. And Casey says that half the staff talks about how incompetent Teletubby is all over this building, though they do so carefully. I suppose I should fear Telebi. He could kill me or my friends. But I'm too old to be scared anymore. Besides, the only person we've met with good enough English to be a threat to us is you. Well, Sarosh is pretty good, too," and here he clapped Sarosh on the back, who was eating a third slice of cake, "but he loves us." Sarosh gave a thumbs up, smiling with a mouthful of cake.

Casey agreed with the sentiment but thought Blake was being a little reckless. "Anyway, we're on top of things. This was our little celebration. We assumed you'd have the preliminary schedule approved, so we wanted to celebrate."

Hamid sighed. "It was. We are a go. Can we do it? They want launch on week 52!"

"Not normally, no. But you kidnapped the right people. We did most of the work already. If you'd kidnapped Cliff and his team…"

Blake snorted. "Cliff talks big, but he's all talk. He promised lunar robots that could do mineral processing. The robots were the size of a dining room table! Nonsense."

Manuel snorted. "And he looks like a Disney villain."

Hamid raised his eyebrows. "I was considering him! He was so convincing. But our informant told us your team was the best."

Casey interjected. "The price of fame and competence. Well, Cliff has swindled more than one investor. But don't you worry. When you chose us, you chose the best."

Abruptly, Manuel stated, "Also, I need some ceramic discs. And a good power supply. Maybe you have an electronics lab I can use?"

Casey laughed, "Not now, Manuel, it's party time. If you need something requisitioned, tell Sarosh tomorrow."

"Yes, whatever you need," Hamid said, Sarosh giving a thumbs up.

Manuel nodded and smiled like a five-year-old who had just got a bike for Christmas, and Casey took Hamid's empty plate, reloaded it, and handed it back to him with a huge smile.

Casey,

I wish I could email this to you, but I can't. I wrote a rather lengthy letter and so am writing this to summarize. I'm leaving this note and the letter with Matt, who will give it to you if you should return, but I don't. I dare not say anything in email. Not with what I'm going to do. If anyone finds out, it'll never work. Only Sue, your parents, and Matt know the truth. I'm coming to get you out. I can't wait to see your face when you realize I came for you, like you came for me.

Love,

Esin

Casey emerged from a deep dive in his laptop, eyes alive with merriment. Nothing distracted him from his existential dread more than a good joke, and this was a great joke. Glancing around the cement and metal lined construction lab, he saw Sarosh humming along to his music, downloading academic articles. They'd made serious inroads with him. He no longer read anything they asked him to get, trusting that they couldn't do any harm in what they downloaded, only if they sent something out. So, they got their articles almost immediately. Sarosh loved this, as it gave him time to research recipes and watch cooking videos. He had unofficially become Blake's cooking apprentice.

Satisfied that their minder was otherwise occupied, he spoke up. "Blake, Manuel, I've done it. I got a bot to translate everything in the servers, so I don't have to constantly translate everything for you two goofs."

Blake replied after glancing at Sarosh. "Excellent. Any salacious details that we can start spreading to undermine the trust of the general further? Maybe if we discredit him, they'll send us home to avoid the shame."

Casey put his feet on his desk and leaned back in triumph. "Hah! You read my mind. Yes, because I automated the bot to translate everything, including some things that were apparently in hidden folders. I have General Telebi's entire personal diary for us to peruse. I'll give you both the highlights when I find juicy tidbits."

Manuel laughed aloud and Blake called, "No, read us some now."

"Alright, alright," Casey said with a lazy smile. "Let me see. This is from two weeks ago. He wrote a poem." He looked sideways at his associates. "Do we dare read his poetry?"

"Well, is it romantic?" Blake asked. "Nature? Horror?"

"Well, the first line makes it seem romantic. Let's set the right ambiance." He glanced at the bare pipes, black topped lab benches, and flickering fluorescent lights.

"Romantic ambiance, check."

"Get on with it!" Blake called. "This isn't a poetry slam."

"Romantic?" Manuel asked in confusion.

Casey cleared his throat. "Very well. I expect the translation bot will have mangled what was probably already unreadable, but here we go. *I feel the flowery...* I'm not reading that. Next... Nope, that's rather disgusting. Next... Nope." He closed the window. "Never mind."

"So..." Manuel began.

"What I read was neither logical nor physiologically probable," Casey replied. "Very violent, though."

Rolling his eyes, Blake turned his screen to them. "Aaaaaanyway, I have completed my revisions of your preliminary con ops and hardware listing. We need to have a full suite of spectrometers and spectrophotometers on this mission to properly catalog the geology of our products."

"Blake, we aren't actually trying to make a working mission. I think we can skimp on the hard science in our designs." He still bent over to see what the list contained.

"No, we can't." Blake turned his screen back, as if to protect the list from Casey's negativity. "We have to do this as well as we have ever done anything. Better, even. Sure, we can put some fundamental flaws into the final design. We can make sure the rocket explodes on takeoff. We can even sabotage all of their computer systems and burn down this building. But we have to do a thorough job of this. We already have 95% of the groundwork done from previous work. The 5% is mounting it to Iranian rockets instead of American. Hamid is too clever by half. He'll figure it out if we fake it and then we'll be stuck."

"If I have to make a working mission on top of fooling so many people!" Casey reined in his anger and stared at the table. He wasn't angry at Blake. He was angry at his anxiety and medication running out.

Casey worked on his emotions while Manuel interjected his thoughts. "Yes, we need to do our best work. We may be arrogant engineers who assume we can do anything, but we can't phone it in."

Casey felt the panic overtake the anxiety and climb out his throat. "This is such an insane project." Impostor syndrome. What did it matter that he had done systems work like this for two decades when his brain did not believe in him? And now their lives were on the line and their families were on the other side of the planet. He had watched General Telebi beat a man over the head repeatedly with a lunch tray in his office last week for looking at him sideways. This was not a stable man.

"More insane than that project the three of us did in numerical methods where we modeled the effects of hypersonic velocities on a cow?" Blake asked.

"Oh, don't remind me." Manuel shuddered. "Why did you have to make the animations so realistic?"

Casey stepped over the teed-up jokes and instead called in anguish, "Guys, I don't think I can do it. Manuel, you're great at this. You'll calculate all the orbits, and you know how to make rockets do their thing. Blake, you'll make sure the robots and mechanical systems work. But I'm supposed to make the balance of system work. I'm not even a real engineer anymore! The last time I did fluid dynamics calculations was before I graduated! I'm the guy who hires the real engineers and coordinates with them because I speak their language!"

Blake stood up, walked over to Casey, and put both hands on his shoulders, staring him in the face. In a deadpan, he spoke. "Casey. Shut up." He then sat back down, leaving Casey smiling despite himself, the tension bleeding out of his soul.

"You're right, of course, Blake. That was very persuasive."

Manuel rolled his eyes. "You two are dysfunctional, you know. What was the subtext? How does telling you to 'shut up' snap you out of your panic?"

"I think it's a language barrier. You don't speak 'Blake.' It's a crude dialect, but each word carries a lot of depth. What he said meant, 'Casey, do you think now is the time for an existential panic attack? Do you think we would be your business partners if we didn't know you could do whatever you set your mind to? Do you believe you can't do this, or are you letting the panic win?' Blake's advanced psychological treatments don't get rid of the panic and anxiety, but it reminds me I'm not alone."

"Well, do you think those things?" Manuel cocked his head and frowned.

Did he? He couldn't lie to them. Not now. "Part of me does. Probably always will. Part of me is scared and uncertain. But then I remember God chooses dysfunctional people to do his work. I mean, how else do you explain the Bible?"

"Easy." Blake winked at them. "I would explain it with mushrooms, aliens, and some very colorful words if you would let me."

"While I would love to take you up on that never, let's get back to deciding on spectrophotometers." Casey took a deep breath and started a most enjoyable argument with Blake on the particulars.

Esin sat in a taxi as they traveled through the maze of streets in Ankara. The streets overflowed with cars and pedestrians and the blare of horns and noise of humanity reminded her of the refugee camp she had suffered in. She loved her home in rural America. It reminded her of her childhood in a quiet village. But the refugee camp was like a city, in violence if not density. She remembered many a day where she was lucky that she was quick and strong.

Flashes of memory took her. Her father buried in the camp. A man creeping into her tent. The flash of a pipe her father had sworn her to carry before he died. A much hastier burial in the sand.

She shook herself and fought the pull of decades old memories. Casey said her trauma was where she got her sense of humor. She reminded him that she had pulled pranks well before the refugee camp.

"Miss? We have arrived. Miss?"

She turned, startled as she realized her taxi driver was speaking to her. "Oh, teşekkürler, sir."

The taxi driver smiled at her butchering of his language and happily pulled her suitcase from the trunk, thanking her profusely for her generous tip. She had been practicing Iranian Persian every spare minute, so her Turkish consisted of about a dozen phrases.

As the taxi sped away, she walked into the office building, going from the noise of a city to a quiet space with the soft sound of fingers tapping on a keyboard and the whirring of a fan that needed its ball bearings replaced. It was a nondescript building that may have been from the time of the Ottoman Empire. It was distinctly not what she had expected for the offices of a Turkish general. More like a hotel lobby from an old movie.

As she entered a foyer full of vases and paintings, a handsome young man greeted her in Turkish.

"Üzgünüm, I don't speak Turkish. I'm American, here to see General Nacar."

"Ah, you are the beautiful wife of General Nacar's dear friend, Casey Scarlett! But the general was not expecting you for another half hour! You made it through Ankara much faster than he expected."

"I am happy to wait." Esin glanced at the overstuffed chairs with a desire to plop down, sink into their luxury, and sleep until next week.

"I will call him now. Please, sit. You must be so exhausted."

Esin sighed with relief as she sat in the overstuffed chair, breathing in the smell of Turkish coffee and something sweet. She closed her eyes and the next thing she knew she heard the sound of footsteps approaching her, old instincts jolting her awake.

"My dear Mrs. Scarlett, you honor me in your visit!" General Nacar stood before her, stout and graying, a broad smile on his well-kept, mustachioed face.

Esin stood and took his hand. "I am so pleased to meet you, General Nacar."

"Please, call me Ahmet, American style. Your husband was such a friend to me. I must be your friend, too."

"Very well, Ahmet, you may call me Esin."

They walked back through the marbled corridors into the building, passing through a very secure looking checkpoint as she assured the general her children were quite happy to be staying with their grandparents.

"I am curious. Why did security not check me?"

"Hah, check the wife of Casey Scarlett? Hardly necessary."

Esin felt growing curiosity over this kind of talk. "Ahmet, what did my husband do for you that makes you regard him so highly and trust him so completely?"

The general stopped and stared at her with shock. "Your husband never spoke of his time in the Middle East?"

"Well, he spoke of his time at the mines and oil wells. He and Blake built a lot of interesting things. He has told me many stories, but the ones with you are all about your heroism."

The general started walking again and spoke with a broad smile. "I wish your husband were here so I could scold him soundly for not telling you the details of his part. He should proudly tell you of his exploits, accepting your regard and admiration. Any woman would swoon to hear of his heroics!"

"Well, my friend, since my husband is now a prisoner in Iran, perhaps you will have to tell me what he did."

They entered an office with a giant cherry wood desk and a few overstuffed chairs that he led them to. She was no longer sleepy at all. He offered her baklava, which she accepted. The taste was rich and sweet, and she savored a few pieces while the general spoke.

21 years earlier–Near Kızıltepe, Turkey–near the Syrian Border

"I still prefer Okey," the mayor said as he collected the stacks. "This Rummikub is not the same."

"Of course not," Casey said, "because Okey came from Rummikub. I like both, and now you know both."

The villagers laughed and gossiped around him as they sat on the patio of the tiny cafe. He didn't get a lot of chances to spend real time with locals when he traveled, as he spent most of his time at the mines. But today, he had taken a mental health day, and he was glad he did. Let Blake deal with that idiot mine manager who didn't understand the fundamentals of ball mill operations. Not him.

"Alright, I think it is time for lunch," Casey said. "Is there any-"

Shots rang out from far too close. Perhaps the edge of the village. A few soldiers had been part of the crowd watching the game and they ran towards the sound as their radios crackled to life. He only caught a single word.

Terrorists.

"Get in the café," the mayor shouted. "They will kill you for sure. They will ignore the rest of us."

He hid in the café, peaking out of a low window. He watched as a truck came barreling down the narrow street and shots rang out between the soldiers and the truck. The soldiers fell under a hail of gunfire.

Men climbed out of the truck and burst through doorways. In shock, he saw them grab several women, teenagers, and even some older children, toss them into the truck, then swing around in the square and head back the way they came.

As soon as they were gone, Casey ran to the downed soldiers but saw immediately there was nothing he could do. He ran back to their jeep and noted the keys in the ignition.

"Mayor, I am going after them," Casey called.

"No, they will kill you!" the mayor replied. "They have many guns and you are one man!"

"Don't worry, I know what I'm doing!" Casey called, giving him a wink.

Do I know what I'm doing? Casey asked himself as he popped the clutch and peeled off after the terrorists. He buried his anxiety under the thrill of action.

As he raced after them, he called Blake on the satellite phone he had for emergencies. He was sure this counted.

"Getting bored?" Blake asked with the sound of a shouting mine manager drifting over the line.

"Terrorist attack. They killed some soldiers and kidnapped a bunch of women and children. I'm trailing them in the soldiers' jeep. I'm going to tag their location. Will you call in special forces to be ready to rescue them?"

"You know, normal people don't start phone calls this way."

"Now, how do I tail these guys without them seeing me?"

"As I know, you're going to ignore me, I won't try to talk you out of this. But there is no good way to not be seen tailing someone in this mountainous country!"

"Little good your Army training did us," Casey quipped. "Okay, so I'll wing it. Coming up on Şenyurt. Looks like they blasted a hole in the border fence into Ad Darbasiyah. Guess I'm going into Syria!"

"Be careful," Blake said. "I only have two friends and am not interested in interviewing for the position again."

"I was born careful."

"Said the guy trailing terrorists without a weapon or any training."

"You trained me! Just now!"

They hung up and he started winding his way through the blasted border. Several trucks were fleeing the scene. He kept his eye on the one carrying the women and followed as discreetly as he could through the busy grid of Ad Darbasiyah. The roads were narrow, but he kept pace.

Once they got out of town, he kept at the edge of sight as they drove. The terrorists had bombed out a checkpoint, the Syrian soldiers lying dead. This had been a planned attack.

Several miles south, just after Kerbetili, the trucks left the main road and headed into the farm country that surrounded the area. He called Blake and gave him an update.

"Casey, the lieutenant here is telling me to tell you to turn back, as he cannot allow you to risk your life for them."

"Tell him my coordinates and to get special forces ready to move. I haven't seen any Syrian military movement that wasn't a smoking ruin. I'll give final coordinates once I see their camp."

"Figures that you have the job that doesn't need Turkish and I'm the one trying to talk to people that speak no English."

Ten minutes later, the trucks ahead disappeared into a clump of trees and, by instinct, he immediately stopped behind a small hill. He leapt from his jeep and ran up the hill, laying on the top to look at the trees. Thank goodness the jeep had binoculars in it.

The trees were sparse enough that he could make out men milling about and one brightly colored headscarf he recognized from the village earlier.

"Blake, I have final coordinates. They're maybe half a kilometer due east of my location."

He gave the coordinates and Blake sighed.

"Alright, hang tight and do not move. Keep hidden and let the special forces take care of it. They're moving in at dark."

"I should have brought a snack," Casey noted.

"You should have," Blake said. "Big men like us need our fuel."

"Blake, you're nearly a foot taller than me! I am not a 'big man' by your measurements!"

"You act like one, so I declare you an honorary 'big man.' If you were here, I'd whack you with a stick to dub you such."

"On the shoulders?"

"Yeah... The shoulders..."

They hung up to conserve power and Casey settled in for a long wait, but only after he checked the truck for snacks. He found a power bar and a few bottles of water, much to his delight.

As the sun disappeared below the horizon, Casey heard gunfire erupt from the camp. He swore and prepared to run, but then heard the sound of helicopters approaching from the north. He hoped the gunfire had been Turkish and not terrorist, but he had no choice but to wait. The helicopters landed as the sound of gunfire ended.

His phone buzzed and he answered, expecting Blake but instead hearing a deep Turkish voice on the other end.

"This is Major Nacar. Is this Mr. Casey?"

"It is, yes. Blake gave you my number?"

"Yes. I am in communication with the special forces. They want to make sure you are well away from the jeep."

"I am on top of the hill I hid the jeep behind."

A missile streaked through the air, blinding in the dark, then his jeep exploded.

"Well, that was dramatic," Casey muttered. "How do I get home?"

"The same helicopter will pick you up. You can stand up now. The enemy is neutralized."

"Oh... Paratroopers?" Casey asked.

"You are a perceptive man, Mr. Casey. I look forward to meeting you back in the village."

"And I you." Casey waved his arm to the incoming helicopter.

"Your husband's actions led to the rescue of all the kidnapped women," the general concluded. "One of those women was my wife. Another was my ten-year-old daughter."

"That is just like him to never tell me he was a hero!" Esin said, smiling. She had heard some stories of her husband's impetuous youth, but never anything like this. Considering how he met her, perhaps she should have known he'd find trouble wherever he went. He had never told this story to anyone that she knew of. He had always only said that General Nacar was a good friend who owed him a favor.

"I owe him the life of my wife, my last two children who had not been born, and of any grandchildren they give me." General Nacar smiled at her encouragingly. "But I suppose Casey does not want to spread his fame afar, if he did not even tell you."

"He is a modest man who acts without regard for himself, only for what is right." She then half whispered, more to herself than to the general, "He could tell so many great stories and jokes about it! Why keep it to himself?"

She shook herself and spoke with earnestness.

"General Nacar. Ahmet... I want to go in and help my husband. I am too much like him. I need to be doing. I need to act. Will you help me go behind enemy lines like my husband and rescue him? I came here to help. I need to save him, like he saved me."

"Lady Esin, you have the heart of a lion, but what could a middle-aged woman do in the belly of the beast that our trained spies could not?"

She realized that this man was a romantic, and she further realized she would have to play to his view of the world to get her way.

"I have seen the beast when I lived in Afghanistan. I have lived the life of a refugee. I do not need training to act deferential and abused. I lived it for years. Have any of your trained spies made their first kill as an orphaned teenager, leaving him buried for jackals to tear? Looked evil in the eye and never flinched? Besides, I am Casey's wife. I know him. I can predict his moves. Do your spies know what it means when he sighs? How he likes coffee when he is happy and how he prefers his tea when he is sad? His every mannerism and each nuance of his voice?"

"No, I suppose they do not," General Nacar said.

Neither do I, Esin thought, *but I'm not telling you that.*

He stood and walked to his window overlooking a beautiful garden. She stood and walked to join him.

"Will you train me?" she pled.

"But what would Casey say if I helped you to your doom?"

"He would ask if I died doing what I thought was right with a joke on my lips." Which was true. He was very adamant that they laugh at every opportunity.

He appeared deep in thought, staring into her eyes with what she hoped was an attempt to see the truth in her words.

She winked at him, the same way Casey often did to his friends.

He laughed and reached for his phone. "Very well, Lady Esin, lioness. Let me see what I can do."

He dialed, speaking Turkish for nearly half an hour while she returned to her seat and prayed, the soft chair a cage holding her back from rushing to Iran right then. When he finally hung up, he turned back to her, startling her from a light doze.

"You promise to be careful?"

"As careful as a lion tamer brushing a hippopotamus' teeth." She replied by instinct, still groggy and so forgetting for a moment he would not know that family joke.

He raised an eyebrow. "Then you are lucky. I know the head of the MIT, our version of your CIA. After three arguments and two threats, one of which I had to nearly carry out, he has agreed to send someone to train you and to accompany you on the mission. We will get your husband back."

Hamid sat down with the Americans and Sarosh, hands fidgeting with his sleeves, eyes downcast. They were on track with their preliminary design, helped as they had done most of the work before he kidnapped them. But how could they possibly meet Telebi's arbitrary one-year deadline?

"You look nervous." Casey laced his fingers together and looked at him. "What's up?"

"He's intimidated by my striking good looks and your hideous visage," Blake retorted.

Manuel rolled his eyes. "Hamid is not attracted to orcs, Blake. I think you have it backwards."

The humor was confusing. *How do they laugh? How do they not fear constantly?*

"I wanted to discuss the schedule you developed for the mission," Hamid replied. "I have reviewed it thoroughly. Can we actually meet this deadline?"

"Yes, if the technicians and engineers are capable of what you said they are." Casey unlocked his hands, tapped on his computer, and showed him a slide. "We have the manpower for this. It'll be absolutely breakneck. We're making some big leaps and counting on our designs working right the first time. It still may not be possible. But why worry about that?"

Hamid inadvertently let the shock he felt show plainly on his face. He stuttered, then asked out loud what he only had pondered before. "You are not worried about that?"

"Of course, I worry." Casey's smile became sad. "Even on my full dose of medication, I worry constantly. But with my team, I can squeak by."

Hamid's worries loomed in his mind. Telebi's vicious face was foremost.

"But if we fail, we die."

Blake laughed. "If we die, then it's not our problem anymore."

Casey put a hand on Blake's shoulder, a look quieting him.

"Blake, I think Hamid is not yet able to process trauma with humor." Casey spoke without his usual laughing eyes. There was instead pity in them.

"That's a real tragedy." Blake's face turned as serious as Hamid had ever seen. "How do we train him to do so?"

"It takes practice," Casey returned his usual smile to his face. "First, let's give him some hope." He turned to Hamid. "You read the Quran much?"

"I used to." Hamid cast his eyes down. "Lately… I can't seem to care."

"Yes, this is late-stage hopelessness." Casey turned to his friends. "Manuel, what did we do for you when you had hopelessness back during your PhD?"

"Made me eat a half dozen cinnamon rolls?" Manuel said.

"After that." Blake smirked.

"Watch *The Princess Bride* on repeat all weekend?"

"Oh, we did do that, didn't we?" Casey chuckled. "After that."

"Made me read selections from the Bible?"

"Correct. But in this case, the Quran will do." Casey faced Hamid and his face became serious. "Does the Quran not say that all who have ever lived will be raised from the dead and will face judgment by Allah?"

Hamid nodded solemnly. "Yes, it does. You believe this, too? You've read the Quran?"

"Yes, to the first question, and some of it to the second. With this in mind, who should we worry about? Not Telebi. Not the Ayatollah. We worry about our heavenly judge, not our earthly judge. That gives us hope. That lets us laugh in their faces, even if they harm us."

"You truly do not fear death?" Hamid felt his heart calm a bit.

"We do not seek death, of course," Manuel noted, "but we do not truly fear it, for we have hope of a better world in Jesus."

"And Jesus was the greatest comedian of all time," Blake said. "He mocked the rulers of his day so bad they wanted him dead! He called them out for what they were, like all the protesters in your streets do today. The best comedians get constant death threats, you know. Besides, we still feel fear, but we do not because of our hope. Does that make sense?"

Hamid sat and pondered on this while the three Americans sat content, fiddling with the projects at hand and letting him think. He felt a tiny seed of courage rise in his heart.

"Teletubby is... he is a fool!" Hamid said, feeling giddy and sick at the same time to speak against the man who had terrorized him for so long.

"That's a start." Casey patted him on the shoulder. "We'll get you there."

"So, what do we have to do to make this schedule work?" Hamid felt an ember alight in his soul.

Esin,

The funniest thing happened this morning. Manuel and I were up and preparing to go to the gym when Blake started speaking in his sleep. He was talking about horseback riding. We started talking to him and he actually got up from his bed and was walking out the door when he woke up. He saw us both and started swearing in Persian, which he has been practicing extensively. He then tripped as he went to his bed and landed on it hard enough that the entire frame shattered!

I realized as I wrote that that it was probably funnier if you were there, but we couldn't stop laughing for half an hour.

Anyway, I have to get ready for preliminary design review. Well, I am ready. But I'm double checking my quadruple checked work. But I'm kind of glad Blake broke his bed. It was good to start the day with a laugh.

Love,

Casey

Waiting in the boardroom, Casey felt nervous, but not his normal nervous. He had the panic of not feeling adequate in his engineering. Today was the preliminary design review for the entire project. The team, including Hamid and Sarosh, were all gathered and waiting for the general.

"You know, Manuel, I've conducted PDRs on four continents, in boardrooms and shipping containers."

"Yes, I know." Manuel continued to stare at his laptop.

"We just gave Hamid a nice pep talk about not fearing death, and I don't think I do. Not my own. But my stupid anxiety makes me afraid, nonetheless. Maybe I am scared of death? Or maybe I'm just afraid of leaving my wife a widow and my children homeless."

"You've never been in the military," Blake interjected. "Every meeting is life or death, for you or someone else. Our families are strong. It tears me up inside to think I might not see my children at their weddings." Blake took a massive breath. "But my wife is my partner and my children are strong."

"You confident in the designs?" Casey idly moved the mouse about the screen where his presentation called the siren song of pending boredom.

Blake squinted at Casey like he was trying to read something important. He then rolled his eyes.

"Casey, you remember Avocado Mining out of California?"

"That's not what it was called, but yeah," Casey said, raising his eyebrows.

"Well, then you remember that the Artichoke Mining executives were all uppity and thought they knew everything because they were from New York and L.A. and we were just ignoramuses from the middle of nowhere?"

"Yeah, and it was called-"

"You remember how those Aardvark Mining execs thought our designs, mine plan, and business case would never work and pulled the plug on us?"

"Of course." Casey sighed. "They thought it was too negative."

"Antelope Mining was bankrupt a year later! And the new owners hired us on the spot to fix the mess that their predecessors left."

Casey nodded, agreeing with the sentiment. Teletubby may be a vindictive idiot, but he had no other engineering companies bribing him to jump ship and take a new approach.

Casey looked around the room. All of them had their laptops open and had been working away when he interrupted them. They were as content to work in a dilapidated conference room as a dilapidated construction lab, which was still nicer than some of the buildings they'd worked at in remote mine sites that needed to be condemned. They had finished their portions days ago but were working on the assumption the general would green light everything they had done. Casey was not so confident that Teletubby would like the status. Executives and generals were often fickle. It was hard to know what to feel. Manuel was so relaxed he appeared to be idly doodling ellipses and rocket nozzles.

"Blake, you ever felt panic from multiple sources simultaneously?"

"Yup. When you're on the phone telling me to hurry because I'm behind on my deadlines and my wife is in front of me telling me to get off the phone and fix something in the house and my kids are yelling in the background. Multiple sources. And we'll be doing that again this time next year."

"But Mr. Blake," Sarosh said, his voice sounding as if he had restrained himself for a long time, "what was the real name of the mining company?"

Casey smiled as Blake laughed. Blake's flippancy always lightened his load a bit. Then he looked at poor Hamid as he walked into the room. His face was pale and haggard, like he had hardly slept in days. Which was probably true. Casey felt sorry for him. He didn't have a Blake.

So, acting on his gut instinct, he walked over and sat by him.

"Hamid, when we're done with this, we are going to go to the cafeteria and celebrate. Will you join us?"

Hamid's face jumped from surprised, to confused, and finally to pleased.

"I would be happy to. But how do you know we will be able to celebrate?"

Casey, still going on the instincts he trusted more than logic, shrugged. "No matter what they say, we have completed the preliminary design of a system that could go to space. It's an accomplishment and we will celebrate."

Hamid's mouth twitched, like he wanted to smile, but wasn't sure he was allowed to do so. Sadly, the smile died on the vine when General Telebi and his staff came tromping in.

With Hamid acting as translator, General Telebi began to speak. Casey ignored the translation, which Hamid sanitized, and listened to the general's own words. He was feeling confident in the Tehran dialect.

"Alright, I want this to be fast and not confusing. You, the talkative one. Talk."

Hamid translated, and that was Casey's cue. The general had yet to learn their names.

"Thank you, General Telebi. I will gladly share our status." Here he brought up their first slide. He had made all the slides in Persian and Hamid had verified them, quite impressed by his skill. "We have completed the preliminary design and have a system that, with the ongoing help of your team, will be able to have the Asteroid Retrieval Probe and Debris Collector Probe both flying in just over ten months."

As he switched slides and showed the schedule, General Telebi interrupted Hamid's translation with a vindictive glee.

"This is not enough. This is an insufficiently ambitious plan. I have spoken to my contact in NASA, and she thinks we should do more. They are holding back. What more can they do?"

Casey's shock probably showed on his face, but he quickly got it under control, even as it tore him apart. *A contact in NASA?* Well, with at least 18,000 people working at NASA, he supposed a spy funneling secrets was likely. But what would it mean?

Hamid had a shell-shocked expression and was no longer translating. Casey waited, feigning ignorance. This was insane. They needed to come up with something, anything to offer, even if they would never be able to deliver it. Something they could fake really well.

Hamid visibly pulled himself together, swallowing, and spoke. "General Telebi, these are the same numbers we discussed last week. With the resources we have, we cannot possibly do anything else on top of what we are doing."

General Telebi scoffed, gesturing to the Americans.

"Why don't you make them suffer a bit? I give Colonel Kazmi here a bit of pain whenever he gives me the slightest provocation."

The colonel spoke up. "Sir, I hardly think now is the time to discuss our professional relationship."

Telebi held up a hand, silencing the fuming colonel.

"But do you torture your people? You have told me you give them physical reminders of their hopeless state."

"Yes, but sir, scientists have proven that to be counterproductive. I'm sure you've noticed that Colonel Kazmi does not produce for you like his previous leaders have said that he produced. He would probably be more productive if you treated him more humanely and with respect."

Casey felt proud of and grateful for Hamid for standing his ground on this. Kazmi's eyes widened and his mouth opened and closed like a goldfish. Telebi's eyes narrowed, and his jaw clenched. Hamid went silent.

"I want more," Telebi barked. "They have more. Get more from them. Now. What we have is not worth their lives."

"May I consult with the Americans on this?" Hamid asked.

General Telebi grunted assent, and Hamid turned to them.

"Blake and Manuel, since you don't understand, I will explain. Due to some kind of information reaching the general from a contact he has at NASA, he wants something more from you. Something spectacular to go with the whole mission. He thinks you are holding back and is threatening your lives for more."

The four of them looked at each other, Hamid looking nervous and ready to collapse if there were any more blows.

"Spies are bad news." Blake used his 'I'll murder someone' frown, which generally terrified people outside their circle. "Like finding out your ice cream has a cockroach in it. You can't be sure what the roach has touched, so you throw out the whole bowl."

Manuel tapped his chin. "How do we throw out a metaphorical bowl, Blake? How do we do anything from here to stop them? It sounds like we need to figure something out to make this project flashier. More exciting. Maybe a fancy maneuver... But how can we do any fancy maneuvers with the piece of junk rockets they have?"

"And what else can we do?" Blake countered. "We aren't experts at everything! We know one thing well. Using garbage to make thrust. We're space trash collectors and delivery drivers."

Casey stared down at his feet, heart racing in fear, the coldness of imminent death pressing in at his already hollow chest, his lack of proper medication making the panic quick to rise. Then a slow smile crept onto his face as his panic fled in the face of an old, untested idea that had sudden relevance.

"Manuel, remember that idea I had when we were arguing about the effects of hypogravity on mammalian physiology?"

"About how irresponsible it was of every space agency to not have a hypogravity space station in orbit before we sent humans to colonize hypogravity planets? The one that you asked a professor about, and he said you'd have to get permission from Arianespace?"

Sarosh, who had been silent, finally spoke. "What is hypogravity? Mammalian physiology? I don't know these terms."

Casey ignored the question for the moment. "Can we do it?"

Manuel's face went into calculation mode, probably iterating through scenarios. He nodded. "As long as Iran doesn't mind ticking off the entire European Union."

Casey laughed, then sobered up his expression at a glare from Telebi. He spoke to Sarosh.

"Hypogravity is any gravity less than 1g. The moon is 1/6. Mars is 1/3. We have never tested the effects on mammals of living in those environments, only in zero gravity. Physiology is how bodies work."

He paused his explanation and felt a distinct feeling that he should speak directly to the general. Not sure why, but trusting God more than himself, he turned and addressed the general in Persian.

"Esteemed General Telebi and staff, while my colleagues do not speak your delightful language, I was fortunate to learn it in Afghanistan and kept this hidden from you on fear you would find my dialect unbearable to your ears, though I have been told it is quite melodious. Pardon my accent, but I feel you should hear the new plan from me directly. Your humble but brilliant servant, Haj Hamid, has enough to do without translating my pitiable speech."

The general appeared stunned, but with no protest, Casey pushed onward.

"I hear your concerns and with our slight weaknesses and vast strengths as a team in mind, I believe there is one idea that would bring glory to the Republic of Iran in the time frame you have mentioned. We can not only do what we are already doing, but we can start by using our Asteroid Retrieval Probe and Debris Collector Probe for a special mission. Your humble, yet strikingly handsome servants have an idea that would involve the capture and re-use of two dozen derelict rocket upper stages from the Ariane 5 launch vehicle, made by Arianespace of the European Union and left comically stranded in an eccentric orbit. By combining them in a ring and spinning the ring up to mimic gravity, they can become a massive space station, far larger than the International Space Station. This enormous space station can easily be spun up to achieve hypogravity or even Earth-similar gravity."

"Now that sounds like something that will be spectacular," the general said with a menacing smile. "This would embarrass the Europeans! Hah, they still have some of my assets frozen. We'll see what they think when I have their assets in my control. Continue!"

Casey was reminded for the moment that Telebi had been a formidable man before. He may still be if he wasn't so lost to his vices.

"Embarrassments galore. The legality of this is an issue that is hotly debated in the Western world, where our governments hate to allow something once in their control to ever leave their control, unlike your munificent government. The Ariane 5 upper stages are abandoned in place and so some claim that maritime law should apply and salvage rights given to those who go and use them. Others say that launched objects eternally belong to the launching company or country, even if abandoned for decades. I believe that in your wisdom, you will clearly see that these are abandoned and belong to those with the will to seize them and use them for their own pleasure."

"I do know how to seize things," the general said, eyes glowing with greed. "I'm amazing at seizing things. I think I seize things every day."

Hamid choked on the water he had been sipping, which Casey ignored.

"In summary, I recommend we astonish the world by your ability to seize things, collect the EU's abandoned rocket bodies, and make the first space station with centrifugal gravity in history! Then you can rent it out for massive profits! I will need an additional team of welders and another mechanical engineer to make it on time, but that is a small price to pay for glory."

The general and his staff sat in stunned silence. Hamid finally finished choking on water and gaped in astonishment, having never heard Casey say more than a few words in Persian. The general turned to Hamid and spoke positively for the first time Casey had heard.

"You made a good choice in this team. They have ideas enough for a lifetime. This is a great idea. We can thumb our nose at the Europeans, then turn around and rent their own rockets back to them! Hah!"

Casey did not like the sound of that. He may have underestimated Telebi.

As his staff joined him in sycophantic laughter, Hamid bowed and spoke.

"I will see it done. Shall we proceed with the preliminary design review?"

"No, I am feeling quite happy," the general said with a dramatic sigh. "I will celebrate our victory this day. See that you meet your schedules. This extra portion must fit into the calendar as well. Requisition more engineers and technicians if you need. Too many idle people on the streets these days as it is. If they won't help, beat them. Make it happen."

They sat silently while the general and his staff left. Hamid turned to the team and said, "I sincerely hope that you know how to do what you just said."

"The ring station is one of my oldest ideas." Casey stood and stretched; glad the meeting was short but annoyed at its result. "I would have done it myself years ago, but didn't want to navigate the nightmare that is getting a large company to let you play with their toys."

Blake grinned, not having understood Casey's speech. "Are you telling me that old crook fell for your space station con? He thinks we can do that?"

"You know it's not a con. But yes, he not only thinks we can do it but is enthused." Casey winked.

"Did you call us handsome in the speech?" Blake asked in amusement.

Casey looked at the ceiling and ignored him. Manuel frowned and spoke, having ignored their banter.

"But the idea is terribly inefficient. The orbital mechanics are such that we will burn as much fuel capturing a single upper stage as to launch one. Well, unless my new rocket design works. Then we could do anything we wanted."

Hamid stood up and appeared to stop breathing. He could barely force out a sentence.

"I thought you said we could do it."

Casey waved his hands in a pacifying gesture.

"We can, we can. But only if we still do a modified cannibal mission. We can use the Ariane 5 rocket nozzles as extra fuel if needed. Each stage will take at least a few weeks to capture. Well, maybe longer. I never did have Manuel check my work. I could be way off. But if we have a cannibal system, we can easily do this."

Hamid paced in fear.

"The general was very excited. And now you say you haven't even checked the numbers? You've never designed this!?"

Casey stood up and reached over, stopping him in place.

"Hamid, I had to say something to appease the general, but it's a logically consistent idea. Trust me and my team. We still have over 10 months. We'll make it work. Now, let's go to dinner. It's time to celebrate. Teletubby didn't kill any of us! That's worth celebrating!"

Hamid appeared slightly mollified as he walked on ahead with Manuel, Manuel telling him all about the calculations he would do as soon as the party was over.

Casey's adrenaline dropped through the floor, the moment of extreme danger over, and he stumbled, only prevented from tipping over by Blake's even larger frame grabbing him.

"Hey now, Casey, you haven't told us everything, have you?" Blake whispered. "You got pretty scared there. I recognize someone pumped up on adrenaline. You promised a lot to Teletubby and his muppets and now the adrenaline is gone, you're in danger of crashing."

"Yeah, that's about right. I told them what they want to hear. There's no way we can do the space station mission in ten months. Especially not in addition to all the rest. Really, there's no way we can do any of what we're promising. I had a bigger panic attack this morning. I hadn't had one in at least a decade! Now I've had four in two weeks. Blake, we're in a lot of trouble."

"We aren't in one lick more trouble than we were this morning. It's all a bed of lies. It's just a new bed of lies. The rocket will fly and the mission will fail, but that's a problem for next year. So, we make them regret messing with the lot of us, and we escape as soon as we figure out how."

Casey looked at his friend, seeing nothing but confidence and faith in the man's eyes. Then a new idea came to him. An idea he never would have considered if his life wasn't on the line. An idea that could help them escape this mess.

"We make them regret it." He stood up straight and smiled. "Can't slow down now, Blake. We're going to miss dessert if we don't hurry! Let's go rescue Hamid from Manuel. Then we have work to do."

Casey,

I apologize I haven't written more. I can't send these notes, so I suppose it will be alright. Training has been brutal. I have had four different trainers. Physically, the hand-to-hand combat has been agony, but I impressed them greatly by my willingness to put my all into every attack. They said I'll have to use my whole weight and all the leverage I can get if my 135 pounds are to be useful at all. They have even taught me some parkour moves! I feel like an action hero when I do those stunts. You'd hardly recognize me, what with wearing robes and veils while throat punching dummies.

The hardest training has been acting like an Iranian cleaning woman. I have felt the panic and fear of my youth come bubbling out, as I have pretended to be what I once was by birth. I hate to say it, but I have not fully overcome those wounds. The pain of being lesser than all around me. Of being beneath notice. They have taken turns verbally abusing me to train me to not lash out. To be silent. That is the worst part. But your decades of respect for me have been an anchor. When I have to act submissive, I remember you and laugh inside.

I have spoken to the children every day. They want to know where I am, but I have told them it must remain a secret. Matt has been an anchor. When I get you home, make sure you recognize his efforts. He's holding the family together.

I love you,

Esin

Hamid was always impressed by how well Casey kept things moving in his meetings. He never ended feeling bored. Even so, there was a lot to cover, and it became exhausting. Where was Sarosh with their snacks? There were two more hours to go!

Casey continued. "So, the con ops revision we started after PDR is complete with the changes made due to the mission scope change. We are nearly done with the mission architecture revision. Now we have to talk through the major system changes. There are some big ones."

Hamid stood in relief as Sarosh came marching into the construction lab.

"Finally!" Hamid frowned. "Where are the snacks?"

Sarosh stood before them, as serious as a tomb.

"Telebi has instructed me to take all four of you to the general's office for punishment."

Blake stood, smirking unrepentantly, stretching his arms above his head and yawning.

"Alright, has Telebi figured out that I have besmirched his honor?"

"I have no idea what that word means, but maybe?" Sarosh asked. "Someone on the general's staff overheard a technician refer to the general as Teletubby. The general got... very angry when they translated it for him, and he called me in to find out which of you called him this."

Blake laughed. "Yes, that was me. That was definitely me besmirching him."

"This is serious, Mr. Blake! What am I to do? If I do not give you 20 lashes, I will die. But if I hurt you, I will be miserable!"

Blake walked to Sarosh and put his hands on his shoulders.

"Sarosh, I can handle 20 lashes from you. I've taken worse. Plus, my back is well padded. Make the general happy."

Sarosh took a deep breath and pulled out a cane and spoke with a strong voice in Persian, the other engineers and technicians overhearing.

"The general instructed me to beat you with 20 lashes in the general's presence. Please, come with me."

Blake led the way, leaving Sarosh behind and heading straight to the general's office. The rest of them followed, struggling to keep up with him. The guards looked confused as he marched past them. As he approached the general's office, one guard tried to stop him and he simply took him by his shoulders, picked him up, and moved him out of his way. This gave Hamid time to catch up, slightly breathless. Blake shoved the outer door open, passed through the secretary's office, and burst into the general's office.

"General Telebi, I hear you are mad at me! I'm here for my punishment."

With that, Blake ripped his shirt off and stood staring at the general, who appeared confused in the face of his withering gaze, but became angrier at the realization that Blake showed no fear.

Hamid belatedly translated.

"Yes," Telebi said, "you have disrespected me and must be punished."

"Then why not do it yourself?" Blake asked, his fiery gaze never shifting. Had he even blinked?

"That was my place as a youth. Now I am the leader." Telebi sneered at them. "Sarosh, on the other hand, is a youth and needs to become hardened. Sarosh, carry out the punishment."

"Make sure it makes a nice slap," Blake muttered as Sarosh approached. "Give him his show."

Blake stretched his massive arms, muscles and joints crackling. He then popped each knuckle of each hand one at a time, his gaze never shifting. Telebi shifted first, Blake's force of will overcoming even Telebi's massive ego.

Sarosh swung the cane, a loud cracking sound filling the room. Blake did not even flinch. Sarosh swung again and again. At ten strokes, Blake had the audacity to yawn.

"It is clear that you are not taking this seriously," Telebi shouted. "It is clear physical pain is of no consequence to you." Telebi's eyes gleamed. "Cease your strokes, Sarosh. I will ponder on better ways to make you suffer."

"Thanks for the massage," Blake said to Sarosh, then turned and walked with slow dignity from the room. Ten welts showed even on his dark back. This was the first time Hamid had seen him without a shirt, and despite him having a fairly large gut, Blake was an enormously muscled man. He could have snapped the guards in half! Telebi tapped his chin, eyes distant. A smile came onto his face and Hamid felt his stomach sink. Blake had made a mistake. He should have cowered.

Hamid took a breath and followed the rest of his team as they followed Blake from the room.

"Who turned us in?" Casey asked as they left the offices.

"That idiot, Kazmi," Sarosh growled, doing a fair impression of Blake. "He's the only one of the staff that occasionally comes into the main facility."

"Why did Telebi ask you to do the punishment?" Casey asked Sarosh.

Sarosh grimaced. "After Hamid assigned me to be your assistant, Telebi called me in and offered me a lot of money to spy on you all. I accepted, of course. I didn't know you and couldn't defy Telebi. What else could I do? But I saw something in you three. You three were different than anyone I knew except Hamid's family. I was an orphan and barely a person in the eyes of my government. Mr. Blake treated me like a person from day one. You all did." Sarosh perked up, smiling like he'd won a prize. "I've been feeding Telebi bad information since I met you."

"Well, good thing I'm such a nice guy!" Blake said.

"Are you not all fearful of what Telebi said?" Hamid's hands shook. "He said he would think of new punishments for you that were not physical."

"Bah," was Blake's only response.

"You can put your shirt back on." Casey rolled his eyes.

"I don't think I will." Blake flexed his back for another pair of guards, whose eyes fairly popped from their heads. "People need to see what the general does to his enemies."

"Liar. You want to show off your giant muscles."

"Guilty as charged." Blake flexed his biceps, which Hamid had to admit were enormously impressive.

"Can we finish the PDR without your shirt on?" Hamid asked. "Because despite all this nonsense, we still need to finish PDR today."

"I could finish a design review naked."

Casey made a gagging sound and bent over like he was about to throw up.

Casey lay down to sleep and felt his heart race, his mind spin, and his stomach turn. A combination of rational fear, inspired by the fact a man held them who would idly torture them and Blake wouldn't take the man seriously, and irrational panic, a gift of his genetics.

He tried to distract himself with a novel he'd borrowed from a technician. 'The Blind Owl' by Sadegh Hedayat. Perhaps this was a bad choice. 'An opium addict's descent into madness.' He read for a time, but felt worse. So, he got up, trying in vain to minimize the squeaking of his ancient mattress and flimsy bed frame.

He paced and felt the agony of the panic attack stabbing him through the heart. At this point, he'd normally have taken a medication that calmed his heart and called Esin and talked through the feelings, processing them one by one. She'd crack jokes, he'd crack jokes, and he would start feeling better.

But he didn't have her. His mind obsessed over that loss. No medication. No phone. No Esin. The panic blossomed and spread through his chest, his arms, his legs, and deepened its hold in his mind. He hugged himself, then swung his arms, flexing his hands in pain. Then he hugged himself again.

He prayed, begging for release. Weeping as silently as he could, his teeth gnashed together in agony as he groaned. He prayed on. *God, release me!* But there was no release. Lost. He felt despair creeping from his heart, into his limbs, into his mind. He battled. *God, I need someone!*

A few moments later, Blake wrapped his arms around him. "Alright now, Casey, you jerk. This won't do. You don't get to have a panic attack alone."

And then Manuel wrapped his arms around Casey from the other side. "This is like back in college. Remember when Casey had that panic attack after he thought he failed his ODE's test?"

"To be fair," Blake said, "there isn't much ordinary about ordinary differential equations."

"And what was your grade on that test?" Manuel asked.

Casey struggled to speak and finally whispered.

"88."

"That's right!" Blake said. "I was so mad at you. You did better than me and thought you'd failed!"

"I only got 2 points more than you," Casey protested, the sobs calming. "The one to be mad at was Manuel. He got 100% and wrote a new question for the teacher to use on future tests."

They stood like that for several minutes as Casey breathed more slowly, his hot tears cooling on his face.

"Thanks guys. I think I'm alright now."

Manuel and Blake stepped back, eyeing him.

Manuel spoke first. "I don't know what woke me, but next time, don't forget we're here. Don't let the panic take root before you come to us."

Casey nodded. "I haven't had an attack that bad since before I got medication. They've been building." He would have to rely on his friends. "Thanks, you weirdos."

"This isn't acceptable." Blake growled. "I'll talk to Hamid tomorrow. You're going to have your medications back."

"Do I want to know how you intend to do that?"

Blake smiled ominously.

Hamid raised his eyebrows and broke out in a broad grin as Blake walked into his overstuffed office. "Blake, what can I do for you? You're not going to drag me to breakfast or something? I already ate."

Blake sat and smiled. "Nope, already ate. Gotta have sustenance when it's time to threaten someone."

Hamid frowned, confused. Blake's smile was somehow ominous. His eyes did not match the smile.

"What do you mean? Who are you threatening?" Hamid shuddered.

"Why, *you*, of course." Blake winked. "You see, Casey had a panic attack last night. First bad one in a long time. He was suffering something fierce. See, he's got panic for the same reason some bloke might have Type 1 diabetes. He was born with the genes. And he's suffering."

Hamid sat tense, not sure what to make of this giant of a man. His voice was friendly, but the timber of his voice was somehow the most menacing thing he'd ever heard. It dawned on him that Blake could kill him with one hand and not break a sweat.

"You have a choice. You will get Casey these medications," he tossed a manila envelope on Hamid's desk, "or we will do no more work. It's one thing for me to take a meaningless beating. But I will not see Casey suffer again."

"But Telebi..."

"Will not be happy if Casey is not functional." Blake then stood and loomed over Hamid's desk. "If Casey is not functional, I will make sure many of your people are not functional, starting with Telebi."

Blake's eyes were blazing and deadly. Hamid knew he was in earnest. This was no idle threat. He suspected Blake did not make idle threats. Hamid's mind grasped for purchase in this bizarre new world.

"But I have never smuggled drugs..."

Blake sat back down, laughing, giving Hamid a genuine smile that comforted him even as it terrified him more.

"I suspected as much." Blake cracked his knuckles, one by one. "This is easy. You get in your car and go to town. Right. Now. You go into the pharmacy with this list and a note from Telebi stating they will provide these medications immediately. A one-year supply. Got it?"

"A note from Telebi? He'll never sign something, and I have never forged anything."

Blake smiled, then leaned forward and tapped the manila envelope. Hamid opened it and read the note.

"This looks like the general's own handwriting…"

"Your brother is a talented man."

"Sarosh can do forgeries? I never knew that. How did you convince him to do it?"

Blake stood and held the door open, gesturing for Hamid to go.

"It was his idea. He is adept at mimicking signatures, apparently."

Hamid stood, checked his pocket for his keys, and headed out the door without another word.

As his car sped along the road to town, his mind caught up with the events of the day. What was he thinking?

"What am I thinking?" Hamid pulled on his goatee with one hand. "Telebi would as soon kill me and my family as not if he finds out I go behind his back. If I give in to the Americans, am I dooming us all?"

He punched his steering wheel, accidentally producing a beep, which startled him. He thought of Casey and felt a fondness that surprised him. In another life, could they have been friends?

"Keeping Casey happy is saving my family. We can't complete the mission if Casey is having panic attacks. Telebi is irrational about this. He's obsessed with pain. If I want to make things happen, I have to do what is best for the mission. Am I in charge of this project or not?"

Happy with the rationale, he relaxed and continued his way to the pharmacy.

Lunch that day was a mellow, quiet affair, if a food fight could be considered mellow and quiet. It wasn't a real food fight. No splattered potatoes on people. No pudding on the walls. No slime covering the floors. But there were crumbs everywhere.

When Blake set his tray down in the cafeteria, painted 70s yellows and browns to make the food even less appetizing, he attempted to butter his roll. Casey had watched Blake eat hundreds of times. Thousands, probably. He always started with a buttered roll. He ended with a buttered roll. When there weren't rolls, he'd butter any form of bread, be it white bread, tortillas, pitas, or baguettes. On one unforgettable day at a conference in Korea, he buttered the ancient saltine crackers that the restaurant had unearthed on a dusty shelf. Truly, buttered carbohydrates were how Blake prepared his palate, and how he cleansed it.

So, when the roll was the same consistency as a stale crouton, he tapped the roll on the table, sighed, and grabbed his other roll. This was also a desiccated remnant that an archaeologist dreams of finding in a five-thousand-year-old hut.

Casey, finishing his vegetables, tried his pudding next and imagined what Blake was thinking. Blake stood and, carrying the offending cardboard pretending to be rolls, returned to the food line. *I go now to seek retribution and justice. These crimes against humanity will not be allowed to stand. I will have what I came for or there will be vengeance.*

Thoroughly enjoying this vision of Blake as the angel of vengeance, he stared with rapt attention as Blake set the offending rolls on the counter and then began to try the other rolls. The pudding was extra tasty as Blake set aside roll after roll. It appeared that Blake's quest for justice was in vain.

Blake's face went red, and Casey continued to imagine the story. *This is where it ends. My life. My hopes. My kingdom. All is vanity! My cause was just but there is no gluten here!!!*

On a whim, Casey felt his roll. It, too, was a brick. *Shall we see if my cause is more just than yours, Blake?* So, he hefted the flimsy thing and, gauging the distance, lobbed it at Blake.

With an audible *doink*, the projectile contacted Blake's slightly graying thick head of hair. Blake jerked upright, then slowly turned, eyes tracking straight to Casey's. The entire room had gone as still as a church where the mom had taken the one baby crying out into the hall. Casey imagined Blake saying, *You challenge me, you whelp?*

In response to this insolence, Casey stood, picked up Manuel's inedible projectile, took a kung fu stance, and signaled his challenge.

Blake began heaving rolls like a maniac. He sent rolls sailing to bounce off of Casey, Manuel, Sarosh, and anyone else unfortunate enough to be eating at the same time they were.

Casey returned the attention and pelted his roll at Blake, then began scooping up the projectiles from other people's trays, all uneaten, and hurled them at Blake as well.

Sarosh got in on the fun almost immediately, went the other direction from Casey, scooped up the manna from the underworld, and pelted Blake unmercifully. Several of the younger technicians and engineers joined in on the fun, though many of the occupants of that hall of battle sat staring dumbfounded at the antics.

Through it all, Manuel sat and steadily ate his way through the rest of the meal. When a roll nearly landed in his food, he deftly blocked it, then continued to work his way through that day's successful attempt by the sadistic chef at making chicken taste like a shoe.

With the subtle but carrying shriek of door hinges, all eyes turned in fear to see what new challenger would enter the war zone. All combatants froze, rolls in hand. Obligingly, Hamid paced in. Hamid, excited, had begun to shout, "I got them!" before the door was fully open. It came out as "I got the..."

Hamid stood staring at the chaos, face a study of changing emotions, from confusion to deeper confusion to abject confusion.

He held up a brown paper bag and, with a quiet croak in his voice said, "I got them!"

Sarosh doinked a roll off his head.

Esin,

When I went to sleep last night, I had my first strong panic attack. Blake and Manuel got me through it, though it took both of them. You could have done it on your own, of course. Neither of them is up to your weight class when it comes to cheering people up.

But there was a miracle! Hamid got me a year's supply of my medications! I am so grateful! God answered my prayers. I suspect Blake had something to do with it. God often chooses him to answer people's prayers. I told him that once, and he said, 'Well, tell God that I ain't no short-order cook.' But he was smiling afterwards.

Please don't give up on me. I worry I will be gone so long that they will declare me dead. I worry that I'll escape in 2 or 3 years and come home to find you remarried. Could you imagine? I'd have to fight the guy for you, and then I'd feel terrible when I beat him senseless.

In good news, I won the food fight today. Don't listen to Blake. He most definitely lost.

Love,
Casey

Esin wore the appropriate robes for a conservative cleaning lady in Urmia. They were hot, confining, and uncomfortable, but hid her face from the people that mattered. She had to glide completely silently through the obstacle course Abdul Demir, her trainer, had set up for her.

It wasn't that the course was very hard. It was just an office building that they were using to practice in. Opening doors, going through corridors, cleaning, all in silence. No, the problem was she had to look submissive and meek while doing it. As Blake had informed her once while brushing himself off after her tripwire had taken him down during a paintball tournament, she hadn't been either since the day Casey got her out of that awful refugee camp.

Abdul slammed his baton against the wall, startling her, but she did not flinch. She had stopped flinching decades ago. She continued her course.

Today was a new twist. She had to get a body out of the office without making a sound above that of a typical office building at night. No louder than the fans recirculating air, the computers humming in low-power mode, and the printers making their occasional whirs.

She found the body in the near pitch black and quickly chose a course. She wasn't strong enough to toss a body over her shoulder like her husband, or to pick it up by the shoulders and drag it, feet screeching as they dragged on the floor. No, she had other ideas.

Grateful this was a weighted dummy and not a real person, she slowly rolled an office chair over, then lifted the legs and wedged the shins cruelly between the seat and the back. She then brought two more office chairs over and lifted the head enough to get it wedged between the arm and the seat of one of them. Pushing these chairs apart, she used the redirected force to elevate the torso enough to get it over the seat of an armless chair. She then dislodged the legs and head from their chairs, tucked the feet in, and slowly pulled the chair along, making much better speed than had she dragged it.

Her mind flashed to the last time she had disposed of a body. Two decades of time now made the entire thing seem farcical. A malnourished, teenage waif, she had bludgeoned a man to death to protect herself the night of her father's death. How in the world had she dragged the body to the sand dunes? *Could I do that again?*

She thought of Casey, laughing in the face of danger. Someone had to be there to bury the bodies for that man!

She felt the tension in her climb as she had to move slowly enough that the feet did not fall, the chair wheels did not clatter, and her breathing did not come out too loudly. But she was out the door and to the finish line only a few minutes later.

As she crossed the line, Abdul and his two assistants appeared as the lights gradually turned on, and they applauded.

"That was the single cleverest method I've seen a person use to get a body out silently," Abdul said. "You have no idea how little variation I've seen. Most of the men try to pick it up. They grunt and breathe hard, then lose. Most others drag, which leads to them also breathing too hard. This will go down in the record books."

Esin smiled, satisfaction filling her. She felt truly like a spy for the first time, then chuckled at herself. Approaching 40, she was not a stereotypical spy. She didn't even have any sexy outfits to seduce the villain with!

"I don't know," she replied. "I thought I was a bit loud when I had to shove the chairs apart and lift the torso to slip the chair in under them."

"You were below specs. Unlikely they'd have detected you by sound. Now, if someone saw," he gestured to the dummy draped in a contorted fashion over the office chair, "you'd be dead. But this was a near dark test. Congratulations. You are the first to pass on the first try. How do you move so stealthily?"

"I have several children who slept like they were veterans in combat zones, and I had to move about their rooms without causing a friendly fire incident."

Abdul's associate spoke.

"Perhaps we should recruit more mothers and grandmothers."

"Agreed. Now, that cut a week off your schedule. You have 8 more modules. I have seen a few finish these in a day. Many in two. We will begin the next tomorrow."

"Today is young."

"No, we'll move language training up to today. You must sound like an ethnic Azerbaijani speaking the dialect in Urmia."

"I also want to keep learning the Tehran dialect. I cannot afford to be limited to only being a local."

He switched to an odd dialect of Persian she had never heard before.

"Very well, let us begin."

As Casey walked through the construction lab, his heart filled with satisfaction. They'd approved his initial purchasing rapidly, and so things were already arriving for his staff of young engineers to catalog and prepare for construction to begin in earnest. Meanwhile, Blake was gleefully supervising the welding teams building the probes. They'd whipped out his designs for the giant space station and had one team making struts to combine rocket upper stages together. Manuel was confident the orbits could pick up all the sections in a lot less time than he'd feared, though it would still take a few months to collect them all. Too bad it would never actually happen. He understood that officer from *Bridge Over the River Kwai*. He would build the best bridge ever, even if he had to destroy it in the end.

Now for the hardest part. He took a walk down the hall and knocked on the door frame of an open office.

"Good morning, Hamid. Can we discuss logistics for a bit?"

Hamid's desk overflowed with papers, and he'd covered his walls with pictures of his young family. Hamid, looking harried and care-worn, glanced up and smiled faintly at him.

"Of course, come in. Come in. How can I help you?"

Casey shut the door, stepped to the wall, and admired a picture of Hamid's small children, each smiling so broadly.

"This is more of a discussion of how I can help you. Hamid, we need to discuss something you didn't think of, but I knew would come up. You see, the first two portions of this mission are very doable. The third part requires a special thing that doesn't yet exist. A zero-g cutting, welding, and assembly robot capable of doing the modifications to the upper stages and combining them together."

"Then how were we going to do it?"

"Did you know that General Telebi regularly raids the nearby city for older children to take to his bed, always by force or drugs?"

"How do you know that?" Hamid sounded shocked.

"Did you know they are developing bioweapons in the locked down section in the east wing?"

"I suspected as much," Hamid said. "But how do you know?"

Casey shrugged, then stepped to Hamid's desk and sat in the chair in front of it.

"We hacked into Teletubby's diary. He has very lax security. I've been reading through all of his personal writings, and he brags about a lot of things. So, that is why I asked those questions. Do you condone these actions?"

"Of course not," Hamid shouted, then quieted. "These are repug-nant actions. But a diary?"

"A journal, but it's funnier if I call it a diary. Anyway, I had to make sure you're not complicit." Casey smiled and sat. "Because we intend to stop him, and you're going to help."

"If I can help stop that man, I will. But what does this have to do with the robot?"

"Telebi says that a robot like that exists. Somewhere in China. He bragged about it in his journal."

Hamid shook his head slowly.

"No, I was not aware of that."

"The designs aren't on your server."

Hamid opened his mouth to speak and Casey waved him to silence.

"Yes, I have full access to that, too. I can't meet our deadline without that robot. Blake could do the design, but it would take too long."

Hamid dropped his head.

"I'll see what I can do."

###

Sherriff Casey stood back-to-back with Deputy Hamid, their revolvers empty and the mob of outlaws closing in. Their horses were dead. Their options were gone. 'Hamid, my friend,' Casey called. 'It's been a pleasure serving with you. I don't think we're getting out of this one.'

Hamid, strong and resolute, replied in his refined tones.

"And so, esteemed General Telebi, I anticipate your approval of the supply of these designs to meet our mission objectives, for the glory of the Islamic Republic, and for your glory."

Casey blinked, having nearly fallen asleep. He had forgotten about the weekly meeting with the general in his office, but it appeared Hamid wanted them there when he asked Telebi for the robot designs. Meanwhile, Casey could sit back and daydream. He had been imagining Telebi as an Old West teletubby. It fit as the man said some truly bizarre things and seemed to think himself intimidating.

General Telebi had begun pacing partway through Hamid's presentation. Meanwhile, Blake sat in his chair slouched, ankles crossed and extended, arms folded on his belly, staring with disinterest.

Savagely, General Telebi charged towards Blake and screamed. Hamid translated literally, sharing what Telebi was saying to Blake.

"Your parents are children of sin, and your life hangs on the line and yet you sit like a beast without a care! Why do you sit so casually! Are you so arrogant as to assume that your designs are perfect and will conquer the stars without concern? Do you not fear for your life after the beating I gave you only days ago, you dog?"

Blake settled himself more comfortably and simply said. "I'm an engineer. Of course, I know my designs will work. I'm staking my life on them. So, no. I do not fear for my life."

Telebi turned and demanded of Hamid what Blake had said. Hamid stammered and so Casey stood and stepped in to soothe ruffled feathers. Kicking Blake in the leg, he stepped in front of his friend, forcing Blake to sit up or fall over.

"Wise and noble General Telebi, what he said was that he was grateful for your input and would, of course, do as you ask. We all are grateful for your feedback on our personalities, weaknesses, and even our designs, recognizing that your insights gained by hard experience are far beyond those of our learning and paltry education. We are but infidels and barbarians and look upon your stunning collection of rugs, plants, stools, tables, and liquors with awe and reverence. Truly, you are as a father to this project, and we eagerly desire your input at these intervals. But we are not nearly as adept as you are at quick thinking. Wouldst that thou would speak to us less often that we could better prepare for your meetings. Weekly is too often for our weak and faltering minds. Perhaps we could prepare better if we met but monthly? Or even every other month?"

Telebi stood stunned. Hamid stared, mouth agape. Blake rubbed his calf, clearly annoyed.

General Telebi stepped back and smiled. "Hmm... What do you think, Haj Hamid?"

Hamid schooled his face better than Casey had ever seen and spoke with only a mild quaver in his voice. "Well, General Telebi, your time is often stretched thin. And I feel I have earned the right to be trusted to manage this project. I have never let you down during any former project."

"You are right. And I was already beginning to think every week was too often. I should let you have more time to get the tasks done that I give to you. I approve of the plan. My secretary will supply what you need." He glared at Kazmi, then snapped a pencil in his hand. "I wish my team was as wise and well-spoken as this infidel. You may leave."

The four of them left the room with many a bow and headed straight to Hamid's office to talk.

Hamid sat down, putting his face in his hands.

"You are going to be the death of me."

Casey turned, placed his hands on his hips, and stared at Blake.

"And Blake is going to be the death of me. Dude, you have to watch your tongue. He could kill us."

"You said you had a feeling we would get out of this alive," Blake drawled. "Your feelings have never been wrong. Why worry?"

"But that doesn't mean we should actively try to taunt them into wanting to kill us! God won't help us if we are actively sabotaging our cause."

Blake opened his eyes and sat up a bit, troubled.

"Huh, hadn't thought of that."

Casey gently slapped himself in the forehead.

Blake laboriously stood and slapped him on the back.

"Now, don't be like that. You always get us out of tough situations. Why should this be any different?"

Hamid sat up, hands on his knees.

"How? How does he always get you out of tough situations? Casey cheekily made a mockery of the general! Now, the general is so arrogant and narcissistic he didn't notice and thought you were actually complimenting him. But you mocked him!"

"People hear what they want to hear, generally." Casey shrugged and picked up a toy from Hamid's desk. "I told him what he wanted to hear. Well, I told him what I wanted him to hear, but in a way that he wanted to hear it."

"Is that how you always get me to do what you want me to do?" Manuel asked with an open and curious expression. "You are manipulating me?"

"Hardly, Manuel." Casey laughed and tossed the toy to him. "I tell you to do astrodynamics and rocket design calculations, which you want to do anyway, and you do them. No, the only one of you two I manipulate is Blake."

Blake stretched his arms above his head and yawned.

"Well, duh. It's the only reason I get anything done. Now I think about it, it's the only reason I asked out Jane in the first place."

Hamid glanced at each of them, eyes wide.

"Let me guess," Casey said. "You think we're all nuts."

"Yes," was all Hamid replied.

"But we're going to get us all out of this alive and even more prosperous than we were. Even you, Hamid. Well, not Teletubby. If I have my way, he doesn't finish this outside prison."

Blake interjected, "Or dead."

They all nodded their concurrence.

"How do you propose we do that?" Hamid asked.

"We're still working on a plan," Blake said. "Don't you worry, Hamid. We're the ones industry calls when things have gone wrong and need fixing."

Hamid cocked his head to the side and queried Casey, "Why do you try to speak Persian like you are an ancient scholar of the Quran when you speak to the general and his staff?"

"I find it amusing to speak like that as a joke. Never thought it would come in so handy."

Hamid rubbed a hand across his face as though pondering the insanity of these men, always laughing despite their captivity. Then he voiced the sentiment.

"How do you guys laugh in these insane situations!?"

Casey raised a single eyebrow. "If I don't laugh, I cry."

Blake sat back, hands on his belly. "If I don't laugh, I rip someone's arms off."

Everyone looked at Manuel. He stared back, then tilted his head in question.

"What? Do I need to do one? Umm... Oh. I know. If I don't laugh, I do math."

Hamid stared as the three men burst out laughing.

Hamid felt amazed by how well things were coming together. Working with the team was going according to plan. Casey kept all the engineers and technicians on a tight line but let them figure out how to do their tasks without excess supervision. His management style was hands off enough to let them flourish but involved enough to give them a sense of real urgency.

But something was wrong. Something he couldn't quite put his finger on. Things were almost too smooth.

So, Hamid called the team to his office for a discussion. They entered, bringing the sound of banter with them like a warm cloak on a chill day. Did they ever not wear it?

"Howdy, Hamid," Blake called. "You missed us so much since this morning's meeting that you had to call another meeting? You know you don't have to have a meeting to see us, right? Just saunter on over." He tried to make a British accent. "Hey Blake, old chap. How's your tea and crumpets this fine morning? Played any cricket this week? I would have gone pro if I hadn't torn my ACL in water polo. Cursed horses!"

Hamid blinked. He opened his mouth to speak, then stopped, closed it, and pressed his eyes shut tight. After a moment, he opened his eyes and replied.

"Blake, I have two questions for you. First, you do know that water polo does not involve horses, right?"

"You sure?" Blake grinned at him, wiggling his eyebrows.

"Yes. Second, I've heard you use at least a dozen different accents. Are you truly incapable of a British accent, or were you doing it that badly to mock?"

Blake's face filled with pretended surprise, then he spoke in an Irish accent. "Why, he may not be as thick as I thought!"

Hamid leaned back, feeling like his brain was rebooting. After gathering his courage, he spoke.

"We need to have a serious discussion."

Blake snorted and continued in his regular accent. "Then why'd you invite us?"

Hamid tried to make his face look stern, but that made Blake and Manuel bust up laughing. Not a mocking laugh. A friendly laugh. Somehow, they could tease him and make him feel loved.

"While I cannot guarantee a serious conversation with Blake present," Casey began, thumbing to his side at the big man, "I promise we are listening, even if we're laughing."

Hamid took a deep breath, shoulders rising and falling dramatically. Then he stared at them for a time.

"Something is wrong. I don't know what, but my instincts scream that you are hiding something from me. Something critically important. But the project looks like it is on track! Everything is going perfectly!"

"Not as perfectly as I'd like." Blake cracked his knuckles. "Your suppliers are criminals."

"Well, yes, we are forced to use the black market, so technically, they are criminals. But that's not the issue. What are you hiding?"

The three of them looked at each other, then back at Hamid. He stared at each in turn. Manuel was smiling with sympathy. Blake's face was full of mirth. Casey's face was happy yet somehow full of pity. Pity for him? Why? It was disconcerting, these men who cared about him. Why did they treat him so kindly?

Hamid sat quietly until the pieces fell together. A feeling of dread and horror spread over him, and he began to tremble.

"You never intended the launch to succeed, did you? You were going along with it in the hopes you could escape or sabotage it or something."

"Fear of death is not something we have in abundance." Blake stood and walked to the window, peaking through the blinds. "Maybe that shows a lack of common sense..."

Casey interrupted, the only method to stop Blake if he was in a mood. "Hamid, what happens if we succeed? Your government is flailing for a handhold as they slip off a cliff into the trash heap of history. Should we provide it?"

"Nice metaphor." Blake stepped over and held a fist out for Casey to bump.

"Thanks. I came up with it on the spot." Casey supplied the required fist.

"Would 'dustbin' have been more à propos?" Manuel asked.

"Shoot, that does sound better," Blake said. "I recall that fist bump."

"No returns," Casey said.

Hamid, utterly confused and terrified, stood and began pacing again. Blake took his seat and Hamid spoke.

"It is not only your lives that are on the line. Mine is. Perhaps they will also threaten your families. What was your plan?"

"Well, we don't have it fully detailed, but we planned to use that rocket to destroy this building." Casey wore an infuriatingly calm expression.

"So, it's tell-all time, eh?" Blake smirked and put his feet up on Hamid's desk. "I ate a bug in high school on a bet. Truth is, it tasted pretty good. Crunchy."

Casey didn't acknowledge Blake, continuing to stare fixedly at Hamid.

"But you would die!" Hamid protested. "You'd leave your families without fathers, your wives without husbands. And for what?"

Manuel rose and approached him, placing a hand on his shoulder. "To protect them and all the children of God from men like Telebi. If we destroy this building, we take not only his hopes of an asteroid capture but also his nuclear and bioweapons research with it. And perhaps we can finish destabilizing this government."

Blake rose and Manuel took Hamid's seat. Blake picked up a model rocket from his bookshelf and pantomimed it crashing into a stack of books on Hamid's desk.

"And who says we'd still be in here when the rocket strikes? We have a lot more months to go on this project. We're clever. With your help, I bet we can find a way out of here, torture Telebi a bit, and cause an international incident or two."

Casey, with a look of compassion towards Hamid that hurt like a dagger to the heart, made a plea. "Help us, Hamid. Help us escape. Help us defeat Telebi. Hamid, I know how to fix all of this, but you have to help us escape and we will help you escape."

"If I help you, my family will die! They will gather my mother, father, siblings, in-laws, wife, and children and stone them to death!"

Casey stood and took the model from Blake, who huffed and sat. Casey walked over and placed a hand on Hamid's shoulder.

"Hamid, you've got a thing or two to learn about laughing in the face of danger. See, I've almost died several times–mostly Blake's fault–and after the first time, I found the best way to survive was to laugh at it."

"I don't know," Blake interjected. "You weren't laughing when you came down with the flu on the flight home from Nigeria."

"Blake, I was delusional with fever and chills. I wasn't even aware of my existence at that moment. And if I recall, you tried to convince the flight attendants to help me dress you up in one of their spare uniforms."

"You'd never have fit in any of their skirts. You are far too fat."

"You two should write a memoir," Hamid said with hesitation, then felt his heart lighten as the three men chuckled at his joke.

"If we live to get out of this, we will." Casey gestured Manuel up and then Hamid to return to his seat. Casey then stood in front of Hamid's desk and became serious. "And if you will promise to help the three of us escape from Iran, I promise you that as God lives and as we live, we will find a way to bring your family out of Iran to safety."

"Give me a minute." Hamid found himself hyperventilating. "I need a minute to think."

The three stepped from the room and the peace that they carried with them faded from the room. He pushed his chair back and knelt, prostrating himself towards Mecca.

Instead of the usual prayers, he said words that seemed to be given to him. He prayed for what seemed an eternity and a moment, then spoke in exhaustion, "Allah, great is thy wisdom, but I know not where to turn. I fear for my family and myself. I want to join the protesters and seek the overthrow of this wicked government, but I am as much a hostage as any. Allah, do I betray my broken nation to save these men and let them try to save my family?"

Hamid felt a wave of confidence pass over him. He looked up at a picture of his family on the wall, heart yearning for their safety. The faces of the three engineers came to his mind, and he saw conviction, compassion, and cheer on their faces. They believed what Casey had said. In fact, they believed they would succeed. These men had true faith in their God and in the words that Casey spoke.

Hamid's heart burned and a feeling of peace and surety settled in him. He reveled in the feeling. The feeling gave him courage, hope, and a conviction to do what was right. His heart spoke of confidence in these men. They would succeed. They would do what they promised. He could right this wrong and his family could be safe, too. He took the first step into darkness.

Hamid rose to his feet and saw that the office was dark. How long had he been? He walked from his office and saw Casey, Blake, and Manuel still at their desks.

"I was getting worried about you." Manuel walked over and stared at Hamid's face. "You have been crying. I'll get you water."

The other two waited at their desks while Manuel returned with a water bottle. Hamid drained it and then spoke.

"Very well, I promise to help you escape, Inshallah, in return for your help getting my family out. What would I need to do?"

"I need potassium nitrate, white sugar, and corn syrup." Blake said while counting with his fingers. "We can make cinnamon rolls,"

"Blake." Casey put his hand to his forehead and slowly shook his head. "I think those cinnamon rolls would be rather dangerous."

Hamid felt very confused as Blake chuckled. Manuel spoke reassuringly.

"Blake is joking. He would not make solid rocket fuel cinnamon rolls. I mean, he didn't even ask for cinnamon."

Hamid looked around the room at the men and realized they had been tense.

"Were you worried I would say no?"

"No," Casey said.

"Yes," Blake replied.

"Blake tried to get Casey to make a bet you would say no," Manuel said. "Casey pointed out that if you said no, Blake wouldn't be able to collect, so the bet was pointless."

"I would not have betrayed you." Hamid placed a hand on Manuel's shoulder. "I would be a terrible person if I could."

"I know we are all tired, but I have questions now that we are all in this together." Casey pulled out a notebook. "That was a terrible segue, but you take what you can get. Who is the NASA contact Telebi mentioned at the preliminary design review?"

Hamid smiled crookedly and sat. "Ah, yes, you deserve to know that. Dr. Devon is in our employ. She is actively funneling us NASA tech. She's paid quite well and is utterly corrupt."

Blake stood, face dark red. Manuel grabbed him by the shoulders. "Sit down and breathe! You're going to give yourself a heart attack again!"

Blake stiffened, then slowly nodded and finally sat down obediently. Manuel led him through breathing exercises while Hamid glanced back and forth between them and Casey. Casey's face had gone blank and pale, eyes cold, hands clenched into fists.

"I didn't realize you would react so strongly." Hamid frowned and fidgeted in discomfort.

"You don't understand the history, Hamid." Casey set his notebook down on Hamid's desk. "Dr. Devon has been a thorn in our sides for years. She has publicly belittled our work, and we know for certain she has used her influence in NASA to prevent us getting at least two small business grants."

"She was instructed to groom someone to be desperate enough to work for us, or at least to be easily fooled." Hamid understood their reaction as he thought about what she'd done. "Though I think she already had some kind of vendetta on you. She sold you out to Telebi cheaply. Telebi sent me to confirm what she reported and to recruit you if I found you as competent as she said."

Blake growled and Manuel snapped his fingers at him.

"You won't get your revenge on her if you're dead."

"You're right." Blake took a few more deep breaths. "I'm already getting some ideas for revenge on her."

Casey began to protest and Blake held up a hand, cutting him off.

"No, I will not use any of the ones we used on that fraternity senior year."

"Alright." Casey nodded, then cocked his head. "I suppose that eliminates a fair number of stupid ideas. But run it by me before you carry any out." Casey then turned. "Hamid, I need to know everything about their communications. Dates, times, funding sources, data dump sites, and everything else you can find on her. Can you get this?"

"I don't know. I will try. This is the kind of thing I'll have to learn to do, I suppose. Maybe Sarosh can help."

Casey shook himself, then closed his eyes and tilted his head forward. Hamid looked at him, then at Blake and Manuel.

Blake snorted. "He's praying, Hamid. He does that to align his chakras."

"I had to sell my chakras online to pay for college." Casey lifted his head. "Praying for me is more like playing pickup sticks with a vindictive toddler."

"I have played that game with a toddler!" Hamid said. "I think the toddler is still more logical that Telebi."

"Hah!" Blake pointed his finger at Hamid. "Now that Hamid is on our team, he's starting to be a little sassy! We'll turn him into a snarky engineer before he knows it."

Hamid raised his head in mock haughtiness.

"Scientist, Blake. I'm a scientist. I have more dignity than you engineers."

Manuel joined in.

"Bah, you're not a real scientist or engineer until you can calculate orbits. Math is the real mark of dignity. Why, I did some Lorentz transformations just this morning, and think I proved that string theory is garbage." They all stared at him in confusion. He meekly added, "Well, as it is currently constituted."

Casey put up his hands in mock conciliation.

"But remember. Without us systems engineers, none of your rockets, mines, or computers would even work. I'll expect bows of respect and adulation going forward."

Hamid marveled at the feeling of friendship these three had. And they'd accepted him into it with nothing more than a verbal agreement to help them. Who were these men?

"Hamid," Blake interjected, "can you get us out of this building?"

Hamid sighed, feeling drained from the high emotional toll of deciding to commit treason. "No, I don't think I can. They take security seriously here since the protests began. And especially after someone bombed half a dozen secret military sites not that long ago."

"Lay it out for us." Blake opened his notebook.

Hamid ran through the compound in his mind, then spoke. "The Revolutionary Guard monitors the perimeter of the compound by a combination of motion sensors and guards every 30 feet. There are no dead zones. They leveled the entire compound and keep it as a lawn so they can monitor it more easily. There is a helicopter landing pad in the yard, but they observe it continuously. They work in teams of two and are all Revolutionary Guard. None of them are local and none of them leave the compound. Telebi allows no relationships in the nearby communities and rotates them regularly so that they don't make friends in the compound. They check every single person to enter or leave the building by face comparison to ID and to the database. I could get fake IDs and hack you into the system, but no one would let you out, even with an ID. They scan every person with millimeter scanners that are as good as the ones at the airport. They X-ray every single item that comes in or out of the building, and trucks are under guard from the moment they enter the compound to the moment they leave it. Truly paranoid, they even X-ray the garbage leaving. The only thing not X-rayed is the garbage they incinerate. Oh, and Telebi's car when he's in it, though Blake couldn't fit in the trunk."

"Locked down tighter than a country club in the 50s when my dad showed up," Blake muttered.

"Patrols in the countryside, too?" Casey rubbed his chin in thought.

Hamid nodded. "Extensive."

"The roof?" Blake asked.

"No access except from the exterior. They made sure of that. You have to climb a very tall ladder on the exterior to get up there."

"Do they have drone flights that watch the roof?"

"Not that I'm aware of, but probably."

"Check on that. Are there labs on the top floor?"

"Yes." Hamid was amazed by how seriously they were taking this.

Casey paced while Blake continued his interrogation.

"Tunneling?"

Hamid raised an eyebrow. "You're the mining guru."

"Blast it all."

"Blake, why do you not swear in English? You swear in so many languages, including Persian."

Blake harrumphed. "Because that spoilsport," he pointed at Casey, "politely asked me if I'd do him a 'favor' and not curse around him in English because he's so sensitive."

"No, I asked you not to curse in English because I didn't want to fall into the habit myself," Casey retorted. "And because my wife tried to wash your mouth out with soap at our wedding dinner."

"Oh, now that was awesome." Blake spoke with his hands in his excitement. "She literally lassoed me with a rope and then tried to force soap into my mouth. That woman is feisty! Glad I married a meek woman myself."

Manuel snorted, which Hamid had never heard him do, and then could barely speak from laughing.

"You think Jane is a meek woman? Jane!? I saw her crush a pair of soda cans against your temples when you annoyed her."

Blake tapped the side of his nose, then gestured with his index finger at Manuel, emphasizing his words.

"Ah, but see, that is very meek of her. She knew that wouldn't hurt me. If she wasn't a meek woman, she'd have used the cast-iron pans to both sides of my head."

Casey sat, staring among them with an intensity that got their attention. He took on a serious tone.

"Well, Hamid, I have the beginnings of an idea, so we have some work to do. Get us the biggest top floor lab. I don't know what to do with it yet, but kick out whoever you need to. That is our space. No one else is allowed up there except Sarosh. We know he's our man. We need to get Sarosh, your family, and all three of us out of this country. And we need to build a space mission along the way that is so convincing, we may have to launch a rocket to do so."

"Don't you want to complete the mission?" Hamid felt a sadness that they would be so close yet so far from finishing their mission.

"Our mission is getting home and foiling Telebi," Casey said. "If I never mine an asteroid but make it home safely, so be it."

Hamid nodded, shocked to find that he felt peace for the first time in months.

###

General Nacar stood with Abdul in the general's office, conversing quietly in Turkish, Abdul giving his evaluation. That did not worry Esin. Abdul had been an excellent teacher of espionage. Esin felt excited and ready.

General Nacar moved to his seat and switched to English.

"Esin, you have impressed Mr. Demir greatly. You have an aptitude for this. You are far better at deception than I would have expected."

"The refugee camps are harsh teachers," she whispered.

"Yes, they are." General Nacar gave a sad smile. "But you are far more capable than you appear. Yet, you can hide it as easily as another puts on a mask."

"Then we are free to begin?"

"Yes. Mr. Demir, who will accompany you, has the full briefing, but I will give you a summary. Our sources have confirmed that the three men held in the Urmia Research Center are your husband and his partners. The center hires cleaning staff from the local community. Mr. Demir will pose as a driver, working for the general. You will be a cleaning lady. The border is reasonably porous. I'd say we should sneak the men out of the base and get them across the border, but your husband would be near impossible to disguise as a Turk or Iranian, and while there are black people in Iran, Blake is so tall that he stands out anywhere outside a basketball league. Besides, they have apparently already become favorites of the base personnel. I don't think a single one of them could sneak around at all."

Esin smiled fondly, thinking of Casey's stories of his trip to Nigeria. Blake blended in fine there, but Casey complained he was stared at wherever he went. Blake, of course, told him it was because he was so ugly.

"Yes, they never could shut up." Esin smiled. "Blake especially would crack a joke at his own execution."

"Be careful, Esin. Your husband may need you, but so do your children. Take no undue chances."

Esin turned serious. "I wouldn't dream of it."

Hamid left his home on a cool, beautiful morning, and smiled at the flowers his wife had so carefully cultivated in front of their lovely village home. She was so wonderful. He glanced at the growing vegetables in their small yard and breathed in the fresh air blowing from the distant lake. Holding these impressions in his thoughts, he steeled himself to go to the soulless research center, where the only bright spots were three mad Americans and Sarosh.

Hamid opened the door to his car and sat down, turning it on. Behind the steering wheel, he found a note blocking his speedometer. He opened it, confused at how someone had placed it there as he had locked his car.

Sir,

We have information that one of the general's staff, Colonel Kazmi, is attempting to influence the general that the Americans are no longer needed. Please, present to the general in your meetings today that he is wrong and how critical the Americans are.

You don't know who we are, but we are your ally. We seek to bring about the Americans' freedom. We must not be seen discussing anything with you, but we will provide you with information intermittently. Continue to trust the Americans and we will work behind the scenes.

Sincerely,

Your friend

Hamid sat for several minutes, pondering what this meant. One thought came to him, bolstering his infant hope. *I'm not alone.*

Hamid walked into the welding shop and Casey looked up. His smile gave Hamid a feeling of calm.

"Ah, good timing," Casey began. "We got the reports back from the X-ray techs and were pulling them up."

"Excellent." Hamid smiled, which he knew also made Casey happy. Hamid smiled a lot more often lately. "That will be far more interesting than watching the latest torture video with Telebi. He has a standing invitation for watching the latest session every week, but I've convinced him the project is too time consuming to spend time on *leisure*."

Blake sat hunched over the tiny shop computer, reading off results. "18, passed. 19, passed. 20, passed."

"Maybe call out the ones that don't pass." Casey folded his arms.

Blake glared at him. "Fine." Then he squinted at the screen, skimming down. "Okay, weld 45 is too thick to fit into the saddle. Grind off 0.02 millimeters and recheck it. Weld 85 failed. That's a tough one, so don't feel bad. I'll re-weld it myself. Otherwise, we're good."

Blake immediately got the welding gear ready while one of the other technicians stepped up and carefully ground a weld for about 5 seconds.

"How did he become such a good welder?" Hamid asked.

"He was a mechanic growing up. Worked with his dad. He got certified and was going to do it in the Army, though he got pulled off that into combat. Showed a real aptitude for war. Did some things that other people regretted. He hated combat, even if he was good at it. He's a bit of a pacifist now, though he'll definitely use his size to let you beat yourself up."

Hamid perked up, feeling a surge of curiosity. "What do you mean?"

"Well, we were at a job at a gold mine in South Dakota, by a little town called Lead. We got off the job real late that night and were starving. The only place still open was a bar. Good burgers. But it had a sour drunk that night. He tried to pick a fight with Blake, who only wanted to eat. Ignoring a punk like that can rile them up even more, so the man dumped a drink on Blake's head. Blake stood and said to the man, 'It appears you are in the mood to make a mistake. This is your only chance to not make a bigger one. Walk away.' Well, that man was a mean drunk, so he went straight for Blake's face. Took a swing, but Blake caught it with one hand. He squeezed, making the man gasp in pain, then he spun him and sent him reeling away. Well, the man was a piece of work. A foot shorter, but vindictive. So he raced back, taking another swing. Blake used some fancy footwork and spun the man around, pitching him headfirst onto the ground! Blake isn't impolite. He didn't want to smash up any of the bar's furniture or anything. Three times that idiot tried to hit Blake, and each time he pirouetted that fool around like a drunk ballerina."

Hamid had seldom been so enthralled by a story.

"But how did he end it?"

Casey laughed.

"Well, that fool didn't consider that the barkeep was also not interested in damage. He charged one last time and failed to notice three constables had come in to join in the fun. Two of them grabbed the fool by each arm and hauled him out of there. The last stepped up to the barkeep and asked if Blake had been part of the fight. The barkeep laughed and said, 'Nah, he was just here dancin'. It was that drunk fool that was fightin'.'"

Hamid laughed in astonishment.

"Blake is that good on his feet?"

"Maybe I was once, but not anymore," Blake chimed in as he walked by. "That was probably a decade ago." He turned and called out, "Alright, re-X-ray those two welds." Sarosh translated for him.

"But you were a fighter?" Hamid asked.

Blake glared daggers at Casey, who smiled back with a face of innocence.

"Yeah, I was once. But if he was telling you the South Dakota story, then you'll see that I try to avoid it. And he always leaves out that the guy ruined a perfectly good taco when he dumped that drink on my head."

Hamid leaned back, pondering on this turn. "But that means you are a real American cowboy!"

Casey began laughing so hard that he cried. Blake tried to frown, but instead chuckled.

"Yeah, I suppose I am." He then glared at Casey. "Now you shut your trap, or I might make an exception and give you a good whoopin'."

###

Hamid stood before the general and his staff and felt himself wilting with fear. But then he remembered the letter. Someone had inside information on this group, and he was aware of it. He had power. Then he thought of Blake. A cowboy. He could be a cowboy, too.

"General, I have received reports that someone on your staff is misinforming you as to the criticality of the Americans to our continued success."

"You have a good source." The general perked up. "That idiot Kazmi was going on and on about how the Americans are not critical and that we have their plans and are a liability. He thinks we should get rid of them."

Hamid concluded he needed to make an enemy here. To discredit the information, you sometimes discredit the informant.

"Yes, from your descriptions of his skill set, you are right to suspect his knowledge and intentions. Colonel Kazmi is not only incorrect, but ridiculously so. I will explain."

Hamid knew Telebi to be a fan of conflict and intrigue among his men. He smiled to himself as Telebi sat back and waved him onward.

"The Americans are not only providing the engineering needed for this mission but are training our staff and technicians in ways that we desperately need in order to succeed in future space endeavors. Manuel spent many years at NASA and is teaching some of our staff astrodynamics, rocketry, and mission operations."

"But they can learn that from any number of textbooks and on-line courses, as well as our Russian friends," Kazmi said, face worried and irate.

"Why?" Hamid shot back. "Textbooks are never as good as professors and hands on learning. Also, there is an American expression. Don't switch your horse mid-stream."

"What are you saying?" Kazmi said. "What do horses have to do with rockets?"

"It means you're a moron, Kazmi," the general shouted. "It means don't whip your horse in the water."

"General Telebi, sir, while that is a fascinating and inciteful understanding, it is not the meaning the Americans ascribe to it, though yours is equally valid, I am sure."

"Alright, what's their interpretation?" the general said with a smile.

Hamid took a breath, thanking Casey for teaching him to be long winded with the general. Hamid had corrected him and left him smiling!

"It means if you are already on a horse as you cross a river, you wouldn't take the risk of changing to a new horse in the middle of the river. The Americans are in the driver's seat for everything right now. Why not learn from them so that we can be ready to take their place? Why give the Russians the satisfaction of having us come to them begging? Are we not a great nation in our own right?"

Had he lied to the general and his entire staff? He felt himself becoming nauseous and fought it down. Blake would not throw up from a little lying, and neither would he.

Telebi turned to Kazmi. "This is why I think you're an idiot. You don't know the most basic strategy. When you have an asset, you don't throw it away in favor of another asset that you aren't sure of. We have three experts in space. We will use them up before we throw them out. So, Kazmi, the issue is settled. Do not bring it up again. We all know you want to take their glory on the mission. Bah! You are old and stupid. You would be my last choice to lead this."

Kazmi glowered while Hamid thanked the general and moved on to report on the success of the probe welding. His stomach settled as he spoke of technical truths instead of political lies.

When Hamid got to his office, he found a note taped to the door.

Esin caught her first glimpse of Casey a week after she and Abdul had entered the compound. Since then, she had seen him often. He'd even spoken to her when he handed her a piece of cake. In her extensive veils and eye screens, he did not recognize her.

That nut job, Blake, had made a tradition of baking a different western dessert every week, and Casey had always loved to feed anyone and everyone he could get within reach. It was agony to be so close to him and not be able to touch him. Not able to talk to him or to see the light of love enter his eyes. And worst of all, he didn't have her to help him refine his jokes. She had tweaks for several.

But she never once doubted his love for her. Even as he was in captivity, he would brag to the staff about her. Abdul had reported that Casey had printed a picture of their family at a reasonable size, and a picture of her on their wedding day cropped with one from last year that was over 2 feet tall! Casey had hung it in their lab, and the engineers and technicians that saw the photo would congratulate him regularly on his good fortune. It filled her heart to know how much he cared. Though it made her job complicated, as she had to stick to a veil all the time.

But that had been weeks ago. A full hundred days had passed since he'd left that conference and she was making progress. None of the other cleaning ladies wanted to be on duty in the staff offices, especially not Teletubby's office. She suspected Blake had given him that moniker. The staff was quick to get handsy, but she let them think she was the general's personal toy. The general never noticed her. So, she could get the offices to herself quickly. Abdul, now known as Abtin, had quickly become the general's favorite as he told him dirty jokes. The other drivers were all too afraid to banter. They had Teletubby now under near 24-hour surveillance.

But they hadn't found anything useful! They had an extraction protocol for themselves, of course. They came and went from the nearby suburbs nearly every day, though she spent the occasional night on site to collect intel. But getting those two lumbering, runaway trains and their spacey partner out of the base would not be easy. Probably impossible. They were so well known and well liked that they could all but walk to the doors of the base uncontested. But the guards that manned the doors were Revolutionary Guard and reported to Telebi directly. They never had interactions with the base staff, and Blake's desserts had not had a chance to woo them. Abdul had no plan for getting past these guards. Neither did she. Sadly, this was no movie where they could sneak out in bags of wheat. Or ride in empty apple barrels. Or get an eagle to carry them. Or meticulously tunnel hundreds of feet to get under the perimeter. Or blast a hole through the wall and then stay ahead of patrols for 40 miles and then somehow get across the heavily patrolled Turkish border. Or ride out in the general's private car with Manuel wearing a fat suit and twirling a hideous mustache.

Esin smiled. Casey had the oddest taste in movies.

But today was another day of cleaning the staff offices. Drab, lifeless, rundown offices that were probably built depressing and had gone downhill since. No one was at their desks. That could only mean staff meeting! *Blast, they're early! I'm missing it!*

She hurried over and passed into the general's soulless outer office, normally manned by his mouse of a secretary. Still soulless, but also empty. All hands meeting.

She carefully opened the general's office door, silent since she'd lubricated its hinges, and walked in, utterly invisible with her cleaning equipment. Not a single eye turned in her direction. She had found they didn't even seem to register her presence, passing over her like furniture. Unlike every other cleaning lady on staff, she did this while the general was present, hoping to catch things he said that could be helpful. Today was a shouting day; unsurprising since every day was a shouting day.

"The fruit selection is deteriorating! I haven't seen a good plum in weeks!"

She thought of another of those ridiculous movies Casey loved and mouthed, *Plum the fruit or plum the color?*

A quiet, shaky voice stammered into the silence. "Sir, plums are out of season. We won't have them again for months."

That was Major Afshar, who the general had working on nothing but fruit. Esin read his private correspondence. He hated the general. Afshar felt the general was wasting his talents.

"They are always in season somewhere! Get them from somewhere tropical! Get them from Florida or California if you have to. They're my favorite. And don't talk back to me! This is probably why I am peeing green! Not enough plums."

Esin knew that trick. Blake had pulled it on Casey often enough. But how had Blake snuck methylene blue into the general's diet?

The unfortunate subordinate bowed and backed away as a small paperweight bounced off his shoulder, hurled deftly by the angry general. The only thing that he was actually competent at was pegging his subordinates with objects off his desk. Wisely, the subordinate grabbed his shoulder, either in pain or to placate the general.

The general stood and walked around his desk to an end table, where he placed an antique pistol each morning as he came to the office. He carried it whenever he left and loved to display it.

"This is my model 1314 Luger P08, bought in 1934 by the Shah from the Mauser company. A delight to shoot, they only made 3,000. I keep it well-oiled and loaded. I use it only on special occasions." Then he turned and screamed, "Like shooting incompetent officers who can't do the most basic tasks!"

He then marched back to his desk and sat, outwardly calm. "Next item?"

Colonel Kazmi took this as his cue.

"General Telebi, we need to discuss the cement costs. The cement for the launch pad has exceeded my projected costs by 25%! I did a complete analysis of the workings they planned. They should not have needed this much cement. Where did the rest go?"

"And how many degrees in outer space science do you have?" growled Telebi.

"None, sir. But I can do math."

A pen bounced off Kazmi's nose.

"You dolts, I keep Hamid on a tight leash. If he says we need something, he knows we need it. Hamid wouldn't risk his life and that of his family on stupid things like overrunning on cement. He was dead on with his own projections, you know. He came in 1% under budget, in fact!"

"But sir," Kazmi persisted, "he shouldn't have needed that much to begin with."

"Bah, next item."

Another man stepped forward, Kazmi sulkily backing up to rejoin the crowd.

"Sir, I have a request from Mr. Jabiri to approve the construction of a helipad on a flat area near where the senior politician viewing platform he's requested will be located."

"Well, approve it already. I was the one who requested the viewing platform on that hill in the first place! Nice and close, for a good view of launch. Quit wasting my time on every trifling thing for Hamid! Hamid is the only competent one in senior management. In three years, he's taken our space program from nothing more than a pile of stolen rockets to a system that will boost my prestige through the roof! Hah, I made a joke! The rocket will boost my prestige through the roof!"

The men laughed sycophantically, and the general wallowed in their approval, looking quite smug.

"Anyway, Hamid has my trust. Don't tell him that, of course. I don't want him getting the idea that he isn't being observed. Unlike the rest of you, he's never given me an ounce of trouble. He does his job. Now, stop wasting your time trying to manage something you don't understand! Why do you think we have a scientist in charge of this? He answers only to me. Not you."

"Now, I have to return to my estates on the Caspian Sea." Telebi's voice dripped with condescension. "I have pressing matters. I will not return for at least two months. Let Hamid be."

Telebi grabbed a handful of grapes and started throwing them one at a time at the group. "Now, who do I have to murder to get me a plum?"

Esin, completely unnoticed even though she'd cleaned the entire perimeter of the office, took that as her cue to slip silently out. She was actually supposed to be off right now, but she worked through all her breaks and only left because Abdul made her. She headed to the general's junior officer guard office to report to Abdul, who hung out with the guards as he waited on the general's whims. The guards knew her as Abtin's wife, though she looked identical to all the other cleaning ladies. She could get him alone with no difficulty.

As she entered, the first guard to see her called, "Abtin, your wife is here."

The guards cast jealous glances at Abdul as he came over and met her. "Shall we go on a walk, my love?" That was simply asking if she had anything to report.

She spoke softly, "That would please me greatly, my husband." That meant that she had something very important to share with him. They walked to the garage, where there were no prying eyes or ears.

"The general has given a blanket command to his staff to approve any of Hamid's requisitions. They are to allow everything, but not tell Hamid about it, so he doesn't get the idea his life isn't in immediate danger or to get greedy. The general will leave for 2 months."

Abdul glanced at her; eyes wide. "That may be the craziest thing I've heard him do!"

"He wanted to rant about not having plums in season. So, we need to do two things. One, we need to make sure that Hamid, Casey, and team all know immediately that they have a 2-month window to get any expenses they want approved without Telebi's oversight. Second, you need to disrupt any fruit shipments to the general. Make sure orders are delayed, and when fruit arrives, make sure that it is overripe. Only allow the fruits that Telebi doesn't care for to be in there. And absolutely no plums. Keep him ranting about fruit for the next several months. It'll make him sloppy, and the staff distracted."

"Brilliant," Abdul whispered. "I'll see it done. And I'll make sure he doesn't try to take me with him."

Esin nodded, worrying about how to accomplish the task.

Abdul spoke again. "How do you endure him not seeing you, but you seeing him?"

Esin smiled, knowing who 'him' referred to without qualification. "Have you met a man more devoted to a woman than my husband?"

"No, he sings your praises to all who will hold still long enough to hear him. I don't know if he talks about space or you more often."

"Space, but only because it is less complicated. Now, what of Haj Hamid?"

"My lady? What of him?"

"I worry he will slowly wear away under the weight and strain of the deceit he is carrying out. He is no spy. He is a scientist and loyal to Iran, though not the IRGC. But when you infiltrated his office, you found he is conspiring with my husband! We must support him more, too. We must give him more hope. He needs to feel like he has allies."

"What about your husband?"

"We have had this argument. He must not know I am here. He would stare at every veiled servant to try to see me. I know him. He would be distracted and worried. And he would give something away to Blake, who can't shut up. I will not reveal myself yet. When we have a plan of escape, or if his hope seems to waver, then-"

Abdul turned, pulling a pistol from his pocket as a shot rang out. Esin dove out of sight behind a car.

"Now where did she go?" a voice called, approaching Abdul. "I got the driver but what about his little accomplice? I saw you leave the general's office, sly one. He would never have noticed. But I followed, and then I guessed where you would go. And you scurried here to tell all."

The man, a major in the general's staff by his uniform, popped around the car, where he assumed she would be crouching. She was not there. He stood up straighter and looked around. A noise sounded behind him where she'd thrown a stone. He turned, and she leapt from behind the car, silent and stealthy, and stabbed him through the side of his neck while he looked away. He struggled, but her placement was excellent. With a rolling gurgle, he dropped to his knees, then crumpled prone on the ground.

Without another glance at the man, she ran over to Abdul. He had pulled off his kufiya and was applying pressure with it to his shoulder.

"He missed. Well, sort of. He missed my heart. Got me in the shoulder. Pretty bad, but I'll live. Well, if you can stitch me up. There's an exit wound, right?"

She looked at his wound carefully and did not share his optimism. "No exit wound. It's still in you. You'll be fine, but not without a surgeon. I can stitch you shut with a bullet in there, but you'll die if you don't remove it soon. I'm grateful the garage is insulated. Probably dampened the sound. At least no guards have come running to check out the gunshot."

She returned to the corpse and spoke to Abdul.

"You're bugging out. Extraction protocol gamma solo." This meant he would drive to an extraction point near the Turkish border manned by a Turkish agent in Serow. He'd have means to get Abdul out. And to dispose of the body.

"Mrs. Scarlett, I cannot possibly let you remain here alone..."

"You're lucky this is a 22, not a larger caliber gun." She added the dead man's kufiyah on top of his, then tied it all in place with the man's coat. She didn't even recognize this guy! Another one of the faceless minions Teletubby inspired. Hopefully, no one would miss him.

"You're going. An injured spy can't help here. You'll die without treatment and that's useless. You can't get surgery here. They'll ask too many questions. I need someone to get the body out of here. The only one that leaves without his vehicle getting searched is the general. That means you need to drive him home. Think he'll notice all the blood all over you?"

"He wouldn't notice if I was naked."

"You'd be surprised. I think that's the only time he would notice. You recognize him?"

She turned the corpse to face Abdul, who shook his head in puzzlement.

"Well, once we get Major Stiff loaded, I'll cleanup the blood and stitch you up. You drop the general and go to extraction. When an officer goes missing at the same time you do... Well, they'll assume you were working together. When neither of you return... Well, that's a mystery for them to ponder. And I'll change my veil and clothing style, so I am another faceless cleaning lady, not your wife. We were never officially connected in the computers."

"You think I'll be able to drive the general home, then 40 miles to the border with this arm?"

"Yes, you're a competent fellow." She pulled a caffeine packet out of his pocket. "Here's something to keep you alert."

He grudgingly opened the packet and chewed the pill, ignoring the bitter taste.

"Alright, help me with this body," Esin called. "I didn't think lifting fat, disgusting, dead, old, lecherous officers would be part of my job description."

"You joke like your husband in crisis mode," Abdul observed.

"He's a bad influence. Anyway, I'll get his lower body. You get his upper body. I don't want to get any more blood on me than necessary."

Together, they lifted the dead man into the trunk, then Esin gathered up his gun and put it in before closing the trunk. She cleaned her knife and sheathed it, then returned Abdul's gun.

"When was the general planning on leaving?" Esin asked.

"I think we have half an hour. Hurry."

Esin rushed to the cleaning closet, hoping the blood on her hands wasn't noticeable. She grabbed one of the med kits she kept squirreled away, just in case. Not running into anyone, she washed and then hurried back. Mop and towels. She cleaned like her life depended on it. Which it did.

After pouring the mop bucket carefully down the floor drain in the garage, she yelled, "Pop the trunk," then pitched everything in for easy disposal.

Nearly panicking, she started into the stitches. She did her best, but shaking hands and the panic of discovery made Abdul grunt in pain.

The sound of the garage door being roughly opened sent her scurrying behind another of the cars, the stitches not quite done.

"Oh good, you're already in the car!" shouted Telebi. "We'll go straight home."

"Very good, sir," Abdul called. He finished the last stitch himself. "I'm dying to get home myself."

Esin shook her head at the joke, then slumped to the ground, head against the wall to try to calm herself from the string of events. She gave herself 15 minutes, then went back to work. It was only her now.

Hamid locked his office each time he left. He didn't even allow the cleaning ladies in, taking out his trash himself.

So, when he walked in that morning and there was a paper on his desk that he did not recognize, his heart raced. He hurried over and sat down, setting his laptop on his desk and taking up the piece of printed paper.

Sir–I hope this note finds you well. I appreciate your prompt actions over our previous missive. In return, I wanted to inform you of logistics developments. In a staff meeting yesterday, General Telebi informed his staff that he trusts you and to leave you alone. You answer only to him. He will be gone to his estates for the next two months. I suspect he will not be reviewing any of your purchases or decisions for the next two months while he deals with more 'pressing issues.' Specifically, fruit.

This dereliction of duty is not unexpected but underlines the corruption in our government. I am well placed to help you. Inform your team of the general's neglect and trust their judgment on what to add to your requisitions. I anticipate they will push you to add a lot of items that are of dubious use to the general's agenda but will greatly aid in their ultimate goal of survival and freedom for all of you.

Tell the men their families are safe and well.

Reach me by putting messages in your top drawer, locked. I will put future correspondence there, as well.

Sincerely,

Your Friend

Hamid sat, stunned, then reread the letter until he had the contents memorized. He giggled, caught himself, and let himself laugh aloud. Then he shredded the note as he had the last one, took the shredded strips, and tore them into tiny pieces. He then took handfuls and dropped them in trashes around the office.

Back at his seat, he slowly got his breathing under control. He wasn't sure if he was more terrified or excited. Telebi would have his head if he found anything amiss. But would Telebi even look?

He pulled his phone out as he whispered, "Whoever said it was a curse to live in interesting times was correct."

"Yes, my brother?" Sarosh answered.

"Send the Americans to my office. Tell them we have some planning to do."

Esin left the apartment she had in the village well after dark, slipping from the single room that was little more than a lean-to added for storage that Abdul's contact had rented for them. With Abdul gone, it was downright roomy, though it would get cold this winter. Eating all her meals and showering at the research center, she only came to the village after work once a week, for one purpose. Communication.

As she never interacted with the other villagers, leaving early and coming back late, she had made no contacts among her neighbors, and saw none now. She made her way carefully to the edge of the village and went to a grove of trees. The grove was isolated and difficult to navigate, with thorn bushes and dense undergrowth impeding the way. Abdul had used this to their advantage, burrowing under a thorn bush to make a hiding place for the satellite phone. She couldn't keep it in her room because of random searches by the landlord. She couldn't keep it at the base. So, she kept it in the underbrush. Now, with Abdul gone, she had to be the one to make the weekly reports.

She pulled the phone out of the plastic bag and swapped the batteries for fresh ones, bought weekly from the village store, and turned it on. She then called the secure number she had memorized. The phone had no memory, so it couldn't be used for information.

She dialed, and they picked up on the first ring.

"Sentry tango 54."

She replied, "Alpha epsilon 68."

He read off new codes for the next call.

"How goes the recovery?"

"His surgery was successful. Status?"

"I'm in communication with Sam and have established a letter drop spot." Sam was their code name for Hamid.

"Good. Any concerns?"

"He seems fearful, but if I know the team," she smiled, "they will have him fearless in no time. Any progress on an extraction plan for the team?"

"We have one option, now they have that rooftop lab. We need to confirm rooftop surveillance protocols."

Esin nodded to herself, recalling what she'd learned. "They have drones, but they are intermittent and focused on the grounds, not going above the roofline. I cannot tell if there are men stationed on the roof, of course, but someone goes up and down the ladder at least once a day. I don't think they station any personnel on the roof, but I cannot guarantee this."

"Copy. We consider that acceptable risk. We're go on the mission."

"Excellent. Entry vector through shaped charges through the roof?"

"Yes, we plan on entering through the area at the far end of their lab, away from the entry doors."

"Negative on the location. Don't go through their lab. If the mission fails, we don't want anyone knowing they were the target."

"What do you recommend?"

"I've confirmed they use lab 714 for bioweapons research. It has ready access to the main corridor. If you send a helicopter with no markings and the men have no uniform insignia, they'll assume you are someone trying to take their research. If the Americans escape, then it won't matter."

"Agreed. We'll plan on hitting the base at 0200 on the morning of the 22nd, in three days. Anything else?"

"Copy, 0200 on the 22nd. Did our friend report our last conversation to you?"

"Teletubby's departure? Yes. He passes his regrets that he will have to leave it to you to disrupt the fruit shipments."

"Copy. Will do. Though hopefully that will be unnecessary."

"Our friend thinks we should extract you immediately. We never intended this to be a solo mission."

Esin's face hardened. "Negative, I will not extract without the targets being freed."

"He also said you would say that. We're trying to get you backup soon. It's proving difficult, as we are not only dealing with Iranian intelligence, but Israeli."

"And the fact you can't give me another 'husband.' Someone is bound to remember I was married if I get a new one. The other ladies at work asked about Abtin. I had hoped they had not connected me. They thought he was very handsome. They were sad that he had to go visit his aging mother in Tehran and wonder when he'll be back."

"Well, we'll come up with something."

Esin sighed, doubtful they would. "Copy. Anything further?"

"Word from the home front continues to be positive. The eldest says, 'The crow flies at midnight. The pigeon flies into oncoming traffic.' What does it mean?"

"Absolutely nothing," she said, truthfully. It was Matt making silly jokes to cope with his mother suddenly being a spy. "Pass on to them that I love them, their father is safe, and to be brave. And say the emu flies parabolically. He'll understand."

Hamid sat in his office and read the latest letter from his new friend, detailing plans to extract the Americans at 2 am the next morning. All he had to do was tell them where to be. But Casey had promised him they would help him and his family escape. Clearly, this was not the plan his new friend had just given him. This plan was from the spies that were working to free the Americans. Could he begrudge them their freedom? What of his own life?

He wrestled with his feelings. He could hold them to their promise. Not give them the details to escape. But who would he be if he kept these men captives? He hadn't enjoyed being the kidnapper. It ate him up until he had finally agreed to help them escape not quite a month ago. He faced the loss of his life and that of his family and asked himself the simple question. What would Blake and Casey do?

Hamid drew out a single piece of paper and wrote, *Understood. I'll have them in position.*

Locking his drawer and office, he headed to the construction lab to let the team know. Now that he'd made his decision, he felt peace. He hoped he wouldn't suffer consequences from this. Maybe he could still save his family. Telebi couldn't blame this on him. Though he would probably try. But he remembered something Casey had said to him. He said it to himself. *I will do what's right, even if it is hard.*

Of course, Blake had then said, *I will make life miserable for my enemies, especially if it's amusing.*

Entering the construction lab, he waved the team to the corner to discuss the situation. Sarosh joined them, and Hamid realized he could possibly still save himself and give Sarosh freedom.

"Guess what?" Sarosh asked. "I had my own idea for a prank."

Blake beamed like a proud father as he said, "Yes, this is a good one."

"Last night, I posted Teletubby's personal phone number to Reddit. I explained he was a... I forget the word. Bad man with children. Anyway, it was upvoted 40 thousand times before I left for work! I suspect he will get a lot of angry calls."

Hamid sat blinking. "Sarosh, that is dangerous! If they caught you..."

Sarosh waved his fears away. "I was behind a VPN and using an account out of Afghanistan. There is no chance. He will probably have to change his phone number!"

Blake and Casey congratulated him, and Hamid waited. As they continued to talk about the prank, he finally interrupted.

"Our new friend has informed me that there will be an attempt to free you at 2 am this coming morning, so not too long from now. Sarosh, you will join them. This will lay the blame on you, and since Telebi trusted you to be his spy, will point the finger directly at him for ultimate blame."

Casey stood, face awash in fear. "But he's your brother! What about you and your family? They will blame you. We promised to help you get out."

"And this will save me and my family. You see, I adopted Sarosh unofficially. They will blame Telebi for ignorance of his background. Telebi doesn't even realize Sarosh is my brother! Sarosh's parents were of the Bahá'í faith, which is considered apostasy from Islam. I have kept Sarosh hidden and protected, but it will be easy to blame his Bahá'í background, exonerating me and my family, and destroying Telebi!"

Casey sat back, glancing at his friends. "We don't like being unable to keep our word. Besides, this doesn't feel like it'll work."

"If you escape in this manner, I will release you from your promise to me. I consider it fulfilled."

Blake leaned forward. "Hamid, I don't know what we'd do if you got in trouble over this."

"No, you don't understand," Sarosh added with glee. "The general's staff all know I am his spy. If I leave, they will sense blood in the water. Telebi will be done for."

Casey frowned but Manuel replied, "What do we have to do?"

Casey frowned even more deeply than before as they moved swiftly and fairly quietly to the freight elevator with Sarosh just before 2 am. A big man like Blake did not actually do 'stealthy.' Casey didn't either, but he could be quieter than Blake's rustling and occasional grunting noises.

They exited the freight elevator on the 7th floor, and Sarosh led them to the secure door for room 714, with a sign reading, 'Biology Laboratory.' He then stuck them in a janitor's closet while he went to the window at the end of the hall to watch through the rebar for the helicopter.

The minutes passed slowly, both because Sarosh had crammed them into a closet with Blake, who was nearly as broad as two regular men, and because they didn't dare talk and draw attention. Casey stood trapped with his own thoughts, which were not happy. Was he abandoning Hamid? He felt excited about getting out, but it felt wrong. He bounced on his toes, trying to stay limber for what could be some running.

The door burst open and Sarosh whispered vehemently, "Run!" He headed straight to the freight elevator as they followed behind him.

As soon as the freight elevator began moving down, Sarosh, gasping, explained. "The helicopter was incoming. I could see it in the lights, flying right over the trees. Well, someone on the roof must have seen it too, because I saw a rocket streak away from the roof, right towards the helicopter! Our pilot must have seen it coming because he veered hard, nearly doing a roll, which I'd never seen a helicopter do before, and the missile barely missed him! We have missile batteries on the roof! Well, that pilot swung around and headed away at a high speed. I think the rescue is off."

"Well, and if that don't beat all," Blake said. "I do wish I could have seen a helicopter do a barrel roll."

"You know what would have been better to see?" Manuel asked, annoyance in his voice. "No rockets and the inside of a helicopter as we left."

"But I've seen the insides of hundreds of helicopters," Blake said. "Jumped out of quite a few, now I think about it. Only one of them was on fire at the time. Wait, two of them."

"Do you mean 'under fire'," Sarosh asked.

"No, on fire," Blake said. "Comes after the 'under fire' part is over."

"You going to blame me for that fire, too?" Casey asked with a smile as they re-entered their barracks.

"Unless you've invented time travel or were in Kosovo fighting for the other side, then I suppose you're innocent in this one instance."

"Why are you and Casey not angry you didn't escape?" Sarosh asked.

Blake set a hand on Sarosh's shoulder. "When you've been in as many scrapes as I have..."

"We," Casey interrupted.

"As we have. Well, you get a bit fatalistic. Are we disappointed? Yeah, sure. Are we surprised? Nope. Now let me tell you about my time in a Pakistani prison."

Casey had heard this question enough he could tell it, so he ignored them and headed to his bunk. He hid his personal items before he went to bed. He felt surprisingly peaceful over this. No one had died, and they were going to still be able to help Hamid escape. They'd have to think even harder on how to get out of here.

"Are you telling me you've never had a deep-fried candy bar?" Blake asked.

Casey rolled his eyes, much to Hamid's amusement, then spoke.

"Blake, why would Hamid have had that? I haven't even had that, and I'm from Montana. No one in their right mind would eat that."

Blake put on a hurt expression. "Are you saying no one from the south is in their right mind?"

Hamid spoke in Blake's accent in a deadpan and, by instinct, did not even pause to think whether what had popped in his head was funny.

"If the shoe fits."

Hamid sat back thrilled as all three of them laughed. This camaraderie was wonderful, and he was learning that he could fit with these men. Men who had no desire for power to be above someone. No, they sought power to lift others up. The laughter filling his office was worth more to him than gold.

Casey, still chuckling, picked up his clipboard again.

"Alright, alright, we have to focus. We're a little over a week into our spending spree and I've had to veto a deep fryer, a VHS player, a foosball table, and a Geo Metro. We don't even have VHS tapes to play!"

"To be fair, I would love a car like a Geo Metro," Hamid said. "I'm still driving a relic from the Soviet era."

Blake perked up. "Seriously? Can I see it? Is it made of cardboard like some?"

Hamid raised an eyebrow but pulled out his phone to show him a picture.

"Blake is a connoisseur of terrible cars," Casey explained. "He doesn't own any, but wants to."

"If that idiot Devon hadn't sabotaged us all those years, I might have been able to afford to buy a few!"

Hamid laughed and handed his phone to Blake, who oohed and aa-hed over the photos with far more enthusiasm than the car deserved.

"Wait," Blake called, "Iran isn't some destitute country. Aren't you one of the largest automakers in Asia? Why do you have a 50-year-old piece of junk for a car?"

"Because I spend all my money to pay for my extended family. My grandparents were supporters of the Pahlavi's before the revolution, in the inner circle, but not high enough to escape with the Shah. I am the first to break out of the poverty they sank into after the Ayatollah came to power."

Manuel's eyes went wide. "Were they sultans?"

Hamid, who understood that Manuel probably only knew about Iranian history from the Bible, smiled. "No, my grandfathers were both engineers. But they all became poor farmers in '79. But my aptitude for school helped me escape. Otherwise, I'd be a poor farmer, too."

"Are they still alive?" Casey asked, a fierce look in his eyes.

"No, they had very hard lives." Hamid sighed. "They were not young at the revolution. But my parents are still relatively young."

Casey grinned in a way that unsettled Hamid.

"Perhaps they will live to see the end of the ayatollahs and the rise of freedom, God willing. Now, let's get this list finished."

"If everyone else is done, can I give you my list?" Manuel asked.

"Yes, what are the non-critical things for your hobby?" Casey asked politely.

"I have made my own list," Manuel said and then, with a flourish, handed him a piece of paper that was passed around the room.

Casey frowned. "You need... I don't even know how to pronounce that."

"It's a ceramic. They are available from the listed manufacturer here in Iran. They aren't special. Just hard to pronounce."

"What are these for?" Hamid asked.

Blake hurriedly warned, "Don't ask, he might tell you!"

Too late, Manuel began to speak.

"The ceramics can handle the radiation and associated temperatures of fusion."

"Well, that was concise. For once." Blake sat back in surprise.

Hamid felt he had missed something. "You can do fusion?"

"Maybe," Casey said into the silence. "Thus, the ceramics. He is trying to test his theories. The math is well beyond me, but the theory is fascinating. He's explained it to me at least a dozen times and I think I'm getting it. In layman's terms, he thinks you can twist electromagnetic fields so fast they will act like a gravitational confinement for the fusion reaction and mimic the fusion of the heart of the sun."

Hamid had underestimated this team.

"Well, I don't doubt that if Manuel can't do it, no one can. What do we do if he succeeds?"

"We don't explode," Manuel said in a rush. Seeing concern, he continued. "I mean, the size I'm doing this, it won't explode. It can't. I mean, if my math is wrong, it could, but so could a lot of things. But we should be fine."

Manuel smiled, unaware of how badly he'd freaked Hamid out. Casey and Blake were nothing but smiles, though, so Hamid put on a sheepish grin.

"Well, let's get him what he needs. And I'll figure out how to keep the cleaning ladies out. The last thing we need is someone to come in here and discover this."

Casey climbed into bed that night, facing the beginnings of a panic attack. Despite his medication, he was fading. It had been a full day of meetings, starting with Hamid and the team, and continuing with several hours of guidance to the blossoming project management team. They were all good at management, but none had done large projects before. He worried about them succeeding in their parts of the project. He worried about being able to get the project together. And he worried about finding a way to escape. The worries piled up until he felt like he was going to suffocate. Not even Blake's sense of humor could reignite his fading hope.

As he adjusted his pillow, he found that there was a paper under it. Intrigued, he pulled the paper out and felt his heart catch. The front had a single word in Persian written across it in a bold hand. It read, 'Hope.' The handwriting was delicate, beautiful, and familiar.

Now trembling, he unfolded the letter and read a cryptic story that no one besides Esin, Blake, and he would understand. The story told of Esin's captivity and Casey and Blake rescuing her. The story then shifted to the present and told of their present plight. It rang with the music of the hummingbird, the chirping words calling to him to hope. He laughed aloud, drawing an odd look from Blake. Casey's heart burned with the joy of knowing they were together, even if so strangely.

Hope!

A bluebird was flying through the wilds and saw a hummingbird in a net, held by a murder of crows. The crows held her fast, waiting for the owl to come and take the hummingbird away in exchange for shiny things. The owl was a cruel and vicious bird, full of desire to hurt, not just to eat. The bluebird saw the hummingbird and knew its fate, so the bluebird hatched a plan.

The bluebird came to the crows dressed as an owl and strutted about with its friend, a falcon. The bluebird called, 'King Crow, I am a mighty owl and want this hummingbird for my own.' The King Crow called, 'Do you have my shiny things?'

The bluebird flashed a bag with many shiny baubles in it and said, 'Crows, if you overthrow your king, I will give you each a shiny thing and the King Crow will have no shiny things!' Then the falcon flashed his talons, and a hawk screeched from above and the crows cowered. They lusted after the shiny things, and so they threw down their king at the feet of the owl who was now seen to be no owl, but rather a bluebird of great goodness.

The bluebird called out, 'Crows, promise you will never take captive the hummingbirds again and you will be free to leave with your shiny things!' The crows, in fear of the falcon and the hawk and in awe of the shiny things called, 'Yes, we swear!' And the bluebird let them go, but that wicked king was given to the hawk in the sky.

Many years passed and the bluebird and the hummingbird were the best of friends. Then a mighty owl swooped in and trapped the bluebird, the falcon, and their friend the robin in another net. The owl was fascinated by the mighty things the bluebird and his friends had done and wanted them close to his nest, so close that the bluebird was ever in the owl's gaze.

Now, the hummingbird has dressed as an owlet and snuck into the owl's nest, seeking to release the bluebird and his friends. But the nest is full of captives. Many birds languish in the owl's prison. The hummingbird rejoices that the bluebird is working to find a way to escape and wishes that the bluebird knew she was helping free him, too. She knows the bluebird must not see her or the owl, vigilant and watching, might take the hummingbird and use her against the bluebird.

And so, the hummingbird, the bluebird, and all the captive birds must find a way to overpower the owl and free all the birds. And until the bluebird is freed from the owl, the bluebird and hummingbird must endure and hope silently, remembering that their love is forever, and that owls are not.

Hope!

Manuel insisted they come look at his experiment that morning before the day got busy. Since Manuel hardly ever insisted on anything, Casey relented and dragged Blake along to the top floor.

"But I don't understand a word that Manuel says when he's talking about his hobbies," Blake grumbled.

"Humor him," Casey said, glaring at Blake. "He's one of your best friends. He listens to you when you ramble about your hobbies."

"That's because he's so smart that he understands all of my hobbies. He could mathematically derive my hobbies from first principles. I bet he could make a robot to do my hobbies for me, giving me more time for more hobbies."

Casey chuckled, thinking that was likely true, especially since Blake's favorite hobby was blowing things up in the desert. But, as they walked into the top floor lab that Manuel had claimed, he stopped and stared in amazement.

"How long since we last came here?"

Manuel looked up and replied, "2 months, 3 days."

In the interim, Manuel had built what Casey assumed was an extremely tiny ion engine attached to a 4-inch box with a mess of piping in and out of it. The box was glowing a faint yellow.

"LEDs?" Casey asked.

Manuel cocked his head, clearly not following what he meant. "What do you mean?"

"Did you use LEDs to make the box glow?"

"No, this is a working model. I don't need LEDs. It glows on its own. I measured and the radiation coming off is harmless. Well, within safe tolerances for industrial exposure in the time frames we are standing around it. I wouldn't lick it or sleep with it."

Casey and Blake glanced at each other, then Blake asked dryly, "You made a working fusion reactor?"

"Yes, as I've been telling you guys the last few months, I've been testing my theories about containing fusion reactions by a warping of spacetime induced by spinning electromagnetic discs charged to oscillating voltages and currents. I had a breakthrough when I threw out the theory that you could contain the fusion reaction merely by magnetic fields. You inspired the idea when you asked about gravitational fields."

Casey's jaw dropped. "You made a fusion reactor using gravity?"

"Sort of. Please let me finish. I will oversimplify, as neither of you took the right math to understand this. I barely understand it. You see, at the Big Bang, something contained the outward force of the immense pressure of the material contained inside the universe. That something was the very structure of spacetime itself. Spacetime, as we know it, manifests as gravity and electromagnetism, which are the same thing, simple curves vs helical spirals. Well, with the right rotational rates and geometries, I can produce both magnetic and gravitational fields that produce a zone that won't allow particles out. I call those null zones. I solved those equations over several weeks near the beginning of our stay. It was very elegant in the end."

Blake sat down and stared at Casey. "He figured out the universal equation of the universe. All I've done is order parts and start training some engineers."

Casey walked closer to the table. "And not just fusion. Cold fusion. It's sitting here..."

Manuel jumped back in. "Not technically cold. Well, the surroundings are cold. The reaction is quite hot, but nicely contained. By making a reaction contained by spinning discs that oscillate in voltage and current, making pockets of repulsive and attractive spacetime around null spacetime, I was able to start producing fusion products. The reactor is self-propagating and is running off of plain water."

"Not heavy water? Just protons?" Casey massaged his temples.

"I'm glad I didn't need heavy water." Manuel tapped a small water pump. "That would have been hard to get. The confinement is so extreme that I can fuse protons all the way to helium, like the sun. I suspect with the right field I could fuse bigger things, like oxygen, though that would be much less beneficial, as some of the fusion products could then undergo fission, and I don't want to deal with the guilt of blowing us all up. I have it in ultra-low-power mode, basically running enough to power itself while venting tiny amounts of helium. In normal mode, it can produce at least a megawatt of energy."

Casey interrupted. "A megawatt from a four-inch square box?!?"

Manuel frowned. "Well, it's a prototype. I expect when I have proper tools and machine shops, I can up that by three orders of magnitude. Now, may I finish?"

Casey bowed and waved Manuel on.

"I used further discs to channel the energy of the reactor into becoming the fuel for a tiny ion engine. Now, this is something you sadly can't watch, but you can witness the results. I'll ignite the rocket for a tenth of a millisecond. Plug your ears." He put a metal slab between them and the ion engine and bolted it down, then flicked a switch. With a bright flash at the other end of the lab, the entire table slid sideways a foot. The room's temperature immediately shot up noticeably.

All three of them looked away, blinking. Manuel apologized. "I don't know how much thrust I'm producing, as I haven't built a test apparatus capable of withstanding that large of a thrust vector. I'd put the table against the wall and run it continuously, but I'd need a lead box to absorb most of the radiation and I suspect it would melt quickly. My measurements indicate we are getting about 50 dental X-rays worth of radiation every time I turn it on, and I have it on very low. I'm estimating that the system is accelerating the particles to at least 0.005c, maybe as high as 0.01c."

Blake said, "Why was the flash of light at the other end of the room?"

"That's where the trail is visible. Particles going that fast collide and produce X-ray light, then lower and lower as they slow down by drag. By the time they are at that end of the room, they're producing visible and infrared light. Don't get in the way of the beam. It'd go through you and cause so much damage. But it wouldn't be visible for a day or so, unless you got enough at once. Then you'd die, not a visible mark on you."

Casey muttered, "Avada kedavra..."

"So, no pretty flame because the exhaust is too fast..." Blake mused.

"The flames are there; you just couldn't see them. This room lit up with X-rays and microwaves."

Blake snorted. "You should mention that part first, before you turn it on."

"Well, it should be safe amounts. I think. And that was an extremely limited thrust. I won't have people nearby when I make a rocket with it."

Manuel dragged the table back to its original location and unbolted the lead slab. After tidying up, he turned to see them still standing there, staring at the setup. He waited for their response.

Casey reacted on instinct. Praise first, problems second. "A hundredth the speed of light... Manuel, you're brilliant and this is the most amazing thing I've ever seen. When we get home, this will surely win you the Nobel Prize and make us filthy rich."

"But you understand we can't let Teletubby and those like him have it?" Blake stood and began pacing.

Manuel frowned, but nodded. "But why would he get it? We can use this to escape. We need to build ourselves a small rocket that can maneuver in atmosphere, which I can do in my sleep, then cut a hole in the roof above us and fly out of here."

Blake turned to Casey. "You think we could do it?"

"If anyone can do it, it's Manuel," Casey replied.

"But it's spitting helium ions out at a fraction of the speed of light! The radiation trail will be massive! It'll kill us!" Blake appeared flustered.

Casey countered, "But his thrust to fuel ratio is probably also massive. We can get lead shielding on the entire back side of the rocket, no sweat. And you love flying. You have that ultralight you go out with on weekends."

"That has propellers, not fusion powered rockets!"

Manuel chimed in. "So, we have about three weeks until our luxury of this open purchase order expires. Can you help me make a list so I can get the parts and start building our escape ship?"

Blake paused his march, glanced up, and started mumbling. He then resumed pacing the lab, this time looking around at the landmarks. He whipped out a tape measure, so Casey pulled out a notebook.

"Fourteen-foot ceilings. Sixty by thirty square feet. Major ceiling interferences include water and natural gas pipes that run right down the middle. Reroute or we'll have a problem. Air ducting is off to the side. Shouldn't be a problem. The major structural beams are through the walls. Lateral support beams are steel but are only for supporting the roof, so they are disposable. We'll need thermite sufficient for sixteen four-inch beams. But that doesn't answer how we can build a rocket in a room where we need to take the ceiling down."

Manuel shrugged. "The rocket can be in half the room. We then take off and hover across and out the hole."

Casey wrote everything down. "Okay, this is quickly turning into a bad episode of Star Trek. Frankly, I think we need to figure out a simpler solution. Why don't we all take some time and evaluate our plans? We have some time to figure this out. But in the short term, I am sure we're agreed–Manuel needs to build a rocket."

Manuel grinned and Blake walked over and clapped him on the back. "And fly us all the way home to America!"

###

As they left the lab, Blake turned and whispered to Casey, "He has to survive. I don't care if we die. Those designs will change the world for the better."

"Only if we're with him to make sure. You know he has no guile. At least, none he hasn't learned from us over the last couple decades. If we die but he lives, someone will take advantage of him and use those designs for their own purposes. Remember Seon Kim?"

Blake grunted in response, and Casey gritted his teeth. Of course, they both remembered that rat. Manuel had been a young college student and had developed a fancy algorithm. A fellow grad student had talked him into sharing the code and then sold it as his own, making millions. Manuel, betrayed and confused, came to them, his best friends, to figure out what went wrong. After they explained liars and crooks to him, he agreed to not show anyone his inventions until they had seen it. They'd been protecting him ever since. Blake and Casey had sworn to each other that if Manuel didn't get rich off his own ideas, no one would.

"Then we'd better figure this out," Blake said with a scowl. "His rocket may work, but I have no idea how to make our crazy idea work to get it out of this building."

Casey stopped, his shoes squeaking loudly in the hallway. Manuel, several yards ahead, turned and came back. He and Manuel patiently waited as Casey's mind raced. They knew what this face meant. He was having an idea.

"A telescope," Casey said. "We'll build an observatory!"

Manuel smiled, "I like that. I wouldn't mind seeing the stars. But they wouldn't let us on the roof."

Casey grinned. "They don't have to. They have to build it directly over our lab and to our specifications. Then we can take down the ceiling at our leisure."

Blake's eyes blazed with delight. "And we can build it out of balsa wood. Then we can blastoff right through it!"

Manuel cocked an eyebrow at Blake and Casey quipped, "What, you think this is a Michael Bay movie?"

Esin,

Manuel has done it. He has solved the fundamental equation of the universe. I don't know if we fully comprehend what that means. It does mean that we can now control matter using artificial gravity. I asked

Manuel, and he doesn't think we can just turn on gravity and people in orbit will stick to the floors. But he thinks we'll be able to have constant thrust on ships and so go places at constant 1g thrust. That's revolutionary! It's like that depressing book series where terrorists drop asteroids on Earth, except we're going to make sure that can't happen. We're going to build the first practical deep space rocket!

I can't wait to show you a prototype. As soon as we execute a plan to get out of here.

Love,
Casey

Esin sat at Kazmi's desk, perusing the purchase orders that the team had put in that day. At her instruction, Hamid put in all his purchase orders at 7 pm. Esin sat down to Kazmi's laptop at 7:05 pm and approved all but a few of them, meaning Kazmi never saw any that were even remotely questionable. Every time she sat down and logged into his laptop, she laughed. No super spy skills needed to hack this laptop. He had written the username and password on the whiteboard in his cubicle.

Today she also continued adding some incriminating contents to his laptop. She didn't have to do much. He was already corrupt. But she added some emails to Mossad, the Israeli intelligence service, asking where his payment was from the information he'd passed on last month. He had passed information on to Mossad last month. Well, she had. For him. Hopefully, they acted on that soon. The Israelis loved to blow things up in Iran and giving them pinpoint directions to the bioweapons floor was perfect. They knew there were prisoners on the bottom floor, so they would be careful.

As she despised Kazmi and thought she should remove him sooner rather than later, she upped the game. She found General Telebi's wife's email address in the database and began an email.

Fatemeh,

I have longed for you since the first day I saw you. Sweet woman, I know how you suffer with that tyrant of a husband. Tell me the word and I am yours! Be mine! Let me know and I will be there for you tonight, while the general is with his mistress. Let us make rapturous love without him ever knowing!

Your ardent admirer,

Behrouz

She clicked send and spent a few minutes snooping elsewhere when the email notification dinged.

Behrouz,

I have longed for you, too. But you waited too long. The idiot is back tonight, and I must be with him. I will write you when it is safe to come.

Love,

Fatemeh

Esin blinked, thinking, *Am I living in a farce? This is a farce.*

Forcing herself to think of something more pleasant than Kazmi and Mrs. Telebi, like dog vomit, she locked the computer and headed to her next task. Incriminating Major Afshar. Then Major Ali. Then the rest of them.

Casey lay in his bed and re-read the letter from Esin. It was a morning tradition. The stillness of the morning and the love of his wife in his hands.

The stillness was broken by the most obnoxious sound in the world. Blake began his morning song. Normally this song amused Casey to the point he'd hum along, but he'd had a lovely daydream going and hated the interruption. This song was a special level of anti-romance. Blake had taken a catchy children's song that repeated on itself endlessly and replaced the lyrics with vulgar words from a dozen languages. The verses cycled through Russian, Navajo, Chinese, Turkish, Swiss, Swahili, Quechua, and more. He added a new verse almost every year.

So Casey rolled over and moved to tuck his letter away.

Manuel had crept up on him and was sitting next to him.

"Hey Manuel, what's up?"

Blake's song drifted into the distance as he left to the bathroom.

"When were you going to tell us Esin was here?" Manuel was not accusatory. That was not his nature. He was curious.

"I was not planning on it. I don't want Blake letting it slip." Casey always tried to answer Manuel's directness with equal directness.

"You're afraid he would talk about it too loudly and someone would find out?"

"Yes, precisely."

Manuel sat thinking about this for about ten seconds, face unchanging. A smile crept out. "She's Hamid's spy friend, isn't she?" He laughed and rose to his feet. "Your wife is nearly as amazing as my own."

Casey smiled as Manuel headed towards the bathroom. He could not ask for better friends.

Blake's song built as he reappeared. Casey realized he could ask for friends with better tone and pitch.

Later that day, Casey led the way into the lab, with Hamid and Blake trailing behind. Sarosh and Manuel were already there, busily assembling a fusion reactor coupled to an ion engine. They would build three ion engines and the rest of the rocket plane would be normal airplane parts. Sarosh was integral to the success of the project. He may have been assigned to spy on the team, but now he was acting as a double agent, leaking what they wanted to the general. Sarosh appeared loyal to Blake above all else and had proven very resourceful.

"How goes the battle?" Casey called.

"Good," Manuel replied. "These new parts are far better than the parts I got for the prototype. More precisely machined. They'll allow for a lot finer control over the reactor and the channeling through the ion engine."

"Well, you'll be happy to know that I got the last of your specialty items ordered and paid for so the general won't ever see them." Hamid stood, turning his clipboard nervously in his hands. "He came back to town last night, though he may or may not come to the office anytime soon."

"You know, the people here are a lot happier than I'd have thought they'd be working under a totalitarian government with a psycho like Telebi ever over them," Blake commented.

"That's because we are not in the heart of Tehran and Telebi is vicious, but lazy. He only abuses senior personnel directly, and he doesn't let most of them have time to abuse junior personnel. It's a fluke that this staff is so different. I take all the abuse for them. I'm so glad our friend is providing us info on all of the senior staff. Did you know Afshar is plotting how to murder Kazmi?"

Casey pondered on this. *Would the removal of the current ruling class free this people? Or does incompetence and greed always rush to claim the throne?*

Manuel sat back on his heels, allowing Sarosh to finish whatever task they had been working on. "When will the aluminum and plexiglass come? The frame of the ship is pretty easy, especially since we can make it a lot heavier than a traditional plane. Blake has been welding the parts that have arrived in his spare time."

Manuel gestured to a mess of metal beams next to a welding rig. The beams were not yet in any recognizable shape, but there were a lot of them.

Blake frowned and slapped the steel like he was a used car salesman. "It's a good thing we have six months, because I'm only able to put about an hour or so a day into this, what with all that is going on for the big rocket."

Casey laughed and patted Blake on the shoulder. "Don't worry, you'll finish your portion on the big rocket soon enough and then you'll have way more time for this. What we should worry about is the observatory. Has there been any grumbling?"

"No, the opposite." Hamid sighed and gripped his clipboard more tightly. "The general's staff caught wind of that and squealed like Americans at a concert."

"Is that a common saying in Iran?" Blake asked, raising an eyebrow.

Hamid winked. "No, I made it up."

When the laughter died down, Hamid continued. "They are excited to use the telescope. I had to make sure the company shipping the telescope would guarantee that the telescope itself won't come until a month after the launch. That way, we can build the building and tell them we'll load the telescope later."

"That's good." Casey took the clipboard from Hamid's hands. "Relax. All the construction materials are scheduled to be dropped on the roof in two weeks. It's going to be a pain for the construction workers, climbing that exterior ladder every day."

Hamid took a deep, cleansing breath, as Manuel had taught him. "But it's an easy build. I made sure none of the materials for the internal components were ordered so no one gets ambitious and builds a frame to prevent your extracurricular activities."

Blake stared at the ceiling. "I'm still worried about taking this ceiling down. That's going to be the five of us. We still haven't decided how to take the ceiling down quietly."

Casey frowned. He'd had lots of bright ideas, but none of them were realistic. Simply put, destruction was noisy, especially when you had to take out a 20-foot circle of ceiling.

"This is easy," Sarosh said with a shrug. "I sleep by day. I cut by night. Everyone else is sleeping. No one notices the noise."

Blake slapped himself on the forehead. Casey laughed and Manuel smiled, clearly impressed.

Hamid spoke first.

"Sarosh, have I told you how amazing you are? You are my brother and will always have a place in my home."

"I will go to the U.S., marry a blonde, and be Mr. Blake's assistant forever."

Blake laughed. "Yes, you better. And when we go to space, you and your blonde wife will be with me."

Hamid walked into the construction bay to check on the status of the interface manifolds when he stopped short. The bay appeared normal. The equipment was where it should be. Welding rigs and machining tables. X-ray machines and wiring benches. Meanwhile, Blake yelled in a mix of Persian curses and English words at the technicians, who found his curses extremely amusing. They were both physically improbable and grammatically unsound. The bay truly was as it should be.

Except for the flies. A dozen houseflies were struggling to fly around the bay with strings hanging from them.

"Blake!" Hamid shouted. "What in the world is going on?"

"Why does everyone always assume it's me?" Blake shouted in reply.

"Isn't it?"

"Well, yeah, it is. But I am offended everyone always assumes it's me."

Hamid marched over to the desk where Blake sat next to Casey. Casey had the nerve to wave nonchalantly and go right back to work. Hamid tried to look stern, but Blake's attempt at offended dignity was amusing enough that he sighed.

"Why do the flies have strings dangling from them?"

"Would you believe me if I told you they were building nests?" Blake asked and wiggled his eyebrows at Hamid.

"No." Hamid reached up and grabbed one by the string as it lumbered by. "Superglue?"

"Yup. You catch 'em in a cup, shake 'em up real good to stun 'em, then use some tweezers to hold 'em in place while someone puts a dab of glue on 'em and sticks a bit 'a string on their wee underbellies."

Hamid sighed again, releasing the confused creature. Thinking deeply, he realized he had never sighed as much at anyone as he had at Blake, which made him sigh again.

"Where's Manuel?"

"Teaching your launch engineers the finer points of countdown procedures," Casey mumbled through a bite of a plum. Their secret friend had intercepted the general's plum shipment, and Hamid now had four crates of plums to dispense.

"Well, that's alright," Hamid replied. "The general called. He's back in the office and wants an update on 'critical matters.' Not sure which ones. He's never actually cared about actually critical matters. It's probably more to do with fruit. It's always about fruit."

Casey sighed even more deeply than Hamid had, closed his laptop, and stood. "Well, I should get to my own meeting with the project managers. I finished that mission in Kerbal, anyway."

"You were playing Kerbal instead of working?" Hamid raised his eyebrows in surprise.

"I know the developers," Casey said, leaning in close. "See, they have a super-secret version of a pre-release of Kerbal 3 that has full physics and can do a full mission design, but it takes a beefy computer. I had this laptop built to handle it."

"Really?"

"No, I was running schedules."

Hamid felt oddly disappointed, but smiled at the joke. "You got me there. I think I believed you for a moment because I actually want it to be true."

"So do I, Hamid, so do I."

Hamid walked into the general's office, finding only Colonel Kazmi and a few of the other senior members of the general's staff present.

The general barked, "Where are the giants and the short one?"

Hamid found it amusing that the general called Manuel 'the short one' when Manuel was 10 centimeters taller than the general. "You did not ask for them, General Telebi, and they would be underfoot in this type of meeting with the need for translation."

Surprisingly, Telebi nodded and launched into his real purpose. "Hamid, I have important things to discuss with you today. We are only half a year away from the launch and we need to make plans for how we will best show our magnificence to the world. Please tell me you have thought about this and have begun plans."

"Yes, General Telebi, we have plans well in place. The launch platform is nearly complete and will be provided with a significant number of cameras. A special grandstand with an adjacent building for dining with government and military leaders beforehand will begin construction in a few weeks on a hill a safe distance away from the launch but close enough for an amazing view."

The general's smile would have curdled milk it was so self-serving. "Excellent. I will have their full attention. Move the viewing platform closer. I want them to feel the power of the launch and be awed."

"Sir, the safety factor-"

"Bah. We know you engineers are too concerned with safety. Closer. I want them to practically singe their beards."

"Yes, sir." Hamid struggled with this as he knew if he did what the general asked, Hamid would be in trouble for the consequences. But... he would not be here to receive the consequences. He smiled.

"To continue, all of the facility staff will be on a different hill, still able to see the launch, but not so close as to interfere with your special time with the dignitaries. Iranian citizens who make the trip may watch from a variety of vantage points that have the roads to accommodate the traffic."

"I still laugh that our lovely spy was able to convince NASA this is a peaceful mission," Telebi said.

"And mission control?" Kazmi asked. "What about them?"

The general shouted a vulgarity concerning Kazmi's heritage and a goat, but Hamid raised his voice to answer the question.

"The launch command center is being built at the Urmia television station building, where we will have excellent communications."

"Very well." Telebi picked up a date and frowned. "Now, let us talk about food selection. Especially fruit. Major Afshar..."

The general's voice trailed off as he squinted into the space between him and Hamid, where a single fat fly was toiling to carry its single string as it flew between them.

"What in the world is that?"

"A fly, sir," Kazmi said, disdain in his voice.

"You idiot, I know it is a fly. What is that dangling from it?"

Colonel Kazmi spoke again. "A string, sir."

General Telebi turned and stared at him. "I know it is a string, you idiot! I'm trying to ascertain why a fly is carrying a string through my office! This is a strange occurrence, and someone is going to explain it to me."

Every eye turned to Hamid. The staff all knew he was a scientist. If anyone in that room could explain why there was a fly carrying a string, it would be Hamid.

Hamid panicked. His brain screamed, and he spoke the only thing that came to his mind. "Nesting, sir. The fly is nesting."

The general's mouth dropped open in surprise, then he sat back, clearly pondering on this. "Really? I've never heard of flies nesting."

Hamid, now committed and still panicking, dove deeper. "Yes sir, they're a special type of fly indigenous to this region. They aren't very common, so this is a special thing to see one. They are the only nesting fly in Asia. There are several varieties in Africa and one in South America. They are world famous among entomologists. We are very fortunate."

The general stared, apparently enthralled by the spectacle. "Well, we can't sit here and do nothing. Kazmi, get off your fat butt and carefully get that fly out of here. Make sure you get it safely out of the building. Be very gentle."

Kazmi, absolutely stunned, attempted to catch the fly, but despite the fly's handicap, it was several attempts before he could catch the string.

As Kazmi led the fly out the door, the general sighed and said, "Isn't nature amazing?"

Esin stared in amazement as she saw Kazmi come walking out of the general's office, leading a fly by a string. If she didn't recognize Blake's handiwork, she'd have thought she was hallucinating. Kazmi fumed, stomping through the office like a petulant child. She wished she dared take a photo of this.

Hamid left the meeting and went straight to the cafeteria, finding all three Americans there, as they were without fail, with their faithful friend, Sarosh. They never missed dinner. When asked why they treated dinner time with near religious zeal, Blake blamed the Army, Casey blamed older brothers, and Manuel was too focused on eating to answer him.

Hamid wrapped up his tale. "And the general sighed. Literally, sighed, and said, 'Isn't nature amazing.'"

All three men laughed so hard at that point that they couldn't keep eating. Blake wheezed like an asthmatic and Manuel kept repeating the general's words between laughs. Casey had passed verbal expression and occasionally took a breath and appeared to be trying not to fall from his chair. Sarosh had tried to follow the story in English but had failed and so was asking Hamid clarifying questions, finally getting the story understood as the Americans could finally breathe.

"Oh, this reminds me," Manuel said. "I want to get some super-computing time on your mainframe. I assume you have one?"

Casey raised an eyebrow. "Manuel, how in the world does a story about flies on strings remind you of super-computing time?"

"The general approves computer time, doesn't he? The story was about the general."

Hamid smiled. "No, he finally delegated that to me. I can approve some super-computing time. What is it for?"

"Oh, I am trying to extend my knowledge of our new ion engine by calculating the resonances of a different high-temperature spinning ceramic disc. I also want to see what happens when the applied oscillating voltages and currents are varied with itinerant excursions out of spec to see if the resulting loss of containment can be overcome by careful design of the polyhedra to prevent plasma ejection and allow…"

Hamid raised a hand.

"Manuel, I appreciate you wanting to share the details, but while I seem to know all the words you are using, I do not understand how they relate in connection. I assume it is important? Okay, how about I just trust it is important, and I will set you up for as much access as you need. We under utilize our supercomputers as it is, so I doubt anyone will complain."

Manuel looked like he'd just received the best present ever and stood up, at which Blake yanked him back down.

"After dinner, Manuel. He'll set you up after he eats his dinner."

###

Esin,

You would not believe what happened today. You know that trick with flies and strings that Blake pulls every summer? Well, a little thing like being in captivity wouldn't stop him from continuing his antics…

Hamid walked into the general's office for their 8 am meeting and realized he was alone with the general. He had the occasional meeting with only the general, but he normally walked in on him while he shouted at his staff. The general sat furiously typing at his computer. Another rarity. He had secretaries for that. Of course, 'furiously' only meant that he typed as fast as he could 'hunt and peck' his way across the keyboard.

Telebi looked up with a deer in headlights look that made Hamid nervous. "Oh, good, Hamid. I need you to make the Americans presentable. We are going to dinner tonight."

Hamid waited for another sentence to clarify what he meant, yet Telebi had gone straight back to typing.

"Sir, dinner where? When? With who?"

"Oh, right, you weren't with my staff last night." He shook himself, frowning. "The president is coming with some members of the Majles, and a few scientists from the Iran University of Science and Technology. To Urmia. Tonight. They want to meet you and the Americans. Make them presentable. Tell Casey to not speak in Persian or let on he speaks it. I haven't passed that along."

Telebi began to turn back to his computer, but Hamid asked, "Sir, we are taking the Americans into the city? To a restaurant?"

Telebi eyed Hamid coldly. "Yes. Can you keep them on a tight leash for the night? You and Sarosh will be translating. I have word you are too lenient with them. Discipline, Hamid. Discipline. They are likeable. If any of the staff side with them, deal with them."

Hamid groaned inwardly. "Yes, sir."

Blake laughed even as he spoke. "And then... He asked you... To keep us on a 'tight leash?' That's priceless!"

Neither Hamid nor Casey laughed. Hamid felt sick to his stomach.

"Blake," Casey began, "this is more serious than you are treating it."

Blake sobered up, still chuckling. "Yeah, I know. But Telebi's delivery is a crackup."

"So, we're not going to have any dinner disasters, like we did in the past?"

"Nope."

"We won't have a repeat of Houston five years ago?"

"Nope." Blake winked. "I learned my lesson. No shellfish."

"And D.C. three years ago?"

"It's not my fault our congressman has no sense of humor."

"And no explaining Nietzsche and the meaningless of life?"

"You know, I didn't mean to make those interns cry! Bunch of babies."

Casey rolled his eyes. "Anything else?"

Blake pondered for a moment. "I suppose no crop dusting the guests when I go to the bathroom?"

Casey sighed. "Do you need to ask?"

"Can I at least show them how to make straw rocket launchers and pelt Telebi in the face?"

Casey stared at him.

"Well, this is going to be plain boring." Blake slapped his knee.

Casey looked to Blake's other partner in crime.

"And Manuel?"

"Yes?" Manuel replied, perking up in his seat.

"No honesty. No cutting-edge math."

"This is that kind of dinner?" Manuel said, sagging.

"Yes, afraid so."

Manuel turned to Blake.

"You are not wrong. Very boring."

"There, that's taken care of," Casey said. "Now, we don't exactly have fancy dress. We each have a reasonably nice outfit that we were wearing at the conference that we all decided to save for the day we get out of here, but it sounds like today needs to be that day. Too bad we can't plan a daring escape, but with no prep time and Hamid's family still in danger, we'll have to be content with our more insane plan."

Hamid continued to worry. The team was so much fun! But that was a deadly characteristic in the upper echelons of a dictatorial government. Even Casey, as cool and collected as he was, was prone to say things that could be very dangerous.

Casey's face lost the amusement.

"You're not comforted, Hamid. I understand. You've only seen us at a formal dinner once, and that was with you, and we were ourselves, which is a lot. Look, I know this is concerning. But what's the worst that can happen? We say something offensive and they ship us off for torture? We're 'cursed infidels,' are we not? They're expecting offensive."

Blake replied for Hamid.

"Right, worst case - torture, dismemberment, and feeding to a pack of lobsters."

Hamid's stomach churned and his face twisted, but Casey replied with cheer.

"Exactly! Pain and death! Unlikely at a formal dinner, sure, and I'm not going to seek out pain or death, but I've passed a kidney stone. Pain comes, it goes. It's awful. But it passes. It may only pass with death, in our case, but seriously, why stress? If it's our time to go, we'll go laughing in their stupid, underworld-bound faces."

"Scream laughing. Because of the torture," Blake added helpfully.

"Right," Casey said with a nod. "Scream laughing in Teletubby's face."

"And maybe they'll be mad at Teletubby and torture him, too! See, there is always a bright side!" Manuel added with a smile.

Hamid marveled at the look on Casey's face as he stared out the window of their car, face alight with joy. For the first ten minutes, Casey had pointed out each thing he hadn't seen in over 6 months except through a barred window. Now he was in silent contemplation. How could a man still in captivity, in a car with men carrying machine guns, take such pleasure in the trees and fields they drove through?

Casey finally broke his contemplation with an observation. "I wonder what Blake and Manuel are thinking in their car? Sarosh is probably getting a running commentary on geological formations from Blake. Manuel is probably ignoring him and calculating orbits in his head. Sarosh is probably trying to learn all the geology terms that Blake is spouting." He changed his voice, mimicking Blake's accent. "That stack of rocks there is a metastaphic pile of chondritic sediments that was deposited in the tristocene epic by volcanic eruptions that disrupted the crystal structures of the existing platytrace."

Hamid scrunched his brow and pursed his lips. "That was perplexing. I did not know some of those words."

Casey smiled. "Good. I made up at least three of them and used the rest wrong."

"Okay, that is an interesting game. You know just enough about a subject that you can make it sound like you know something, but you are saying nothing?"

Casey nodded and put on his professor expression. "You see, in psychology, it is when your pre-frontal cortex interferes with your amygdala that you have discombobulation of the pituitary glands that causes intense bouts of transcranial interference."

"You made up some of those words?"

"Not a one, but I used them all completely wrong. Try it."

Hamid stared out the window at the beauties that he enjoyed every day. What did he know about enough to speak so wrongly and yet sound so knowledgeable?

Hamid smiled, then hesitantly began, pausing occasionally, but plowing through the sentence like a locomotive through a herd of cows.

"The direct phase reduction of the inverse tangential flux in the electrical discharge of a plasma colloidal crystal matrix is critical in trimming the oscillations in the capacitance of the transformer."

"And that is one of my favorite games." Casey chuckled. "Blake is also a master. Manuel struggles as he already speaks like that, but isn't speaking nonsense. It just sounds like it. He tries to understand what we say, and it frustrates him, so we play the game without him. Most of the time."

Hamid looked out the window again. "What do you miss most about your freedom, Casey? Besides your wife and children."

"That's a tough one. The comedian in me answered 'Colby Jack cheese' without hesitation. But in all seriousness... Being able to get up and choose my consequences."

"What do you mean by choosing your consequences? Don't you choose your actions?"

"Well, sure, but actions have logical consequences. If I cheated on my wife, there would be many consequences. I'd have betrayed my core self. I'd experience self-loathing, hatred, and disgust. Oh, and Blake would murder me before my wife even found out. I don't like any of those consequences."

Casey then pointed to the guard in the front seat of the car. "Take this fellow? I could choose to fight him. There would be consequences. Do I know for sure what those would be? No, but I can guess. He might shoot me. I might kill him. It might lead to Blake and Manuel being killed. Or you. Or your whole family. I could choose that. Are there any good consequences of that? No."

"So, right now, your choices are limited, so your consequences are limited."

"Exactly. If the three of us chose not to work, Telebi would see us beaten, maybe even killed. That's not a real choice. That's a choice of only two consequences at the point of a gun. At home, I had many consequences as possibilities. I could choose so many! Hundreds of consequences a day were available to me! The diversity of consequences for a free man is breathtaking. So, the first thing I'm going to do when I'm free is to choose a consequence. Probably I'll choose the consequence of making my wife smile. And how will I get that consequence? I don't know, but there are dozens of actions I can take to get to that wonderful consequence!"

Hamid sat and pondered the remainder of the drive as they passed into Urmia. Was he truly free to choose his consequences? Was it possible that he was as much a slave of Telebi as Casey? Perhaps even more so?

After a round of introductions, they all sat down at the table filled with Telebi and the dignitaries. Hamid had spent the day planning how to survive this meal. For starters, Hamid sat between Blake and Casey. Sarosh sat between Casey and Manuel. That put Blake away from any of his friends. Sarosh was much less likely to do something Hamid would regret without Blake to egg him on. And since Blake and Manuel could not speak Persian, neither would have anything to say to their neighbor. A very logical, orderly plan.

Blake often said that no plan survives first contact with the enemy. Hamid wished he'd asked him to clarify what it meant.

With his accent turned up to an eleven, Blake faced the man across the table from him and said, "Howdy, my name's Blake, what's yours?"

Hamid's heart dropped. The president was a cruel and terrible man who never deviated from the hardline IRGC policies the Ayatollah spewed. And Blake said 'howdy' to him?

The man, the president of Iran, spoke enough English to know what this meant and was surprised enough to respond in that rudimentary English. "I am President Sharifi. Pleased to meet you."

"Well, pleased to meet you, too. Beautiful day out there now, in't it? Why, I reckon I saw the purtiest flowers I done saw since beating the snot out of a couple hoodlums in Amsterdam. You been to Amsterdam?"

The president, dumbfounded by this onslaught but sensing the extremely friendly nature, seemed to have caught the last sentence. "Yes, I went to Amsterdam."

Meanwhile, Manuel was also speaking to the man across from him, a leading scientist from Tehran.

"Integrate the function here by partial fraction expansion..." he doodled what he said right on the tablecloth, "and you get a tractable polynomial you can solve for lambda, there."

The man smiled, took the pen, and speaking in Persian, continued the equations on the tablecloth and added, "Then you can do a trigonometric substitution with the original partial differential equation and the Hamiltonian falls out!"

Casey sat demurely, eating with the most careful attention to manners and etiquette possible. He carefully ate with only his right hand. He ate slowly, but with obvious relish. And he smiled at everyone.

One of the Majles members stared at Hamid and said coldly, "Translate for me." He then turned to Casey and spoke. "You are the leader of the American infidels. How do you find your time here?"

Casey smiled after the translation and said, "I am a captive and a forced laborer. How do you think I find my time?"

"I have reports you are often found laughing and making light of your captivity? I am here to evaluate you. To verify you are not bringing your heathen ways into our land."

Telebi paled and Hamid struggled not to laugh at his expression or, worse, mimic it.

"I am a happy and jovial fellow," Casey replied. "I make the best of my circumstances. Does not the Quran say, 'To God belongs the future of the heavens and the earth, and all matters are controlled by Him?' Why then should I fear?"

Hamid trembled in his own fear as he translated. *Casey, you madman! You are quoting the Quran to a politician!*

The man replied, "Does the Quran not also teach that 'Excessive laughter kills the heart.' Also, 'If you knew that which I know, you would laugh little and weep much.'"

"But the words of my God, Jehovah, Jesus Christ, the judge of both quick and dead, have commanded me to rejoice in my salvation! To lift up my heart and rejoice in my deliverance from death and sin at his hand!"

Hamid trembled even more as he translated this, wanting to stop but feeling some compulsion to see Casey's gambit to the end.

"You dare speak so openly of your religion? You dare to challenge me when I have the power to end your life if you speak words of blasphemy?"

Casey gave a gentle smile, full of something Hamid could not identify. "I do, for if I did not speak of my joy in my God, the very walls of this building would echo with the words I was not allowed to speak."

The translation complete, the men stared at each other. Blake's voice continued to drag the president from one topic to another. Manuel continued to solve complex math with the scholar to his side. And Casey sat with eyes full of that indefinable something as he stared fixedly at the learned man.

Hamid's eyes widened. *Compassion. Casey has compassion for this man.*

The man snorted. "I like you. You are fearless in your beliefs. Would that our people were so fearless in true Islam, perhaps we would have eradicated the scourge of the infidels from this world. Now, you are a Christian dog, yes? Let us discuss the bizarre occult tradition of transubstantiation. I want to know from an infidel like you why such things are believed."

Hamid sighed inwardly with relief, but had no chance to think. Hamid ended the dinner starving, as he had to translate a constant dialogue between the two throughout.

Meal complete, Blake, Casey, and Manuel gathered to the side while the rest of the guests gave their parting words. President Sharifi and the Majles member took Telebi aside. President Sharifi got straight to the point, speaking without concern for anyone overhearing.

"So, Ahmet, these Americans seem like friendly, intelligent types. They will finish the project and deliver?"

"Yes, President Sharifi," Telebi replied. "They are on track. Hamid has them on a tight leash. We are on schedule."

Sharifi nodded as the lackey spoke. "Well, it is too bad we will have to kill them when this project is over. But they are merely infidels. Make sure Hamid absorbs everything they know."

Hamid glanced at Casey, who only showed he had heard and understood by a slight frown that was gone almost instantly.

The dignitaries took their leave, and Telebi took Hamid aside. "Good job. I had an uninterrupted conversation for once. The Majles normally interfere with my meal. Having a religious debate? Brilliant!" He clapped Hamid on the back and went to his car.

Back in their car, Hamid asked, "When did you learn the Quran?"

Casey handed Hamid a cloth napkin that was wrapped around a bundle of something lumpy and replied, "I've been reading it for almost 20 years to understand the people I work among better. I've been memorizing key parts this last several months. Now, I saw you didn't get a chance to eat, so I swiped as many of the breads and cheeses as came across the table as possible and stored them up for you. Hope this makes up for an exhausting night."

Hamid glared at him. "That depends if you got some Lighvan cheese." Unwrapping the precious bundle, he smiled and bowed. "You are forgiven."

"What do you mean it is tonight? It's supposed to be tomorrow night!" Esin struggled not to jump to her feet under the thorn bush. She squeezed the satellite phone with her hands until her knuckles ached.

"I'm sorry. We have no say in timing. They saw an opportunity. You have maybe an hour."

"Gotta go."

Esin crawled out of the brush and sprinted towards town. She headed straight to her neighbor's van. She'd stolen a key months ago for just such a crisis. Willing no one to notice a woman driving, she weaved through the village and onto the main road, praying she wouldn't be too late.

At 0220 in the morning as Casey and Sarosh worked on moving ceiling pipes in their 7th floor lab to prepare for the observatory completion in a few days, Casey's heart nearly skipped a beat as the formerly locked door burst open and a veiled woman stepped through. She shouted to them in Persian.

"Incoming attack. Run!"

Not waiting, she fled.

Neither of them needed any further convincing. Sprinting from the door, they saw the woman heading down the stairs and followed. As they reached the fifth floor, the floor shook, knocking them to their knees. The sound of a blast rumbled through the building.

"Bioweapons," the woman called as they caught up to her. "Get to your dorm." She veered down a corridor on the fourth floor.

Casey ached that he wouldn't be able to even talk to her. He hadn't seen his wife in over six months.

Blake stood outside their dormitory as they emerged from the first-floor stairwell. He looked wild-eyed and confused. Manuel stood nearly hidden behind him.

"Was it us? Did we do it?" Manuel asked.

"No, for once, we aren't the source of the mysterious explosion," Casey assured them. "The bioweapons research wing was attacked. Let's see if they'll let us evacuate to the outside."

They went to the door of the facility, but the guards only yelled at them to go back to their rooms.

"Is the building on fire?" Casey shouted. "We will not stay and be burned alive!"

"No, everything is under control," the guard in charge said.

"Then why did the floor shake?" Casey asked.

"A... an airplane flying low..."

"Big enough to shake the entire building?"

"Yes, so go back to the barracks," the guard replied.

A group of men covered in soot came bursting out of the stairwell and ran from the building, yelling at each other about the smoke.

"An airplane?" Casey asked again.

The guard cursed. "Take them outside and put them all next to that truck." He ushered them outside. "Guard them!" They all heard gunfire in the distance. The guard turned on his radio and shouted, "Send reinforcements to the main gate. It is under attack!"

They lay down on their stomachs to look toward the gate through the gap under the truck. The sky was alight with a full-scale battle.

"Ask them what is going on," Blake called.

Casey shouted in Persian, "Guards, who is attacking us? What is going on?"

One guard, crouching at the edge of the truck, screamed and fell to the ground, blood spurting from his shoulder.

"It appears conversation will have to wait," Casey said.

He grabbed the man by the ankles and pulled him to the center of the truck for protection. The man wasn't moving, so Blake drew the man's knife and started cutting off his shirt, exposing the wound.

"Casey, lift enough to see. Did it go all the way through?"

Casey lifted the shoulder and said, "Yes, nasty exit wound."

Blake ripped his pajama top off and gave it to Casey, who placed it under the man. Manuel took his off and Casey placed it on top.

Casey turned to the rest of the guards, who huddled behind the truck in obvious shock, and shouted, "I need two of your belts, right now! Now, you fools, he'll bleed out!"

One of them removed his belt and then Manuel removed the belt from the bleeding man.

Manuel tossed both belts to Casey, who lifted the man enough to get the belt under him. Blake attached the belts together, and they cinched them as tight as they could, slowing the bleeding.

Casey then crawled over to the group and said, "Who has a radio? Speak up, you fools if you want him to live!"

The coherent one raised his hand and Casey held his hand out expectantly. The man handed the radio over.

"What's your group call sign?"

The man muttered and Casey clicked the radio on. "Base, this is Pay Aliph squadron. We have a man down, requesting medical attention."

"Copy. What's your location?"

"Twenty feet in front of the front doors."

"The fighting is that close?"

"Negative, still at the gates. In fact, it looks like it's dying down."

The firefight appeared to move away from the walls. A helicopter arose in the distance, firing at the ground as it flew away. The sound of gunfire was replaced with the sound of the screams and moans of the injured.

"If he's stable, leave him and go find more wounded."

"Copy. I can't guarantee he's stable, but he's breathing, and the bleeding is slowed."

"If that wasn't Mossad, I'd be shocked," Blake added.

Casey slapped a few helmets, getting the six squad members' attentions. "The fighting is over. Come. We will help with first aid."

"But our orders..."

Casey barked in frustration. "You'll have to shoot me to stop me from saving lives, so get on your feet and let's go!"

Blake stood, pulling a canteen from the injured man. "Manuel, stay with him. Someone needs to give him water and keep him from moving if he wakes up."

The next hour was a blur. The two of them and Sarosh each took two of the soldiers and directed them in first aid. Blake used swear words and gestures, while Sarosh and Casey used less traditional methods, like clear, verbal direction. Altogether, they stabilized a half-dozen men and bid farewell to at least a dozen more. They found no enemy troops among them.

Hamid pulled up and leapt from his car as the first man they'd treated was the last placed on a helicopter bound for Urmia.

"What happened?" he asked Casey, eyeing their wild appearance. "Who attacked the base?"

"Probably Mossad," Blake said. "No one else has the guts for this kind of operation. The bioweapons are toast."

Casey looked at himself and Blake. They were both down to boxers, their clothes all having been used as emergency bandages. They were covered in blood and dirt. Manuel was shirtless, but not as grimy. He panicked at too much blood. The fact he'd helped get the belts and gave up his shirt was a testament to his good heart.

"Well, that was enough excitement for one night," Casey quipped to Hamid. "Tomorrow, you are buying all three of us new pajamas."

"Why didn't you all escape in the confusion?"

Blake snorted. "Because even in the confusion, there were a half-dozen men with rifles to shoot us. And because we had no food, water, or way of navigating to the Turkish frontier. Hamid, escapes aren't something you can do without a plan." He placed a hand on Hamid's shoulder. "Don't worry. Our plan will work."

Sarosh came into the construction lab, concerned. His abrupt entry and distressed face drew the eyes of all the engineers and technicians working that day. "Teletubby is back from the inquest in Tehran and in a foul mood! I think that was an hour ago, and he has been raging! Rumor has it they blame him for lax security, but he weaseled out of it."

Casey knew what that meant. Someone would be tortured. So far, only Blake had been tortured among them. They had heard some of the general's staff were tortured, including Kazmi, as well as a handful of technicians.

"Who do you need to torture? I'm sure Telebi got raked over the coals and needs to feel powerful."

Sarosh waved his hand, eyes wide. "No, he hasn't asked me to do it. He didn't even ask me to his office. The staff said he invited someone they'd never seen before to do it!"

The door burst open, and two guards entered, followed by a man so pale he made Casey feel positively tan. The man reminded Casey of no one other than the Russian boxer in Rocky IV. Except this man exuded a barrage of friendliness.

The jovial man spoke English with a moderately pronounced Russian accent. "Good afternoon, my friends. I am George. George Smith. I will be your torturer today. Isn't that delightful?"

Hamid came bursting through the door, saw 'George,' and paled to a shade of green Casey had never known possible.

With more boldness than he normally mustered, Hamid stepped forward. "Can I help you, Mr. Smith? I am in charge here."

George cheerfully turned to Hamid and smiled with a tremendously friendly smile. "Not today, Mr. Jabiri. I am in charge. You may ask my dear friend, General Telebi. You see, he wants a highly professional film today. Our lovely amateur friend, Sarosh," he gestured to the hapless man, "produced a wonderful moment for General Telebi with our friend Blake, but it lacks that special something I can put into my work. You see, I am a filmmaker. I specialize in the form of entertainment only the most refined of palates can truly enjoy. Torture is an art, you see. Truly, causing pain is my forte. And Telebi made a reservation with me the moment Mr. Blake's torture failed. After his difficult week at the inquiries in Tehran, he needs something to vent his excess spleen on."

Moving quickly to Hamid's side, Casey said, "Very well, Mr. Smith. If you need to torture someone, you may choose me. It is my place."

The smile never left, but now Casey could see his eyes. The smile did not enter his eyes. They were a sink of madness.

"No, no, my friend. Casey, correct? I am so pleased to meet you. I expect I will have the opportunity to torture you in the future. Yes, he has fine things planned. But no, today is not for you, or for your large and formidable friend there. Blake, I presume? No, today's torture is for our dear, innocent Manuel."

Blake hefted a massive pipe wrench with one hand and soundlessly charged the closest guard. He bludgeoned one guard aside while Casey charged and grabbed the other guard, swinging him to the ground. As Blake swung the pipe at Mr. Smith, he froze, seeing a gun pointed not at him, but at Manuel, who had not partaken in the extracurricular activities.

Mr. Smith's smile was somehow even more delighted. "My, my, Mr. Blake, you are truly as strong as your size indicates. Perhaps we will have to do something gladiatorial for your torture. But that is for after the project is complete. No, this is to give you the proper motivation. I'm afraid Sarosh's punishment was not sufficient to cow you into fear. We must rectify this situation." He gestured his other hand towards two chairs. "Now, Casey, Blake. Sit."

Furious, they stepped to their seats. The guards arose, though one appeared to have a broken arm. The uninjured one walked to Manuel, took him by the arm, and led him out of the room. Manuel's face had not changed through this entire exchange. Confusion. Complete confusion. Casey's heart screamed. *Not Manuel!*

Mr. Smith turned. "Now, because you were so entertaining, I will be kinder to Manuel than I would have been. I so enjoyed seeing Blake break that guard's arm. That was a masterful stroke. Your follow through! Beautiful. Why, you had that club in position at the end of the stroke so that you could have felled me with no excess motion. If I'd been any slower on the uptake, I'd be dead now! Beautiful. A piece of art. I wish I'd thought to record it. But another day. Now, until we meet again."

Mr. Smith left, the other guard trailing behind him, glaring at Blake with undisguised hatred. Blake glared in return.

Hamid rushed over. "What do we do?"

Casey stared at the ground, his thoughts a jumble. He could handle his own life being in danger. Or Blake's. But not Manuel! He was so good and innocent. He had no guile and had never harmed anyone in his life with malice or planning. *How dare Telebi do this!*

Blake spoke with a strangled sound of repressed fury. "What can we do? There are guards. This isn't some stupid action movie. We can't go bludgeoning around, knocking people out. We almost killed that monster because those guards were sloppy. I'd have left him dead, and then we'd have taken our chances on escape, even if they were futile. But now they have Manuel. If we fight, they'll torture him worse, or kill him."

Blake stood with a frustration-filled roar of fury that set lab equipment vibrating, then paced the room, occasionally grabbing something and tearing it in half.

Casey fell to his knees, bowed his head, and prayed. He prayed for a miracle, then got up to do what he could to make a miracle.

Casey looked up to see Hamid kneeling prostrate, forehead pressed into the ground, weeping soundlessly as his lips moved.

Casey rose from his knees and looked at Sarosh, who stared back, his face filled with horror.

"Sarosh, go to the laundry and get extra pillows and blankets. Take them to Manuel's bed and have them ready for when we bring Manuel in. Have boiled water and clean bandages ready in case. Also, Tylenol,

Ibuprofen, and something stronger if they'll give it to you. A full med kit."

Sarosh nodded and ran silently from the room.

Casey turned to Blake, who had torn a fire extinguisher bracket off the wall and bent it into an unrecognizable piece of modern art. It would have sold well in New York or London. *Rage of the Giant* or some nonsense.

"Blake, Manuel will need us to be calm, collected, and ready with a joke. Start praying and coming up with all the jokes you can about torture."

Blake stared without comprehension, so Casey walked up and put his hands on his friend's shoulders.

"Blake, come back to me."

Nothing.

Casey slapped Blake across the face. Not with all his power, but hard enough that his head moved a bit. It hurt his hand.

Blake swore. "Right, right. Jokes. Praying. Got it."

"What about me?" Hamid asked, standing.

"Food," Casey replied. "You will need to have meals delivered for all of us to our quarters. We will not be working until Manuel is better. If the general protests, I will gladly come to his office and explain it to him. He will be dead by the end of that conversation, so help me, he will."

Hamid nodded and began to leave.

"And a large screen to watch some movies on," Casey added. "We will need access to some silly, mindless movies. Anything with Jackie Chan. They're his favorite."

Hamid nodded and started from the room, but stopped and stared at him.

"Manuel would want us to laugh, wouldn't he?"

"He would be angry if we didn't," Casey replied.

"It feels insensitive, but I'll try," Hamid replied. "An Italian spy was captured and tied up with his hands behind his back. They tortured him for hours and he never spoke. Finally, they gave up and threw him into a cell. Another spy asked him, 'How did you not crack?'"

Casey cocked his head and even Blake stopped to look at him. Hamid finished.

"The Italian spy said, I couldn't talk–they tied up my hands."

Blake groaned and gave a slow clap while Casey smiled.

"Thanks Hamid," Casey said. "Tell it to Manuel when he's out. He'll appreciate it."

Casey and Blake stood in the room, praying aloud when so moved, and then wandering the room, preparing themselves mentally. Blake appeared to have finished destroying things, so Casey scooped the items up and put them away. Casey knew he was imagining it, but he could swear he could hear screams.

After what felt like days, they heard the door open, and both rushed to it.

Two guards, and not the one with the broken arm, entered, dragging Manuel, who was unconscious, between them. Seeing the giant Americans coming, they let go of their load, but Casey and Blake arrived in time to catch Manuel. Casey helped to gently lift Manuel into a fireman's carry on Blake's massive shoulder as the guards fled. Blake hefted Manuel with no difficulty, immediately starting towards their barracks. Casey knew he was slowing himself down so he wouldn't jostle Manuel.

As they approached the room, Casey rushed ahead and opened the door. Hamid and Sarosh were waiting and helped position pillows as Blake set Manuel down as gently as if he were an infant being tucked into a crib. Casey felt that odd mix of rage and helplessness only known by protectors who had not been able to protect their charges.

Casey called to Blake, "Alright, let's triage him."

"Pulse is rapid, but not too rapid. Maybe 120. Breathing is steady but labored. Pained."

Manuel's eyes fluttered, and he groaned. "Señor, ¿dónde estoy? Sediento." He licked his lips and Sarosh instantly provided Casey with a cup full of ice water and a bendy straw.

Hamid entered the room and stood looking helpless.

"Estas seguro ahora," Casey whispered gently. "Estás con Blake y Casey." He put the straw to Manuel's lips.

Manuel sucked greedily, and his eyes focused. "Then why are we speaking in Spanish? That giant doesn't speak the language of heaven."

Tears streamed down Blake's cheeks, which made Casey cry. Blake drew in a deep breath, got control of himself, and said, "I can't think of anything funny to say in response to that. I'm failing at my job!"

"Let me guess," Manuel said with a weak smile. "Your job was to come up with jokes to tell me when I came back to distract me from whatever they'd done."

Fighting the sobs that were trying to escape from his barrel sized chest, Blake grinned.

Casey wished Esin were there. She was so much better with injuries and sicknesses.

"I'm glad you don't sound like they permanently damaged you," Casey said through his tears.

"No, not permanent," Manuel said, his smile fading. "There were a lot of tiny needles. Mr. Smith... I do not think that is his real name. He lied, didn't he?"

"Yes."

"Well, he said he would not do me any damage if I would tell him what he wanted to know. He said I would be sore for a day or so, then would be fine. But when he stuck those needles in... Then he made me move while they were in... It hurt so much, Casey! I did not know such a tiny needle could hurt so much! I blacked out in the end."

"What did they ask you?" Blake whispered.

"Who gave information to Mossad." Manuel took another sip of his water. "I told them I didn't even know who Mossad was. Who is Mossad?"

Casey placed a hand on Manuel's shoulder. "You don't need to worry about that. You just focus on getting better."

Hamid, who had stood watching since entering, relaxed a bit. "No permanent damage. Not physically. Mossad to blame. I'll have a talk with our friend." He came closer and put a hand on Manuel's shoulder. "Manuel, my friend. I have a joke for you."

Hamid shared the joke from earlier with Manuel. Manuel smiled, much to Casey's delight.

"Do you know what they call 'water boarding' in the U.S.?" Manuel asked.

"No," Hamid said, cocking his head.

"Tactical baptism."

All of them burst out laughing at this one, Casey relieved. If Manuel could joke like this, he was going to be okay.

"I am so glad you are safe; if suffering," Hamid said. "I will leave you in the capable hands of your friends. I believe any of these three men would do anything to protect you. I must go now and work through a way of protecting others from Telebi. To make sure this doesn't happen again. I will return when I have that idea ready to present."

"Well, that was very dramatic," Manuel whispered as Hamid departed.

"I believe it was more melodramatic," Casey corrected. "We are a bad influence on him."

"No, he was always like this," Sarosh chuckled. "It was buried under years of working for Telebi. You are archaeologists, unearthing an ancient personality under years of sediments. I think that we just watched the last layer get washed away. I suspect what returns tomorrow will be the real Hamid."

"I do think you are right," Casey nodded.

Esin made sure to be in the general's office first thing in the morning, hoping to catch him making phone calls. Today he sat there looking smug. *Monster.* She aggressively scrubbed the underside of the shelves of his liquor cabinet, as his office was about as clean as it could be. She had never felt more furious than after the gossip reached her that Telebi had had Manuel tortured. Manuel! Dear, sweet, innocent Manuel.

She hoped and prayed that the despicable Mr. Smith would be there to report to the general, and she could learn something to prevent any torture from happening again. She kicked herself that she hadn't known he was coming, but the general had said nothing about it in his office, and she couldn't be with him all day.

She desperately tried not to cry. But how did one not cry when things like this happened?

As if in answer, she remembered a story Blake had told her years earlier. Casey had a co-worker tell him you couldn't laugh at work. Casey took a piece of paper, wrote on it and stuck it to the man's forehead. He'd written, 'This is a humor free zone.'

Esin came back to the present and smiled. This was another stupid situation, like the ones Casey and she had always overcome. She could do that now.

After finishing the undersides of the shelves, she started cleaning the liquor cabinet exterior again. Anything to linger longer. The general never even glanced at her, so she was in no danger.

The door burst open, and Mr. Smith came waltzing in like he owned the place, with his smile wide and uncanny. A sickeningly friendly smile, utterly false and disturbing. His wardrobe was perfectly matched, all black with too tight pants, too tight shirts, and ruffles at the sleeves and neck.

The general glanced up and clapped his hands like a child receiving a present. She wanted to scream.

In immaculate, only slightly accented Persian, Smith spoke with a flamboyance and relish that made her feel disgust by even hearing him. "General Telebi, my dear friend, I am so glad you called me in for this job! It was truly a pleasure. It was fortuitous for you I was already in Tehran for the Ayatollah's birthday celebration, for Manuel was such a dear and sweet choice for your enjoyment." He swept a jump drive out of his pocket, holding it like a cheap stage magician doing a trick. "Voila! I have what you seek right here." The general held out his hand in excitement, but Smith held it back and played with the general. "I only ask that you allow me the pleasure of returning and make a similar recording for Manuel's dear friends. Casey and Blake are feisty creatures and I have a vision of drugging them so they hallucinate. I will convince them that the other is trying to kill them. Then we will watch them fight to the death!"

The general positively tittered with glee. "You can do this? There is such a drug?"

"Yes, my dear friend, there is. It is a special cocktail I have perfected over the years. Now, let me look at my calendar."

"You can't have them kill each other until the launch is ready," the general said with downcast eyes.

"Yes, I have your cute little launch on my calendar. Shall we do it after the launch?"

"Can you do before? They will not be needed at the launch. They will be done before then."

"Very good. Let us say three days before launch?"

"Yes, that is perfect! Oh, how exciting! I wonder who will survive?"

"Well, enjoy your video! I will be off! Thank you for your prompt payment and do recommend me to your friends."

With a flourish, Smith swung the door open and strode with horrific joy out of the office.

Esin didn't wait for the general to play the video, following Mr. Smith in case she could learn anything further.

Hamid stepped out onto the roof, completely winded. Climbing a 7-story ladder was exhausting, even after doing it once a week for the last few weeks. As he walked away from the edge, he saw the observatory and felt pleased it appeared complete. It was only 2 days later than he'd anticipated.

The construction manager, who had led the way, was all smiles as he showed Hamid around the observatory. But Hamid only half paid attention. Each time he had come up, he had kept his eyes on alert, trying to see where the rockets were stored. It would be just wonderful if Blake flew that ship up through the observatory and had a missile come after them.

Interrupting, Hamid asked, "How did they bring equipment up here? Helicopter, I assume. What about the missile batteries on the roof?"

The construction manager laughed. "Haj Hamid, I asked the same question, worrying about my men who were working up here. What if the missile thought the observatory was a target? Well, they removed the missile batteries during construction. They said they want to put them back up, but one guard told me the missiles will see the observatory as a target, and so they have had to leave them off while someone figures out how to program them to exclude the observatory!"

Hamid smiled. "Well, that's funny. We'll keep that to ourselves."

"Yes." He held out a remote. "Now, would you like to play with the controls? You can make the doors open and close and the entire top of the observatory rotate."

Hamid smiled and played with the controls until he was well versed in their capabilities. Besides it being important to know how to operate it, he had loved remote control toys since childhood. This was a very large toy.

The afternoon after the torture session, Hamid walked into the dormitory where the Americans and Sarosh were playing cards. His heart ached with the screams he could still hear coming from Manuel's innocent frame. Telebi had called him into his office as soon as he got off the roof and made him watch the torture session. Some kind of sadistic bonding, he assumed. He'd vomited in the secretary's office garbage can as he walked out. Praise Allah he'd made it that far.

He spoke without preamble. "The roof missiles are removed while the observatory is there. The observatory keeps coming up as a target. We don't have to wait. Five months remain. We could get you out that way now. A few days of work to get a Blake sized hole into the observatory, and the four of you are out of here."

Casey and Hamid looked at each other, then Casey shook his head. "No, we're in too deep. We should never have tried it last time. They will blame you and you and your family will die, even if Sarosh gets the blame. We need your family to get out, too. This is good news, though. Manuel's rocket is a lot safer to fly without roof mounted missiles. We can out accelerate any shoulder carried missile, considering human reaction time. And after the Mossad incursion, security is going to be extra tight."

"And Russians take a long time to reprogram anything." Blake laid down his cards on the flimsy with a flourish, eliciting groans from the others. "They're distracted by their foreign wars."

"Is escape on an untested rocket plane safer than extraction by helicopter?" Hamid asked. "Maybe I can smuggle my family in here and then we take a helicopter?"

"Even if you could smuggle them in, no helicopter could carry your whole family and all of us. Fast attack helicopters don't have that kind of carrying capacity." Casey shook his head and collected the cards. "It's only a few months. And besides, we're getting to do paid product development, and the investor doesn't even know it! And we'll get to keep all the tech!"

"In short, what's the difference between escaping now or in five months?" Blake waved Casey to hurry with the shuffling. "Yeah, it stinks to be captive for five months, but I once spent a six-month stint at a mine in Siberia, living underground!"

"Ah yes." Casey smirked and began dealing. "I avoided that one by having my appendix rupture two days before the trip."

"Yeah, you jerk. Anyway, if we stick it out, we'll have our system designed, equipment built, and hopefully fly straight home with a working technology!" Blake set down two cards. "Not that what we're building for your rocket is even relevant anymore. Not with our fancy new fusion rockets. We'll be able to fly around and pick up garbage or capture asteroids without much hullabaloo."

"Don't forget the opportunities for giant space stations and moon and Mars settlements." Casey handed out cards and then pushed all his chips to the center. Potato chips, that is. "I think space debris will be mostly ignored, as usual."

Hamid pulled up a chair and sat down across from them, head hanging.

"Alright, what is it?" Casey smiled as the rest of the group folded and he collected the pot. "You still look worried, but we've argued about escape enough that you know we aren't going to risk escape prematurely. You're worried about something else."

Hamid looked up, a feeling of surety growing in him. *What would these three do? Do that!* But that is crazy! These men were mad! Yet he loved their madness. Their hope. His country was in the grip of the despair of tyrants corrupting their worship of Allah for their own enrichment. For power. Prestige. If he had the chance to cripple the efforts of the likes of Telebi, could he pass it up? He sat up straight and spoke with a surety that he was only beginning to feel he could own.

"We have to decapitate my country's research efforts. Cripple them. Maybe even embarrass them. And I think I know how."

All three Americans wore huge grins. Sarosh had a look of wild excitement in his eyes. Those of the Bahá'í faith had known nothing but persecution for almost two centuries. Hamid had heard Sarosh tell of the deaths of his parents at the hands of the IRGC. He hated the Iranian government. Hamid found him loitering around a government building in Urmia. He looked ready for violence, but Hamid convinced him to come to his home for a meal. His wife decided they would adopt him as a brother that day. Hamid had bribed an official to get him into a school and lied to get him his job. Sarosh was now attempting to learn the faith of his parents, helped by Blake's urging to expand his mind. Freeing the rest of his people, who the government still repressed, would always attract Sarosh.

"I have identified key members of my staff that have become indispensable to Iran becoming a spacefaring nation. I intend to recruit them, with Sarosh's help, to join us in escaping to America. I spoke to them, saying nothing about our plans, but to a man, they despise Telebi and blame our government for letting him be in charge. All of them sympathize with the protesters, though they cannot join, or they and their families would immediately die, as surely as I would. The curse of a government job."

"How will they escape?" Manuel set his cards down, game forgotten. "We can't fit anyone else on our rocket plane."

"While the three of you escape on your rocket plane, the rest of us need to steal the helicopters my government brings to the launch and fly out. I'd offer to take you, but Telebi has insisted you will *not* be allowed to attend the launch."

"Excellent plan," Casey mused. "But don't many of them have large families? How will we get them all out?"

"This is an issue." Hamid nodded with concern. "I will ask my special friend what we can do. But the helipad near the launch site is my best bet."

Blake sat back, hands comfortably resting on his belly. "Your Ayatollah will come. So will the president, and as many of the Majles as can fit. This is a huge event. The first real launch of a space mission by any proud nation is not to be missed. But helicopters don't have a ton of space for passengers. Even our president's helicopter is only meant for

14 passengers. The largest helicopter in the world, the Russian Mi-26, only holds 63."

"How do you know that?" Casey asked, raising an eyebrow at his friend.

"What, you never had to carry out a kidnapping of a Chechen terrorist flying a stolen Russian helicopter over the mountains of Kosovo before?"

In his usual deadpan fashion, Manuel replied. "No, Blake. I have not had to kidnap a Chechen terrorist before. My largest prey has been capturing my toddlers when they were holding the cat hostage."

"Now that's my boy," hollered Blake. "You've been getting good at the zingers! Nice use of figurative language!"

"Your point with the helicopter seating being?" Casey asked.

Blake said, "We'll probably have a limited number of helicopters and so need to limit how many we can get out. How many dignitaries are coming?"

Hamid smiled, excitement struggling to burst out of him. "The number keeps climbing. Telebi invited the governor-general of Yazd province and he bragged to someone else, and now every governor intends to be here. We are over 1,000 and climbing! I have to build a larger helipad! So here it is by the numbers. There are 36 key personnel. I have their files–we surveil everything. They average 12 people per family, including parents, in-laws, spouse, and children. We can't go any further or it grows exponentially. I'm afraid siblings are going to be at risk. With Sarosh, that's 433. We'll leave a little extra room, just in case."

"And you have a list of helicopters?" Blake asked.

Manuel raised an eyebrow and asked in a tone of confusion, "Why not planes?"

"Because the launch is fairly remote. Easier to come via helicopter so you can get right to site, rather than drive from the airport."

Hamid pulled out his laptop and pulled up the list. Blake skimmed over it.

"Okay, the Saba-248's are tiny, and I doubt they'll have enough fuel for any great distance. Scratch them." He scrolled further. "Oh, that's nice. We've got a bunch of KA-32's. Sixteen passengers and a couple of crew."

"Our government licensed those recently from Russia," Hamid said. "We have 50 of them and that is what the Majles will come in. They'll be flying in 36 of them."

"That's it, then," Blake said, tapping the screen. "You get us 18 pilots capable of flying a KA-32, we're golden."

"Seventeen," Hamid said. "I'll be flying the eighteenth."

"Now, how do we run interference with the Iranian Air Force?" Blake asked.

Hamid closed the laptop with a satisfied smile. "Our special friend said to not worry about that. So, I won't."

"I hate to put a damper on this whole plan," Casey interjected, "but how will we make sure we don't have a leak? Thirty-six people... Someone will give it away."

"We don't tell them." Sarosh said with a smirk. "We don't give them a choice until the last moment. Hamid, my brother, you are too kind to see this, but if we give them notice, they will fear and question. No, we will surprise them."

"But how will we get their families there?" Hamid asked.

"As a prize." Sarosh opened his arms like he was showering gifts on them. "You will tell the 36 people you have identified that, in honor of their great contributions to this project, they and their close family are invited to watch the launch from a private viewing platform next to the helipad. At the last moment, we tell them to get on the helicopter because it is an emergency, and we fly!"

"But that is kidnapping them!" Hamid shouted.

"No," Blake said, "that is good tactics in battle. Casey, what game now?"

Hamid sat, quite stunned, as Casey shuffled two decks together. Hamid supposed that kidnapping people to take them away from tyranny was better than what he'd done to these three Americans, but it was still hard to swallow. Could he justify doing this to his staff and their families? He made up his mind.

"Can you all truly forgive me for stealing you from your families?" Hamid hung his head, tears welling in his eyes. "I think of losing my family and feel I deserve to lose mine for what I've done."

Casey set his hand on Hamid's. Blake and Manuel's followed.

"Hamid, you are a prisoner surviving." Manuel delivered their judgment with his usual bluntness. "We have forgiven you. We miss our families, but the fault is Telebi's and the Ayatollah's, not yours."

"Alright." Hamid raised his head. "Let's do it. I'll also send our spy friend our detailed plans." He smiled. "Now, deal me in. What are we playing?"

"We just finished up poker." Casey took a bite of a chip. "But as I won the entire pot, I think the four of you can do Pasur while I deal."

Blake swore. "I know Sarosh and Manuel cheat somehow!"

Manuel's sly grin was all the answer he gave.

###

"Now, can you do it?"

The radio went silent as Esin sat in her hiding place, waiting patiently for a response. Finally, after at least two minutes, the radio crackled to life.

"Please confirm, you want how many helicopter pilots on launch day?"

Matthew sat up late in the kitchen of his grandparents' house, working on a presentation he would give to an investor next week. With the taste for business under his belt, he was on a roll. The profits from his first business were now paying for the development of a second. Last month, they'd successfully shown that the technology he was funding had converted an acre of barren desert sand in western Utah into a thriving plot of ground. Now a venture capital group was paying attention. For being barely sixteen, he had a lot on his plate.

The work kept him sane. Dad being gone was no fun, but dad had been traveling for work to exotic places Matt's entire life. But on those trips, dad had video called every day he wasn't on an airplane. He was almost always available at least once a day.

But mom was never gone. Even working as a handyperson around town, she would be gone at most for a couple of hours a day and would be there for everything important. Having both of them gone drove him to bury himself in busyness, and that had become business.

The sound of a low-flying helicopter distracted him from a chart explaining desert recession rates. He stood and went to the window, looking to see if he could see the noise-ordinance defying flight. Was it Life Flight? The trees in his grandparent's yard began to blow.

The sliding glass door burst open in a shower of glass and two men in black carrying military-style rifles came charging in, pointing the guns at him. They'd covered their faces and had no insignia.

A third man walked in, face also covered, and held up a picture, comparing Matt's face to the picture in his hand. He nodded and one of the men grabbed Matt, who struggled. But the second man stepped in, and their much greater physical maturity overpowered his gangly sixteen-year-old muscles without difficulty. They bound and gagged him, then threw a bag over his head. His senses swam as he struggled, and he felt himself going limp.

###

Matt experienced his trip as one long, strange nightmare. He came to in the helicopter, as they'd pulled the bag off his head. The helicopter ride, his first, was in complete and deafening silence, the only action being when they took his phone and smashed it thoroughly. When he tried to speak, the noise of the tiny helicopter overpowered his voice. He understood then why helicopter pilots all wore headphones.

They landed at a regional airport, and they quickly loaded him onto a small jet that took off as soon as he was on board. The two thugs took it in turns sleeping as they flew, keeping an eye on him. The flight attendant spoke no English, so he tried his Persian. He was not as good as his parents, but his mom spoke only Persian to him, so he had a grasp of the language.

"Where are they taking me?"

The flight attendant jumped. "You speak Persian? You sound Afghanian. I thought you were American."

"I'm actually an international super spy and speak all known languages," he replied, still in Persian. When the woman looked at him with confusion, he sighed and said, "I am American, but my mom is Afghanian. Where are we going?"

"I am not supposed to talk to you... I'm sorry."

She scurried away, looking uncomfortable.

He kept his eyes on the window as they flew, but he drooped from too many late nights and eventually slept. Twice they landed and refueled, and each time, he tried to get information from the flight attendant. She simply apologized and made sure he had food and drinks as often as he asked.

The day dragged on and on, and with nothing to do, he tried speaking to his guards in Persian. Again.

"What is the time, friends?"

The man squirmed in his seat but replied. "It is almost 7 am at our destination."

"And where is that, kind sir?"

"We will land soon. We have had to take a very long route. We have been flying a long time. But I don't think I am supposed to tell you."

"It's Iran, isn't it? That's where they took my dad, we think. That's where you are taking me."

The man's face screamed his discomfort, but he nodded, pointedly ignoring further attempts at conversation.

When they began to descend to land at their final destination, the guard broke the silence and said, "The general is not a patient man. Do not try to be funny, as your father and his friends are. The general is... dangerous."

"You have met my father?"

"Only seen him in meetings. He is a very foolhardy man."

"Please, tell me why," Matt said, desperate for any kind of human connection after so long with almost no communication.

"I should not say... But you seem a nice young man. You have been so polite and your father seems a good man." He looked around, then spoke. "The general was yelling at Mr. Jabiri and your father spoke up. Let me see if I can find what he said."

The man pulled out his phone, then searched for a minute, finally tapping something and holding it up. His father's voice came out in Persian. Not a colloquial Persian, as the guard spoke. No, the formal style that Matt's father would use when he was trying to make Matt's mother laugh. Which was most of the time.

"Esteemed General Telebi, I must intervene for my poor yet esteemed colleague, Mr. Jabiri, and save you and your team from the misapprehension you are under. You see, while your diligent staff informed you that there would be an available seat for you to fly on this mission, I must sadly inform you they were ill-informed or seeking your doom. Great General Telebi, if a human were to ride on the rocket selected for this mission, the acceleration would slam them down so hard into their chair, they would become a jelly. Thus, dearest leader of our heart, you must not get your hopes up for this mission to grant you the title of astronaut. It would only grant you status as a pancake."

The guard tapped the screen, ending his father's speech.

"Young man," the guard said, face imploring. "The general may not be as young as he was, but he is still dangerous. Your father walks a terribly dangerous line. Be careful."

They led Matt out to a car and a new set of guards drove him for half an hour to an imposing building that he assumed was the same his mother had told him about after her trip to Google. The Urmia Research Center, home to General Telebi, the man who had destroyed the peace of his life once again.

Telebi called the entire team to assemble in his office before lunch, which was a strange time in Casey's experience. The general was a man of routine and habit, eating at precise times every day. If he broke that habit, something big was going on.

Casey grew even more concerned when they walked in to find a dozen guards around the perimeter of the office, armed to the teeth. Two of them were nearly as large as Blake, though still shorter. Casey and Blake both looked at Manuel, but he smiled. He had shed the memory of the torture rapidly or was faking it really well.

"This can't be good," Blake muttered.

Worry grew into near panic as Telebi turned in his seat, smiling as if he were a cat who had vomited in Casey's shoes. Both of them.

"Gentlemen, sit down." Telebi spoke with a near giggle in his voice.

They all sat at his tiny dining table, which had extra chairs from the foyer set around it, though all faced Telebi's desk. Hamid translated for Manuel and Sarosh for Blake.

"You are doing an excellent job, but I am most disappointed by your lack of fear. You see, I wanted you to fear me so that you would truly appreciate the gravity of your situation. But it seems you have not feared me enough."

Casey did not like where this was going. They'd escaped almost 200 days with nothing more than captivity, and now the general was turning up the thumbscrews. Torturing Manuel wasn't enough?

"Meet my new assistant? Bring him in!"

A young man came through the door, face angry, not fearful. The young man wore an Iranian junior officer's uniform, but he was no junior officer.

There were several snaps and cracks as both Casey and Blake tore the arms off the antique chairs they sat on. But neither stood. Men with assault rifles surrounded them. Matt, Casey's eldest son, was not rescuable if they were dead.

Casey felt his entire body seized by a hatred and revulsion for the man that threatened to snap his mind. He teetered on the brink when he felt Manuel's hand gently touch his arm. He glanced and saw Manuel was touching Blake's arm, too. They both looked at the hand on their arm. Casey felt a calm wash over him. In that calm, he cried, *Oh God, protect my son! And give us all rational thought so we may act to save him!*

Telebi lamented with a glee that twisted his face. "Now you see why I have so many guards! You spoiled those poor chairs with your bare hands! Why, Blake appears to have crushed his to splinters! Casey, you are not far behind that giant in sheer strength, even if you are so much shorter. My, what a pair you will make in the gladiatorial arena. I do hope that can be arranged."

The general walked over to Matt and clucked his tongue like a disappointed parent. "Unfortunate, though. He is not my type. He is far too tall and muscular. He takes after you, I suppose, Casey? Too bad. But I suspect this will be sufficient motivation to keep all of you focused on completion of your tasks? On avoiding outside entanglements?"

Casey slowly and ponderously stood, every muscle in his body screaming at him for action. "May I speak to him?"

"Yes," the general spat.

"You okay?" Casey asked in English.

"Peachy," Matt said, winking at his dad.

"Hamid, translate for me," the general shouted.

Hamid's translation was literal, and the general looked confused.

"What does 'peachy' mean? Why would he say that? Is that code?"

While Hamid attempted to explain idiomatic expressions and the general shouted at him to stop being so condescending, Casey spoke loudly enough for Matt to hear.

"You know about... the situation here?" Casey gestured about them.

"Yup. The tooth fairy already visited me, and she said I'd get three wishes."

"That's wonderful," Casey said, sighing with relief. "I wish I could see the tooth fairy, but I will have to wait."

The argument with the general wound down, and Hamid turned back to them, ready to translate.

"How are things back home?" Casey asked, going back to innocuous for the general.

"As well as can be without you," Matt said. "I started an auto repair shop and sold it. You'd be surprised how easy it was."

"Be strong," Casey began.

"And laugh in the face of trouble," Matt finished, smiling at him.

"Enough," Telebi said, already bored. "Casey, your son's life hangs in the balance. I know you have been collaborating with my enemies. Now, give me the name of your co-conspirator or you will watch your son lose a finger."

Casey folded his arms. "Even if I were conspiring with your enemies, how do I know you won't do him harm, anyway?"

"If you tell me, I will release your son to return home."

Casey's mind raced, and he struggled to maintain a relaxed exterior. "Afshar is funneling information to and from us from Mossad. He also is embezzling funds from your estate to pay for an assassin to take out Kazmi."

"That is a lie!" Afshar shouted. "I've never even spoken to the Americans!"

"Why did you not consult with me before this, General Telebi?" Hamid asked, tears running down his face. "If I'd known, I could have stopped Afshar. I thought he was in your good graces. He spent many hours with the Americans and when I asked him why, he said it was on your orders!"

Chaos reined as soldiers grabbed Afshar, restrained Kazmi from murdering him, and Telebi shouted at Afshar.

Casey met Matt's eyes across the room. Casey mouthed, 'I love you,' to him, and Matt returned the same. Matt looked on the verge of hysterical laughter, which was understandable.

"Your first time being taken hostage is always traumatic." Blake looked between Casey and Matt. "He's handling this well."

"How many times have you been taken hostage?" Manuel asked.

"Umm... Four times. No, five, if you count that time Casey made me go to the symphony."

The shouting stopped as a single shot echoed through the room. Afshar crumpled to the ground.

"Justice is done." Telebi tossed a cell phone onto the corpse. "Jew loving swine."

"Yes, General Telebi, justice is done." Hamid stepped in front of the still armed man. "Now, can you please give the orders to return the boy to his home and I will return these men to their work?"

"No." Telebi walked to his desk and disassembled his gun to clean it. "There is a rot here and I want this boy here to prevent the Americans from being tempted to work with any others. The boy shares their fate."

Hamid glared at the man with more vehemence than Casey had ever dreamed. It warmed his heart even as he wanted to strangle Telebi.

"I will get them back to work." Hamid spun on his heel and signaled to Casey and crew.

"Time to go, gentlemen," Casey muttered and waved farewell to Matt. As soon as they left the office, he muttered a translation of all that had happened.

"Good thing that friend of ours had dossiers on the staff," Blake said.

"You okay, Casey?" Manuel put a hand on Casey's arm as they walked. "I know I'm not okay."

Hamid stopped in the corridor and screamed. Casey had never imagined such a sound coming from the quiet man. A rage burst out of him and tapered off as he sunk to the ground.

"What do we do?" Tears streamed down Hamid's cheeks.

"First, we thank you." Casey sat down next to Hamid. "Your lies saved us all. How did you get tears like that?"

"Those were real." Hamid pulled out a pack of tissues and blew his nose. "But in a panic I asked, 'What would Blake do?' and the words, 'Throw Afshar under the bus,' came to mind."

Blake chuckled, reached down, and pulled both of them up to their feet. "We'll figure this out, fellas. You both did good. Normally, I wouldn't say to do what I do, but it seemed to work out better for you than me. Now we figure out how to help Matt."

Casey's mind was clear, his fury acting as the pavement over the last of his anxiety. He suspected he would have no further medical anxiety until his family was home safe. The crisis was upon him, and he never had anxiety when the crisis involved his children. He knew his wife was somewhere about. He'd have to trust her on this one.

"Never mind Matt. We don't worry about him. We give it to the spy. Spies can get a single person out of places; no problem. We do our job. That's all we can do." He smiled despite the rage in his heart. "The spy will know exactly what to do for him."

"General Telebi, may I train your new assistant on where things are in the office? I think he will be more useful if I do."

The general looked at Esin, surprised at her presence, even though she was there every day for most of the day.

Telebi blinked a few times.

"Oh, what? Yes. Good idea. You do that."

He waved her away, then went back to his game of solitaire. He only played solitaire when he appeared especially stressed. She supposed losing his favorite lackey would be stressful.

Esin gestured to Matt, and they crossed the room, where she started pointing at things.

"I think we'll have more time to talk today. Thirty seconds yesterday was not enough."

"In Persian? My Persian is... poor."

"I'll speak clearly. Can't have anyone hear me speak English."

"Makes sense. You're okay, mom?"

"I was going to ask you the same thing. And call me Madam, just in case."

"I'm fine. It was scary but I'm your son. I'm handling it. How are you? You've been here for what, six months in this awful man's office? Wow, my Persian is better than I assumed."

"Of course it is. You're my son. And it's only four months, though I have to clean the staff offices, too. But I mostly sleep on site, so I have plenty of time to spy." Esin looked closely at Matt's face. "Are you really alright?"

"Mom, I'm fine."

"Madam. You'll tell me if you start having nightmares. Or insomnia. Or tremors. Or panic attacks."

"As those were clearly not questions, I suppose I just have to say yes."

"Now, I'll have to actually teach you things, too. This is the most important thing in the office. He's going to have you make him liquor. I began a week ago to spike all of them with Depakote I stole to make Teletubby calmer. It's a mood stabilizer. It's enough to not kill him if he gets drunk, yet mellow him. Hopefully, he won't be so excited to torture people."

"Teletubby, huh? Nice nickname. Blake come up with that?"

"You bet he did," Esin said with a smile. "Now, did they do anything to you? That man is a vile pervert and if he's done anything…"

"Nothing except look at me like I was a side of beef, and he was the butcher. But he sniffed and said, 'Too tall.' Whoa, mom, you look like you want to murder him and I can only see your eyes!"

Esin tried to school her face, but the rage was nearly impossible to keep from shouting from her every feature.

"Because I do. He laid violent hands upon my son."

"Mom, I've been praying and thinking. I realized something. I want him to live after we escape. You know why?"

"Why?"

"Because he will face the consequences of his failure at the hands of his own government. I think him facing failure and death will be far more fitting than one of us killing him."

Esin considered his words and replied, "You are a wise young man, Matt. I'm proud of you."

"It's like killing a spider," Matt said. "It's always better to have someone else do it."

"You're right," Esin said. "We'll make a plan that will result in his demise at his own leaders' hands. Now, training. Teletubby likes to throw things at people. You should keep a handful of pencils and pens at all times in your pocket. If he gets mad, pull them out of your pocket and offer them to the idiot for his throwing pleasure. And if he pegs you, pretend it hurts."

The wind was hot and dusty against Casey's face as he leaned his head back against the pole he was bound to. A tumbleweed blew by, between him and the firing squad, standing a mere 25 feet away. He had refused a blindfold. He'd face his fate with no fear. A woman cried in agony in the crowd, while children wept. He stared daggers at the general as he handed each man a single bullet. Casey reached out with his magic but could not sense the bullets. Aluminum? Rust and ruin, the general was better funded than he'd thought. How would he get out of this one?

Casey chuckled to himself at his line of thinking as he waited on the general. Stories always reduced his panic. He'd promised himself to never stop telling them, even in the face of the devil himself. He always felt like he was a doomed man when he had to give tours. Casey did not enjoy giving tours in the best of times. These were not the best of times. He'd shown dignitaries around mines, processing plants, and refineries. Never for someone who had the vindictiveness of a hornet and the temperament of a honey badger.

Next to him, in both presence and purpose, Hamid stood far stronger than Casey had seen before. He was not trembling and fearful like he'd been the first month they'd been there. Casey felt proud of the man Hamid had become in their time. He showed no fear of Telebi anymore. No fear of anyone.

"You think he'll be more mellow now that the spies have him drugged up on mood stabilizer?" Hamid asked. "I still can't believe they pulled that off."

"Oh, I think our spy is mighty competent," Casey said with amusement. "And it will only work if he's been drinking enough."

Like a thundering roar, Telebi and his minions came tromping into the construction bay, Telebi yelling and disparaging his team.

"Obviously not enough..." Casey muttered.

Casey's eyes went straight to his son, and he waved with a fake smile on his face. It hurt like nothing he'd ever known to see Matt in danger.

Matt smiled broadly, then gave him a huge, melodramatic wink, lingering at the back of the crowd. Casey knew what that meant. Expect anything, and it was Matt's fault.

As was wise in the face of an invasion of overgrown toddlers, Casey had had the technicians clear everything fragile out of easy reach as dignitaries liked to touch things. Even so, he led with, "Welcome, please do not touch anything. Many things are dangerous in this room."

"Natural selection," Telebi said with a vindictive laugh. "Let them touch things if they are stupid enough to flaunt your warning."

"Sir, they might break some of the items," Hamid said boldly. "This will cost us money and lead to delays."

While he didn't care about his men, Telebi cared about time and money. "You heard the man! Touch anything and I'll see you flogged!" The general then faced Casey again. "Alright, get on with it. I have a lunch to be at."

Casey kept his face schooled, not allowing his loathing of the man to show on his face.

"Yes sir. I'm excited to show you the Asteroid Retrieval Probe and the Debris Collection Probe, as well as some of the hardware that we will use to mount them to the rocket."

He walked them over to the first. "The ARP will be mounted permanently to the second stage of the rocket. When the whole system reaches orbit, the DCP will be ejected to begin gathering debris. The ARP will take over navigation of the second stage, dissecting the rocket bit by bit, sending it through the refinery, here, and using the ion engine, here, to thrust the entire system into intercepting orbits with the Ariane 5 upper stages. The entire system is powered by massive solar panels, which are coming from a Russian supplier and will arrive on schedule. The robotic system you see on this table will piggyback on the ARP and is being built to climb up and down the rocket and even leap to capture the target upper stages. The system can capture three upper stages at a time and then will have to return to the desired orbit to assemble the space station."

The general's phone rang, emitting an ear piercingly high-pitched song that sounded like the theme song from an anime. The general emitted a tiny scream of unbridled rage. He took out the phone, looked at it, flung the phone to the ground, then looked around like a wild man. Seeing a toolbox, he ran over and yanked drawers open until he found a hammer. He then stormed to his phone, still singing, and beat it, letting out bestial cries of rage with each stroke of the hammer. Finally, the music stopped. He stood and gathered himself, taking a breath and trying to sound calm despite his rapid breathing.

How many times has that gone off today? Matt, be careful!

"Make a note, Major Ali," the general said. "I need another new phone. And if this next one does this again, I will shoot you." He patted the pistol at his waist, then turned to Casey, took a deep breath, and said, "Continue."

"Yes, sir," Casey said, blinking rapidly. "The robotic system can then take the structural beams, which are in fabrication at a specialty shop in Tehran and connect the upper stages in series. The system will then repeat the collection process, consuming most of the second stage rocket as it collects all the Ariane 5 upper stages needed for a complete space station ring. At that point, the ARP will leave the robotic system behind and head on its asteroid retrieval mission while the robotic system will cut into the cryo tanks in the upper stages and begin welding airlocks in place. These airlocks are also under construction in Tehran and Urmia."

Another staff member's phone rang, making the same shrill sound that the general's had. The general still had the hammer and threw it at the man, clocking him in the head, dropping him to the ground. The general's secretary, with a look of resignation, took the man's phone from his pocket, collected the hammer, and then smashed the phone soundly, tactfully setting the hammer onto a table when complete.

Casey smiled, pretending nothing had happened, and led them to the second probe. He fought the urge to laugh even as he fought the urge to shout at his son to be more careful. What did a manic episode feel like? Was he going to have his first ever manic episode? The group left the fallen man behind as if this were a perfectly normal aspect of a tour.

"The DCP is a more subtle beast than the ARP. The DCP will take each piece of debris it captures and tack weld it to another piece of debris with these elongated arms you see. When the load becomes significant, it will return to the site for the space station and will attach the debris collected to one of the Ariane 5 upper stages for storage. It will then repeat this indefinitely. It also has significant solar panels. This claw you see here will be attached to a long tether that is being assembled in China using a technology we learned about last month, greatly increasing our reach. The microelectronics in the tether can each be activated separately, causing the tether to 'whip' itself in any direction. It makes the tether essentially an articulated arm with almost a million articulations. This means the claw can grab debris at over 100 meters distance and up to a 4 meter per second difference in orbital velocity."

The general scrunched his face up, then pointedly yawned, so Hamid interjected, "It's like Indiana Jones' whip. It can grab space junk from far away."

"I knew that," Telebi said like a petulant child. "But I suppose these idiots didn't."

Several of his men nodded. Kazmi glared hate at Telebi.

Hamid picked up at this point.

"Now, the rocket is not at this facility, of course, but the two stages are being combined in a month at the rocket assembly building before these probes are completed."

Casey could tell Telebi was losing interest when Kazmi proffered a question. "The schedule is intact? No slips?"

"No sir," Casey said. "We baked into the schedule the potential for delays and have definitely had our fair share of those, but we are on track for completion on schedule. As you can see, our probes are on track for completion in one month, at which point we begin flight qualification testing."

Telebi wacked Kazmi across the head, knocking his hat off.

"Idiot. You could learn from these people. They keep their promises, unlike you. I still haven't seen that report on the status of plum harvests and the potential to start a plum orchard at my villa."

Casey knew Telebi was not complimenting them. He was using their competence to insult others. It was a strategy he'd seen before. He had underestimated this man for too long.

"Sir, I'm not a botanist," Kazmi spoke through gritted teeth. "You shot the closest thing to one we had."

Telebi dismissively ignored him. Kazmi's hands momentarily lifted towards Telebi like he wanted to grasp his throat. Hamid and Casey glanced at each other in concern.

"Are we done?" Telebi shouted. "I'm hungry. Everything looks great. We'll leave you to your work."

Without another word, Telebi turned to leave. Kazmi's phone rang, the same ringtone as before. Kazmi immediately bolted, sprinting out the door. Telebi grabbed the hammer from the table and walked after him like a serial killer, confident his victim had nowhere to hide and would probably be in the shed full of chainsaws, anyway. Two of the staff helped the man with a head injury out the door. Matt was the last to leave. Casey smiled and lifted his hands in silent applause. Matt bowed and followed the entourage out the door.

"Could you please requisition us a new hammer?" Casey asked as the door finally closed.

"So, how did Matt do that phone thing?" Hamid asked in awe.

"He's a clever kid. I doubt it was hard for him to mess with all of their phones. The kid is too much like me for my blood pressure's sake." Casey rubbed his chin and sighed. "And Hamid? Tell our secret friend about Kazmi's obvious desire to murder the general..."

Hamid nodded solemnly, but then asked, "Would it be so bad if Kazmi killed Telebi?"

"Do Iranians say, 'The devil you know is better than the devil you don't?'"

Hamid considered this and replied, "We say, 'The yellow dog is brother to the black jackal.'"

"What's the origin of that?" Casey asked with interest. He did love a good idiom.

"My mother would tell it to me this way. There was a black jackal that would bother the people of a village. He got so obnoxious, they united to drive him out of the village. He would try to come back, but they would throw stones at him. But the jackal wanted to be with the people, for he delighted to torment them. So, he rolled himself in yellow dust and entered the village as a yellow dog, which the people loved. But he continued to torment people, though this time more secretly. But then it rained, which revealed his fur. The people drove him off saying that the yellow dog is brother to the black jackal."

Casey considered this and opened his mouth to speak. Then he closed it. Then he opened it again and said, "Hamid, I don't think those sayings mean the same thing at all!"

Esin sat in the security office perusing the tapes. It shocked her they were still using VHS tapes for most of their security cameras. She checked them regularly for anything she could use against Telebi or for her husband. The guard slept soundly, as he always did this time of night. The drugged cup of tea she delivered him every night ensured her a solid four hours of study time.

She fast forwarded through the tape of the cafeteria. She wished for the hundredth time that she could have witnessed the great food fight of their second month. The cleaning ladies spoke of it like a strange battle of foreign armies.

She stopped fast forwarding as she reached dinner time. Casey and crew came bustling in. She watched as they gathered their meals, joked, laughed, and ate. She sighed and was about to fast forward further when she paused the recording in shock. Kazmi was poking his head into the cafeteria. He stayed only a minute, then left before anyone noticed him.

She hadn't figured that man out. He should have been implicated in the Mossad incident, but Casey had chosen the harmless Afshar. Well, harmless to them. He was a horrible person, but not to them. He had connections she needed to find. He was too dangerous to allow to freely spy on her husband.

Manuel handed out welding goggles and Casey gladly put his on. "Are you sure this is enough eye protection?"

"Casey, if this isn't enough protection, then it's because it vaporized us." Manuel moved to position by the computer, put his finger on the button, and put his welding goggles on.

"Test sequence alpha zero one point three, initiating."

A flame saturated Casey's welding goggles, and he smiled. A nearly perfect ion engine circular flame appeared and then ended.

"Clear." Manuel removed his goggles.

Casey and Blake followed suit.

"How's the thrust?" Blake asked.

"Lower than expected." Manuel moved his mouse furiously with his right hand, typing with his left.

"How bad?" Casey asked.

"Bad, bad. It means I'm doing something wrong with my math. I think there must be some variables I don't know about. What other variables could there be?"

"Did you remember air pressure?" Casey had asked that question a hundred times in his career. People forgot air pressure often, even scientists and engineers.

Manuel stopped and stared at Casey, eyes wide as saucers.

"I'll take that as a no?" Casey chuckled.

Manuel swore, making Casey and Blake jump.

"If he swears, do I get to swear?" Blake rubbed his hands together.

"No." Casey stepped next to Manuel. "Manuel, talk to me. You're having feelings?"

Manuel typed and moved his mouse furiously.

"Manuel?" Casey put his hand on Manuel's shoulder.

"I need space!" Manuel snapped.

Casey and Blake stepped back. They'd taught Manuel that strategy in college. They went to a table and sat quietly. They knew not to talk, so Manuel didn't think they were talking about him.

After five minutes, Manuel walked over and sat at the table. They sat in silence for another few minutes.

"I don't know how you do it, Casey." Manuel finally looked up at Casey, then back down at his own hands. "I hate the feeling of panic. What if I fail?"

Blake jumped in first. "You think Casey owns panic? At a time like this, if you didn't feel panic now and then, you'd be crazy."

Casey opened his mouth to speak, but Manuel preempted him.

"But I never panic! I don't have an anxiety disorder. My emotions are normally so still."

Casey again tried to speak, but Blake spoke.

"You were kidnapped and torn from your family. Anxiety disorder or not, trauma like that causes occasional or constant panic."

Casey waited, assuming Manuel would say something. When he didn't, Casey finally spoke.

"Just remember, we both know what you're going through better than anyone else. We're here with you."

"What if I fail?" Manuel's agony hurt Casey. "What if I never get back to my family? What if we explode?"

"We do our best and let God make up the difference," Blake said. "And should we die, then we leave our family in his hands."

Casey stared at Blake, eyes wide. "Who are you, and what have you done with Blake?"

They laughed and Manuel stood.

"We have work to do. I fixed the calculations to account for air pressure. Makes sense we'd lose thrust to displacing air. I suspect it was pushing it out the side channels. Stop sitting! Let's go!"

Casey gave Hamid the wrench and let him tighten the last bolt on the Asteroid Retrieval Probe. As Hamid pulled the wrench away, the staff cheered. Construction was complete. The Americans stepped back as the Iranians all gathered for pictures.

"I can't believe we're done," Blake said with a smile.

Manuel fidgeted with apparent concern. "But it is not done until flight qualification says it is ready for…"

"Yes, we know," Casey said, interrupting him before he could get started. "Remember, Manuel, photo op."

"Ah yes. Photo ops are where you lie with photos."

Blake grinned and slapped Manuel on the back. "We'll teach you social norms yet."

"Like not saying whatever pops into your head?" Casey asked, one eyebrow raised in amusement.

As usual, Blake played the situation up to full effect. He placed his hand up to his heart in mock outrage. "That is a time-honored tradition and very much a social norm. If humans didn't say what popped into their heads, they'd be so civilized that no one would get married or have any fun. Why, if I hadn't told Lucy what I thought of her dancing skills, I wouldn't be a happily married man today."

"Who's Lucy?" Casey asked in surprise. "You married Jane."

"Exactly. Lucy was the girl I was dancing with the weekend before I met Jane. Why, if I hadn't been so quick to say what popped in my head, she might have gone steady with me and then Jane would have been a stranger in the night, like that stupid song they always play at dances."

"Blake," Manuel interjected, "you are actually insane."

Someone noticed them and tried to drag them in for photos, but Hamid vetoed that.

"Photo ops are when you lie with photos," Manuel said.

Hamid laughed aloud.

"Right you are, but we can't have you guys in any." He turned to the group. "Thank you all for coming. The general and staff will be here in a few minutes for their own photos. I highly recommend you all head out. The Americans will take you to their party while I have the real fun."

The crowd laughed but headed with all possible speed out of the construction bay.

Casey lingered. "Say 'Hi' to Matt for me if you get a chance. Give him this." He handed over a small device. "Tell him to attach it to the bottom of the bedframe of the general's bed. It's got a magnet to hold it in place. It's powered by a micro-fusion reactor. Smallest we've made so far. It will vibrate the bed at about 6 hertz, inducing terrible fear in the general as he sleeps. If he sleeps elsewhere, move it to follow him. He'll be in constant terror as he sleeps and never know why, since he can't hear it."

Hamid held the device in awe. "Between this destroying his sleep and the drugs calming him down, he's going to be completely useless. You guys are terrifying. Remind me never to get on your bad side."

###

Matt shook his head in wonder at how Telebi exemplified everything negative in one afternoon. They'd left the photo shoot and headed straight to dinner, though Kazmi veered off at the last moment. No loss there.

"Matt, what do you think of the fruit selection? Quite impressive, is it not?"

"Yes, General Telebi, it is quite extensive." *But not as extensive as my grocery store's fruit selection, you egotistical moron. And you still can't get plums despite shouting about them every day!*

Telebi drank heavily, and the mood stabilizer seemed to have an impact, too, as he became quite introspective.

"I do wish you were prettier, Matt. You are just such a large young man."

Matt hedged his bets against this man's distorted proclivities.

"Yes, I take after my father. As you can see, he is a massive man. I will never be described as petite. I'm far too masculine and large to be considered pretty. In fact, I will probably become quite fat soon."

"Yes, a pity. A pity." Telebi took a long draw at his wineglass. The other guests were looking downright sleepy after their multiple glasses of wine. Matt wondered if any of them would react poorly to the drugs in the liquor?

Matt listened as the general rambled for several minutes, letting slip his plan to sell Matt into slavery in Kazakhstan. Matt poured the general another full glass of the drugged wine and watched as the general greedily drank it down.

"Mr. Matt," the general's personal waiter said, "the general is only to have a single glass of wine at dinner."

Matt barked a laugh and handed the general the entire bottle, daring the waiter to do something. He may not actually be as burly as his dad, and neither of them were anywhere close to Blake, but he had all of his dad's reasonable height and used it to tower over the waiter.

"A toast!" Matt shouted. "To General Telebi!" He took a glass from the table and held it aloft. "Drink to the general!"

The men all drank more and Matt topped off all of their glasses, emptying three bottles of the general's wine stores.

"A toast to his vision and foresight!"

The general swayed in his seat and glared at all the men, who all downed their glasses of wine under his gaze. The general took a pull at the bottle he was holding.

His mom said there was a plan that would see him out of here with her on launch day, and dad and his friends too. He prayed that would work.

"A toast to his greatness!" Matt shouted, having passed one last time among them and topping off their glasses. As each finished their full glass, heads crashed to the table and a few men slipped from their chairs to the ground. Telebi laughed like a mule, then crumpled, wine spilling all over his front.

Matt looked around the room. Telebi had not allowed him to join the meal, finding it amusing to make sure he was hungry when there was a feast. Matt took Kazmi's unused plate, dished up a massive pile of food, then sat down and ate, staring down the few inebriated men who remained conscious. One by one, they stood and left like beaten dogs, leaving him alone with the wait staff and the drunk general. Matt ate his way through a sizable portion of the remaining food before settling down on the floor to sleep. The general would probably sleep the entire night in that chair and be a terror in the morning. The new toy from his dad would wait until tomorrow.

Hamid sagged with exhaustion by the time he'd finished all the photos with the general and his ridiculous staff, but he had got Matt alone long enough to explain the device. Matt's face lit up like he was in an American Christmas movie. Afterward, Hamid stumbled into the cafeteria and came to a stop, amazed. When the Americans had said they would throw a party to celebrate completion of construction, he hadn't thought it would be quite so... elaborate. So many decorations!

As he walked in, he saw Sarosh at one end manning a new grill and wearing a Japanese Hibachi uniform. He was grilling up heaps of meat and veggies. The crowd cheered as he made a flaming onion. What was going on?

He turned for answers and found only questions. He saw Blake wearing an enormous chef's hat and apron, handing out plates of tiny pastries. He saw Manuel dishing up heaping plates from a giant tray of shrimp and rice. Then he saw Casey and a few of the technicians dishing up potatoes and veggies.

Then the music pushed itself into his consciousness. He recognized it as jazz music. Big band.

He walked up to Casey.

"What is going on?"

Casey raised an eyebrow but answered exuberantly.

"What do you mean? It's an American party! Now eat, or my wife will haunt you. She insists that people eat at her parties and everything I know about having a good time, I learned from her."

"But how did all this get approved?"

"Remember when Teletubby stopped checking our work? Obviously, you approved a few things without realizing it, too!" Casey winked, then laughed at Hamid's expression and handed him a plate, waving him over to Manuel's stand.

"Hamid, mi amigo! Good, you have space on your plate." Manuel put a big scoop of shrimp and rice on Hamid's plate. "Welcome to the party! Get another plate and get some food from Sarosh! He's been practicing his Hibachi skills for months, ever since Blake showed him a video of a professional at work."

Hamid glanced at Sarosh as he launched a piece of shrimp from his spatula directly into the open mouth of one of the engineers.

"Well, that is not something I would have expected to see."

Hamid sat down at the Hibachi table next to one of the cleaning ladies who he saw in the general's office nearly all the time. "I thought the general didn't let his staff come to these events. What's your name?"

"He doesn't but I'm not on his staff, just part of the cleaning staff. I'm Leila. You are Haj Hamid, yes?"

"Yes, pleased to meet you, Leila. Are you a local?" The accent was not quite like the local Urmians.

"No, I am from Tehran. I came here for the work. I am the only woman on the cleaning staff who can handle the general and his staff. They are terrible men, but they do not see me."

"Speaking of the general, please make sure he doesn't hear about this."

"Never you fear, Haj Hamid," Leila said with a laugh in her voice, "I wouldn't want these parties to end. No information ever passes from down here to the general's staff. Not if I can help it."

Leila got up and went to watch a part of the party Hamid had missed. A bucket of water had apples floating in it and people were trying to get them out with their mouths!

Hamid turned back to his food just in time, because Sarosh had been calling his name and lobbed a piece of shrimp at Hamid, which he deftly caught in his mouth to cheers from his staff. Hamid began to see the appeal of an American party.

Esin thoroughly enjoyed the party. She spent some time at each station and then stayed close to Casey. Hearing him talk about her with almost everyone had been like a shot of joy directly into her veins, buoying up her heart. He always had some fresh story about her in the most mundane situation, yet he made her seem the veritable angel. His Persian was becoming truly fluent at this point. He had even given her dessert.

Then she saw Kazmi come in. She wanted to alert them to his presence but didn't dare speak near Casey, as he would recognize her voice in any language. She hurried over to Sarosh, who was still at the grill, and whispered, "Kazmi is here. Beware."

Sarosh glanced at her, stared at her eyes for a moment, then turned and saw Kazmi. He quickly handed his cooking implements to another technician, apologized to the guests, and went to Casey, who was now making caramel apples.

Casey looked where Sarosh pointed and frowned. Esin wondered what he would do.

Esin followed as Casey and Sarosh approached Kazmi, who was lingering near the edge of the party.

Casey spoke with his usual exuberance. "Colonel Kazmi! It is so kind of you to join this party. We are celebrating the probe completion."

"Yes, this seems to be an out-of-control abomination against the worship of Allah."

Casey handed a caramel apple to Kazmi.

"These are caramel apples. A delicacy in my country. I would love for you to have one." He then took a large bite of his apple, showing thorough enjoyment. Sarosh started handing them out, then took a bite of the last one.

Kazmi threw his to the ground. "I will eat nothing given me by an infidel. You are a fool."

Kazmi backhanded Casey across the mouth.

Except this did not get him what he thought he'd get. First off, Casey, while petite compared to Blake, was still at least nine inches taller than the diminutive Kazmi, and Casey had the bone structure of a heavy-weight fighter. At least, that's how Esin saw him. Kazmi was slight of frame and did not exercise even a minute a day, let alone an hour a day like Casey.

Kazmi's knuckles made more a cracking sound than a slapping sound, and Casey's head did not move. The poor colonel grabbed his hand, making a strangled sound of agony, then he stormed out of the room, leaving them to enjoy their party.

Casey felt his jaw. "The idiot hit my jawline with his knuckles. My toddler hits harder."

Esin left the party and followed Kazmi swiftly, sure he was up to no good. She could have warned Casey that kindness would not work on Kazmi. He had a reputation for ruthlessness, even if Telebi treated him poorly.

She followed Kazmi into the staff offices and silently moved among the cubicles. She heard his voice speaking on the phone. She crept closer, seeking to hear what he said.

"Yes, I think I have evidence against one of the senior engineers. No, I will not tell you who. I want to get the credit myself." He paused, listening. "No, Telebi is a fool. He has his staff run so ragged that no one has bothered to go down to the rest of the facility in months. Did you know the Americans were having a party tonight? They are turning our people away from Allah one decadent dessert at a time." Another pause. "Well, most of them are decadent. I think I got a bad one tonight."

Esin's pulse quickened. Telebi's indolence and her careful monitoring had kept the general's staff apart from the facility for months. Would this man ruin things?

"I blame all of this on the talkative American. I cannot believe that Telebi has agreed to let the Americans build this entire mission! I intend to get the credit for the finish myself. I have analyzed the status of the mission and I think the Americans are superfluous. We can do how the Americans say in baseball and be the close-out pitcher. Then Iranians will get all the glory." A pause. "How hard can flight qualifications be?"

Esin's mind raced. She had to stop him. But how?

"I'll take care of them tonight... Yes, tonight." A long pause. "Bah, I'll just shoot them and claim self-defense. Two of them are huge. They're very dangerous. Look, I need to go. I'm hungry and I'm missing the general's dinner." He sighed. "He will probably throw food at me. Now, make no move until you hear from me."

Esin felt a buzzing inside her head and her vision narrowed while her heart raced.

She came to herself lying next to Kazmi, whose head was facing the wrong direction relative to his body. Sweaty and disheveled, she looked about her. Cubicle wall leaning. Chair upended. Dead man. Her shoulders ached.

"How did I do that?" she whispered. "Surely, I didn't just do that."

She looked about her some more.

"I definitely did that."

She lay there trying to remember what she did, but all she got were flashes. Did she parkour off the cubicle wall?

"I'm going to be so sore tomorrow. Stop talking to yourself. You're going into shock."

She pulled herself to her feet, looking down at the body of the colonel. He wasn't breathing and stared with sightless eyes at the world. Don't think about that now. Feelings were a later problem. She'd need to do something and quickly. She checked his pockets, broke his phone, and pulled the battery out. She straightened the cubicle wall and went to the front of the office to retrieve her rolling garbage can.

She did not want to remember the rest of the cleanup. With a fair amount of blunt force, she folded him up into the garbage can.

"Alright Esin, you've snapped a man's neck in a berserker rage and shoved him in a garbage can. But none of that is nearly as weird as Blake in a chef's hat, so I guess it isn't that bad." She stifled a laugh. No time for laughter. No time for tears.

She then went into the general's office, drank a glass of water, and washed the glass. Heart still racing, but feeling more in control, she smoothed out her dress and robes and tried to regain her normal composure. Finding that impossible, she tied the bag over the body and pushed the garbage can laboriously across the floor.

Her mind raced, edging towards panic. What could she do with the man? The dumpster was out. They X-rayed all garbage leaving the facility. She no longer had Abdul to drive the body out with the general. She couldn't leave him sitting around. It occurred to her that there was only one place. But she wouldn't be able to do it on her own.

Without knowing why, she headed to the party. Slipping into the cafeteria, she saw they were wrapping up. Some of them were cleaning. She desperately wanted to go to Casey and throw herself into his arms and weep. To ask for help to dispose of this burden.

She realized with a start that her veil had come loose in the chaos, and so she quickly fixed it. She then prayed. She cried, *Oh God, I have killed another! I have killed three men! Why, God, why have I had to kill so many?*

Manuel walked up to her. In a passable attempt at Farci, he handed her a plate and said, "Extra food. Take." Then he smiled and walked away as Blake began singing a sea shanty. One of her favorites.

Then Sarosh sat down next to her and spoke barely above a whisper. "I saw your face when you came in, Lady Scarlett, and will protect you with my life. You have had some difficulties this day, that is clear. Even now, your eyes say you are in agony."

"How did you recognize me?"

"I have seen your photo every day in the lab. You are so beautiful that it is only a blind man who could not recognize you, even if he only saw your face for a moment."

"Sarosh, you risk your life…"

"Blake is my father, Casey is my uncle, and Manuel is my brother. Therefore, you are family. I live and gain freedom with them or not at all. Now, you need help."

"My garbage can in the hall holds Colonel Kazmi, dead by my hand. He planned to kill my husband and his team. I need to take it to the incinerator."

Sarosh rose, eyes wide.

"You are truly as great and terrible as Casey says in the stories. You have had an exceedingly difficult day. I will dispose of it. You stay here. Stay with friends. But keep your face down or others may see your eyes and recognize you."

Without another word, he headed out the door, leaving her feeling relieved of a massive burden, allowing her to enjoy the banter of the friends in the room.

"I'm telling you," Blake shouted, "shrimp cannot be kept as leftovers. It's a sin against the natural order of seafood."

"Since when is there a natural order of seafood, Blake?" Casey countered. "You want an excuse to eat all the leftover shrimp."

"Well, duh," Blake said, stuffing another handful into his mouth.

Sarosh came back as Casey approached Esin. With cleaning done, his radar was drawn to her suffering.

"My lady, are you alright?" Casey asked.

But Sarosh intervened before Esin had to reply.

"Yes, Mr. Casey, I was helping her. She had a bad run in with one of the general's staff and did not think she could finish her chores. I took care of her garbage and will now walk her to the shuttle to go home."

"Sarosh, this is why I love you. You are so good." Casey then turned to her. "And lady, if you need more help, do not hesitate to ask anyone on our team." He clapped Sarosh on the shoulder and walked away.

As Sarosh walked with Esin to the shuttle, he slipped a cell phone into her hand. "I always have a few false phones since I joined Blake's family. This phone does not retain messages, except to and from the contact labeled, 'Mother.' Read them so you know their content and add new messages every day. I will reply, in case the police read it. The contact in there for your 'brother' is the important contact. You can text me on that, and the messages will disappear as soon as you hit send. When I send you messages, they will stay for 30 seconds after you read them."

"You will not tell Hamid or the team that you are in touch with me?"

"No, for while I love him as a father, Blake is a loudmouth."

"Agreed. Casey knows I am here, but I cannot speak to him for fear we will be discovered. All watch him and would notice me talking to him. I will talk to him through you. If you need help, you can ask him."

"Yes, Lady Scarlett. Now, sleep well. I will return."

Sitting at the shuttle stop, she looked down at the neatly foil wrapped plate, stacked 4 inches deep in who knows what food from that wonderful night. She glanced at the phone, a lifeline in this mission of solitude. And she allowed herself to weep silently behind her veil, in relief, sadness, shock, and gratitude. She was known, she was heard, and she was loved.

Casey put his feet up on his desk in the lab and hummed to himself. The party last night had been a great time. He still marveled that Sarosh had taught himself to be a Hibachi chef from internet videos! *What a great kid.*

As the rest of his team and Hamid's team leads came into the lab, he greeted them with enthusiasm. With the team gathered, he stood up to give a motivational speech, Sarosh translating for Blake and Manuel.

"Dear friends, you have done an amazing job these last several months. I cannot begin to tell you what a challenging endeavor we've been asked to accomplish. But you're on schedule. And that means that you get to experience the most nerve-wracking part of preparing for space flight. Flight qualification. We get to spend the next several weeks trying to break what we've built, hoping it doesn't break, but knowing some things may fail. It's not the end of the world if things don't work. We still have three months to finish in. In fact..."

He paused with his mouth open as none other than the Teletubby himself came waddling through the door, followed by Matt and a few minions.

"He smells like narcissism," Blake muttered.

Mentally switching to fancy Persian, he greeted the rotund man even as he gave a subtle, underhanded wave to his son. "Good morning, General Telebi. It is most illustrious to see you on this grand morning as we begin flight readiness tests."

"Yes, yes, it is always nice to see me. Unless you're Kazmi. He seems to be avoiding me. Have any of you seen that villain since last night? I scheduled to meet with him an hour ago and he never showed up. I called his home and was told he never came home. I had security trace his phone, and it was in the office until it shut off near the end of my dinner party. No one saw him."

"The last I saw him was a week or so ago when he tried to sneak into the cafeteria and take a dessert," Casey said with a bow.

"Yes, sounds like him," Telebi barked with a laugh.

"General Telebi," Sarosh said with a tone of subservience very unlike his normal tone, "he told me he was going to the brothels with your permission. He said if anyone came looking for him, he was not to be disturbed and he would not be back for several days. He said something about Tehran."

Telebi's eyes bulged and his face reddened. "Why that conniving, self-centered, greedy, bootlicking..." He paused to catch his breath. "Well, I guess he'll miss out on the glory he was always going on about! Namazi!"

A stout man poured from the same mold as Kazmi, but with less intelligence, stepped forward.

"Yes, General Telebi?"

"Alright Casey, Major Namazi here is going to job shadow you for the rest of the time here. He is to stick by your side and learn everything from you he can."

"But sir, I am not adept at science or math," the unwillingly promoted man protested.

Casey, despising and yet pitying the man, helpfully added, "Or engineering?"

"Yes, I have no skills in science, math, or engineering," Namazi said, nodding furiously.

"Well, learn what you have to," Telebi said with a glare. "Engineering can't be that hard. You will lead teams in the future to flight qualify and launch new missions. So, you better learn everything he does. Ask questions. Be there for everything he does. Hah, sleep in his room with him! Anyway, you'll be working the next launch without the Americans, so do your homework."

Telebi patted the stunned Namazi on the shoulder.

"And Casey?"

"Yes, General Telebi?"

"He's my nephew, so treat him well." Telebi left the room, leaving behind a stunned silence.

Casey looked at Blake and Manuel as Sarosh caught up on the translation. Blake swore in Greek, Turkish, and Russian in rapid succession.

Namazi was worse than useless, as Casey rapidly learned. He spoke no English. He hadn't taken a math or science course since barely graduating high school, and he hadn't read or even heard a word about engineering in his life. He had never done project management. He had never run a business. In fact, he appeared to have been lifetime military. And not the useful kind. The 'uncle is important and so nephew gets promoted quickly' kind.

"Major, tell me how you would order your men into combat," Casey ordered.

"I have never done so, so I do not know," Namazi replied.

"Well, how would you order your men to pick up a gum wrapper?"

"I have never done that, either."

"It was an example, Namazi. What have you ordered your men to do?"

"I have ordered them to make me coffee," Namazi said. "And to drive me places."

Casey turned to Blake and vented his feelings in English.

"This man is worse than useless. It appears they promoted him far above his competence. So far that his competence is in a deep oil well and his position is in geostationary orbit."

"Is he the type to yell at to get results?" Blake asked. "I only yell at groups of people and not individuals, but there are some people that you gotta yell at."

"Blake, I haven't yelled at someone in anger in five years and I'm not going to start on this guy."

"So, give him a job that has maximum visibility and zero impact," Hamid interjected.

Casey and Blake both turned to him, and Casey applauded softly, feeling proud. Hamid was quite good at navigating a dictatorial bureaucracy.

"Alright major, you have some serious gaps in your training," Casey said in Persian. He did not say his thoughts out loud as Blake would have. "You are to begin your training by reading several textbooks. Then I will have Sarosh give you a list of videos to watch. Once you have completed all of that, you will be competent enough to start job shadowing me."

Namazi's eyes widened. "But this will take me a long time, won't it? I have to learn what you're doing in only three months! And Telebi ordered me to be with you all the time. Even sleeping."

Casey groaned. *He follows stupid orders? Bother.*

"No, Major Namazi, you will not be sleeping in my quarters. New members of the staff sleep in the janitorial closet until they have proven themselves worthy. You want to be part of this mission? You want to learn what I do? Start by gaining the background I gained."

"Did you have to sleep in the janitorial closet when you were a new engineer?" Namazi asked, eyes wide.

"Not literally," Casey said, the man's lack of understanding of hyperbole killing his attempts at humor. "It was exaggeration to get a point across."

"What was the point?" Namazi replied, confused.

"Never mind," Casey said, feeling deflated. Humor didn't work when the other party would not play along.

"But I can follow you around while I read the books, yes? I have to do that. I think Telebi will forgive if I don't sleep with you, but not if I'm not with you during the day."

Casey could feel his anxiety building, and he gritted his teeth. Instead of saying what he wanted to about the whole situation, he said, "Yes, of course. We will find you a place to sit."

Hamid's respect for Casey's patience grew by leaps and bounds that day. Namazi seemed to get underfoot at every inopportune moment. Casey would politely but firmly order him back to his corner chair, where Sarosh had supplied him with a tablet and a laundry list of books to read. And Namazi had the attention span of a gnat. In fact, Hamid wasn't certain the man could actually read. Casey sent the man to the corner at least half a dozen times, but like a prizefighter, he always got back up.

So it was that Namazi stood centimeters behind Casey, peering around him to see what he was doing. Casey demonstrated the procedure for mounting one of the probes to a vibrational table for the first flight qualification test and stepped backwards into Namazi, sending Namazi reeling, landing flat on his back, and cracking his head hard on a table leg.

Casey turned, fire in his eyes, but seeing the man curled up, holding his head, blood seeping between his fingers, the fire went out and pity replaced it. Hamid's mouth dropped open in astonishment. Telebi would have had the bumbling oaf beaten. Casey leapt into action.

"Ehsan, get a shop towel! Farbod, call the med techs! We'll probably need a stretcher."

He then knelt next to the man. The blow had left him dazed and confused. Casey took him by the shoulders.

"Major! Can you tell me your name?"

Namazi stared in confusion, but mumbled, "Dana Namazi."

"Are you sure?" Casey said, his normal twinkle coming back into his eye. He took the towel from the lab tech.

"I'm pretty sure," Namazi said in reply. "Is it not?"

"No, I think you are right. That is your name. I'm going to put this cloth to your head to help you. While I do that, tell me what you used to do during the summer as a child."

Namazi, wincing at the attention to his wound, rambled about picking fruit in the orchard and wandering the hills by his home.

When the med techs came in, Casey calmly explained, "Major, these men are going to take you to get stitches in your scalp. Maybe staples. Have you ever had those before?"

"No, Mr. Casey. Will it hurt?"

The med techs helped the man onto the stretcher, and Casey continued to speak. "Less than your head wound. You be brave. You probably have a concussion. You can have two weeks off to recover. You can't read or watch TV or think too hard. Lay there and be still. I'm sure that will be very difficult, but I believe you can do it."

"Yes, Mr. Casey."

Hamid saw something he had never imagined from one of the general's staff. He could see adoration in Namazi's eyes. Had the man been so starved of affection that a single act of kindness could completely win him over?

As the med techs took the man out, Hamid came closer to Casey and whispered, "He will probably be destroyed in Telebi's wake if our plan succeeds. Why bother with words of kindness? Won't that make it harder?"

"Perhaps, but if I didn't trust anyone deep among my enemies, I would not have you or Sarosh as my new brothers, now would I?"

Blake, who had overheard, said with his wisest voice, "And if we can win that little goof over, Namazi could be useful. Teletubby may want one of his staff in the flight control center. Instead of sending one of the awful ones that we want dead, we can make sure a harmless one like Namazi gets assigned."

Hamid laughed.

"Blake, you and Casey are so different and yet so alike."

Blake patted Hamid on the shoulder.

"Yes. When Casey met me, he was a sentimental pushover who always tried to help everyone and got walked on relentlessly. I was a ruthless jerk, stomping on people. But when I stomped on him, he gave me mercy and compassion. He made me feel like he loved me despite me being a jerk. Well, he started me on the path to being a better man. Saved my marriage once or twice, for sure. But I've done him a favor, too. I've taught him to have a backbone and stand up for himself. But pitiful whipped puppies like Namazi still make him sentimental."

Casey rolled his eyes. "You weren't ruthless. A jerk? Yes. But you had PTSD. I reminded you of your humanity and harassed you until you got the mental health treatment you needed."

"And that's why my wife bakes him a boysenberry pie every single Thanksgiving, all for him. He's not even allowed to share it."

Casey grinned and patted his belly.

"I never do." He then shouted in Persian, "Alright, enough excitement for one day. Let's get this test started!"

While the general camped out in the bathroom that night, Matt waited for an opportunity. Telebi's wife had a routine. She scolded him for taking too long in the bathroom at 9:30. She sat on the bed calling him names until 9:35. Then she called him something Matt didn't understand, but he assumed was vulgar and went to use the guest bathroom. Clockwork.

At 9:36, Matt slipped into the bedroom, raced to the bed, placed the device from Blake on the frame, and turned it on. He felt no vibration, which was comforting, since infrasound was below human hearing and normal tactile detection. But it induced fear in humans. He'd read about it on the latest phone he'd stolen from an inattentive officer on the general's staff. Elephants' and lions' roars could travel miles because they contained some infrasound components, and that caused fear. Well, this time, the general would experience it. Maybe it would make him see some ghostly images in the corner of his vision if the frequency matched the vibration of his eyeballs. Matt could only hope.

Slipping back out of the bedroom, he went to his room and waited for 10 pm. The general finally exited the bathroom at precisely 10 pm every night. Probably had an alarm. Matt snuck into the hall and listened at their door.

After only a few minutes, Mrs. Telebi spoke. "Firouz, I'm worried. Did the staff turn off the stove?"

"Of course they did, woman. Go to sleep."

A few minutes later, he heard Mrs. Telebi get up. "Something is wrong. I'm going to check it out."

Matt slipped back into his room, then followed Mrs. Telebi at a distance. She seemed tense, but when she reached the kitchen, she relaxed and sat down. Matt made some noise in the hallway and then came out, making his face look groggy.

"Oh, it's you, boy. Why are you up?"

"I'm hungry, Lady Telebi. The general, in his wisdom, does not feed me enough. I am too big, he says."

"Bah, the man is a fool. Eat! Here, I am not so useless as him. I will make you some food."

Matt took a seat in the kitchen, and Mrs. Telebi proceeded to fry some chicken with a variety of spices, rapeseed oil, yogurt, and rice, making a delicious smelling dish.

"Jujeh kabab, though not in kabab form. No time for that for growing boys! You are a tall one. You must eat your poor mother out of house and home."

"Yes, but now I am here, she will save money on food."

Mrs. Telebi's eyes moistened. "I hate that he has taken you from your mother. I told him... But he is not a good man. You know this."

"Why are you married to him?"

She bristled a bit. "He was a good man once, you know. He was. But he became proud. He became hard. And there is no divorce in Iran. Not like in your heathen America."

Matt nodded, pausing as he ate to say, "You are strong to endure him. Thank you for the delicious meal. It is amazing." He then took a last bite, at which the woman's eyes grew wide.

"You eat like there is a famine in the land and you must prepare! My goodness, do you want more?"

"No, Lady Telebi. I am now full. I will be hungry again in the morning, but for now, I am full. It was truly magnificent."

Leaning back, happy to finally be full, he looked at the chessboard on the table. The general played him every night. Matt let him win, though Matt always made it a close thing.

Seeing his gaze, Mrs. Telebi asked, "Do you play?"

"A little, Lady Telebi. A little."

"We should play sometime. I never play my husband. He hates that I always beat him."

A scream sounded from upstairs. Mrs. Telebi walked briskly up the stairs, followed by Matt.

They found the general screaming.

"He has not had a night terror in a long time. I will go in first."

She opened the door and went in, calling Telebi's name. He did not reply but screamed again, then shouted, "No, the blood! The blood is on my hands!"

"You are asleep, you fool! Wake up!"

Matt peered into the room, his eyes adjusting to the dark. The general, half strangled in his own blankets, thrashed like a madman.

"Well, I can do nothing for you, you fat old fool. Defying Allah with liquor. Defying Allah by overeating. You get what you deserve. I will sleep in the guest bedroom." She matched her words by collecting her pillow and leaving the room, shutting the door behind her.

"If he is too loud for you to sleep in your guest room, there is a guest room on the top floor that is quite nice. An excellent view of the grounds. Goodnight, young man. May Allah preserve you."

She headed away, a dignified grace in the face of a cruel, perverse world.

Matt took her up on the top floor guest room, as the general was annoyingly vocal in his terrors.

Two weeks later, with flight qualifications well underway, Namazi returned. As Casey had requested, the flight technicians gave a cheer and Namazi, confused but happy at the positive attention, went straight to his chair in the corner.

"Namazi," Casey called, "we have a job for you. Come over here to this table."

Namazi approached, looking confused, and walked to the table in the center of the room. He took the seat Casey had proffered.

"Feeling alright?" Casey asked. "You don't need more recovery time, do you?"

"No, Mr. Casey. I think I could have come back a few days ago, but I stayed away for two weeks, like you said. I will be more careful to do what you say and not stand right behind you. You are a large man and sent me flying. Not as large as Mr. Blake, who I think is a giant."

"Major, I want you to be our timer." Casey handed over a shiny stopwatch. "You will run the stopwatch. When they yell start, you will start the timer. When they yell stop, you will stop the timer. You will then make a note on this notebook of the time. We are doing a very important round of testing and accurate timekeeping is critical. Can you do this?"

Namazi looked at Casey with excitement.

"You will trust me with this important task?"

Casey felt for the man. Years of abuse in Telebi's office had made him ridiculously easy to manipulate and please.

"Yes, you can do it."

"Thank you, Mr. Casey. I will be very diligent." He then practiced the timer a few times, making sure he knew how it worked. It was a simple timer, not even having lap functions. Tap once to start, once to stop, and once more to reset. Repeat. A child could do it.

Casey patted him on the shoulder and walked away.

Sarosh approached Casey and whispered in English, "Are the tests not measured by internal digital timers?"

"Yes, but why spoil his fun? This does two things. He feels appreciated, thereby feeling loved by us. And we've got him occupied, so he doesn't break something or get stepped on again."

"Very cunning!" Sarosh said with a grin. "Make him love us and he will betray Telebi for us!"

Casey smiled, but inwardly he felt a twinge of guilt. Was he only trying to win Namazi over for his own purposes and not for that man's benefit? Had he done that with Hamid, Sarosh, and all these technicians and engineers? *God, forgive me for self-serving motives in befriending these men. I hope I have moved beyond this and now love them for their own sakes.*

"Alright, commencing radiation testing on probe alpha," an engineer called. "Timer ready?"

An enthusiastic voice called, "Yes!"

"Begin timing."

At the same time, in Telebi's office, the general had a right temper tantrum. He threw everything on his desk to the floor and pulled things out of the drawers. Finally, he told everyone to leave, even Matt, then sat staring out his window. As usual, he didn't even notice Esin.

Esin went to the wet bar to quietly dust the liquor collection. It was a spotless liquor collection after all these months. It also had a very dangerous cocktail of medicines in each bottle. The Turks had told her that giving these to anyone in the doses she was giving them would give them all sorts of mental health issues and reduce their lifespan by years. She'd assured them that was not a concern. Abdul had told her he was both terrified and impressed by her bloodthirsty attitude. She'd just told him, 'You don't mess with a mama bear.'

Telebi pulled out his cell phone and viciously poked at the screen. After a minute, he spoke. "Telebi, authorization code 853421. Put me through to Devon."

Esin memorized the code and then realized she knew the name. That was the NASA traitor! She wished she could hear both sides of the conversation.

"Devon? Telebi. Yes, pleasure to speak to you and all that." A long pause. "Your Persian is pitiful. You can't compare to that Casey fellow. Why, he sounds like my grandfather, and my grandfather was a poet. Loved that man. His wife was an awful shrew."

Esin made a note that Devon spoke Persian, though not very well. Casey would want to know that.

"Yes, yes, I'll get to my point. Can't let an old man wax philosophical? Anyway, we're closing in on finishing flight qualifications. Hamid says it is hard, and we have failed over 100 points already! Is that normal? Oh, so when they said we should take 3 years, they weren't just being lazy? Well, shows what a bit of fear and hard deadlines can do. We'll have this off the ground in only a year."

The general sipped at his drink and listened before speaking. "So, you're suspicious of the quality of their work? I've watched the robotics work. They can pick up objects, they can cut things, and they can weld things. Watched it myself. Well, maybe we Iranians are better engineers and technicians than you thought."

Another long pause.

"No, I don't think we need any more consulting in the near future. This mission has consumed a lot of my budget, and until I get income from NASA and the rest of the world, I won't have more to give you. You've been lobbying your administration to prepare them to rent from us when we have our space station ready to go? Good. When they rent the first berth, then and only then will you get paid your next fee."

What a strange idea. Did Telebi really think that NASA would bow to Iran in this?

He hung up without further discussion, finished off his glass, then looked towards the liquor case, seeing her.

"Excellent. Will you bring me the bottle of whiskey? Oh, you won't know what that is. The brown bottle. Oh, that's not helpful. Umm, the bottle second from the left. Yes, that's the one. Bring me the bottle and a glass. Would you care for one?"

"It is forbidden," she whispered.

"I suppose it is. Any interest in something more? I suppose not. Well, off with you."

Esin left with more excitement than she'd felt in days, a lot more to tell Hamid and team than before.

"Acoustic test 14 complete. That's a wrap."

Hamid clapped along with his men as they celebrated the accomplishment. Flight qualifications were complete and on time, and they'd identified over 200 items to repair. Casey said that was quite impressive, considering that they were going at a ridiculous pace to complete a ridiculously complex project in a ridiculous time frame. He also pointed out that they had skipped a large number of irrelevant tests and it didn't matter if they actually fixed everything, as the mission was not going to actually operate beyond launch day.

Blake sidled up to Hamid.

"Any word from our secret friend about the special package?"

The special package was a virus to wipe every government computer in Iran. Hamid would plant it in critical systems to kill everything as soon as the launch was obviously not taking off as planned.

"Yes," Hamid said with his best conspiratorial smile, "they provided me a jump drive with the special package on it yesterday. It took some iterating on the specs. Apparently, it is a very special package, straight from your NSA, via Turkey. But I can't place it until the five-minute mark. I don't know how I'll do that as I'll be getting on a helicopter."

"I have an idea," Blake said.

"That's not cryptic at all."

"Your sarcasm is getting better. Good job."

Hamid rolled his eyes, but only internally, knowing Blake wouldn't be able to keep the secret long if he didn't show interest in the secret. So he stood stoically and waited.

Not 30 seconds later, Blake said, "We'll give it to Namazi the day before as a 'special mission.'"

Hamid laughed out loud.

"You devil! That's amazing. I love it. But can we trust him?"

"Of course. Casey has been giving him more and more responsibility. He's been positively blooming. The technicians and engineers are even taking to him. He needed an actual job and someone to care for him. He told Casey he will never go back to Telebi if he can help it. I hope he can succeed."

"Think he'll realize the virus is from his jump drive?"

Blake leaned back, hands behind his head. "I'll come up with some story to tell him."

"I'm going to go take a nap," Casey said. "Manuel wants help tonight."

Hamid sighed. He wanted to help Manuel, too. Fusion reactors and engines!

Hamid entered for the private meeting he'd requested with General Telebi. He'd need all his wits to get the general to agree to this. Or so he thought.

The general walked up to him with a frantic look on his face. "Did you hear it? As you were coming in? Did you hear the sound?"

"No sir, I didn't hear any sound."

"The high-pitched sound. It only goes away when other people come in. When I'm alone, it is always there. Always whistling! The boy doesn't hear it! He says he hears nothing! Nothing!" Telebi laughed hysterically for a few seconds.

Hamid suspected this was what Blake had expected from the device he had given Hamid to give to Matt last week. A glance at Matt's face confirmed his suspicions. When asked what it was for, Blake had simply said, 'Terror.' That was enough to make Hamid wash his hands of it. Hamid glanced at Matt, who winked at him. *Allah preserve us, that boy is just like his father.*

The general slumped back in his chair, looking forlorn, but turned his eyes and said, "Alright, on with it."

"Yes, general, as you wish." This brusqueness would normally have thrown him for a loop, but nine months with the Americans had taught him to speak or they'd leave him behind. Conversationally, at least.

"I have asked for no benefits or boons for my work on this project, General Telebi. I have sought no personal favors or advancement. I will not do so, save one thing. I would like the chance to have my family and the families of the leads on my staff to be here on the launch day to see the launch, that they may see what our life's work has led to."

"You don't ask for much, do you? Huh, your loss. If you don't ask, you never get anything. But you have done good work. Why not? But not with the dignitaries. Can't have that.

"No sir, I would have them on a hill of their own where we can watch the proceedings. And I would have them arrive the day before and stay in the empty base barracks."

"Excellent. Go ahead. And if you keep being competent and asking for things, you may make some advancements. You're still a bit squeamish about violence. Once I cure you of that, you'll be ready to advance high."

Hamid bowed, thinking, *You have no idea what I'm capable of.* "Thank you for your benevolence, General Telebi. At your leave?"

Telebi waved him away, and he marched out the door, leaving the general staring out the window. As he reached about 10 feet away, before the door closed, he heard the general yell something vile and heard something heavy bounce off the door.

"The thrusters are working, but the controller is in Russian," Manuel said.

Casey hung his head. "I'll take them to the main lab tomorrow and get Hamid to help. He reads Cyrillic."

Manuel nodded and then stepped over to the rocket plane frame. His job today was to pull wires and land them on the terminals. Without the controller, he couldn't test it.

"I'll work on installing the seats." Casey moved to the jet fighter seats scavenged from an ancient Iranian fighter.

They worked in silence for a few hours. Blake was incapable of working in silence, but Manuel and Casey enjoyed it on occasion. It freed up their minds.

"Is Esin okay?" Manuel asked, startling Casey.

Casey stopped bolting down the seat he was on and looked at Manuel.

"I haven't heard anything to indicate she isn't."

"Sarosh says Kazmi still hasn't been found. Do you think that was her?"

"Well..." Casey hadn't thought about that. The last he'd seen the man, Kazmi had hit him. Had Esin taken revenge on the man?

"Esin has a hardness in her. A hardness that is close to the surface. I've seen it before when your children were bullied."

Casey stepped away from the frame and sat down, elbows on his knees.

"You know, Manuel, you don't often say much, but when you do..."

"Maybe you should pray for her not to break against the evil in this place."

Casey felt tears well up and didn't fight them. He never did with Manuel.

"I will, my friend. I will."

Exhausted from the aftermath of the general's staff meeting, Hamid sat as Telebi and his minion's left the conference room. "Namazi sure has lucked out, getting away from that crew."

"You know," Casey said with a touch of relief in his voice as well, "while we're all here, we might as well do a last discussion of outstanding issues. I haven't heard. Is the flight computer sabotaged?"

"You bet it is," Sarosh enthusiastically confirmed.

Blake gave him a thumbs up. He'd been teaching him American idioms and Sarosh was using them constantly.

"Alright, you tested that it'll switch to our program at the 10 second mark?" Casey opened his notebook to document their discussion.

Ever enthusiastic, Sarosh nodded with a giant grin on his face. "Yes. It was super easy."

"Barely an inconvenience," Blake said, chuckling to himself.

Casey raised an eyebrow at Blake, who seemed highly amused at his joke, though Casey didn't get it.

"And Manuel, they haven't discovered the code to lock out the flight controllers and reroute the launch?"

"They'll never find it." Manuel smirked. "It's so deep they would have to reinvent binary to find it."

"I assume that is some kind of uber nerd boast," Casey said with a chuckle. "Alright, and the dignitaries are all still scheduled? We'll have enough helicopters?"

"Yes," Hamid confirmed. "The number has continued to climb. I had to add a second grandstand down the hill slightly."

"So, what are we missing? We have 6 weeks. What have we forgotten?"

"Roof missiles?" Blake asked.

"Still out, as far as I have discovered," Hamid said with relief. "The programming is Russian, and their IT support has been less than stellar."

"More like non-existent, I'd suspect," Blake said.

"It helps that they assigned me to liaison with the Russians on the repairs," Sarosh bragged.

"You speak Russian?" Manuel asked, perking up.

"Not a word." Sarosh stood there, as proud of ignorance as only an acolyte of Blake could be.

"The general still intends to leave us here for the launch?" Casey asked, ignoring Blake's laughter.

"Yes, he wants all glory for the Iranians," Hamid said, rolling his eyes.

"Well, that means the rocket plane is still a go. You all as terrified and yet excited as I am about flying an untested fusion powered rocket plane out of the roof of a secret Iranian research facility?"

"Hah!" Blake shouted. "Are you saying it that way to convince yourself we're not insane?"

"Yes."

"And the spy is certain they can get Matt on your helicopter?" Manuel asked, getting them back on track.

"Yes, no change," Hamid said. "You all worry too much. We are scientists and engineers. When everything goes wrong, we will improvise."

"And that is why you cannot grow plums on your family farm."

Major Ali sat down, terrified, as Telebi fumed, then took a sip of his drink.

Matt put a hand over his mouth to cover his smirk. Major Ali was in trouble.

"You're saying my soil is too alkaline for plums?"

"Yes, sir."

Telebi threw a pencil at the major, shouting, "Then make it acidic!"

"That's not how soil works, sir. The minerals in your soil themselves are leaching alkalinity into the ground. We'd have to dig down deep and replace the ground itself to make the soil match."

The general fumed. "Who told you this nonsense?"

"An arborist, sir."

"What in the world is an arborist?" the general asked.

"A tree scientist, I believe," Major Ali said.

"You believe?" the general hissed.

"Well, I have not looked up the word to find out its meaning, sir. But they study trees, I think."

"You think?" the general said, now sounding dangerous.

"Yes, sir."

Telebi sagged back, anger visibly bleeding from him. "Bah, you're not worth my trouble."

Matt smiled. The drugs his mother was giving Telebi were working nicely.

"Now, on to my calendar," Telebi continued. "Mr. Smith confirmed he'll arrive on site at noon, three days before launch. I will have no appointments after noon that day. Period."

Matt's stomach lurched.

"If anyone interrupts me, they will become Mr. Smith's newest plaything."

Not if my super-spy mom and I can help it.

###

They completed rework on the rocket almost ten days early, meaning they could mount the payload to the rocket early. Casey was jealous of Hamid. Telebi would not relent to allow any of the Americans to visit the rocket assembly building, so Hamid was there with his phone streaming video to Sarosh's phone, which was being cast to a computer monitor.

"Here is the mounting assembly for the second stage," Hamid said. "Visually, it looks ready for mounting the payload."

"I know they tested the crawler when they put the second stage on it," Manuel asked, "but when was it last checked?"

Hamid's voice rang tinny over the speakers. "It has had rotating checks by your schedule, Manuel. We'll be able to test it when we do the rehearsal in two weeks."

The camera panned up. "The payload is approaching now."

Sarosh covered the mic on the phone and leaned over to them. "When will the... what is the word in English? The covering? When will it go over it?"

"The fairing will be mounted last," Casey explained.

They watched with excitement as the technicians lowered the payload to mate up with the payload adapter on the rocket. When it was lowered into place, the technicians quickly put bolts, washers, and nuts in place and secured the assembly in position. Casey and team shook hands and slapped each other on the back in their excitement.

"Why do we need weeks to do this last part?" Sarosh asked. "Isn't it ready to go now?"

"We'll be doing checks on every bolt, nut, and washer," Blake explained. "We'll be checking every little thing to make sure we did it right. The mountings need to be within micrometers of ideal or it can all go badly. It takes days to do everything correctly. The rocket, both stages, was already built when we started, so they went through their tests all year long. The weeks we have left are hardly enough time for this, but we'll make it work."

"Looks great, Hamid," Casey called. "Wish we were there to turn a wrench with you."

###

Esin,

Do you know how bitter a taste I had in my mouth as I watched my payload mounted on a doomed rocket? How angry it made me to know that because of wicked men like Telebi, my system was doomed to die a fiery death? I don't know how we did it, but we took our unqualified system and we built it and flight qualified it in a year. We cut a lot of corners. We used best judgment and made guesses at times. But we got lucky. Our system passed the important flight qualifications. I didn't fake those. This system worked. And in less than a month, I have to watch it burn. Better lucky than good? Best to be both, and I have the best team ever.

I suppose I sound bitter. I feel bitter. I will have to process these emotions. I will have to find peace with my life's work becoming ash. I suppose I can take solace that Manuel's new design will be able to go to and from an asteroid, bringing it along, with no refueling. But just because you have a new Ferrari doesn't mean you don't still love the 25-year-old Toyota pickup truck you drove in high school. This mission is my pickup truck. That truck died when I went to college. This mission will die so I can return home. That's a worthwhile sacrifice. But it's still bittersweet.

Love,
Casey

Hamid walked into the construction lab to hear Blake's near deafening laugh and see Casey smiling amused but disapprovingly at Sarosh.

"Now what?"

Blake slapped the table.

"Sarosh, tell it again to Hamid!"

Hamid, who had jumped a bit at the slap, sat and turned expectantly to Sarosh, who looked embarrassed but pleased.

"It is only a small prank," began Sarosh.

Hamid buried his face in his hands.

"Should I be expecting a call from the general? The shower in the staff bathroom is still green!"

"Matt helped on that," Sarosh bragged. "Our finest work."

"Until now!" Blake bellowed.

Sarosh leaned in and spoke loud enough for Hamid and associates to hear.

"I learned of an amazing prank from Blake, whose grandfather taught it to him. I took a small nail, and I bent it around the metal screens at the general's house. It has to be real metal, not those flimsy new screens like most new homes. I then tied a long carpet string to the nail, and I unreeled it as I went into the trees by his house, up the hill slightly. I then took some rosin, like for a violin, and coated part at the end. I pulled it taut and played it like a violin. The string did not make much sound, but the metal screens vibrated and every window in the house screamed like a thousand screaming cats!"

Hamid sat with mouth agape. The general at his own residence? Sarosh was crazy!

"I did this once, 2 weeks ago, then left the string attached, planning to play it again. I came back a week later, but it was beyond my dreams. Not only was it still there, but every time the wind sighed at the right speed, the windows screamed! Matt says that the general abandoned his home yesterday. His wife moved back to the villa. The general slept in the bed in the staff office and Matt slept in the guard office. And yesterday I found out that no one will go to his screaming house, for they say it is haunted!"

Hamid felt something in him shift. The fear of Telebi withered and died in that moment, and the seed of understanding of how Blake and Casey thought took root. He laughed. He laughed an honest, deep chested, fully invested laugh for the first time in many years. He laughed until tears came to his eyes and then laughed at the look on his staff's face, seeing him overtaken by mirth.

Sarosh spoke with a laugh to Blake and Casey.

"You know how I said the torture cleaned off his true personality? I take that back. I think we see him most truly now."

When the laughs finally subsided, Hamid accepted a tissue from Blake, wiped his eyes, and spoke.

"No wonder he's been so tired lately. He has also been terrorizing his staff."

Settling back, he looked at his hands and then smiled mischievously at the group.

"What other pranks have you pulled on him? Any we can do these last two weeks?"

###

Climbing into the burrow in the grove, Esin pulled out the satellite phone and made her call. She heard a familiar voice and, after security checks, spoke with a broad smile on her face.

"Hello Abdul. How's your wife? You've been married 2 months now?"

"We are very blessed. She is pregnant!"

"That's wonderful! I'm glad you could finally marry her."

"Yes, getting shot had its benefits. Now, what is your report?"

"Telebi has approved launch. One day early."

"Alright, we'll move our timelines up."

"To confirm, you'll have fighters patrolling close to Urmia to escort their rocket plane and Hamid's fleet of helicopters over the border."

"Yes. You'll be on one of those helicopters."

"If my husband is safe, I will be in a helicopter."

Abdul sighed.

"My lady, the Father of Cheer will escape, but he will never forgive me if you are not there at his return."

Esin ignored this.

"And the pilots?"

"We will begin moving them across the border three days before launch. There is a cave in the countryside our agents have stocked with food and bedding. The hiding places are dug next to the helipads?"

"Yes. I've inspected them myself. The helipad is enormous. This is going to be quite impressive. Hamid has insisted that all helicopters arrive early so we can refuel them for safe return trips."

"And the Russian?"

"I have a plan. I will handle him."

"You won't take any unnecessary risks?"

Esin smiled. "Not a one."

"Excellent. I think things are well in hand. We will talk again as scheduled."

"Confirmed. Tell the wife congratulations from me."

Abdul's voice sounded excited.

"Oh, I most definitely will."

Esin sat in disguise in the general's office not long before lunch, chatting with Telebi amicably. A steady prayer that her plan would work filled her mind.

Telebi spoke with a leering attention.

"I am shocked that the late colonel never told me of his son! You are such a beautiful young man. I wish I had known. I would have made your acquaintance sooner."

Esin felt nauseated but forced herself to speak on. False nose, eyebrows, and mustache and months of practice with makeup and she still wasn't convinced of her disguise, but Telebi had no problem believing she was the effeminate son of a lately deceased friend. The outfit of a rich Iranian young man helped.

"Yes, General Telebi, sir. My father spoke highly of you and said you had a fondness for young men with my particular... affliction."

Telebi continued to leer.

"Yes, I most definitely do. But this is most fortunate timing! Another dear friend is arriving in only a few minutes. He is here to do work on making a video with the Americans. It will be positively breathtaking work. Would you care to stay? It is gruesome and magnificent."

Esin wanted to vomit. "Why, that sounds positively dreadful. I would love it!"

The moment lingered, and she desperately looked for something to keep the conversation going while they waited.

"I see you play chess. Are you in the middle of a game?"

"Yes, I play that young man that I sent for lunch with my secretary. He's quite good, though not as good as me."

Telebi oozed smugness, which galled Esin, knowing her son was throwing the games.

Mercifully, the door burst open and Telebi and Esin rose.

"My dear friend, I am so pleased to see you again!" cried the false smile of Mr. Smith. "And you have a friend! Why, what a beautiful young man! I could use a face like yours in my videos. But where is the young American boy? I heard he is quite the giant, like his delightful father!"

Esin stood and retreated to the general's display table.

"I sent the boy to gather lunch," Telebi said. "He will be back in a few minutes, I'm sure."

Esin knew he'd be back in a few minutes, so she acted on the instant. As usual, the general had set his antique pistol down on the display table first thing as he arrived each morning. She picked it up.

"Well, sir, we must get right to things," Mr. Smith said. "I wish I could stay forever, but I only have today and tomorrow. Must we eat or shall we get right to it?"

Esin stepped forward, took careful aim, and fired three rapid shots into Mr. Smith's chest and one into his head. He dropped like a bowling ball to the ground. She turned and saw the general's shocked face and before he could register what she had done, she fired into his shoulder; her aim true as she hit him where he hopefully wouldn't bleed out. He needed to live to through the launch. He dropped to the floor. She headed over to hit him, but he was already unconscious from shock before he hit. She panicked but saw him breathing. *I hope those medications and his liquor habit don't kill him, despite my excellent aim.*

She then used the last bullets to break the general's window. She used the end table to make a person sized hole in the window, producing her false 'escape' route.

Praying with gratitude that the general's office was soundproofed and with hopes that the rest of her plan would work as well, she rushed to the door and entered the secretary's office. Matt had dragged the secretary along to help him retrieve the food, so she met no one as she raced to beat their return. She tossed the pistol on the desk, tore off her mustache, nose, and eyebrows and stuffed them into a pocket. She then slipped her cleaning lady robes over her form, put on her headscarf and veil, and sat down on the floor next to the door inside the general's office.

Not a few moments later, the outer door opened. Matt, the secretary, and some of the staff hurried into the outer office and straight into the general's office, Matt pushing a lunch on a cart with a floor length cloth covering it. As planned, he stopped inside the general's door and gasped melodramatically as she climbed into the empty space hidden by the cloth. He pulled the cart back out the door and set it to the side in the secretary's office. The secretary screamed and ran to the general, the staff following. Telebi, who was feebly coughing, had come to and was cursing weakly. As soon as Matt found only himself and his mother in the outer office, he tapped on the frame of the cart. She rolled out and stood, straightening her clothes.

"Fancy meeting you here, mother," Matt said in a cheesy British accent.

"Quite fancy," she replied in an equally cheesy accent. "Why, I haven't seen you since the last time I saw you."

"Is that so?" he said as medics came running past them into the office. "I don't believe I've seen you since I last saw you either."

"Well, all the more reason to catch up," she replied, ignoring the shouting in the general's office and in the office outside. "Care for a spot of tea? We can discuss the cricket scores."

They heard a helicopter through the broken window and glanced into the office to see the medics lift the general onto a stretcher.

"Quite, quite," Matt said. "I love cricket. Almost as much as I love tea. Cause I'm British."

As the general rolled past them, he looked at Esin and weakly gasped, "Clean up my office while I'm gone!"

They were left alone again as the door out of the secretary's office clicked shut.

Esin stared at Matt, whose face reflected her own disgust at the general.

"We did it," Matt said in a quiet, slightly rattled voice. "How did you do it?"

"Matt, he is the fourth man I have killed in my life. I am getting far too adept at this."

Matt took a step back in shock, so she explained.

"There was the man in the refugee camp, the man who nearly killed my fellow spy, the man who was going to kill your father, and now this man. No big deal. I did what I had to."

Matt sat back, a look of profound respect coming over his face.

"Mom, you are a bonified super spy!"

Esin smiled sadly under her veil. "I am a mamma bear. No one threatens my family."

A moment later, two men came struggling out of the general's office into the outer office, lugging a body bag. The remains of Mr. Smith. Matt, ever the gallant hero, approached them.

"Gentlemen, may I interest you in using this food cart? I can clear the food off and you can put the body on it for easy carrying."

The men nodded appreciatively, and Esin and Matt cleared the food and cloth off, leaving the bare metal cart. They had removed the body from the room when the general's chief guard came out of the general's office.

"I must ask you both questions. Were either of you in the room when this happened?"

"No sir," Matt said, "I had gone to get lunch for the general and his guests." He gestured towards the food.

"And I was cleaning the staff offices outside," Esin said. "Sir, the general told me to cleanup as they took him out. Do you want me to start?"

"Fine, fine, we should clean up," the guard said with annoyance and turned to Matt. "Young man, did you see the person's face?"

"Yes sir, short, pretty young man. Moderately large nose. Thick eyebrows and a mustache like yours."

"Neither of you saw this person leaving the office?"

They both shook their heads.

The guard swore, shouting as he stormed out of the secretary's office. "The man is a ghost, apparently! No one saw him leave at all and the security cameras have been broken for a week!"

Esin smiled behind her veil at Sarosh's handiwork at breaking the security cameras. She glanced into the general's office. "Empty. Time for the cleanup crew."

She went to his phone and called the cleaning office number. After several minutes of asking, pleading, begging, and finally threatening, they agreed to send her four women to help with the cleanup efforts.

She went to the table where she'd left the pistol and found it still there, untouched. So, she swiftly took it apart, cleaned it with alcohol wipes, and put it back together. She took a thin dagger from the general's display stand and stuck it in the barrel.

"Mom, what are you doing?"

She did her best to bend the barrel, then handed it to Matt. "Bend it. Only a little."

Matt smiled, torqued it until the barrel groaned audibly. He looked down the barrel and smiled. "That'll never shoot straight again."

Esin took both items, then returned them to their proper place and contemplated cleaning the room with disgust.

Matt pointed to the secretary's desk. "That was terrible, but I'm ravenous. Is it wrong to eat the lunch?"

"No, you're a growing boy. You go ahead and eat. I'm not hungry."

"What's going on?" Casey peered out the door of their dormitory. People were running every which way and the guard who had marched them back from the lab was preventing them from leaving.

The guard was also rather noncommunicative.

Casey shut the door. "Manuel, use our back door and see if you can figure out what is going on?"

"Already on it. I'm in the general's chat account." Manuel paused to read. "He's getting a lot of messages wishing him a speedy recovery. Is this translation right?"

Manuel held up his laptop and Casey walked over to verify the Persian.

"Yup."

"Well, launch is in three days," Blake said. "We don't have time for anything to go wrong. I only came down to get more welding supplies. I still have a good two days of welding to get our rocket ready for escape."

The day lingered on with them trapped in their room. Not a soul came in and they were just glad they had their laptops.

Casey felt the familiar throes of panic rise. Something happened to Telebi and now they were trapped in their room, unable to finish their escape plan, and he, his son, his friends, and probably his wife, were all going to die.

What were their options? Had they found something?

He paced. Pacing relieved a bit of the nervous tension he was experiencing. He paced as there was no choice. After all this effort, they would fail in their final stretch.

Dinner time rolled around and Blake was verbally berating the guard for not providing them food.

"How do you say goat-faced again?"

Casey gave him the phrase and Blake called the man a variation of the insult that made the guard's eyes widen in surprise.

Sarosh shoved the guard aside and entered the room, shutting the door in the surprised guard's face.

"You're not to be let out until after launch." Sarosh began pacing.

"But... We have to get out!" Blake roared. "I still have a day's welding to do. I can't optimize the aerodynamics until I have the ailerons correct, and the nose isn't even attached!"

"Then let me do it." Sarosh grabbed his hero by the shoulders. "You've taught me how to weld. I'll get it ready."

Casey, Blake, and Manuel looked at each other, as they always did in times of stress. What else could they do but trust him?

Blake spoke in his most dangerous growl. "Alright, here's what you've got to do."

Matt sighed as he gave the general some knock-off gelatin pudding, having to endure Teletubby yelling at the doctor.

"Do I sound unable to go? I feel fine. Better than I have in months! Release me. I have a launch in two days that I have to be at!"

The doctor bowed his head and said, "Please give me 24 more hours. I will release you tomorrow."

"Sir, you wouldn't want to overdo it," Matt said. "The assassin obviously wanted you dead. Don't give him the satisfaction."

The general glared at Matt, then smiled.

"The boy is right. Okay, one more day. But I will leave tomorrow!"

Matt smiled, thinking, *He'd better. I need to be at that launch, too.*

"Father, mother! Welcome to Urmia Research Center!"

Hamid's mother hugged him and promptly chided him, "Couldn't be spared long enough to meet us at the airport?"

"No, mother, tomorrow is launch day. It is only by the grace of Allah I can spare the time to have dinner with you tonight. Now come, see your grandchildren. They have grown so much."

The feast that night, including Iranian, Spanish, and American delicacies (meaning Americanized foods from all over the world), was delightful, and Hamid was only embarrassed by Sarosh a few times as they told stories about him to his family.

"And then I hit him square on the head with one of the rolls!" Sarosh said, finishing the story.

"I like that story almost as much as the flies with strings," his father said. "Hamid, my son, you have had a very busy year!"

The party was wonderful, including all of his research and construction staff, his family, the Americans, and even the facility cleaning staff. They ate for well over two hours, with singing and toasts throughout. With the addition of over 400 family members from the 36 key personnel, this was a giant party. Hamid hoped they would be as enthusiastic about joining them in their escape as about the launch. He knew some would be furious, but in the end, his government's attempt at space would be crippled.

As the feast concluded, Hamid gave instructions to the staff and their families.

"To all our families, you will meet at the front gate no later than 6 am to be taken to your viewing site. As they say in Latin, per aspera ad astra. Through difficulties to the stars!"

Esin,

This is my last entry. I'm giving this notebook to Hamid so I can make sure you get it if I am delayed. These next few hours will decide every-thing. There is no more uncertainty. There is no more doubt. There is only action. The plan is in place, the rocket is on the pad, and the only option left is to launch. No matter what happens, I will be yours for all eternity and I praise the knowledge that you will be mine.

Love,

Casey

T-minus 6 hours

Walking with an excess of energy into the upper floor lab, Casey broke into a huge smile when he saw Hamid there waiting. Blake and Manuel were a few minutes behind, as they were tying up the guard so no one would find him for at least the next six hours. Sarosh had his radio to run interference. It was just Casey and Hamid in the room.

Casey marched over and fake saluted. "It has been a pleasure being kidnapped by you." He winked at Hamid.

"Of all the people I could have kidnapped, thank Allah it was you three," Hamid said with an easy smile.

Casey then wrapped Hamid in a bear hug, slapping him on the back vigorously. Hamid returned the gesture.

"Please give this to my wife when you see her," Casey said as he pulled out his private notebook and handed it to Hamid. "In case I am delayed."

"I will do so," Hamid said solemnly, taking the notebook reverently and putting it in his coat pocket. "But you will be there. Inshallah. But I have a letter for you, too. It is from our spy."

Casey's eyes brightened, and he took the letter solemnly, eager to read it.

"See you in Turkey," Hamid said.

"See you in Turkey," Casey agreed.

Hamid left then, and Casey opened the letter.

Patiently, the bluebird and the hummingbird waited, their love enduring beyond the pain of separation and captivity. And the bluebird burst his bands, and the hummingbird joined his flight, and their son rose with them, and they and all the captives left the owl's nest, the force of their departure burning the owl and his nest to ash.

Love,

The Hummingbird

Casey smiled fondly, folding the note carefully into his laptop bag. Somehow, they all still had their laptops and laptop bags from that conference a year ago, though they would not try to take their clothes on this flight. Medications, laptops, and themselves. That was it.

Blake and Manuel came sauntering in a few minutes later.

"Hamid caught us on the way out," Blake said. "It's weird saying goodbye when you know you're going to see him in a bit over 6 hours. But it feels all dramatic and the like. Just cause we're going up in an experimental rocket and blowing up a top secret military base along the way... I guess that's why it's so dramatic. Now, where's Sarosh? I had a notebook to give him so he could give it to my wife, in case."

"I get it. He's over there. But we'll make it, Blake."

"I know, Casey. I know. But just in case." Blake mused for a moment. "You know what I would regret most if we die?"

"What's that?" Casey asked.

"Every time you guys made me eat healthy food. There is a lot of bacon I have not enjoyed because of you two!"

Manuel dropped his head into both of his hands and groaned.

"Yes, that is normal in the countdown sequence." Casey spoke to the flight director calmly and reassuringly while doing the last checks on his own rocket. "Correct. You are doing fine. I'm monitoring with you in real time. I appreciate that you wish I was there, but you have this in hand. Trust me, I recommended you to Hamid for this on purpose. Now, take a few breaths. Good. I'll talk to you when you need me."

Blake lowered his multimeter to look at Casey. "Was that the flight director?"

"Yes, I feel so bad for him. He is the only one we can't take with us, though we haven't taught him anything not on the internet. He has talent, though. He absorbed everything I taught him like a sponge. Hopefully, I taught him enough to get through countdown. Then it's all down to Manuel's coding."

"Did you get this from a giant?" Manuel called, swimming in his flight suit acquired by Esin through her Turkish friends.

"That one might be mine," Blake said with a laugh. "Let me check. Yep." He tossed a flight suit across the room. "This one is yours."

"Do you think the mission control team will be okay?" Manuel asked.

"If our plan works at all," Blake laughed, "I think they'll be hunky dory."

Manuel raised an eyebrow.

"What is this word, hunky dory?"

"You've been in the U.S. since college and never heard the word 'hunky dory?'" Blake put his hand to his chest with mock horror.

"Blake, that word was old when our grandparents were kids," Casey countered. He turned to face Manuel. "Don't worry, Manuel. Blake is a crotchety old man and hasn't updated his slang since 1943."

"I'm only 5 years older than you two, you know," Blake countered.

Casey attempted to appear serious as he replied with great solemnity, "And what a difference 5 years can make."

"I went through a final systems check," Sarosh said, joining them. "Reactors are nominal. Ion engines are nominal. Everything is go for flight."

"Sarosh," Blake frowned, "I already did all that 20 minutes ago! You should have left to go to the extraction site."

"I worry about you, Blake. You are the father I never had. I must take care of you. You are my father and my friend."

Showing what a big teddy bear he was, Blake sniffed once, eyes glistening, then stepped over and scooped Sarosh in a giant hug, picking him up off his feet.

"Blake," a strangled voice whispered, "if you murder me now, how will I come to America and get my blonde wife?"

They all laughed, and Blake set Sarosh down, wiping his eyes. Manuel was openly crying, and Casey was tearing up.

"You're all a bunch of babies," Blake said, getting his crying under control, but grinning. "I never knew one of the things missing in my life was a 20-year-old Iranian with bad breath."

Sarosh smiled, eyes welling with his own tears. "Well, I'd best get to the extraction point. You'd better survive this flight."

T-minus 2 hours

As they waited at the helipad, Telebi, in a foul mood, ranted. As usual. Hamid ignored 95% of it but perked up when Telebi mentioned something Hamid had hoped to hear.

"And we finally found the source of the smell in my office! Some stupid mouse died under the carpet! One of my oafish staff must have stepped on it, and they didn't mention they'd stepped on something lumpy. The cleaning staff says it will take a week to air the place out! It's been driving me mad for a week already!"

Hamid exulted inside. No wonder Sarosh loved pulling pranks. He wished he'd started months ago. It had been simplicity itself tossing the mouse under the edge of the carpet while Telebi stared out the window at their meeting almost two weeks ago. The man was so dramatic, always going for the backlit look as he stared out over the compound. What a loon.

The Ayatollah was the last to arrive. Hamid bowed deeply next to Telebi as the older man descended from his massive helicopter, accompanied by the highest-ranking ayatollahs and clerics in the country.

The Ayatollah glared down at them. "General Telebi, I hope this is all you have made it out to be."

"Rahbar, I am humbled by your presence and believe that this will be all I have said and more."

"It better. Now, I understand there is a banquet."

"Yes, Rahbar, a car is waiting for you."

"That is a large rocket. The grandstand looks very close. Is it safe?"

Hamid lied with confidence now.

"Rahbar, it is the same distance as the president and other dignitaries sat when they watched the Apollo missions."

The comparison had its effect.

"Ah, very good. I will go." The man walked away. He appeared arrogantly confident in his power, driving with Telebi to the pavilion.

As soon as they were gone, Hamid looked about and saw Sarosh stood at the edge of the helipad. Hamid signaled him and Sarosh gestured to the dignitaries' pilots, gathering them to take to the general staff viewing platform. The pilots appeared as excited to see the launch as anyone, so they went freely. Once complete, Sarosh would begin loading all the families onto the helicopters for their 'private' viewing party and secure the Ayatollah's own helicopter for their departure. Cell phone jammers would prevent any panicked calls from family as they loaded onto the helicopters. Sarosh had made them under Blake's tutelage.

Once the three vans containing the pilots were all gone, Hamid waved both hands above his head. Out of the ground popped seventeen pilots, dressed identically to the Iranian pilots he'd sent off to view things. They swiftly moved to the helicopters and did pre-flight checks and top off fuel reserves.

Hamid smiled, adrenaline pumping, and headed to his car to go to the pavilion, where Telebi expected him to mingle, all the while asking himself what would go wrong first.

Hamid had never wished that he drank more than that morning. In the last hour, he had greeted every single general, member of the Majles, the Guardian Council, and most other top level government officials that had come. He knew he should feel shock that they were so arrogant as to allow the entirety of the heads of government and the military to be in one place, but if Casey had taught him anything, it was to not be shocked by the level of stupidity to which a government could climb. They milled about, eating and drinking in the temporary building Hamid had had built for the dignitaries. They would go to their seats to watch the launch 50 meters away on the grandstands he'd had built. The rocket stood beckoning, far too close for safety, but exactly as far as Telebi wanted to be. Everyone bought his statement that this was how close-up the Americans were when they watched their launches. Maybe he secretly wanted it to explode and decapitate the government.

Hamid kept glancing at his watch. He needed to head to the helipad soon. His family was probably very confused why they were being loaded into helicopters. They would know soon enough why that was a good thing.

General Telebi strutted about like a peacock, dragging Hamid from group to group, bragging about how he had nurtured this project and how he had guided Hamid's success each step of the way. It was nauseating.

"But do you think this will actually work?" one politician asked.

General Telebi, acting slightly offended, replied with head held high. "Of course! The rocket is the finest we have ever produced!"

"Then where are the Americans you used to design it? Should they not be here to accept praise or punishment at the end?"

Hamid thought, *Oh. This is where things go wrong.*

Telebi, slightly drunk, said, "You are right." He pulled out his phone, called the guards at the base, and ordered them to bring the Americans down.

Hamid pulled his phone and texted Sarosh, hoping he could get the message to the Americans before it was too late.

T-minus 50 minutes

Esin waited near the helipad in a truck she had commandeered. Her gut told her that if anything went wrong, it would be here. Her pocket suddenly vibrated, and she pulled the phone from Sarosh out, answering with surprise as he'd never called her before.

"Yes?"

She listened to him speak for 15 seconds, realizing it was not here that the trouble was coming, and replied. "On my way."

T-minus 35 minutes

Manuel buckled himself in, then tightened his straps.

"You know, I'm glad we don't have to get strapped in like in the Apollo missions. Remember in Apollo 13, the guys standing on their shoulders, shoving things down. But these fancy flight suits Hamid got for us are so compact it's not much worse than wearing a tuxedo."

Blake, who was not having an easy time strapping himself in, cursed at his belt in Persian.

"Manuel," Casey said, "giants like Blake and, to a lesser extent, myself, do not have the same experience getting buckled in that you do. I expect Blake may need some help. Somehow, he has gained weight in our captivity."

Blake cursed further at this, then made a karate-like yell before finally succeeding at buckling his belt. He then groaned and said simply, "Ow."

Casey stood in his seat, ready to close the canopy, when the door rattled, then a key sounded in the lock. When that didn't work, they heard a single shot. The door opened to reveal two of the Revolutionary Guard entering, rifles at the ready.

"I didn't think that worked on locks," Blake said.

Casey turned, faced the new entrants, and spoke in a friendly tone.

"Hello gentlemen, how can we help you?"

The men ogled the space plane, positioned and ready under a giant hole leading to the observatory.

"The general has invited you to join him at the gala. He wants to show you off. But I think he will want to see this far more. You will come with us." They pointed their rifles at Casey and stepped into a convenient position to cover all three of them.

Casey watched as a silent figure crept in the open door. One of the cleaning ladies, but moving with abnormal stealth and care. Their backs to her, the guards were unaware as she glanced around the room, then sprinted to the workbench where Manuel kept his original prototype, modified to resemble a gun. She hefted it, holding it with uncertainty.

"Yes, that is an honor," Casey said. "These two will need to unstrap." He stepped down the ladder as slowly as he felt he could get away with. In English he said, "The big yellow switch, quick on/off."

She ran toward the men, getting Casey and the ship out of the line of fire, then flipped the yellow switch on and off before they had realized she was there. A bright light appeared a few feet behind the men, and the gun shoved Esin back, nearly off her feet.

The guards turned, but their movements rapidly became uncertain. They stood for a few heartbeats, unmoving, then fell to the ground, blood beginning to pour from their eyes, nose, mouth, and ears. Otherwise, there was not a mark on them, though Casey knew the bodies were already falling apart from the ridiculous numbers of helium nuclei that had torn through them, producing microscopic rips through their organs.

Casey stared for a heartbeat, then ran to the woman who set the prototype down on the table with a look of the same horror he felt. She sat down in apparent exhaustion.

"You turned it into a death ray and didn't tell me!" Blake shouted with annoyance.

"You would have insisted on playing with it!" Manuel protested. "It's not a lot of radiation, but it's non-zero. Some gamma and the like. We're probably okay, though I think we should get checked out before too long."

"I can't undo these stupid straps!" Blake replied.

Casey stood next to Esin, uncovered her face, then kissed her gently. "You saved us."

"And strained every muscle in my body doing it," Esin groaned.

"How did you plan to get out of here? We don't have much time."

Casey stood and helped her climb to her feet.

"I have a truck," Esin said. "It's only a 10-minute drive to my extraction point. As much as I want to stand here and make out with you, I'd better go."

"Is that Esin!?" Blake shouted, still trapped by his straps. "How in the world? Okay, I need an explanation."

Casey ran her to the door, ignoring the smell of seared flesh and burning clothing, rejoicing in holding Esin's hand once more.

Esin kissed him briefly, then ran through the door shouting, "See you soon! And seal this door!"

Blake swore creatively, then shouted to Casey, "Get your butt over here and explain!"

"As soon as I use Manuel's toy to weld the door shut. Manuel, how do I turn down the power? I need it to be hot and not bake me with radiation or throw me across the room."

Manuel explained, and Casey sealed the door shut.

"We almost forgot to do something about this death ray. We can't leave it in case the building survives."

"Press the red button twice, the green button twice, then flip the switch four times. Then toss it into the corner and get in here."

Casey did so, tossed it in the corner, then climbed into the ship, closing the canopy. A bright flash filled the room and Manuel said, "And it's destroyed."

"That was rather small, considering it is a death ray!" Casey said. "Wouldn't it explode?"

"This is the real world, Casey," Manuel said. "The flash was from the containment failing. The fuel is merely water."

"So, no boom?" Casey asked with a frown.

"No boom," Manuel said, patting him on the leg, which was all he could reach.

"Alright, start at the top," Blake ordered. "How long has Esin been here?"

"Not now. We have less than 20 minutes. Let's do a final check. Weird to be skipping so much, but we aren't going to space."

Casey began the checklist, with Manuel or Blake confirming.

"Engines?"

Manuel called, "Go."

"Navigation?"

"Also go," Manuel stated.

"EECOM is go, though without A/C on this beast, does the 'environmental' part even apply?" He sighed, then continued. "Control?"

Blake grunted, "Go."

Casey tested the broadband radio. "Looks like external communications are a go."

They continued to do checks until Manuel called, "T-minus 12 minutes to launch."

Blake growled. "We have 10 minutes before we start take off sequences. Now talk."

T-minus 12 minutes

Hamid finally saw a chance for him and Matt to escape when Telebi went to the restroom. He finished the conversation with the dignitary and then excused himself, implying a need for the restroom as well, and left the grandstands, Matt following. They headed to the back of the structure and sprinted out the doors towards the parking lot. With launch only ten minutes away, all the service staff had left, as he had instructed them most assiduously. They were barely going to make it up the hill to the helipad before the fireworks began.

Outside the north door, a woman from the cleaning staff was waiting in a truck. In English, she said, "Let's go, Mr. Jabiri. You're cutting it close."

Nervous, Hamid asked, "Who are you?"

Matt smiled and said, "That's my mom!" He hopped into the middle seat of the truck.

"I am Esin Scarlett, Casey's wife. I infiltrated the base. I've been sending you intel for months. It's time for us to bug out."

Hamid grinned foolishly and climbed in next to Matt, relief and adrenaline causing him to laugh out loud, nose wrinkling at the smell of smoke. She floored it, sending them careening to the helipad. "Sarosh said he got someone to take care of the guards. I assume he meant you?"

"Yes. They're taken care of. And when I told him my success, he mentioned you were late, so I came to give you a ride."

"How long has he known how to reach you?"

"Months, Hamid. He's a smart one. But he agreed I needed to stay anonymous."

"Mrs. Scarlett, I feel like I have known you for a year. Your husband sings your praises to the skies, and it is clear he has not exaggerated. Speaking of him, I have a notebook to give you. He wanted you to have it."

T-minus 9 minutes

General Telebi walked out of the bathroom and saw Hamid and Matt as they sprinted into the parking lot. His drug-addled mind struggled with the implications but finally caught up. Betrayal broke through his torpor. He trotted as fast as he could out the back of the building, away from the dignitaries, and to his car. He watched Hamid drive up towards the helipad. Checking that his antique pistol was present, he climbed in and grabbed his encrypted radio.

"Escort flight, this is General Telebi. If you see any abnormalities in the sky besides our rocket, shoot it down."

"Copy that."

Namazi felt so excited he could barely sit still. The Father of Cheer had given him a critically important mission. If he didn't put this jump drive into a computer after the five-minute mark on the countdown, the Turks could infiltrate the system and prevent the launch. Namazi kept his eye on a computer right next to him. It was running, but no one was using at the moment.

Namazi slipped the jump drive into the port at the five-minute mark, then hurried and left, as he'd been told to do. Because of this, he was blissfully ignorant of the consequences of that little drive.

The virus was a subtle one. The NSA had tuned it so that it would start its job the moment he put it in. It infiltrated every computer in the control room and set a virus to activate the moment the launch countdown hit 5 seconds. Then it waited.

The countdown continued.

T-minus 5 minutes

The flight radio sounded, "T-minus 5 minutes to launch."

The flight controller texted Casey. "Anything you want to say to the team?"

"What is about to happen will change the world, Inshallah," Casey replied.

Blake asked for a translation then quipped, "Think they'll realize what happens is our fault?"

"Not initially," Casey sighed. "They'll think it's all their fault."

"We can't worry about them right now," Manuel said. "We have to focus on our survival. All the people we have come to care for are safe. As for the rest? Well, God willing, they will not live long enough to hurt anyone ever again."

"Alright, cut the chatter," Blake said with uncharacteristic seriousness. "I have to focus on flying this tub of lard you lunatics made for me."

"It's not our fault you're the best pilot," Casey retorted. "And besides, you welded 90% of the thing."

"Then I'm naming her Bessy."

"No, you will not!" Casey shouted.

"Too late. You admitted I did the bulk of the work. That means naming rights are mine."

"Well, then I call dibs on naming our first real spacecraft."

"Can I name the fusion reactor and thruster system?" Manuel asked meekly.

"Of course, Manuel," Casey said, grateful for Manuel's kind heart. "You could claim right to name all of this. It's your inventions that make it possible."

"La Propulsión de la Rosa."

"The Rose Drive. Your wife will love it."

"Rosa's favorite color of rose is yellow, like the reactor's glow." Manuel then glanced down at the timer. "T-minus 2 minutes."

They watched the countdown, knowing that whatever happened, the next few minutes would be monumental.

T-minus 30 seconds

The helicopters were all spinning up their blades as Hamid and crew arrived. Sarosh smiled and waved.

"You made it, Hamid! Lady Scarlett and noble son, welcome! It is time to load up. I had no problem getting anyone on board."

Hamid smiled, hearing the loudspeakers hit ten on the countdown.

T-minus 6 seconds

"6, 5, engine start, 2, 1... Liftoff... wait. What?"

The two-stage rocket, the largest ever assembled by the Iranians, had ignited as planned and blazed brightly. It lifted up beautifully, as planned. However, mission control in Urmia quickly became exceptionally confused.

The mission controller called, "Casey, we're showing an irregularity in launch sequence, but we have lost control. We are locked out!"

They received no response from the Americans, but every screen in flight control began showing a stream of strange symbols as Namazi's virus viciously wiped the flight control system in Urmia, as well as the entire base computer system, and then spread to every connected government computer across Iran. All personnel turned to stare at the lone TV monitor still in operation as the rocket lifted from its moorings.

The dignitaries, absolutely deafened by the liftoff, were far too close for comfort, though they were reasonably safe from all but hearing loss–if they didn't have any heart conditions. But unhappily for many of them, a significant number of the Majles and ayatollahs, including the Ayatollah, had lived lives of excess and vice. The deafening roar, shockwave, and shaking startled them so badly that most of those with weak hearts suffered from heart attacks. Most of them, if not all of them, would have survived, but the cell phone jammers that Sarosh had installed in the grandstand and the pavilion had kicked on at the ten second mark and so no medical help was forthcoming.

The firefight that erupted among the IRGC when they saw the Ayatollah dead made things worse for everyone. Those with the best claims to take his place were killed by rivals within moments.

As Blake later commented, "The pavilion would have been the perfect distance, but the conversion from metric to imperial got screwed up. Three and a half miles somehow became 305 meters. So tragic."

As a testament to Manuel's mathematical skill and Russian rocket construction, the rocket lifted high into the air and then tilted over right on target, acting as a ballistic missile rather than a space bound rocket. The rocket roared through the lower atmosphere and slammed into the center of the empty Urmia Research Center, save for the Revolutionary Guard left to guard it. The hydrogen and oxygen, torn loose from their tanks by the force of impact, ignited and sent gouts of flames racing through the research center. With all of the staff, including the onsite fire department, sent home by Hamid, the fire burned until all of the physical remains of Iranian nuclear and restarted bioweapons research were erased from existence and the only sound from the base was crackling fire and groaning metal.

T-minus 6 seconds

"6, 5, engine start, 2, 1... Liftoff... wait. What?"

Hamid was jogging to the helicopter when he heard a car coming, but the warning came too late to do anything more than leap to the side. The car narrowly missed him. With a screech of metal, the car crashed into a fence post, producing a spout of steam from the hood. Hamid pulled himself to his feet, bruised and scratched, but fine. Then, like a decrepit phoenix rising from the now smoking car, Telebi, or Teletubby, as he preferred to call him, opened the door, screaming curses, and climbed out. He pointed a pistol at Hamid.

"Mr. Jabiri, you are a traitor. As such, I will see you dead." With that, the general fired, but the pistol exploded in his hand, knocking the general to his back.

Hamid ran to the general, followed by Matt and Esin. The man's face was a ruin of black and red and his shoulder wound reopened by the trauma and poured blood. He gasped, one good eye staring at the three of them.

Hamid leaned over and spoke. "I will forgive you, but that will not save you."

The man sighed, his body shuddered, and he went still.

"Nice work, mom," Matt said. "Bending his pistol was the right call."

"Lady Scarlett, that was an excellent idea. Well done." Hamid checked the general's pulse, verifying for himself the general was dead. "Having known Casey, I am not surprised at all that his wife is his equal in competence and cleverness. Shall we?" He gestured toward the waiting helicopter.

With the dead general no longer a risk, the three of them entered their helicopter where Hamid took the pilot's seat and the fleet of 18 helicopters took off, flying low towards Turkey.

"6, 5, engine start, 2, 1... Liftoff... wait. What?"

At 6, Casey pressed a button that opened the telescope doors on the observatory. They had not built it out of Balsa wood, like Blake wanted, but rather, had made the opening wide enough for their ship to fit through. Casey muted the mission control at their shout of confusion and focused on their escape.

Blake had initiated thrust at the call of liftoff, the reactors giving thrust within milliseconds. Easing them up, wary as he'd never been able to test this live, he reached the observatory as the doors opened. With only a slight scrape, he passed them up and out of the observatory.

"Would have been cooler if we burst out," Blake muttered.

"Flight radar engaged," Manuel called. "The rocket is on course, as expected. Four bogies, two in range to intercept us."

"All systems green," Casey called. "You're nominal for vertical thrust."

Blake called, "Copy," even as he accelerated them at an uncomfortable rate to get to a speed so that he could turn lateral and have the flight control surfaces become useful.

"Two bogies are moving to intercept, as expected."

"Are the other two anywhere near the helipad?" Casey called.

"Yes, they are."

"Then we give them a target. Blake, fly with best safe thrust towards the other two bogies. I want all four engaging us while those helicopters get out of sight."

Their radio crackled, and the fighter pilots called in, "Unknown aircraft, identify yourself."

Casey spoke to them in Persian, "We are experimental flight fourteen, on assignment by General Telebi. Please disengage, authorization code 853421."

The Iranian fighters called back, "Unable to comply, Casey, the general gave orders a few minutes ago to shoot down anything that flew besides the rocket."

Casey cut the mic and switched back to English. "How'd he recognize my voice? I thought my accent was better than that. The general ordered everything shot down beside the rocket. Time to intercept?"

Manuel called, "One minute. The rocket is well into its turn."

Casey had an idea.

"Flight, you don't want to do this. You know Telebi kidnapped us. We are escaping. Do you want our innocent blood on your hands? And watch the rocket. Do you see its trajectory? It goes to destroy the bioweapons and nuclear weapons research your terroristic government would use to kill millions. Don't shoot us until you watch it burn."

"Five seconds to impact... Impact. Wow, that's quite pretty."

They looked over their shoulders to watch the fireball engulfing the building.

"Flight, disengage. I repeat, disengage," Casey called.

A new voice came on the radio in passable Persian. "Iranian Air Force, this is the Turkish Air Force. We have six flights of four fighters each bearing down on you. If you engage those Americans, we will shoot you down. They are under our protection. Fly home and we'll leave in peace."

"Twenty-four bogies appeared on radar," Manuel said in awe. "They must have been flying so low!" He paused. "The Iranians are in missile range. All four bogies are in missile range."

"I can't dodge a half dozen missiles," Blake called. "I might be able to outrun them, but we would probably pass out. Turning off max thrust safeties."

"This is Iranian flight. Disengaging."

As Casey sighed with relief, three of the bogies turned away, but a single voice came on, "No! You traitors!" And one Iranian fighter launched a pair of missiles at them.

"Hold on to your butts," Blake called, then slammed his controls down.

The sound of the fighters arguing with each other was drowned out by the sudden pressure on Casey's entire body. They were accelerating faster and faster. 6g's. 8 g's. 10 g's. His vision started to go black. The flight suit engaged to keep him breathing, but it was not designed to do this forever.

As soon as the missiles realized they were losing, they exploded, the shockwave buffeting them. Blake cut the thrust, and they felt the pressure release, their breathing going back to normal.

"The three Iranian bogies are flying to base at speed," Manuel called. "I don't see the fourth on the radar. The Turkish flight is shielding the helicopters. God bless Hamid; I pray he makes it to rendezvous safely. 15 seconds to the border."

Casey called, now in Turkish, "Turkish flight, this is American flight. Permission to enter Turkish airspace."

The response came in English.

"American cowboys, your flying is amazing! You are crazy! How many g's was that? Did you pass out? Yes, come, come to our space."

Casey relaxed until Blake called, "We've lost drives one and two. Drive three is compensating, but I think it's going to fail."

"Confirmed," Manuel called, "we're going to have to glide and then use the parachutes."

"Turkish flight, those missiles damaged our engines. We are going to have to glide to reduce speed and then use our parachutes to land. We're anticipating landing in..." He glanced at Manuel, who was typing furiously, then showed him on the map. "North of Yuksekova by a few miles."

"Copy, American cowboys. Agent Esin, would you care to say something?"

A feminine voice Casey recognized immediately came onto the same channel.

"Turkish flight, this is Agent Esin. I have a lot to say to the American cowboys, but for now I'll only say, all passengers and helicopters accounted for, and Telebi died of his own arrogance."

Casey whooped in relief and joy. He knew she'd make it out! Blake smiled and Manuel began to tear up, even as they focused on the work of gliding to a safe parachute speed.

Blake grumbled, "Of course she infiltrated Iran, snuck into the most heavily guarded secret research facility anywhere on Earth, and then never stopped by to say hi."

The pilot spoke with cheers from his co-pilot echoing in the radio. "Copy, Agent Esin, you are cleared to proceed. Do you have room for 3 American cowboys?"

"Copy, flight. Direct us."

"American cowboys, that helicopter has three seats with your names on them. We will watch their six, too. They'll be not too long behind you."

Launch +10 minutes

Esin smiled. "Copy that, Turkish flight, I have the coordinates for the landing site."

Hamid laughed out loud as he changed course to go pick up the 'American cowboys' the Turkish pilots said needed a lift.

"My family, the Americans I told you about have made it safely to Turkey! We get to pick them up and take them with us."

His family, cheering at the news, shouted questions to him which were mostly lost in the noise of the helicopter. After 10 minutes, they came to the landing site and found the Americans standing in their rumpled conference clothes at the side of the smoking ship, wearing laptop bags and staring at a rock in Blake's hand. It very much appeared that Blake was lecturing them about geology!

As he landed the helicopter, the three came running up and climbed in the side door that Sarosh held open for them, Blake still holding his rock.

As soon as he climbed in, Esin climbed into the back and rushed to Casey, hugging him tightly. Casey wept as he scooped her up, holding her with her feet off the ground. Matt then hugged both of them. Casey disengaged with his wife and hugged Matt, too. The three of them sat, Casey between his wife and his eldest son, holding both around the shoulders. Hamid wept openly as he saw the joy on both of their faces.

His family also cheered. Casey called for a headset and Hamid overheard a snippet of the family's conversation as he put the headset on.

"...yet you came all this way to rescue me?"

"I wasn't going to redo the kitchen by myself. I came to make sure you do your fair share."

Casey then put the headset on properly. He called, "Hello, Hamid, thanks for the ride." Then the man had the audacity to speak Turkish to the flights circling above them!

"What did they say?" Hamid asked after they had taken off and Casey quit talking.

"They want us well clear of the border. There are some strange happenings reportedly beginning in Iran. We're to go nearly due west. You're not going to believe the name of the city they want us to refuel in."

"Why?" Hamid asked Casey.

"Blake, Manuel, you will never believe the name of the city where the Turks want us to refuel." Casey smiled with a look that Hamid had learned meant that he was going to make a ridiculous joke.

"Then tell us, you cretin!" Blake shouted.

Casey laughed. "Batman."

Manuel and Matt started laughing like Hamid had never seen them laugh. Blake looked momentarily shocked, then began laughing so hard that Hamid thought he might pass out.

"This is funny because of the movie character with the same spelling?" Hamid asked, smiling.

Esin, who also laughed, but with far less gusto but equally visible joy, replied, "Yes, that is part of it. But also, because we are so relieved to be going home that something a little funny becomes a LOT funny."

"Hopefully they have a sign that says the name and we can all take a picture in front of it to show your families."

The first thing Casey did when they arrived in Batman was to call the American embassy. The next thing he had to do was to tell their story to his old friend, General Nacar, who had flown in special to meet them. They shared the details as they flew to Ankara. Casey was simply blown away as he heard Esin's part of the story.

Upon arrival in Ankara, they were whisked to the American embassy where Casey presented Hamid, Sarosh, their families, and the girls they had rescued as political asylum seekers and Casey, Manuel, and Blake recommended them for asylum as American citizens. The fact they had no passports was no problem, as Esin had her passport and everyone treated her like a celebrity. In fact, the embassy treated them all like dignitaries. The Turkish military, having been informed of the basics of what happened to protect them, had immediately leaked the news, which spread like wildfire across the whole world.

Casey balked at cooperation only when they asked to debrief him immediately at the embassy. "I think I can speak for Blake and Manuel when I say that we will not be able to focus until we have called our families."

The consular agent expressed shock that they hadn't yet had the chance to call and immediately provided three cell phones and three private rooms. All three were already dialing before any of them had the door to their room closed.

Casey's father answered the phone groggily, which made sense, as it was early in the morning back home.

"Dad, it's Casey! I'm with Esin and Matt. We made it out! We're in Turkey and will be home in a day or two!"

His dad, ever calm, said, "That's wonderful." He then spoke to his wife. "Sweetheart, it's Casey. They all got out. They're in Turkey."

A breathless, much more excited voice came on the line. "Casey! My boy, you are all safe?"

"Yes, mom. Matt and I were kidnapped. That man who paid us so much was actually an Iranian agent. But we won him over to our side in the end. He helped us escape, and we rescued his whole family. We got to design and build a space mission, but it was all a red herring so they wouldn't know we were planning to escape. We blew up a secret Iranian base that was making weapons of mass destruction! With a rocket we built! We planted a virus that probably killed every online government computer in Iran. And we escaped on our own rocket plane and got shot at by an Iranian fighter jet, but we dodged the missiles. We didn't get to go to space yet. Blake flew the rocket! And Matt and Esin flew out of Iran in a helicopter and picked us up in Turkey. Esin snuck into Iran and was a super spy at the base and helped keep us safe and get us out. And now I'm in Ankara at the embassy and will probably have to tell the whole story to a bunch of people."

Casey's father, voice now choked with tears of joy, asked, "Will you be able to come home soon?"

"I sure hope so. It's getting late here, so we'll probably sleep soon and then we'll get debriefed for at least a day, if not more. Then we'll be able to come home. So, a few more days."

Casey and Esin's children had clearly been woken by the shouts of joy. They made their own cheers in the background. Casey and Esin caught snippets like, "Daddy blew up a base!" and "Mommy is a super spy!"

After their grandparents hushed them, Casey said, "My dear children, I would move heaven and earth to be with you for even a moment. I literally built a spaceship, a rocket plane, and blew up an Iranian base to get home to you!"

They spoke for a long time, but eventually the pleas for debriefing prevailed and they said goodbye for a few days.

Hamid glanced up from his laptop to his cell phone, where a single notification flashed.

We landed safe.

Hamid smiled and walked across the shared office the U.S. Embassy had him in while things worked out with Iran. He grabbed a fresh cup of coffee, then pulled up a news channel in the U.S. on his laptop. What a joy to freely access any website and not worry about who was watching.

A talking head appeared, and he turned up the volume. "...rumors of American involvement in the death of the Ayatollah are completely false. The death was called a 'fortuitous accident' by the new interim government. Nevertheless, there were definitely at least three Americans near the site of the rocket incident. Will we get answers from them now they are back on American soil?"

Hamid ignored the rest. He was the one making the news now, after all. No time for watching redundant things.

Interim President Zarei—In response to your request for comment, I believe the issues of state are best addressed by the representatives of the people. I will state that I believe universal suffrage, common law for men and women alike, and a secular government that honors religious freedom are crucial to Persia becoming the nation we believe it should be.—Regards, Interim Director Jabiri

A change in the newscast caught his attention, and he flipped back to the streaming tab. Casey, Manuel, Blake, and Sarosh were shown exiting the airport, police providing a security perimeter. Ever since the Ayatollah died, most of the government was killed by infighting of the IRGC, and someone in Turkey leaked the rescue operation for the Americans, the news media had been obsessed with the story. Especially since the leak had included only enough to be enticing and not enough to be informative.

He wept as he saw the men hugging their families, and then most of them hugged Sarosh, who had been standing back. Hamid laughed when he saw Sarosh step back and Blake's oldest daughter join him. He thought hard. Her name was Angel and one brief camera shot confirmed she was as beautiful as Blake's pictures had shown. Perhaps more so, with her dark skin and hair. Hamid was no matchmaker, but he knew Sarosh and he suspected Sarosh's desire for a blonde American had already departed.

Casey finally stepped up to the podium, and Hamid wiped his eyes to focus on his words.

"Thank you for your interest in our well-being. As you can see, we are safe and happy to be home. We will perhaps give detailed interviews of our dramatic abduction, our strange captivity, and our even more dramatic escape, but for now, I will simply say it is good to be home."

One reporter shouted louder than his neighbors. "Were you part of the events that reports say led to the decapitation of the old government in Iran and the new Persian government that came to power a few hours ago?"

Casey looked surprised. "Well, now wouldn't that be a crazy thing? We're just a team of engineers. Besides, I've been on a plane or in airports for close to 16 hours. I haven't seen the news."

The reporter continued. "The new government was officially formed only an hour ago. The missile test was a tremendous blow to the existing government, and the survivors stepped down and fled or were killed. There is even talk of reforging ties to the West. You weren't involved in those events?"

"Fascinating. That would be wonderful. The people we met in our time are kind and loving at heart. They had a few bad apples in government. I'm grateful they could overthrow their own leaders. If they can have a period of peace and freedom, that would be wonderful for the whole world."

Another cacophony of questions blared out, but one dominated. "Were you aware that a NASA engineer was arrested and charged with espionage this morning?"

Hamid laughed aloud as Casey innocently raised an eyebrow.

"Who?"

"Dr. Stacy Devon."

Hamid was now crying from laughter as Casey replied with utter diplomacy, though Hamid noticed Blake was smirking in the background.

"Well, that's a shock now, isn't it? If she is innocent, I hope she is exonerated promptly. If she is guilty, I hope justice has its day. We'll take no more questions."

The cameras followed for a minute, but then returned to the talking heads speculating, which was not interesting. He closed the tab on his browser and sat thinking about all that had happened. A year ago, he had deceived those three men in the name of saving himself and his family. Now, they were some of his dearest friends and he was free of those same tyrants. The world was an odd place.

His phone rang, and he answered with delight. "Nice camera work. You should become a reporter."

"Yuck, don't wish that on anyone," Casey replied with disgust in his voice. "I'd as soon gargle mouthwash up my nose."

The call was on speakerphone, as Hamid clearly heard Blake speak.

"Why you gotta remind me of college? I still haven't forgiven you for cracking jokes while I was gargling."

Casey ignored him. "Good job on our NASA problem."

Hamid felt an insane amount of pleasure in receiving thanks from these men. He realized it was the respect that did it. "I gave your State Department so much information on Dr. Devon that I think the entire bureaucracy had a collective aneurysm. It was quite fun."

"And the rumors of the new Persian government?" Manuel asked.

"That's even better news! The new Persian government is making indications it could be friendly with the Americans and the Turks! There are rumors they are in discussion with NATO and the EU."

"And the protesters are being heard? What about the Revolutionary Guard?"

"There is still a lot of violence, with the Ayatollah dead, but the Revolutionary Guard is mostly fighting each other, not the people. Many blamed Israel, but the evidence Esin planted on Teletubby came to light. It was most convincing. The word is spreading that it was Teletubby that did it all. The news is even calling him 'General Teletubby!' The new government is in talks with the Phoenix Project of Iran and every other group, even the Pahlavi clan, trying to make democratic reforms and welcome back the Iranian diaspora from around the world. They want Persians to return who have fled the former government. I think most will wait to see if they maintain power. I will wait for a time. I want to see if they will hold to their word and have elections. If the people will vote yes on the reforms. But I cannot wait long, for they have given me a job offer."

"Now that sounds like an interesting thing," Blake said. "You were instrumental in overthrowing the old, so I suppose that the new would like you."

"Yes, well, the new government wants me to run our new Iranian Space Agency! If they are true to their word, I will accept and make sure we are a full partner with NASA and sign the Artemis Accords. My first act will be to fund whatever mission you three envision! But with your new tech, I think asteroid retrieval has become much more doable! I will expect great things from you three!"

"Congratulations, Haj Hamid," Casey said. "Soon to be Director Jabiri, I hope. We look forward to letting our imaginations run wild."

The End

About the Author

Hyrum W. Hawks is a lot of things, but first and foremost identifies as a child of God, a disciple of Jesus Christ, and a child of the covenant. He is a devoted husband and father of seven children. He began his career by getting master's degrees in chemistry and chemical engineering, and recently earned one in outer space resource engineering. He spent his career in heavy industry, especially mining, oil & gas, and outer space resource mining and processing. He is also a patent agent and has written hundreds of patents for clients, and is an inventor on over forty granted patents himself. He is beginning the process of moving to being a full-time novelist since he began to learn about creative writing in early 2022 when a few of his children expressed interest in writing but didn't take the initiative to learn. He decided to learn how to be an author and teach them. Instead, he's found the first hobby of his life that has lasted longer than a month. His goal is to go full time within five years.

Check out ReamStories.com/HyrumHawks, where you can read short stories and the beginning of his works in progress as a subscription. His books include hard sci-fi, sci-fantasy, and whatever pops into his head.

The book you have just read is a product of my experience in outer space resource engineering and heavy industry over the last fifteen years. I spent some of that time in Turkey, not too many hours from Iran. I try to stay up to date on world news, especially on regions I travel. I also am very much aware of the realities of space mining. I had the idea not long after I attended a space resources conference and thought about how cool it would be to escape from Iran into Turkey. And that's how the idea was born. Casey, Blake, and Manuel are all a bit of me and a bit of my colleagues and friends in the engineering and heavy industrial fields.

I wrote the book in the summer of 2022 in just a few weeks and spoke to an Iranian American woman about the book and its ending, who I will call M. M did not think it likely that regime change would ever happen and suggested I leave the ending more vague. I wanted to keep it.

A few weeks later, the protests began in Iran and M started to believe it just might be possible. I put words from a few Iranian friends in here. Their hopes and desires. May *Woman, Life, Freedom,* become more than a slogan, but a reality in Persia.

A Note from G, a young Iranian woman who came to school in the US just before the protests began and now can't go home:

I am a newcomer immigrant! I have been in the United States for less than a year now. In Iran, I made every effort to qualify for a Ph.D. program in the United States and have more freedom and prosperity. I am happy that I no longer have to be in a challenging situation for my basic freedoms. I am glad I am studying at a university that supports me academically and socially. I have found new friends and built a new life that aligns to a large extent with my aspirations. But I can say that if Iran respected my future and my abilities more, neither Iran would be a hell nor America a paradise! I love Iran for its four seasons, its cuisine and fancy restaurants, the hustle and bustle of its streets, and the way people value appearances in life! Another good thing here is that I am not caught up in trivial matters, and I can focus on the most important aspects of my life!

من یه مهاجر تازه واردم! الان کمتر از یک ساله که به آمریکا اومدم. توی ایران که بودم همه جور تلاشی کردم تا شایسته تحصیل در مقطع دکترا در امریکا باشم و بتونم در زندگیم آزادی و رفاه بیشتری داشته باشم. راستش خیلی خوشحالم که لازم نیست برای آزادی های حداقلی در چالش باشم. خوشحالم که توی یه دانشگاهی که در جنبه های مختلف تحصیلی و اجتماعی کمکم میکنه درس میخونم. دوستای جدیدی پیدا کردم و زندگی جدیدی ساختم که تا حد زیادی با خواسته هام انطباق داره. اما میتونم بگم اگه ایران، به فردیتم و تواناییی هام احترام بیشتری میگذاشت، نه ایران یک جهنم بود و نه آمریکا یک بهشت! من ایرانو بخاطر طبیعت 4 فصلش، بخاطر غذاها و رستوران های شیکش، و بخاطر شلوغی خیابون هاش و نوعی که مردم به ظواهر زندگی اهمیت میدن دوس دارم! و خوبی دیگه اینجا هم اینه که درگیر حاشیه ها نیستم و روی اصلی ترین جنبه های زندگیم تمرکز میکنم!